ROCHESTER'S WIFE

ALSO BY D. E. STEVENSON

Rochester's Wife

 D. E. Stevenson

HOLT, RINEHART AND WINSTON
NEW YORK

Library of Congress Cataloging in Publication Data
Stevenson, Dorothy Emily, 1892–1973. Rochester's wife.
I. Title. PZ3.S8472Ro 1978 [PR6037.T458]
823'.9'12   ISBN 0-03-042616-2   77-26134

First edition published in the United States
in 1940. Second edition published in 1978.

Printed in the United States of America
10 9 8 7 6 5 4 3 2 1

With the exception of Jem, all the people in this novel are imaginary and bear no relation to any real people who happen to have the same name.

CONTENTS

Rochester's Wife

CHAPTER I

THE STONE BROTHERS

WHEN Kit Stone landed at Southampton he took the boat train to London and made a bee-line for his brother's house in Halkin Street. This was quite a natural thing to do, for his brother was his only surviving relative and they had not met for four years. It is true that Kit had not thought about Henry very often—he had had too many other things to think of—but, now that he was actually on his way to see Henry, he realised that Henry meant a good deal to him if only for the reason that they were of one blood. For four years Kit had knocked about the world and he had enjoyed it tremendously and had prided himself upon the fact that he was free to do as he liked and had no ties of any description . . . but, now that he had set foot upon his native land and was once more amongst his own people, he felt an unexpected glow of happiness, of friendliness. He felt he had come home.

It was February, but the afternoon was warm and dry and sunny and, when Kit emerged from the tube at Hyde Park Corner and looked about him, a strange little thrill of pleasure and excitement stirred his heart. He felt that he had been away for a hundred years, yet London was just the same—it had not changed a whit.

The passersby were curiously indifferent to the fact that a young man had returned from wandering over the face of the earth and was greeting them silently as his fellow countrymen; they hurried past, bent upon their own affairs, and ignored him completely . . . but Kit loved them all—even the ostensibly unlovable old villain who was selling matches at the corner—his heart yearned over them.

He stood still and looked about him and it seemed to him that only half of him was here; only half of him had arrived here, at Hyde Park Corner, and the other half was still wandering in foreign lands. He seemed to see, transposed upon the glittering marble arch which stood at the top of Constitution Hill, the glitter of the sun upon the small blue waves of the Southern Seas; and he seemed to hear, beneath the roar of passing traffic, the rustle of palm trees bending before the wind.

The illusion was so strong that it gave Kit quite a shock for he was a practical young man and not used to hallucinations; but after a moment he was able to laugh at himself, and swung around and set off down Grosvenor Place with a battered suitcase in either hand.

Henry's house was tall and narrow and, despite the fact that it had been painted and there were crisp white curtains in every window, it looked a little gloomy to the wanderer. As he went up the steps he thought, But I needn't stay long. . . .

He was not expected, of course, for it had never occurred to him to let Henry know that he was coming, but he managed to convince the somewhat suspicious parlourmaid that he was her master's brother and, leaving his suitcases in the hall, he followed her up the stairs to the drawing room where Henry and his wife were having tea. They were astonished to see Kit, for the last communication they had received from him was a postcard depicting a Maori warrior with the simple words "A Merry Christmas to you both from Kit" written across the middle, but despite their astonishment they welcomed him cordially and Mabel directed the parlourmaid to bring another cup.

". . . unless you'd rather have a whisky and soda or something," said Henry, who was suddenly assailed by the feeling that tea was scarcely a suitable refreshment to offer a man arriving straight from New Zealand.

"Tea please," said Kit promptly, "and I believe I see crumpets —how lovely!"

"If you had let us know—" said Mabel, as she busied herself pouring out tea for her guest.

"I didn't know myself, really," Kit explained, "I just suddenly thought I'd like to come home, so I took the next boat. I came by Tahiti and Panama."

"I see," said Henry—who didn't see at all.

"Yes," said Kit, "it was Christmas, you see, and it felt all wrong—Christmas in the middle of summer—and I felt—well, I suppose I was homesick or something."

"I'm glad you're here, anyhow," said Mabel, smiling.

"You could have wired from Southampton," Henry pointed out.

Kit saw that this was true but the truth was he had never thought of it—the idea of wiring from Southampton had simply never crossed his mind—he explained this and Henry accepted the explanation and said it didn't matter.

"We're delighted to have you, of course," Mabel added.

"Delighted," agreed Henry.

Henry was looking older. He was fatter and paler, and there were little pouches under his eyes. Kit added seven years to his own age and discovered that Henry was thirty-six; he looked much more than that, but of course the life of a London business man must be very wearing. Kit decided he would rather be a tinker than a successful stockbroker chained to an office and, catching sight of his own lean brown face in the gilt mirror which hung on the wall, he grinned at the reflection. I'd make quite a good tinker, he thought.

"What are you smiling at?" Henry enquired.

"Myself," said Kit. "Myself and you, really. Nobody would think we were brothers."

"We've both got father's nose," said Henry seriously, and he felt his own straight, well-shaped nose with some satisfaction, for old Dr. Stone had been a very good-looking man.

"Yes," agreed Kit. "You're very like father in lots of ways."

"You're more like mother—except for your nose," Henry said gravely. "You don't remember her, of course. She had dark blue eyes like you, and a long shaped face. She was tall and slim with long bones," he added, glancing at Kit's long fingers which were stretching across the table for another crumpet.

"I remember nothing about her except a pink dress," declared Kit, "a soft pink dress—perhaps it was velvet."

They talked about their old home after that, and compared notes upon the various incidents which they remembered: the day when Kit had fallen into the river and Henry had fished him out; the day which they had spent together on the moors and when Kit had shot his first rabbit; a cousin's wedding at which Kit had officiated as page. They talked about people too—"What's become of Jack Kelston?" Kit enquired, "and where are the Bartons, now?" Mabel did not know the places or the people, but she was a good wife. She sat and sewed and listened sympathetically and thought how nice it was for Henry to have his brother to talk to, and what a pity it was that Kit did not live quite near so that they might indulge more often in this harmless pleasure. Mabel had two sisters and enjoyed nothing better than a chat with them over old times.

Presently there was a pause in the conversation and a significant glance passed between hostess and host—a glance which said, "Now is the time."

"What are you thinking of doing, Kit?" Henry enquired.

"Doing?" echoed Kit in surprise.

"Henry means," said Mabel quickly, "Henry only means have you any plans? Of course, you can stay here as long as you like. We shall love having you, Kit."

"We were talking about you the other day," Henry put in.

"Haven't you had your fill of wandering? Isn't it about time you settled down?"

It was a new idea to Kit. Just at the moment it seemed rather pleasant to be home again, rather pleasant to be with his own people and to chat with Henry about old times, but to "settle down" had a dull sort of sound.

Kit had always wanted to be a sailor—his mother's people had seafaring blood in their veins—but Dr. Stone had been so grieved to find that neither of his sons was desirous of following the medical profession that Kit had not the heart to oppose him. Dr. Stone wanted Kit to become his assistant; it was the dream of his heart to have his son working beside him, to see Kit established at Garbury where the Stones had been doctors for three generations. It seemed to Kit that he had no option in the matter, he was bound to his father by ties of gratitude and love, so he agreed to fall in with the plan, and went up to Cambridge to take his degree.

Kit worked hard and his interest in medicine quickened, but when he was in his sixth year his father died quite suddenly of heart failure. So the well-laid scheme miscarried, and the practice had to be sold and presently Kit found himself the possessor of a degree and not much else. There were several openings for him of course, for his degree was a creditable one, but Kit refused them all. He remembered now how his very real grief at his father's untimely death had been tempered by the realisation that he was free. He was free to go where he would, to voyage to the ends of the earth, to visit all the glamorous lands he had hankered for—and, best of all, he possessed in his head and hands the wherewithal to earn his bread and to earn it usefully and honourably wherever he should go. The price of the practice was divided equally between the two brothers, and Kit's share was invested as an insurance against accident or old age. This done, Kit offered his services to a well-known shipping company and shook the dust of London from his feet. All this had happened four years ago and since then Kit had wandered over the world. He had wandered deliberately obeying every impulse to stay or go, taking pleasure in the feeling that he was as free as air, working off the restlessness which years of hard work had engendered in his adventurous nature.

Kit thought of all this and it was a few moments before he answered Henry's questions, and even then his answer was vague.

"I don't know if I want to settle down," Kit said thoughtfully. "Why should I, anyhow?"

"We think you should," said Henry solemnly, "you're getting on for thirty, aren't you?"

Kit agreed that he was. "But I don't feel it," he said, "and I haven't any ties—"

"That's just it," Mabel pointed out. "You ought to have ties. It's so lonely for you wandering about by yourself."

"A rolling stone gathers no moss," added Henry.

Kit laughed, "But I don't want moss," he declared. "I shouldn't know what to do with it if I had it. You gather enough moss for the whole Stone family."

"Henry works hard," said Mabel quickly.

Kit knew that this was true; and, although he had no desire to emulate Henry, he admired him for his industry. Henry deserved all the money in the world—if that was what he wanted.

"Is business doing well?" he enquired politely.

"Moderately," replied Henry with a complacent air. "The 'change is very jumpy, of course, but our firm is managing not so badly. We've taken another partner—but I told you that in my last letter, didn't I?"

"Did you?" said Kit, and then he added, "oh yes, of course." He had received the letter at Auckland and it had seemed to come from a far distant planet: the fact that the firm of Godfrey

& Stone had added another name to their official designation
had seemed of little importance at Auckland, but now that Kit
was back in London he saw the fact in its true proportions.
"Oh yes," said Kit, trying to make up for the lack of interest
he had shown, "oh, of course. It was—it was Winchester,
wasn't it? The fellow's name, I mean."

"Rochester," said Mabel with a reproachful look. Godfrey,
Stone & Rochester—it sounds well, doesn't it?"

Kit agreed that it sounded very well indeed.

"And that reminds me," said Henry, "it was really Rochester
that suggested—I mean—" and he looked at Mabel for help.

Mabel flung herself into the breach. "It's like this," she
explained. "We had the Rochesters to dinner one night—they
live at Minfield, you see—and Mrs. Rochester happened to mention that their doctor is getting old—"

"He's looking for an assistant," put in Henry, "and of course
Mabel and I thought of you. We didn't know where you were,
of course, so it wasn't much good . . . but still . . . we thought
of you . . . and now, here you are."

"It seems like fate, doesn't it," Mabel said thoughtfully.

"But I—" began Kit. "But I mean—"

"It sounded so nice," Mabel said.

"Why not try it for a bit?" suggested Henry.

"But look here—" cried Kit.

"You've roved about for years," Henry pointed out. "Four
years, isn't it, since you went away? Try settling down for a
change."

"You needn't stay if you don't like it," Mabel pointed out.

Kit listened to their persuasions, and he began to think that
it might be rather nice for a change. It might be rather interesting to practice medicine seriously, to settle down in an English
village and, of course, as Mabel said, he need not stay. Nobody
had the power to bind you down. You could always escape
when you wanted to. Kit smiled suddenly as he thought of all

the money he had forfeited by sudden whims, by the sudden urge of wanderlust, by the sudden desire to move on, to see more of the world, to visit another country.

Mabel was watching his face. "Why not try it?" she urged.

"Well . . ." said Kit doubtfully, ". . . but he might not take me, of course."

It was decided that Henry should speak to his partner about it and the matter was shelved for the time being. They spoke of other things; they dined and went to a play. Kit enjoyed himself immensely. Henry and Mabel were very set in their ways and bound by conventions, but they were extremely kind and obviously anxious to make Kit's visit as pleasant as possible.

They were all somewhat surprised when Dr. Peabody's letter came, for the doctor seemed to take it for granted that the whole thing was fixed. Kit read the letter without comment and passed it to Henry, and Henry put on his glasses and perused it with care.

"Most unbusinesslike!" Henry said, "really very odd—so vague and unsatisfactory."

"What does he say?" enquired Mabel eagerly.

"I'm to go for a month on trial," Kit said. "He wants me next week. I don't see anything vague about that."

"I should have thought he would want to see you," said Henry, "and you ought to see him. You don't know what he's like."

"The Rochesters like him," Mabel pointed out. "Mrs. Rochester said he was a dear."

"And the letter is couched in the most unbusinesslike language," added Henry, turning over the sheets and studying them carefully. "He says, 'Of course, you will live here and feed with us and we shall do our best to make you feel at home. I hope you have a car. We can settle everything later'. That's vague to the point of lunacy in my opinion. You want it all settled before you go, not after."

"He's a doctor, not a lawyer," said Kit. Somehow or other the very vagueness of the old doctor's letter attracted Kit. He did not like things cut and dried.

"But Kit!" cried Henry, "he doesn't say what he intends to pay you!"

"Perhaps he wants to see what I'm worth," returned Kit with a grin.

Henry sighed; this was not his way of doing business, but as he was extremely anxious to get Kit settled he held his peace and let matters take their course. A certain amount of telephoning took place and the whole thing was arranged.

"It's bound to be all right," Mabel declared. "The Rochesters wouldn't have recommended it unless they liked Dr. Peabody."

"It was Rochester's wife who arranged it," Henry pointed out.

"What is she like?" enquired Kit, for it seemed rather strange that a woman whom he had never seen should play such an important part in his affairs, and he was anxious to know more about her.

"She's Scotch of course," said Henry.

"She's tall and thin," said Mabel, "and not very smart. She could be smart if she liked because she had a nice figure and they're very well off—aren't they, Henry?"

"Seem to be," Henry agreed.

"But what's she like to talk to?" asked Kit.

"She doesn't talk much," Mabel told him. "As a matter of fact she isn't easy to talk to."

"Awkward manner," Henry put in.

"Yes, she *is* rather awkward . . . and silent."

"Rochester is an amusing sort of fellow," Henry said. "He's got plenty to say for himself, hasn't he, Mabel?"

"Plenty," said Mabel smiling.

The description of Mrs. Rochester did not sound very attractive, and Kit lost interest in his unseen benefactor. He was very busy, of course, for now that he had really got his job it behooved him to buy some clothes—his wardrobe was in a parlous condition. Henry helped him to sell out some stock and Mabel helped him to spend the money; she was very knowl-edgeable on the subject of clothes. He needed instruments (those he possessed had belonged to his father and were com-pletely out of date) and he needed a small car. The instru-ments cost a good deal, but the car was cheap—he obtained it for the sum of twelve pounds and was delighted with his bar-gain—it was an ancient sports car, with a shabby cape hood and incredibly battered wings. Henry and Mabel were shocked beyond measure when they saw this contraption and they offered to lend Kit enough money to buy a new one, but Kit disliked borrowing and the car did well enough. As a matter of fact he was proud of the thing, for although he had driven other people's cars he had never had one of his own.

"It has a history," declared Kit.

His brother and sister-in-law were bound to agree, for its body bore evidence of a checkered career, but unlike Kit they preferred a vehicle without a history, a vehicle without a past. Kit never knew how sorely it irked them when he left this relic of a bygone age standing outside their door, nor how many times they were obliged to explain its presence to their friends.

"It belongs to Henry's brother," Mabel would say with a whimsical lift of her brows, "a dear boy—we both love him— but such a madcap, so wild and impulsive. Henry wanted to get him a decent car, but he wouldn't hear of it. He went off one morning and came back with *that*—isn't it frightful? Henry teases him unmercifully about it, and says he must have picked it up at the Caledonian Market."

It was in this car—which had been christened Tabby—that Kit started off one fine March morning to take up his new duties. He piled all his worldly goods into the tonneau: his brand new suitcase full of brand new clothes, his old battered suitcases which had accompanied him round the world, his case of instruments, a wooden case of books and various other small bags and parcels.

"There," said Kit, coming into the dining-room where his host and hostess were finishing their breakfast. "It's all in— every bit of it. Not bad, eh!"

"Splendid!" agreed Henry without much enthusiasm.

"Come back if you don't like it," Mabel said.

"Take an apple—take two," suggested Henry hospitably, "you can eat them on the way."

Kit accepted the apples, and after a cordial farewell to Henry and Mabel (who had been extremely decent and had put themselves out a good deal on his account) he started up his engine and set forth upon his journey.

CHAPTER II

THE DOCTOR'S HOUSE

IT WAS by no means the first time that Kit had started off
for an unknown destination, but, strangely enough, this seemed
a much bigger adventure than any he had undertaken before.
He discovered an unfamiliar constriction in his chest and
thought—Good Lord, I'm frightened! How funny, I'm actually
frightened!

As he threaded his way through the traffic of the London
streets he tried to find out the reason for his "fright" but it was
not until he had left London behind him and was spinning
along the broad main road which led to Minfield that he
found the solution of the mystery. It's because I'm tied down,
he decided with some alarm, it's because I've let them bind me.
Kit had always told himself that he was not bound—even for
the month of probation to which he had agreed—because, if
he didn't like Dr. Peabody, or if Dr. Peabody didn't like him,
he could just walk out and forfeit his salary, but now, quite
suddenly, he saw that he couldn't do that. He couldn't do it
because of the Rochesters, because Rochester was Henry's
partner and he couldn't let Henry down.

It was such a disturbing thought that Kit pulled up at the
side of the road to consider the whole thing carefully, and the
more he considered it the more he saw how completely they
had succeeded in binding him. They had done it between them
—Henry and the Rochesters and Dr. Peabody—yes, Dr. Peabody had helped, by his very vagueness, to bind Kit all the
faster. It was a gentlemen's agreement that they had made and
therefore more binding than a cast-iron contract. He saw that

14

he would have to stay for a month at least, and he saw, too, how frightful it would be if he did not make good.

This craving for complete liberty was really sort of an obsession; it was a complex deeply rooted in Kit's nature. The thing had grown in secret during his thwarted boyhood, had lain dormant during his medical training and had flowered when he had found himself free. He had decided then that nothing should interfere with his freedom—nothing ever again —and now he had let them bind him. Kit felt almost sick, and for a few moments he actually considered whether he should turn the car westward and disappear; whether he should escape here and now before it was too late; but of course it was an absurd idea, he was crazy to think of it. . . .

He sat there for some minutes and ate his apples and looked at the countryside, and presently he began to feel calmer and more content. The air was fresh and invigorating after the stuffiness of the city (it was English country air, and there was none better in the world, Kit thought); the road was quiet and there were fields of dark brown earth and meadows and trees as far as eye could see. It was now the beginning of March, and the sun was warm and the dark brown fields were covered with a faint haze of green, like green smoke. The trees were bare, of course, but there were fat brown buds on the chestnuts and, in the little copse by the side of the road, there were rooks flying to and fro and cawing lustily. They are building their nests, thought Kit, it's really spring. It's the loveliest time of year in the loveliest land. . . .

He finished eating his apples and moved on towards his destination.

Thirty years ago Minfield had been a village and a small village at that, but now it was a residential area. The fields and meadows which surrounded it had sprouted houses, houses of every sort of shape and hue, but they were all "nice houses" and each stood by itself in a pretty piece of garden. The main street of the village was still much the same, though the shops were larger and better and the cobbles had long since disappeared. As Kit drove along he noticed a small old-fashioned inn, and this pleased him for it was years since he had seen its like. He promised himself a pint of home-brewed ale in a pewter mug, and perhaps a pleasant chat with some of the habitués. The sign which swung over the door had been newly painted and proclaimed in large letters that the name of the inn was "The Fig and Thistle." It looked a pleasant clean sort of place and as he passed he saw a rosy-faced barmaid gazing out of the window. At the other end of the street Kit found the doctor's house; it was at the corner opposite the bakery. The house stood back from the street and was enclosed by a fine old stone wall with two green doors in it, and several trees peeping out over the top of it. Kit drew up at the first door which was decorated with a large brass plate proclaiming the doctor's name and medical degrees. The plate was highly polished and winked cheerfully in the bright sunshine. He noticed that the house was old and large and occupied the whole of the corner site; the windows were clean and nearly all of them were open and their crisp white curtains swung and danced in the breeze. It's nice, Kit thought. It's clean and neat and prosperous. I believe I'm going to like it.

He got out and rang the bell, and presently the door opened, apparently of its own volition, and Kit, pushing it open further, found himself looking into a small garden enclosed in high walls with one or two large trees in it. A pathway of pink bricks led up to the door of the house and on either side of the path there were small green plots of grass and small neat beds in which daffodils and tulips were marshalled in rows. The whole effect was so orderly that it was impossible to imagine a weed having the impertinence to force its way in, or of any flower daring to grow an inch out of place.

Kit looked round the garden with interest and then he looked at the house and in the doorway he saw a young woman, obviously waiting for him. He hesitated, for he did not know whether to advance and explain who he was, or to return to the car for his luggage. The young woman put an end to the awkward moment by coming towards him down the path. He saw that she was about his own age, neatly made and neatly dressed in a brown tweed skirt and a rust-coloured jumper. Her hair was fair and wavy and her eyes were brown.

"You're Dr. Stone, aren't you?" she enquired, holding out her hand. "How d'you do. I'm Dr. Peabody's daughter."

"How d'you do," returned Kit, shaking hands, "yes, I am. I hope I'm—not late or anything."

"We didn't know when you were coming, so you couldn't be late," replied Miss Peabody gravely. "Come in, Dr. Stone."

"I'll just—er—I'll just fetch some things," babbled Kit nervously. "My car—I mean—"

"Tupman will bring in your luggage and take your car to the garage."

That was all very well, but Kit did not like the idea of leaving his precious new instruments and his fine new suitcase outside in the street. He was used to looking after his own belongings, and he had found that it paid to look after them well. He therefore rushed back to the car and collected the most valuable of his possessions and, having done so, signified his willingness to enter the house.

"I suppose you're afraid they'd be stolen," said Miss Peabody. "They wouldn't be, you know. Minfield is a very law-abiding village."

She spoke with calm amusement which Kit found somewhat annoying, for it made him feel small and foolish and very young.

"I'm not taking any risks," he declared.

The house looked crowded, for it was an eighteenth century

house and was full of solid Victorian furniture. The ceilings were too low for the massive cabinets; and mahogany tables with fat shiny legs were stationed in corners and alcoves too small for them, but, because the furniture was shabby and worn and had the air of having stood where it was for generations, the effect was less incongruous than it might have been.

Miss Peabody led Kit through the hall which was dim and shadowy after the glare outside, and was lighted only by a stained glass window. "That's the dining-room," she said, pointing to a door, "and that's the library," she added, pointing to another; "the consulting room is down that passage and has an entrance-door on the street."

"Very convenient," said Kit politely.

She did not reply to his remark but led him up a steep flight of stairs and along a twisty passage, through a door and up three steps and round a corner to the left. Kit followed her as best he could, stumbling a little over the uneven floors.

"It's an old house," Miss Peabody pointed out.

Kit had suspected as much. "Yes," he said, "Queen Anne, isn't it?"

"I don't know," replied Miss Peabody casually.

"I love old houses," Kit continued, panting after his guide. "There's something very attractive about these twisty passages. I wonder why they built them like this."

"Just to be annoying."

"What did you say?" enquired Kit, unable to believe his ears.

"Just to be annoying," she repeated in an unnecessarily loud voice. "Just to make more work for people who have to keep them clean."

By this time they had reached Kit's room and Miss Peabody opened the door and showed him in. It was not very large but it had a comfortable homelike air. The window, set deep in the thick wall, looked out into the back garden and garage.

"There's Tupman with your car," Miss Peabody said.

Kit leaned out of the window and saw his car being driven into the yard; it was a stable yard with cobblestones, but the coach-house had been converted into a garage—a large one with double doors. In the garden there was a huge old apple tree with gnarled branches.

"An apple tree!" Kit said.

"Yes, but the apples are worthless—small and green and bitter," said Miss Peabody grudgingly.

Kit drew in his head and became practical. He asked whether anything was required of him at the moment or whether he should unpack his things before lunch.

"I don't know," she replied. "I suppose you'd better unpack. Father didn't say what he wanted you to do."

She seemed so casual and disinterested that Kit was quite pleased when she went away and left him to his own devices. He cast a practiced eye over his new quarters and decided that he liked them. He had been in so many rooms all over the world and each one—so Kit had found—had its own particular flavour and atmosphere. This room was fresh and peaceful, there was a leisurely feeling about it, an atmosphere of a bygone age when life had moved more slowly and was more dignified. The wall paper had a pattern of small pink roses, which had faded into a pleasant blur; the carpet, patterned also, was mellowed with age; there was a large mahogany wardrobe with a mirror in it, and a chest of drawers and dressing table to match—plenty of room for all Kit's clothes, old and new. The bed was a four-poster which had obviously boasted a canopy and curtains, but the canopy had been removed and the carved posts cut off. This was vandalism, of course, but Kit forgave the deed for he was too fond of fresh air to have enjoyed sleeping with a canopy over his head.

Kit was looking round and examining everything in the room when suddenly there was a loud knock on the door and a man, very short and broad and exceedingly bowed in the legs, staggered into the room with the box of books on his shoulders and a suitcase in his hand.

"Where shall I put it, sir?" he asked in a deep throaty voice.

Kit sprang forward to help him. "That box is heavy," he said, "I'd have given you a hand with it if I'd known . . . yes, put it here . . . thank you . . . it's books, you see. That's why it's so heavy."

"I'm strong," declared the man as he stood back and wiped his forehead. "I'm strong, I am. A liddle box like that don't worry me—not nohow."

"You're Tupman, I suppose."

"That's roight, sir. Tupman, that's me. There ain't no more to come up 'cept your 'at-box, an' Master Jem's fetching that."

"Who?" enquired Kit.

"Master Jem, the doctor's grandson," replied Tupman jerking his thumb towards the door.

Kit looked round and saw a small boy standing in the doorway with the hat-box. "Oh, thank you," he said.

The boy stood on one leg and looked at the floor, and Kit could find nothing to say. He had never been much in contact with children and he had not expected to find one in this strange old-fashioned house. There was an awkward silence while Tupman undid the straps and went away.

"Come in, won't you," said Kit at last.

The boy came in. He put the hat-box on the floor and held out his hand. "How d'you do," he said.

They shook hands solemnly. Kit decided he must be about seven years old. His face was thin and freckled, he had a wide mouth and a pointed chin and his eyes were round and very blue. His hair was the colour of straw and was very untidy, and there was a large tuft on the crown of his head which stood straight on end. Later, Kit discovered that this tuft was the bane of its owner's life for nothing would make it lie down.

"My name's Jeffrey Ethridge Manson," said the boy gravely, "but Grandfather calls me Jem so now everybody does. It's my initials, you see."

"I see," said Kit.

"I live here, you know," he continued. "I've lived here ever since I was a little boy. I'm learning to be a doctor."

"You're starting early," Kit said, trying to look solemn as befitted the occasion.

"Yes. It's good practice for me—being here I mean. I know a lot already."

"I bet you do," said Kit.

The boy looked at Kit suspiciously but Kit's lean brown face was perfectly grave.

"Oh well," said Jem, "of course I know I've got a lot to learn before I can be a doctor."

"Yes, there's a lot to learn," nodded Kit.

The boy sighed. "I know," he said. "Sometimes I wish I could have my head opened and all the things I've got to learn put into it."

Kit considered this operation. "It would save time," he agreed.

"But they couldn't," Jem said. "They couldn't get it into a small enough space. I'll have to pack it in myself," he looked very thoughtful for a few moments and then smiled up at Kit engagingly. "You've got to help Grandfather until I'm ready, and then you can be my partner if you like."

"I should like that."

"It'll be a long time of course—about eighteen years I should think—but you're quite young, aren't you?"

"Twenty-nine."

Jem did some arithmetic on his fingers. "Forty-seven," he said. "It's quite a good age."

"I shall be in my prime," agreed Kit, gravely.

Having settled this important matter to his satisfaction Jem enquired if he might help unpack and, his offer being accepted, he set to work with a will. The ice was broken now and the unpacking went forward rapidly to the accompaniment of talk and laughter. Kit liked the child, he was a strange mixture of wisdom and naivete, he was eager and interested and full of life.

"What a neat sort of collar-box!" he exclaimed. "It's just the right shape, isn't it? I'd like to have one like that when I'm grown up . . . and what's this thing? It's like a little mowing machine for cutting the grass."

Kit looked around. "That's my razor," he said. "Look out, you'll cut yourself—"

He spoke too late. Jem had run his finger along the blade and was standing looking at the slit in amazement.

"Blood!" he exclaimed.

"Well, what did you expect?" enquired Kit, somewhat irritably. "Haven't you ever seen a razor before?"

"Not like this. Grandfather has things like long knives—one for every day." He looked at the razor again and added in an incredulous tone, "it cut me so—so *gently.*"

Kit took the small hand in his: it was a beautiful hand, delicately but strongly made with the long flexible fingers of a born surgeon, but unfortunately it was extremely dirty. Kit decided that it would have to be washed before he could dress the wound, and he was more annoyed than ever.

"It's quite a clean cut," Jem pointed out, "you can put a bit of plaster on it, can't you."

"The cut may be clean but your hand isn't. I'm not taking any chances with it, my lad," replied Kit.

Jem's hand was washed, and a wet dressing prepared and

bandaged into place with professional skill, the patient taking an intelligent interest in the proceedings.

"I'm quite glad I did it," he declared. "It's been a lesson to me."

"A lesson not to play with razors?"

"No, a lesson in bandaging."

"Well, next time you want a lesson in bandaging you can have it without the wound."

"Will you really?" Jem enquired eagerly. "Will you teach me how you do it criss-cross like that? It's so neat," he added, looking at his finger with pride, "so *very* neat. I should think you must be a very good doctor. I'm glad I'm your first case."

"Well, I'm not glad," declared Kit. He felt it was a bad start and he had been so anxious to start well.

CHAPTER III

DR. PEABODY

THE unpacking was finished now, except for the books which could be left until Kit had more time. He was standing by the dressing table sorting his ties when he heard a gruff voice announce, "I'm strong, I am. A liddle box like that don't worry me, not nowhow."

He swung round in some surprise and was just in time to see Jem dump his empty suitcase on the floor and stand back wiping his brow in ludicrous imitation of Tupman's action.

"Why, Jem!" he exclaimed laughing. "What a fright you gave me! I thought it was Tupman."

"Did you really?" asked Jem, blushing beneath his freckles. "It's just a game I play sometimes—rather a babyish game."

"It's a very amusing game," Kit declared. "Do it again, Jem."

"Shall I really?"

Kit nodded.

"I'll do it properly this time," said Jem. "I'll go outside the door," and he seized the suitcase and departed forthwith.

There was a little pause and then a thundering knock, and the pseudo-Tupman staggered in, balancing the case on his shoulder. In some strange fashion Jem had managed to assume the outstanding characteristics of the man—the screwed up face, the awkward carriage, and the incredibly bowed legs—it was such a life-like imitation that Kit had difficulty in keeping serious.

"Where shall I put it, sir?" he growled.

Kit sprang forward. "It's too heavy for you!" he cried. "It's books, you see. I'd have helped you with it if I'd known. Put it down here, please."

Between them they lowered the empty case on to the floor. "I'm strong, I am," declared the young actor, as he stood back and wiped his forehead. "A liddle box like that don't worry me—not nohow."

"I suppose you're Tupman?" enquired Kit gravely.

"That's roight, sir," he replied, touching his forehead, "Tupman, that's me. There ain't no more to come up 'cept your 'at-box. Master Jem's fetching that."

"Who?" enquired Kit.

"Master Jem, the doctor's grandson," declared the pseudo-Tupman with a jerk of his thumb.

The play was over now, and Tupman changed back into a small boy with sparkling eyes. "Oh!" he cried ecstatically, "oh, wasn't it *good!* It's far more fun when you have somebody to do it with."

Kit thought it had been extremely good. He was aware that Jem had been much better than he had—not only more word-perfect but also better in his rendering of the part—and this was odd because Kit's part should have been much easier to play since he was merely representing himself.

They discussed the performance gravely and at some length. "I listen, you see," said Jem. "I listen with my mind you see, and then I can play it properly."

"I see," said Kit, nodding, "I shall have to—"

"Wait!" cried Jem, suddenly cocking his ears like a terrier at the sound of his master's voice, "wait . . . I believe it is . . ." he rushed to the window and peered out. "Yes, yes it is . . . I thought it was . . it's Grandfather's car. Come on, Dr. Stone."

"Come where?"

"Come down and meet him."

Kit did not want to. He was frightened again—absurdly frightened—but Jem would not listen to his excuses.

"He'll want to *see* you," cried Jem excitedly. "Of course

he'll want to see you. He'll be in the library *now*—do come on."

It was fortunate that Kit had his new friend to lead him through the house for he would have had some difficulty in finding his way alone. He followed Jem along the twisty passages and down the stairs feeling like an ocean liner in tow of a fussy tug.

"Here we are!" cried Jem. "Come on, Dr. Stone," and he opened the door of the library and dragged Kit in.

The old doctor was standing by the fireplace warming his back. He was a big man, heavily built, and his broad shoulders stooped a little with the weight of his years. He was like a lion, Kit thought, blunt-featured and shaggy, his big head was covered with quantities of grey wavy hair. His brown eyes were sharp and keen, they peered out up on the world from beneath a pair of thick grey eyebrows.

"Hallo, what's this?" he asked in a deep rumbling voice which matched his size.

"It's him," declared Jem, dragging Kit across the room by one hand. "He's come, and I've just been helping him to unpack. I knew you'd want to see him—"

The old doctor's somewhat grim face broke into a smile, "Of course I want to see Dr. Stone," he said, as he shook hands with Kit, and then he added, "I hope Jem hasn't been making a nuisance of himself."

"I've been making a helpfulness of myself," cried Jem, dancing about from one foot to the other. "I've been telling him things like where the bathroom is and what time we have lunch, and I folded up his vests and pants and put them away in the drawer. . . ."

"You've made a friend already," said Dr. Peabody, turning to Kit and smiling at him.

"I hope so, sir," replied Kit.

Jem had seized his grandfather's arm and was hanging on

it and chattering up into his face—it was easy to see that Jem was a privileged person, and was fully aware of the fact.

"Dr. Stone has got two steffy—steffo—scopes," he cried. "He's got a funny black one like a trumpet—it's very old, you see because it belonged to his father—and he's got a new one with two ear-things like yours. . . ."

Kit watched the little scene with interest, and because the doctor's attention was fully engaged by his grandson, Kit was able to examine him, and to size him up at leisure. He decided that Dr. Peabody might be a bit of a bully, he probably had firm opinions and would stick to them through thick and thin, but there could be nothing small or mean about such a man—his nature must match his appearance. It amused Kit to see that Dr. Peabody was more than a little embarrassed by the revelations of Jem, and was doing his best to put a stop to them.

"Yes, yes," he said. "No doubt, no doubt . . . but perhaps Dr. Stone would rather . . . after all it's his affair, not ours. . . ."

"He's got a new suit," chattered Jem, "it's grey flannel, and he hasn't worn it yet, so you'll have to remember to pinch him when you see him in it . . . and he's got a little car with a hood. It's green and it goes like smoke and he's going to take me out and let me hold the steering wheel. . . ."

"Yes, yes, very good of him," said Dr. Peabody, "but I think that's enough, Jem. What have you done to your finger, eh?"

"I cut it," Jem said proudly, "I cut it on his razor. It's a funny sort of razor like a little mowing machine. He boiled some water and put a wet dressing on it—look how neat it is! Look, Grandfather!"

"I see," he said, and he looked at Kit and smiled, "I see I've got a very careful assistant," he added.

Kit smiled too. "It was a very dirty finger, sir."

"No doubt, no doubt."

"I'd been cleaning the rabbit-hutch, you see," explained Jem.

The meeting, which Kit had dreaded, had gone off very well and Kit was extremely grateful to Jem for his unconscious support. It's going to be all right, Kit thought, we're going to get on like a house afire.

There was no opportunity for any serious conversation before lunch. Miss Peabody appeared and they all went into the dining-room and sat down at the table. Miss Peabody's appearance had put a stop to Jem's chatter and the old doctor was silent too, so it was left to Kit to carry on a conversation with his hostess. He began to talk about the weather—they discussed it at length and decided that it was rather cold for the time of year—and then Kit enquired whether Miss Peabody had seen "Snow White and the Seven Dwarfs" and was informed that she had seen it "months ago". "I've been abroad, you see," said Kit, who somehow felt that an apology was necessary.

Miss Peabody said she was aware of that.

As a rule Kit found it fairly easy to make conversation, but Miss Peabody defeated him. She was not exactly rude, but she made him feel foolish and it was obvious that she had not the slightest interest in his affairs. He thought that she seemed to resent his presence in the house—it was an uncomfortable feeling.

The pudding course had been served before Miss Peabody noticed Jem's finger and enquired what had happened to it, and Kit was so thankful to find a topic of conversation that he seized upon it at once and explained the circumstances at some length. He was half way through his story when, suddenly, he became aware that Miss Peabody was not amused.

"It's quite all right," babbled Kit. "I mean it's just a scratch ... it will be perfectly healed in a ..."

"I told you not to annoy Dr. Stone!" exclaimed Miss Peabody looking at Jem with a thundery frown. "Why can't you mind your own business? Perhaps this will teach you not to meddle with things that don't concern you."

"But I wasn't annoying him!" cried Jem indignantly, "I was helping him to unpack. I like helping people."

"Helping!" echoed Miss Peabody. "I never knew you liked helping people. There are plenty of things you could do for me if that's what you like."

Jem was silent for a moment and then he said in a low voice, "But you aren't pleased when I try to help you . . . and anyhow they aren't *interesting* things."

"Interesting things! No, perhaps not," agreed Miss Peabody, her voice suddenly shrill with anger, "but how do you suppose the necessary work would get done if people only did the things that they like doing? Do you think it interests me going on day after day ordering food for other people to eat? Do you think I enjoy mending holes in your socks?"

"My dear Ethel," said Dr. Peabody, raising his head and looking at her, "I think your philosophy is too advanced for a child of seven. . . . Go on with your pudding, Jem," he added.

Jem took up his spoon and obeyed.

CHAPTER IV

AN IMPORTANT DISCUSSION

"THE trouble is, you're far too young," Dr. Peabody declared.

The words came as a shock to Kit for he had imagined that he had made a good impression, and that all was well. They had finished lunch and had come into the library together, the door had been shut and the old doctor had taken up his favourite position on the hearth rug.

"Yes, you're far too young," he repeated irritably. "It won't do at all."

"But I'm not really . . . I thought you knew . . ." began Kit in dismay.

"Knew what?"

"My age."

"It was the Rochesters who told me . . . Mrs. Rochester, of course."

"Did she tell you my age," enquired Kit in bewilderment.

"Said you were thirty-five."

Kit was more bewildered than ever. "She can't have said that," he declared. "She doesn't know me."

"That was what she gave me to understand. She said—er—now what was it she said? Let me think . . . yes, she said your brother was over forty—about forty-two and you were seven years younger. Thirty-five that would make you, and you needn't tell me you're anything like that!"

Kit could not help smiling. "My brother is thirty-six, but I admit he looks more."

"So you're twenty-nine . . . and you look less."

Kit laughed.

"It's no laughing matter," grumbled Dr. Peabody. "It's damned annoying, that's what it is. You're no use to me."

"I've had quite a lot of experience—"

"Experience!" snorted the doctor. "It's your looks I'm complaining about. I've got all the experience I need. I want somebody who can diagnose whooping cough and measles and write a prescription for dyspepsia—but he must look like Solomon in his prime."

Kit burst out laughing.

"Curse it," exclaimed Dr. Peabody ferociously, "curse it— I like you, and the boy likes you—curse it!"

"I'm sure I could—"

"No, it's no use. You look about twenty-four. It's no use at all."

"But Dr. Peabody, I assure you—"

"It's the Hill I want you for," continued the old man in an explanatory manner, "that's the devil of it. The Hill would have a fit if I sent you to them . . . the Hill is the curse of my life. If it wasn't for the Hill I could carry on by myself quite easily."

Kit did not understand. "But what is the Hill?" he enquired, for as yet he had not learned that the right way to manage Dr. Peabody was to let him run on in his own fashion. If you sat back and waited patiently the bits of information—tossed out haphazardly—fell into place like the pieces of a jigsaw puzzle and the picture became clear.

"Building!" exclaimed Dr. Peabody, waving Kit's question aside. "They call it building: tossing a few bricks together, sticking in windows, clapping on a lid! That's building nowadays. *This* house wasn't built like that, and it'll be standing when every house on the Hill has fallen down."

"It's a building scheme, then?" murmured Kit.

"What is?"

"The Hill."

"Of course. I told you that, didn't I? Slum clearance, that's what it is."

"I see," said Kit. "They're on the National Health Insurance, then."

The old doctor laughed grimly. "I wish they were," he said. "Panel patients are easily dealt with, and you get paid for them, too. No, the people on the Hill come from the slums of Kensington, from the tenements of Mayfair—la-di-da society women with jangled nerves. Their husbands eat too much rich food, and their children scream in the night—I can't be bothered with them."

Kit said nothing, and after a few moments silence Dr. Peabody sat down and began to fill his pipe. "It's like this, Stone," he said, in a calmer tone. "I've never dealt with people like that before—I don't understand them, and I can't interest myself in their footling ailments. If the women took a reasonable amount of exercise, and the men starved themselves for a week they wouldn't need barbiturics and bicarbonate of soda. I've lost my hair once or twice and told them so—and they don't like it. Minfield used to be a quiet country village . . . I know where I am with quiet country folk. The place has grown like a beanstalk."

"I see," said Kit, "but really I think it would be all right. I've knocked about a good deal, you see. I was in New York for a bit as assistant to a fashionable doctor and I got on all right. That was an experience, I can tell you!"

"New York!"

Kit nodded. "It's a fantastic place, a glittering roundabout. It takes your breath away."

Dr. Peabody was gazing into the fire. "I can't tackle the work," he said. "Getting old, that's what's the matter. I'd have been glad of the extra work when I was young; but now—and I have no son. He died, d'you see! He'd have been thirty-five now. Yes, thirty-five years old. He was twenty-four when he died."

"I'm sorry," Kit said uncomfortably.

"It was a hard blow. The hardest I've had, and that's saying something. The girls are all very well in their way—I've three daughters, and two of them are married—but Jeffrey was . . . he was very special, d'you see? I'd set such store on Jeffrey . . . all my eggs . . . well well, it's no use talking."

Kit made a sympathetic noise.

"Never put all your eggs in one basket," advised the old man, looking up with a faint smile, "it's a bad thing to do. I did it once—and now I've done it again—Jem."

"A most attractive youngster!"

"Attractive! Yes, he's like his mother. She's my eldest daughter. She married a tea-planter when she was thirty and went out to Ceylon. She'd looked after me, d'you see, and brought up the little ones, and then this fellow Manson came along—a good fellow. They're happy."

"So you've got Jem."

"Yes, they can't have him in Ceylon—thank Heaven! He's the only child—my only grandchild. I've had him since he was two years old. His aunt is supposed to look after him."

Kit said nothing. He had learned a good deal about the Peabody family and he was beginning to hope that the doctor was relenting in his attitude. He did not think that the doctor would have told him so much about his private affairs unless he intended to give him a trial.

"It's a pity you look so young," said the doctor at last in reluctant tones.

"Jem said—" began Kit, and then he stopped.

"Eh? What did Jem say? What did the young rogue tell you?"

"He said I was just the right age."

"He did, did he? And what does he know about it?"

"He offered me a partnership when you retire, sir," replied Kit with a grin.

The old man laughed delightedly. "That takes the cake!" he declared. "A partnership when I retire ha—ha—and how long will you have to wait for it?"

"Eighteen years," replied Kit. "He counted it up on his fingers, and decided that I would be in my prime."

"Ha, ha, ha," laughed the doctor. "What a lad . . . he's got it all cut and dried . . . well, well . . . it almost looks as if I'd have to try you out. . . ."

"That's what I thought, sir," agreed Kit.

Strangely enough this seemed to settle the matter. Dr. Peabody drew in his chair to the table and began to discuss the cases he intended to hand over to his assistant.

"There's Mrs. Thorne," he said. "You can take her and make what you can of her. I wouldn't care if I never saw the woman again—eats like a horse and plays bridge from morning to night, and wonders why she can't sleep—"

"Yes," said Kit, scribbling hastily in his note book.

"What are you writing down?" enquired the old man suspiciously. "Good Lord, that'll never do! You'll go and lose that book and there'll be hell to pay!"

Kit handed over the book without speaking.

"Humph!" grunted the doctor. "Shorthand, I suppose. I don't know anything about shorthand but other people do . . . looks like beetles and spiders. . . ."

"It's my own shorthand, sir," Kit told him. "Nobody else could read it. I invented it when I was laid up with dysentery at Cairo—it helped to pass the time."

"Dysentery, eh?"

"Yes, I had rather a bad—"

"Take Gilbert Furnival," interrupted the doctor.

"What did you—"

"Take Gilbert Furnival, I said. He's just come home from Palestine with dysentery—you'll know more about it than I do."

"I know a good deal about it," agreed Kit, with a wry smile.

"H'm, of course you do. The Furnivals are nice people, they're worried to death about Gilbert. He's the only son and they think the world of him. See what you can do."

Kit took down the particulars of the case. He took over about a dozen cases with particulars of each. He was surprised to find that Dr. Peabody had no notes, but seemed to carry all his data in his head. He tumbled it out to Kit in a haphazard manner which was somewhat bewildering (this is frightful, thought Kit scribbling away for dear life, this is positively frightful. The old man doesn't know what he's doing. I shall never get this straight) but afterwards, when Kit had got the information sorted out and classified correctly his opinion of Dr. Peabody was revolutionized, and he saw that the old man had a firm grasp of the essentials in every case.

"Supposing they don't like me!" exclaimed Kit suddenly.

Dr. Peabody laughed. "That's your lookout," he replied. "You've got to make them like you. I'll come if they insist on having me and I'll come if you get into difficulties and want my advice . . . but if too many of them want me . . . then you'll go."

"I'll go!" echoed Kit in bewilderment.

"Back to London or Cairo or New York," explained Dr. Peabody with a smile. "I'll be sorry, of course, but it has to be like that."

Kit saw that this was reasonable. He would be no use at all to the doctor if the patients refused to have him.

"You've got a month," continued Dr. Peabody. "That was what I said—a month's trial. During that time you've got to make up your mind whether you can bear me, and my patients

have got to make up their minds whether they can bear you—
that's all."

"And you, of course," said Kit, smiling at him, "you've got
to make up your mind whether—"

"I can bear you all right," said Dr. Peabody.

CHAPTER V

PRACTICING AT MINFIELD

KIT settled down very quickly at Minfield for he was used to adjusting himself to different conditions of life. Indeed, when he had been there for a week he felt like a fixture in the doctor's household, and was on excellent terms with everyone —except Miss Peabody. He found Miss Peabody difficult to understand. It was obvious that she was unhappy and discontented, but he could see no reason for it. She had quite a good time—she played golf and bridge and belonged to the Minfield Dramatic Club, and had plenty of friends, both male and female. Kit had seen her in the village surrounded by a chattering group of contemporaries, and he was aware that she entertained her friends for tea whenever she so desired. Fortunately for Kit she did not expect him to enter into her activities, the tea-parties took place in the drawing room and he and Dr. Peabody had the library as their own private preserve. From the very beginning Miss Peabody made it obvious that she did not intend to be friends with her father's assistant. She treated him with distant politeness and Kit accorded her politeness in return. They conversed politely at meals, and wished each other good morning and good night, but to all intents and purposes they remained strangers.

Kit had promised himself a pint of real English beer at a real English inn, and he lost no time in redeeming the promise. On his first free evening he walked down the street to the "Fig and Thistle" and joined the assembled company in the bar parlour. At first he was received with suspicion and reserve for he was the doctor's assistant, and a "foreigner" to boot, but Kit had no airs or graces, and was ready to stand a round or

participate in a game of darts or to take his part in any discussion which happened to be in progress. It was agreed that
he had no nonsense about him and, this important point settled,
Kit was accepted into the circle forthwith.

The old doctor raised no objections to this mild form of
entertainment, indeed he encouraged Kit to spend a couple
of evenings a week at the "Fig and Thistle" for he was of the
opinion that this was an excellent way for his young assistant
to become acquainted with the village people, to gain their
confidence and to study their mentality. Kit would learn far
more of human nature by taking part in the confluence at the
"Fig and Thistle" than if he frequented the local picture house,
and the study of human nature was an important part of a
doctor's training. Miss Peabody's views upon the subject were
otherwise. She said nothing at all, but Kit was in no doubt as
to what she thought of his partiality for strong drink and low
company. Miss Peabody was a past mistress in the art of ex-
pressing disapprobation and contempt without the aid of
words.

So much for Kit's private life at Minfield; his professional
duties occupied a much larger portion of his mind. The doctor's
patients received him in different ways, some of them dis-
trusted his youthful appearance and clamoured wildly for
Dr. Peabody, others accepted Kit's ministrations with resignation. Kit adopted a grave demeanour and assured them that
he had a world-wide experience and was older than he looked.
He had half a dozen children recovering from chickenpox and
two recovering from minor operations, and he found, somewhat to his surprise, that they liked him and were willing to
listen to what he said. He treated them with the same respect
as their seniors, and when he had time he sat on their beds and
told them about the South Seas. Besides these, he had Mrs.
Thorne and several of her ilk—people who liked nothing better than to talk about their aches and pains to a sympathetic

listener. Dr. Peabody had had no patience with them, but Kit dealt with them faithfully. He listened to all they said, he looked as grave as a judge, he examined them with elaborate care and gave them harmless medicines.

Gilbert Furnival was the only serious case which Dr. Peabody had handed over to his assistant, and Kit gave a good deal of time and thought to the young man's condition. Having suffered from dysentery himself, Kit was better able to put himself into his patient's skin, and he was aware that hope and confidence was the best medicine he could give. When he had observed the case carefully and had carried out the usual tests he decided on a plan of action and started upon it forthwith.

"I was much worse than you are," he told the young man, not altogether truthfully, "and you've got advantages over me in other ways. The food and the climate, for instance."

"They don't understand," declared Gilbert Furnival, with a heavy sigh. "They won't tell me anything. . . ."

Kit nodded. "I know," he said, "they tried that game with me, but of course I knew a good deal about it. Now look here, I'm going to tell you all I know, and we're going to work together. Is that a bargain?"

It was a strange bargain, but it brought a glint of hope to young Furnival's eye. They shook hands upon it gravely and Kit proceeded at once to carry out his share of the pact. He discussed Furnival's condition frankly, he changed his medicine, regulated his diet and gave him new hope. In less than a week there was a perceptible improvement in Gilbert Furnival's condition; he acknowledged it himself and declared that Kit was the best doctor in the world. This was exactly what Kit had hoped for. He was aware that the improvement was due not so much to the alterations in treatment, as to his personal influence and encouragement. He was aware that there were bound to be ups and downs before his patient was once more a fit man, but, now that he had gained his patient's confidence, the battle was more than half won, he could go forward to victory with a light heart.

Mr. and Mrs. Furnival had been somewhat distrustful of Kit's boyish looks and of the new medicine and diet which he had prescribed but the improvement in their son's condition set all their doubts at rest and they declared themselves more than satisfied. They sang Dr. Stone's praises to their friends and, as they knew everybody and were exceedingly popular in the residential area of Minfield, their championship was well worth having. Kit's stock went up by leaps and bounds and he began to find messages upon the telephone pad asking for him by name.

Dr. Peabody chaffed him in a friendly manner on his success. "It's unbearable," he declared with a twinkle in his eye. "It's more than human flesh can endure . . . to be ousted from my own practice by a whipper-snapper. Here are half the people on the Hill clamouring for Dr. Stone."

"I thought that was what you wanted, sir," said Kit, with an innocent air.

"What I wanted!" cried the old doctor. "Good Lord, what made you think that? I wouldn't have minded so much if they had accepted you with a decent show of reluctance, but they're *all over you.* They haven't clamoured for me once . . . it's rank ingratitude. There's Mrs. Thorne, for instance," he continued, shaking his head regretfully, "I've spent hours listening to that woman's complaints, and longed to give her a good smacking —which would do her all the good in the world—and now she's lost to me, she doesn't spare me a thought."

The more Kit saw of Dr. Peabody the more he liked him and respected him. He was old-fashioned, of course, but he was honest and wise and exceedingly kind. It was true that he had little patience with people who made a fuss about nothing, or who failed to carry out his behests, but when his patients were really ill he could not do enough for them. Kit was at first somewhat alarmed at the old doctor's methods of diagnosis for they were based upon instinct rather than science, but Dr. Peabody had seen so many sick people during his practice that he was seldom wrong.

"How on earth do you do it?" Kit asked (he had discovered that he could say what he liked without fear of giving offense).

"How do I do it!"

"Yes," said Kit nodding, "I want to know."

"Well, bless me," said Dr. Peabody, frowning with the effort to explain the inexplicable. "Well, I don't know how I do it to tell you the truth. I take a good look at them, d'you see, and something tells me what's gone wrong ... it's a look they have ... and there's a feeling about the skin ... I can't explain it, somehow."

The dispensary adjoined the consulting room; it was a slip of a place with a sink and shelves and cupboards and the usual apparatus for mixing drugs and carrying out tests. The air was permeated by a smell of ether and antiseptics and aromatic oils, and on this particular afternoon (when the foregoing conversation took place) Dr. Peabody had followed his assistant into the dispensary and was watching him at work. He was a little scornful of Kit's "new-fangled" ideas—or at least he pretended to be.

"You're wasting your time, young man," he declared. "I could have diagnosed that woman's condition in two minutes. She needs iron, and raw liver and plenty of fresh air. I've told her so half a dozen times, but she won't listen to me."

Kit was slightly nettled. He had spent some considerable time analysing the woman's blood and had come to the same conclusion as Dr. Peabody.

"I'm not a wizard," he said, with a half-hearted smile. "I'm just an ordinary mortal."

"Don't you get too cocky."

"Cocky?" Kit exclaimed, "but I said—"

"You said you were just an ordinary mortal, and when any-body says that to me I begin to look out for squalls. If you thought you were an ordinary mortal you'd keep quiet about it, d'you see? That's how we're made. Human nature is a queer mixture but the principal ingredient is vanity—yes, vanity. It's not a bad thing to have a good percentage of vanity, for we couldn't get far without it—no, we couldn't get very far—but it's got to be kept in check, d'you see, and a doctor more than any other man on earth runs the danger of getting too pleased with himself."

"I believe that's true," said Kit thoughtfully.

"Of course it's true. How can it be otherwise when every patient you visit treats you like an oracle, and all their rela-tions hang on your words and bind themselves to carry out your behests? Yes, they hang on your words, poor souls, and demand of you 'Will he live? Will he die?' and they're con-vinced that your drugs will cure every ill from cancer to housemaid's knee."

Kit sat on the edge of the sink and thought about it. "Not all of them," he said.

"Most of them," declared Dr. Peabody. "The faith they should vest in their Maker is vested in us. It's a humbling thought—or should be."

There was a little silence.

"I suppose you think I'm a failure," continued Dr. Peabody at last, "you think I'm a failure because I'm only a G.P. in a little country town—an old-fashioned G.P.—eh?" The words were shot out fiercely and the grey brows beetled in a frown.

"No," said Kit thoughtfully.

"Eh?"

"No, I don't think you're a failure. I don't think anyone could do your job better. You know your patients and they trust you."

Dr. Peabody's frown faded. "H'm!" he snorted. "Yes, they

trust me . . . I shouldn't be much good if they didn't. By the way what's that thing you were talking about yesterday—that electric machine?"

"You mean the lamp for infrared rays," said Kit steadily, but his heart leapt with delight. (He had suggested that this apparatus for the treatment of rheumatism and neuritis should be installed in the consulting room, and Dr. Peabody had refused point blank.)

"Infrared rays," said Dr. Peabody. "H'm, well . . . you'd better find out what it would cost. We'll think about it, d'you see, but we're not going to launch out into any other new-fangled ideas. They've got to be proved first, you understand, and we'll let other men prove them."

Kit said nothing, and for a few moments there was silence.

"It's difficult to steer straight," said the old doctor at last. "Life's a queer set-out, Stone. In the old days the innovator was a figure of suspicion, he was laughed at, he was scorned. The Florentine Church tortured Galileo, and Lister was persecuted and ostracised for his antiseptic surgery. Yes, the way of the innovator was strewn with boulders . . . nowadays it's too smooth. It's dangerously smooth."

"You mean anything new must be good?"

"So they think. Anything new—any new machine to send electric current through their bodies, any new treatments, or diets, or inoculations! Well, well, there may be good in some of them but we'll just go warily, you and I. You'll keep me up to date and I'll keep you from flying off the handle. H'm—and how's Gilbert Furnival doing these days?"

CHAPTER VI

A CHEERFUL TEA-PARTY

IT WAS a wet Sunday afternoon. Kit was sitting by the fire in the library and Jem was curled up beside him in the huge leather chair. Jem's lithe body fitted very comfortably into the space between the arm of the chair and Kit's lean frame. They were engrossed in the "Adventures of the Swiss Family Robinson"; it belonged to Kit, and had come to the doctor's house in the case of books which Tupman had carried up to Kit's room. Kit had not read it since he was a child—had not even thought of it—but now he was remembering it, and enjoying it both on his own account and through the enjoyment of his young friend. He was obliged to simplify the language for Jem, and to explain a good deal of it in his own words, but he considered himself well repaid for the trouble when he saw Jem's delight and the intense interest he was taking in the story.

"Penguins and flamingoes!" said Jem, in a dreamy voice. "Just think of them, Dr. Kit."

"Yes," agreed Kit. He forbore to point out that penguins and flamingoes could not really be found in neighbourly juxta-position—except perhaps in the Zoo—for it was obvious that Jem believed every word of the story, and why shouldn't he?

"They *were* lucky to be wrecked," continued Jem. "I wish I had been there . . . but I was there, really. Jack is me."

"Frank is you because he's seven years old—."

"No, he was a mutt," Jem said. "He was a mutt and clung to his mother and cried. I wouldn't have done that."

Kit remembered that he had felt the same; he had always been Jack, the dare-devil.

The book slipped to one side, the fire burned slowly in the grate and the rain beat on the windows.

"Aunt Dolly's coming," said Jem suddenly. "Did you know? She's coming to stay here."

"Is she?" enquired Kit in a sleepy voice.

"Yes," said Jem. "She's married, you know. It was fun when she was married. We had a lovely party." He thought for a few moments and then enquired, "D'you think Aunt Ethel will ever get married?"

"I don't know."

"It would be nice," Jem said. "I like weddings. Everyone's so nice and jolly and jokey . . . but I don't believe she will. I don't believe anyone would want to marry her."

Kit was disinclined to enter into a discussion upon the subject of Miss Peabody's chances of matrimony. "Tell me about Aunt Dolly," he said.

"She's nice," said Jem promptly.

"Is that all you can tell me about her?"

"It's lots," declared Jem. "She's—she's happy, you know, and she says funny things and makes you laugh. I like it when people do that."

Kit agreed that it was extremely pleasant. He began to wonder what Mrs. Dorman would be like and what effect her advent would produce upon the Peabody household. In spite of Jem's assurance that she was nice, he found himself resenting the arrival of a new member for he had now made himself a place in the household and had settled down comfortably. His place would have to be remade, and various adjustments would be necessary. It was a nuisance, he thought.

"It's cosy," said Jem in a sleepy voice.

"Yes—cosy," agreed Kit. He felt Jem settle down more comfortably into the crook of his arm . . . and then . . . his eyes closed.

He had no sooner closed his eyes than he was asleep, and

almost at once he began to dream. He dreamed that Miss Peabody came into the room. She was dressed in white with a bridal veil and orange blossoms in her hair. Kit was not at all astonished to see her like this for, somehow or other, he was aware that this was her wedding day. He looked at her and she looked at him, and smiled in a pleasant way without any undercurrent of bitterness. "Hallo, Kit," she said, "I'm just going down to the Fig and Thistle."

Even this extraordinary statement did not surprise Kit, for it seemed quite natural that Miss Peabody should want a drink to fortify her for the ceremony in which she was to take part. He was about to reply and offer to accompany her when the dream faded.

Kit awoke with the sound of Miss Peabody's voice ringing in his ears, and the first thing he saw when he opened his eyes was the figure of Miss Peabody standing before him on the hearth rug. She was dressed in her usual neat fashion, in a tailor-made coat and skirt, and she was carrying a green leather hand-bag. The bridal dress and orange blossoms had vanished, and so had the smile—her face wore an expression of annoyance and disgust. Kit was still sleepy and he was also somewhat dazed at the sudden change from dreaming to reality. He gazed at her without moving and she gazed back, and the curl of her lips showed her scorn; *this is a fine way to be spending the afternoon,* she seemed to be saying. He could not think why she was so much annoyed, for it was his free afternoon and if he chose to spend it sleeping by the fire it was none of her business. He might have gone out and walked in the rain, but why should he?

They were still gazing at each other in silence. Kit wondered whether she expected him to get up—he had always made a point of treating her with respect—but if he moved it would disturb Jem. He glanced down at the boy's face and saw that his eyes were closed and his long silky brown lashes were spread out upon his cheeks like fans. Like most children Jem was pathetic in his sleep; he looked like an angel, delicate and other-worldly. Suddenly Miss Peabody took a step forward as if to rouse the boy, and Kit raised his free hand to his lips.

"Hush, Jem's asleep," he whispered.

She hesitated for a moment and then tossed her head and turned away. The door closed softly behind her.

Kit was wide awake now, but bewildered by the incident which seemed quite inexplicable. Why had she come? What had she wanted? He was further muddled by the atmosphere of his dream which still hung about him. In his dream Miss Peabody had been like a different person. He was aware that dreams have no significance and are merely the wanderings of the subconscious mind, but it seemed very queer that even in a dream he should have seen her completely different from what she was, completely different from what he had ever imagined her to be. Kit was meditating upon this and wondering whether Miss Peabody had it in her to be friendly and pleasant, and whether the fact that she was neither the one nor the other could be due to some unfortunate turn of Fate, when suddenly he felt a strange shaking in the chair beside him and looking down he saw that Jem's eyes were open and his whole face was creased with laughter.

"Jem!" he exclaimed in amazement.

"Oh, wasn't she cross!" cried Jem, abandoning himself to mirth. "Oh, wasn't she in a rage. Doesn't she hate us to be friends!"

"Does she?" asked Kit incredulously.

"Of course she does. It makes her squirm . . . didn't you see her squirming, Dr. Kit?"

Kit looking back upon the incident, saw that Jem's reading of it might be the true one.

"We don't mind, do we?" said Jem smugly.

Kit could not dismiss the affair so easily for he liked to be comfortable with his fellow human beings. He had wondered about Miss Peabody a good deal, for she was the pea in the mattress of his otherwise pleasant life. He had tried very hard to make friends with her, he was willing to go out of his way to propitiate her, but he was certainly not willing to give up his friendship with Jem. If that was the only way to gain her friendship he would relinquish all attempts to gain it. He was still considering the matter when Tupman appeared with the tea and proceeded to lay it on the solid round table which stood in the middle of the room.

"You look roight comfortable, sir," he said, as he spread the cloth.

"We are," Kit replied, smiling.

"That's roight," said Tupman benignantly. "Out 'alf the noight, wasn't you? I 'eard you come in about foive."

Kit admitted the fact ". . . and it was only a tummy-ache after all," he added somewhat regretfully.

Tupman nodded. "That's loife, that is," he pointed out. "Nointy-noine cases out of a 'undred it's the stomach-ache an' the 'undreth case is appendicitis. I've 'eard the doctor say it toime and again."

He laid out the plates and cups and saucers deftly and went away, and a few minutes later Dr. Peabody came in.

"Don't get up," he said smiling.

"It would be difficult, sir," replied Kit.

The doctor sat down by the fire and put his feet in the grate. His trousers steamed gently.

"I suppose it wouldn't be any good asking you to change, sir?" enquired Kit mischievously.

"Not a bit. I've gone about with wet feet for sixty years or more—it does me no harm. Where's Ethel?"

"I don't know," Kit replied. "She came in when Jem was asleep—at least I thought he was asleep—"

"Well, I might have been asleep," said Jem.

"I'm afraid I *was* asleep," admitted Kit apologetically.

"And why shouldn't you be asleep," enquired Dr. Peabody. "Why should it be a crime to be asleep in the afternoon?"

"We were reading, you see," explained Jem sitting up and smoothing his tuft of hair, "and then we were talking—Dr. Kit's a very listeny sort of person—and then we just slid off to sleep . . . at least I was only pretending."

"So that was the way of it?"

"Yes. Can we have tea?" he enquired, glancing at the table.

"I see no reason to wait," replied his grandfather. "Ethel must have gone out—though why anyone should want to go out on a wet Sunday afternoon is more than I can fathom."

"I needn't wash my hands, need I?" said Jem. "They're quite clean really and let's sit where we are, it's nice and cosy near the fire."

They moved the table onto the hearth rug and started. Dr. Peabody poured out the tea and handed round the cups. Kit had been long enough a member of the household to be aware that if Miss Peabody had been present Jem would have been sent upstairs to wash his hands and the whole party would have been marshalled round the table—but Miss Peabody was absent.

Jem took a piece of bread and butter in each hand and bit them turn about. "I'm like the Hatter," he declared, waving them in the air as he spoke, "look at the neat little marks of my teeth in the butter—look at them, Kit."

"Did Dr. Stone give you permission to call him Kit?" enquired his grandfather mildly.

"No, but he doesn't mind," declared Jem. "We're friends, you see."

Kit did not mind at all. He did not even mind when Jem dropped crumbs upon his waistcoat and borrowed his handkerchief to wipe his buttery fingers; he minded nothing that

Jem did. It was by far the most enjoyable meal of which Kit had partaken since his arrival at Minfield, and the reason was not far to seek. They're very much alike, Kit thought, looking from Jem to his grandfather and smiling indulgently, they're both being as naughty as they can and glorying in their wickedness.

Dr. Peabody's wickedness was relative to cherry jam—he had taken a helping twice as large as usual and was eating it with his teaspoon with obvious enjoyment—Kit was aware that Miss Peabody would not have tolerated such a procedure; for one thing she was propriety personified, and, for another, she was of a frugal nature. Miss Peabody liked to economize, and especially to economize in jam; she rationed Jem strictly and sometimes, when occasion seemed to warrant the liberty, she would point out to her father that jam in general and cherry jam in particular was exceedingly bad for his acidity.

"Cake," said Jem suddenly, *"cherry*-cake. Two pieces, please."

"But you haven't got two mouths," objected his grandfather.

"I've got two hands," replied Jem, grinning widely.

He leaned forward and held them out and received a piece of cake in each. This was rank spoiling of course, but Kit looked on indulgently for he was infected with the spirit of liberty—not to say licence—which filled the air.

"You should call on the Rochesters," said Dr. Peabody suddenly.

Kit nodded, he had decided that he must do that sometime, but the days slipped past so rapidly and there was so much to do that he had put it off indefinitely.

"You should call," repeated the doctor, "they were instrumental in bringing you here. I saw a good deal of them when they came here first about three years ago—he had a whitlow and she weighed in with a sharp attack of gastritis—but I haven't seen much of them lately."

"I'll call tomorrow," Kit said.

"Yes, call tomorrow . . . You'll like them. They're pleasant people, and devoted to each other. Mrs. Rochester is a Scot, and she claimed me as a fellow-countryman before I had been in the house ten minutes."

"But you aren't—"

"My mother was," declared the doctor, "so I'm half and half. I used to spend all my summer holidays in Scotland—"

"And you fished," cried Jem eagerly. "Tell Kit how you fished in the river and about the day you caught a whopping big fish."

Dr. Peabody smiled but did not comply. "Strangely enough my mother's family is distantly related to the Macfarlanes. Mrs. Rochester was a Miss Macfarlane of course—so we decided that we were cousins and immediately became friends. A distant cousinship is a very strong bond between Scots, you know."

Kit nodded. He was aware of the fact already, for he had met many Scots during his travels and had seen, and sometimes envied, their clannish tendencies.

"More cake," remarked Jem, with his mouth full of crumbs.

Dr. Peabody demurred. "You've had two pieces," he said. "Why not have bread and butter now?"

"No. *Cake,*" said Jem firmly. "Cake with butter on it, please."

"Cake with butter on it!" exclaimed the doctor, and his astonishment at the request was so ludicrous that Kit threw back his head and roared with laughter.

Dr. Peabody laughed too. "Well!" he said at last, "well, what do you think of that, Kit? Cake with butter on it! Did you ever have cake with butter on it when you were seven?"

"No," said Kit, trying to look grave.

"No, I should think not. Cake with butter! Bless me, what will the child ask for next?"

"Cake with jam on it!" cried Jem, bouncing up and down with excitement. "Cake with cherry jam—"

Kit assumed a serious professional air. "I should be inclined to prescribe cake with butter," he announced. "Butter is an exceedingly wholesome fat; the nutritive value is high." He cut two slices of cake and began to butter them.

Dr. Peabody laughed heartily. "Why, bless my soul!" he cried. "You're as bad as I am! You're worse!"

CHAPTER VII

A FIRST CALL

ON THE following day Kit started forth upon his afternoon round with the intention of polishing off his patients quickly and neatly and calling on Mrs. Rochester at tea-time. For this purpose Kit had donned his new suit and a gaily coloured tie and had covered his finery with an old waterproof to protect it from oil and dirt; but, alas for his plans, Monday was one of those "bad days" with which every doctor is familiar—it was one of those days when everything seems to go wrong—when every bronchitis seems to be heading straight for pneumonia, and when every scratch seems to be turning septic. Visits which normally would have taken ten minutes absorbed half an hour, and patients and relations insisted on discussing their symptoms at length.

"I scarcely slept a wink all night. . . ."

"He doesn't seem so well today. . . ."

"She's had a good deal of pain. . . ."

Kit listened to the anxious bleatings and soothed them as best he could. He was sick at heart and worn out physically and mentally when he returned, late for dinner, to the doctor's house.

"Well, did you call?" enquired Dr. Peabody, looking up with a kind smile.

"Did I call!" echoed Kit in despairing tones. "Did I *call!*"

"It was like that, was it?"

"It was," said Kit. "I've decided to give up medicine and start growing tomatoes—or cabbages or something. . . ."

Dr. Peabody chuckled. "I know," he declared, "I've often felt the same . . . but cheer up, tomorrow will be better. Just wait until tomorrow before you buy your seed. You'll find everybody much better tomorrow."

Strange to say Dr. Peabody was right and on the following day Kit found his patients better, and more cheerful. He finished his afternoon round in record time and drove up to the Rochesters' house to make his call. The door was opened by a tall angular parlourmaid with a very efficient manner; she led him through the house and into the garden.

The brief glimpse of the house as Kit passed through gave him an impression of comfort and peace, of soft colours and pleasant shapes. The rooms were large and airy and there was plenty of room to move, the floors were of polished parquet with Persian rugs upon them. Kit followed his guide through the French windows of the drawing room onto a sunny sheltered terrace and down some steps of crazy paving into a wide shallow hollow which had been converted into a rock-garden. There was a woman here, kneeling amongst the rocks, and, as Kit approached, she rose in one graceful movement and came to meet him.

"Dr. Stone," said the parlourmaid distinctly. Kit took Mrs. Rochester's hand and found himself looking into grey eyes which were almost on a level with his own . . . she *is* tall, he thought.

"I'm so glad you've come," Mrs. Rochester said. "I would have asked you to dinner, but I knew you would be busy settling down."

"Yes," said Kit.

She was smiling at him encouragingly. "You're not like your brother," she said, "but why should you be? Brothers are often quite unlike each other."

"Yes," said Kit again. He was aware that he was not playing his part very well but he could not help it, for he had been taken by surprise. He had heard so much about Mrs. Rochester, and he had made a picture of her in his mind—quite subconsciously, of course—and Mrs. Rochester did not resemble the picture in the very least. For one thing she was much younger and more attractive . . . and for another she was much more human and friendly. Kit decided that the reason he had been so taken aback at Mrs. Rochester's appearance was because he had expected to find a stranger; but this woman was not a stranger. He had never seen her before and yet he knew her quite well.

They were walking back to the house together now, and Mrs. Rochester was talking easily and pleasantly about her part in arranging Kit's affairs.

"I'm not as a rule an interfering sort of person," she was saying, "and I began to wonder if it was going to be a success."

"Oh yes," said Kit, "at least it is from my point of view."

"It *is* a success then," she declared, smiling at him. "I've heard quite a lot about Dr. Stone, and I've heard nothing but good. The Furnivals think the world of you."

"I like them very much," said Kit uncomfortably.

"They're dears," she declared, "and I've been so sorry for them—especially Gilbert, of course. It's hard for a boy of his age to feel weak and ill and fit for nothing . . . you've done wonders for him, you've given them all new hope."

"I've tried to," Kit said, "and as a matter of fact you've hit the nail on the head . . . I've altered their outlook and made them take an optimistic view."

Kit had now begun to recover his wits, and he found Mrs. Rochester easy to talk to. He had intended to stay for ten minutes—his first call was to be on strictly conventional lines—but presently he found himself sitting in the drawing room accepting a cup of tea. It was easier to look at his hostess now that her hands were occupied, and Kit wanted to look at her. He wanted to find out, if he could, why she had had such a strange effect upon him. She was not beautiful, nor glamorous (he had seen plenty of women who were both and they had not moved him at all) but there was something about her which drew him to her as a magnet draws steel. So while she poured out tea he examined her critically to find out where this attraction lay. It was an unusual face, he decided, the eyes were grey, very clear and candid, and they sparkled with life and twinkled with humour as their owner talked or listened, but in repose the whole expression changed, and became sorrowful. Her hair was slightly wavy—it was dark brown with reddish lights in it—and her complexion was pale. She was tall and slim, and long-necked, and she showed in every movement the strange awkward grace of a young colt. He had seen this awkward grace in the first moment when she had risen in one lithe movement to greet him.

Mrs. Rochester raised her eyes and smiled at Kit. "Don't you think so?" she enquired.

"Er—yes," stammered Kit, "yes, of course I do."

She laughed. "You haven't the least idea what I said, have you?"

"I'm terribly sorry—"

"Why should you listen? Why should we be obliged to listen to people when our own thoughts are more interesting?"

"Do I know you well enough?" he asked, smiling at her.

"I feel as if I knew you quite well," she replied with a thoughtful air.

He was glad to find that she had the same feeling—the feeling that they were not strangers, meeting for the first time. He would have liked to pursue the subject, but it was too soon. Later when he had known her longer he would re-open the subject. . . .

"Doctors must have such a lot to think about," continued Mrs. Rochester. "It must be difficult to stop worrying about one patient before they go on to another. It must be difficult to come back to ordinary everyday life when they shut the door of a house behind them."

Kit nodded. "You look up at the sky," he said, "and you take a deep breath . . . and then you go on to the next house. Perhaps the most difficult thing of all is when you leave one house with the shadow of death hovering over it and go on to another to find someone making a fuss over nothing at all."

"You haven't got used to it yet?"

"I suppose you would get used to it in time. This is my first experience of private practice in England."

"Mrs. Stone said you were a great traveller."

Kit smiled suddenly—it was the sort of thing Mabel would say (in fact he could almost hear her saying it in her thin, rather high-pitched voice. "Kit is a dear boy—we're both so fond of him—he's a great traveller of course.")

"I never thought of myself as a great traveller," Kit declared. "I've been to lots of places, of course. I like seeing new places. There's so much to see."

"I'd like to travel. I feel as if I wanted to see *everything*."

"Rather a large order."

"I know, but that's how I feel. It seems wrong to stay in the same place day after day when there's so much to see. It seems —wasteful."

"Wasteful?" he asked in surprise.

"That's what I feel. It's a selfish feeling, really. One isn't so important as all that. It isn't really wasteful that there should be so many beauties in the world unseen by me. . . ."

"I felt that too!" Kit exclaimed. "I was gathering all the interesting things I saw for myself."

"Why shouldn't you?" she asked. "You have no ties. What is right for you would be wrong for me." She smiled at him and continued, "But I do travel sometimes, you know. I travel in space very easily and quickly and you can be back for dinner."

"To Babylon by candlelight!"

"Of course . . . I see you understand."

"I used to do that," he told her, "before I was free."

"What a nuisance bodies are!" she said. "How terribly heavy and cumbersome and helpless! They must be conveyed from place to place at vast expense by train or ship or air. They must have a place to sleep every night and constant supplies of food. Wouldn't it be marvellous if we could leave our bodies behind when we want to travel and see the world?"

This was a new idea to Kit, and it was rather an intriguing idea. He considered it quite seriously before he rejected it. "You would lose a good deal," he said at last, "because a great many of the impressions you receive are received through your body. Different kinds of food, for instance . . . perhaps that sounds rather greedy, but, to me, the food is an important part of travelling. It helps me to understand people better if I eat their kind of food. . . . I like eating dates in the desert if you know what I mean. . . ." He looked at her to see if she understood.

"Go on," she said eagerly.

"And the feeling of things," said Kit, searching for words. "The warmth of the sun, the grittiness of the sand, the dryness of the atmosphere—you would lose all that, wouldn't you? And you would lose the smells. I don't know anything more wonderful than the first smell of land, rich and spicy with tropical scents, after weeks at sea."

"You've made your case," she told him. "To Babylon by candlelight is a poor second best."

"Perhaps you'll travel someday."

"Perhaps . . . but I'm not really a wanderer—not a true nomad. I'd love to travel but I should always want to come back . . . and I should be miserable unless I had a place to come back to, a little piece of my own land that belonged to me."

He looked round the room, "I don't wonder—" he began.

"Not here," she said hastily. "Not this place. It doesn't really belong to us, it's only rented."

"I like it," Kit told her. "It's peaceful and pretty. I like the way the house is situated on a little shelf or terrace with the ground sloping away from it into the valley."

"That's why it's called the Lynchet. It means a terrace."

Kit liked the name.

"It *is* nice," she added, looking round, "but you can't feel the same about a place that doesn't really belong to you. We've got it on a ten years' lease but it doesn't *feel* the same."

"Your home is in Scotland?"

"My old home is sold—it had to be sold when my father died —but I've still got a foot in the soil. I kept one of the cottages on the estate. It's quite small—just an acre of ground on the hillside—but it's mine right down far into the earth and right up into the sky—my very own."

She spoke with such intensity that Kit had a glimpse of her heart, and, although he had never possessed a foot of land (and had never wanted to) he understood exactly how she felt.

"I don't go there often," Mrs. Rochester continued, "but I know I can go when I want to—that's the important thing. An old servant lives in it and keeps it aired. She has a pension, you see, and it suits her to live there rent free and look after it. As a matter of fact it's the most satisfactory arrangement I ever made because it suits us both so perfectly." She laughed a little and added, "I seem to be talking a lot about myself."

Kit had not noticed it; he thought the conversation had been evenly balanced. "I was told you were a very silent person," he said.

Mrs. Rochester laughed. "I know who told you that. It was Mrs. Stone. I like her, you know, but somehow or other we haven't much in common, and I'm one of those stupid people who find it difficult to make conversation . . . I was brought up in the country with dogs and horses and books. Mrs. Stone is a town person, isn't she?"

Kit agreed that she was.

"I do try to talk," Mrs. Rochester declared, "but apparently my efforts are unavailing."

Kit rose suddenly. "I must go," he said, glancing at the clock. "I meant to stay for ten minutes and I've been here over an hour."

"But we aren't strangers," she told him. "I feel responsible for your being here—"

"And I meant to thank you," said Kit ruefully. "I haven't done anything I meant to do."

"There's nothing to thank me for. We all like meddling with other people's affairs."

They smiled at each other. "I feel I have to thank you for meddling with mine," Kit told her. "I'm very happy here. I like the work, and Dr. Peabody is splendid."

"I haven't seen much of him lately," Mrs. Rochester said, "we've been so healthy. That's the worst of a doctor—you only see him when you're ill. Dolly used to come here quite often before she was married. You don't know Dolly, of course."

"She's coming to stay with her father."

Mrs. Rochester nodded. "I know. I had a letter from her this morning. It will be lovely seeing her again. She's a dear. I missed her dreadfully when she married her sailor and went away; but they're very happy, and that's the main thing."

"Yes," said Kit.

"And Jem," said Mrs. Rochester, "tell me about Jem. I haven't seen him for ages."

He told her about Jem as they moved slowly through the hall, and recounted some of his funny sayings; and Mrs. Rochester listened and laughed and declared that she must see Jem as soon as possible and renew her acquaintance with him.

"He used to come to tea and play in the garden," she said.

"Dolly used to bring him . . . perhaps you'll bring him some day, will you?"

Kit said he would.

"Come again soon," she added, as they shook hands at the door. "Come whenever you can."

CHAPTER VIII

THE YOUTHFUL DOCTOR

IT WAS after eleven and Kit had gone up to bed. He was thinking about the events of the day, and especially of his call at the Lynchet and his meeting with Mrs. Rochester. He would see her again. He would see her often, and they would talk about all sorts of things. She had told him to come whenever he liked and he would take advantage of the invitation—why shouldn't he? Not tomorrow, of course, thought Kit, but perhaps Friday, that would not be too soon. He felt happy and contented for he had found a friend in Minfield—a real friend —and because of this discovery Minfield itself seemed pleasanter and more homelike. Yes, he was very glad he had met her. He had never met anyone like her before; never anyone so natural and friendly and comfortable, never anyone who understood so well. What a fool he had been to put off his call on Mrs. Rochester! He had wasted nearly three weeks.

Kit thought about her as he took off his tie—he shut his eyes for a moment and tried to see her with his mind—her oval face, and her smooth dark hair with its heavy wave, and the roll of curls round the back of her neck. It was her eyes that he saw most clearly. They were honest eyes, straight and clear and cordial, and the colour of cloudy skies.

What was her name, he wondered. She had worn a little brooch with the initial "M" in brilliants. Could it be Mary, or Margery—no, she wasn't like a Margery, somehow. He tried over several names and matched them to her but none of them suited her very well.

Kit had started to undress in earnest now. He had taken off

his coat and had begun to undo his braces when there was a knock at the door. It opened very slowly and Jem appeared.

"Hallo!" said Kit in surprise.

"Hallo!" said Jem. He was wearing a brown woolly dressing gown with a red cord round his waist; his eyes were large and dewy and his straw-coloured hair was standing on end.

"Why aren't you asleep?" asked Kit, somewhat sternly.

"I can't go to sleep."

"But why? There must be some reason. Have you got a pain?"

"I'm worrying," said Jem gravely. "You can't go to sleep if you're worrying."

Kit was aware of this unfortunate fact. He enquired sympathetically into the cause of Jem's trouble.

"I've broken Grandfather's heart—"

"Grandfather's heart!"

"His heart—thing," Jem explained. "His steffyscope."

Kit was suitably dismayed. "My goodness!" he cried. "What were you doing with Grandfather's stethoscope? Why on earth can't you leave his things alone? You know perfectly well you aren't allowed to play with his instruments!"

Jem bore these reproaches with outraged dignity. "I wasn't *playing* with it," he declared, "you don't play with steffyscopes, you *use* them."

"Well, what were you doing with it?"

"I was using it."

"What for?"

"It was a bird," said Jem gravely. "It was a poor bird that was ill . . . I had to examine the bird, hadn't I?"

Kit looked at the small figure with some amusement but he hid the amusement beneath a grave manner; it was really naughty of Jem to take the stethoscope. Jem was always ready with excuses for anything he did, and the worst of it was his excuses were so excellent and so plausible that they cut the ground from under your feet. You began to wonder whether he really had been naughty or whether you were being too hard upon him, and lacking in understanding.

"Why did you have to examine the bird?" Kit asked as sternly as he could.

"Why?"

"Yes, why?"

"It was ill," Jem pointed out, "and anyhow I must have practice. Doctors have to practice a lot before they're any good." He took a dead bird out of the pocket of his dressing gown and laid it down on the table . . . and sighed . . . "Poor thing, it's dead!" he said in a sad tone. "Poor thing! I couldn't hear its heart beating at all . . . so I knew it was too late."

"It was much too late," agreed Kit, glancing at the small corpse with some distaste.

"It was a pity," Jem said, and his voice had all the sorrow of the world in it. "It was a pity I didn't find it sooner . . . when it was just a little bit ill."

Kit felt his heart melting. He pulled himself together and returned to the point. "That's all very well," he declared, "but you know quite well that you shouldn't have taken the stethoscope."

"I had to see—"

"No," said Kit firmly, "you had no business to take it. I shouldn't dream of borrowing Grandfather's stethoscope—no doctor would do such a thing."

"You've got one of your own," Jem reminded him. "In fact you've got two, haven't you?"

That was quite true, of course, and it was just like Jem to turn the tables in this uncomfortable fashion. "H'm . . . you had better go back to bed," said Kit. "You'll get cold wandering about in your dressing gown. We'll have to tell Grandfather about it in the morning."

"I thought you'd tell him now," said Jem quickly. "I thought perhaps you'd go along to his room and tell him."

"You thought that, did you?" enquired Kit, turning away to hide a smile.

"Yes."

"Why should I?"

"You could tell him better than me," said Jem engagingly.

"But why tell him now? We can't do anything about it tonight."

"Because then I wouldn't worry any more and I could go to sleep."

"Well—" said Kit doubtfully.

"Please, Kit. You could tell him so—so nicely," Jem said, looking up with disarming affection. "Please go and tell him. I'll go back to bed and he can come and tell me it's all right."

"Perhaps he'll come and tell you it's all wrong," warned Kit, as he took his own dressing gown out of the cupboard and put it on.

The stethoscope was produced from the other pocket of Jem's dressing gown and handed over.

"You see it's the ear-thing," said Jem, "it came off when I was putting it in my ear. Perhaps it was loose," he added hopefully.

Kit examined it, and saw that nothing very serious was the matter, but that did not affect the principle, of course. He chivvied Jem off to bed and went along the passage to the doctor's room.

Dr. Peabody was half undressed; he took the stethoscope and listened with some amusement to Kit's account of the affair. "There's no harm done," he said. "It has come unscrewed, that's all."

"But we mustn't spoil Jem," Kit pointed out. "He knows he oughtn't to touch your instruments—knows it perfectly well."

"I'll speak to him seriously," Dr. Peabody promised.

They looked at each other and smiled.

"Very seriously indeed," added Dr. Peabody.

"Yes," said Kit, "yes, you really should . . . if you *can,* of course . . . it isn't very easy, somehow."

"I'll do my best . . . er . . . and look here, Kit!"

"Yes, sir."

"We won't . . . er . . . we won't mention it to Ethel, I think."

"No, sir."

"No, it's nothing to do with her, d'you see. It's just between Jem and me . . . nothing to do with her at all."

"No," said Kit.

Dr. Peabody was now at the door. He paused and looked back at Kit ". . . and *was* the bird dead?" he enquired.

"Very dead, sir," replied Kit laughing.

The following day was Wednesday and Dr. Peabody had told Kit that he could have the whole day off duty. Kit had decided to go to London and see Henry and Mabel.

He did not repeat his previous blunder of arriving unexpectedly but wrote and asked politely if he could come to lunch and received a cordial invitation by return of post. It was a fine dry day with a pleasant breeze, Kit set off early in his small car and reached London without any adventures. Mabel was waiting for him, for they had arranged to go shopping together. She looked very smart in a black coat and skirt and a silver fox fur and Kit felt quite pleased when he found himself walking up Regent Street with her. They shopped satisfactorily and returned to Halkin Street to lunch and found Henry waiting for them. It was very pleasant, Kit found, to be back with his own people. They were so interested in his doings and so sincerely pleased at his success.

"How are you getting on?" Henry demanded as they took

their seats at the table. "What sort of a place is it? Are you going to stay?"

"Yes, I like it immensely, and I'm going to stay," replied Kit smiling, and he told them various items of interest about his life at Minfield.

"I'm glad," declared Henry. "Very glad indeed. I was a bit worried about it to tell you the truth. Rochester was asking me how you liked the job and I wasn't very sure what to say . . . by the by, you should call on Rochester's wife."

"I have called," Kit told him.

"Good!" said Henry nodding.

"That was *quite* right," agreed Mabel. "She took a lot of trouble and recommended you to Dr. Peabody, so it was quite right that you should call. You needn't do any more about it, of course."

"No, but as a matter of fact I liked her," said Kit a trifle uncomfortably. "She was very nice, I thought . . . and she asked me to come again."

"Oh, she's very *nice,* of course," agreed Mabel.

"Nothing much *in* her," Henry declared.

Kit could not let this pass. "I liked her," he said, "and I thought she was interesting. We got on like a house afire."

Henry and Mabel were obviously surprised at this statement, but they said no more about it.

"Have you any serious cases?" Henry asked.

"Just one, really," replied Kit. He did not intend to say more but Henry and Mabel were both so interested that he found himself telling them about the case and his treatment of it, and he found that they understood and sympathised with his feelings. He told them a good deal about his life at Minfield, about Jem, and Dr. Peabody and about his visits to the Fig and Thistle, and he made them laugh by describing Miss Peabody, and her reactions to his sojourn in the house.

"She doesn't like me at all," declared Kit, with a somewhat

mischievous grin, "and I believe it's because I eat too much."

Mabel wanted to know all about Miss Peabody, what she looked like, how old she was, and, when she had obtained every bit of information she could, she sat back in her chair and digested it.

"What are you thinking about?" Henry asked.

"The woman is in love with him," declared Mabel firmly. "Oh yes, you can laugh if you like, but I'm sure I'm right. You had better look out, Kit."

"I'll look out all right," Kit promised.

Kit's visit was a great success, and he decided that they were very nice indeed and that he had not appreciated them at their true worth . . . and strangely enough they decided the same about him. After he had left for Minfield in his small car (which was still battered and dented, of course, but which looked a good deal more respectable owing to Tupman's ministrations) Mabel put her arm through Henry's and said, "He's settling down, isn't he?"

"Yes," agreed Henry, "yes, he's much more serious and responsible. It's a good thing he got that job; it suits him down to the ground."

"He really *is* a dear!"

"Yes," replied Henry, "and I believe he's *clever*, you know. It was interesting about that case, wasn't it?"

"I hope he won't get mixed up with that Peabody woman," said Mabel with a sigh.

CHAPTER IX

THE DIFFICULT DECISION

THE day in town had been very enjoyable but Kit was quite ready to resume his duties on Thursday morning. He was talking to Mrs. Furnival in the drawing room when the door opened and Mrs. Rochester walked in.

"Oh!" she exclaimed, drawing back, "I didn't know the doctor was here—"

"I'm just going," said Kit, smiling at her.

"He's seen Gilbert," Mrs. Furnival explained. "We were just chatting. Come and sit down, Mardie."

Mrs. Rochester came in. "How is Gilbert?" she asked.

"Not quite so well today," Mrs. Furnival said, looking at Kit as she spoke.

"But I warned you, didn't I?" said Kit quickly. "He's bound to have ups and downs before we get him properly on his feet. You mustn't worry, you know. It's bad for him when you worry."

Mrs. Furnival nodded. "I know," she admitted, "but he was getting on so splendidly . . . I can't help being disappointed— but I won't let Gilbert see that I am."

Kit, himself, was disappointed at the slight setback (though he had known that it was almost inevitable). His success in the treatment of Gilbert Furnival was a personal triumph for it was through his own suffering that he had been able to understand and help, and he was aware that nobody else could have done it so well. Kit had begun by being interested in Gilbert as a case, but now he was interested in him as a friend; they had had good talks together and exchanged views on politics.

Mrs. Rochester had brought some books for the invalid—she gave them to Mrs. Furnival and was suitably thanked.

"I can't keep him in books," Mrs. Furnival said. "I change them twice a week at the library . . . the funny thing is he never cared much for reading before."

"I wish Jack . . ." began Mrs. Rochester, and then she paused uncertainly.

"Oh, Jack is a great reader, isn't he?" Mrs. Furnival said.

There was another little pause—rather an awkward one—and Mrs. Rochester turned her head away. "He used to be," she said, "but—but he hasn't much time now."

Kit sensed something uncomfortable beneath her casual words, and, although he had no idea why the subject should distress her, he was sure she was distressed. The slight mystery intrigued him and Mrs. Rochester's awkwardness of manner added to her charm. She's a dear, he thought; she's so crystal clear that you can see right through her . . . but I wish I knew what it was all about. Why is she so upset because her husband hasn't time to read? Or was it something else?

They talked of other things for a little and then Mrs. Rochester rose and said she must go, and Kit found himself offering her a lift home. He offered it somewhat diffidently for he had found a strange reluctance in his friends and relations to entrust themselves to his car. They seemed to imagine that the mere fact of battered wings and dented body made further dents and batterings more likely. Mrs. Rochester had no such foolish fears. She accepted the lift with alacrity and after the usual leave-takings Kit drove off proudly with his passenger beside him.

He knew now that her name was Mardie and somehow the quaint name suited her down to the ground. It was probably a contraction of Margaret—thought Kit—

"Come in for a few minutes," Mrs. Rochester said, "I want to show you my garden . . . but perhaps it would bore you. . . ."

Kit came in. He had two other calls to make but they were unimportant and he could do them in the afternoon. They walked round the garden together and she showed him her flowers.

"I like those best," she said, pointing to a magnificent bed of variegated heath. "It reminds me of home, you see, but sometimes I have a feeling that it's cruel to keep heather in a garden."

"It's tame heather," Kit pointed out.

"But I don't like to see birds in cages."

"Not even tame birds?"

"There shouldn't be tame birds!" she cried. "There shouldn't be! It's a contradiction in terms. Birds have wings—"

They looked up at the birds in the trees, flying backwards and forwards freely and happily.

"There shouldn't be cages," she said, in a low voice. "I should like to break them all—and we shouldn't keep lions and tigers behind bars. It isn't right."

"No cages, and no bars," agreed Kit. "When I'm dictator I shall do away with them all."

She smiled at him. "What else shall you do?"

"I might carry your idea still further," said Kit slowly. "There are human beings in cages too, and that is a terrible thought to me. Imagine what it would be like to be confined in one small space . . . I should die!"

"You are a free sort of person," she replied soberly, "I can feel it, somehow."

"Everybody should be free!"

"But nobody is," she said. "Nobody is really free. People forge their own chains without knowing it . . . and then they suddenly find that they are fettered."

For a few moments there was real tragedy in her face, and then she threw back her head and smiled. "We have come a long way from my heather, haven't we?" she said lightly.

Kit agreed that they had. He thought it was an example of the way their talk grew and blossomed, of the way their minds worked in harmony, of the manner in which they each in turn supplied something to the subject and so moved the other to another deeper thought. Talking to this woman was like dancing with a partner whose steps suited perfectly to his own. It was smooth and effortless and yet full of delightful surprises. Did he try an unexpected turn he found that she followed him faultlessly. . . .

He sat down beside her on a seat beneath an apple tree and took off his hat. "I like your garden," he told her, "the Peabody's garden is too tidy."

She nodded. "That's Ethel Peabody," she said. "Ethel herself is too tidy. She can't let herself go even in the garden, there mustn't be a leaf out of place."

"She's a little—er—difficult."

Mrs. Rochester nodded. "That just describes her. I'm afraid you'll find her even more difficult when Dolly comes home. Ethel and Dolly spend their time trying to annoy each other, and they usually succeed. I'm very fond of Dolly but she is rather naughty, you know, and Ethel seems to rouse all the devil in her."

"That does happen sometimes, doesn't it?" said Kit. "I mean people who are very nice if you take them separately are simply impossible together . . . but perhaps they'll get on better now that Mrs. Dorman is married."

"Perhaps," agreed Mrs. Rochester without much conviction.

"But you don't think it likely?"

She laughed, "Don't look so frightened," she said. "You need not be mixed up in their disagreements. As a matter of fact, I don't think they will get on any better now. Ethel was very difficult indeed when Ralph and Dolly were engaged, she wanted her father to refuse his consent, but of course there was no earthly reason why he should refuse—Ralph is a very nice creature and reasonably well-off. He's a lieutenant-commander and almost certain to be promoted when the time comes."

"It must have been rather uncomfortable for them," said Kit, thoughtfully.

"Yes, it was. Dolly could not ask him to the house unless she knew that Ethel was going out; but they met here whenever they liked and billed and cooed to their hearts' content." She hesitated for a moment and then added, "I'm afraid Ethel will never forgive me for my part in the affair. . . . Poor Ethel!"

"Why do you say that?"

"Because I'm sorry for her, of course," replied Mrs. Rochester promptly. "It can't be pleasant to feel like that, can it? The truth is she's discontented . . . I wish she would marry somebody."

Kit laughed. "You haven't selected me, I hope."

"No," said Mrs. Rochester smiling, "no, I don't think you'd do *at all*."

"It's funny," said Kit after a little pause. "It's funny how completely different people are. Miss Peabody and her father, for instance."

"You get on well with the old doctor?" Mrs. Rochester asked.

Kit nodded. "I like working with him. Do you know I look forward all day to the hour after dinner when we discuss our cases. Last night I was telling him about a case that worried me; I described some of the symptoms and in a moment he was *there*. I knew he was right—he's nearly always right. I had been afraid of something else, something much more serious and obscure."

"You must remember his experience."

"That's only part of the reason," said Kit thoughtfully. "He diagnoses his cases by a sort of sixth sense, and recognises what symptoms are significant. It's a subconscious process, really."

"He's very wise."

"Wise—yes—and you can't learn wisdom out of textbooks. He's old-fashioned of course, and at first he was very scornful of my new-fangled ideas, but he's coming round. He let me have a look at one of his pet patients this morning and *listened to what I said!*" Kit laughed excitedly at the recollection of his triumph.

"That **was** a great honour!" agreed Mrs. Rochester, smiling at him.

"It's funny that it should matter so much, isn't it?"

"It's because you admire him so much."

"He's a grand old man," Kit declared, "and a fine doctor. I'm learning a great deal from him. Diagnosis is his strong point and that's just where I'm weak . . . because I haven't seen enough, but I wish he would let me have more say in the treatment of his patients."

Mrs. Rochester smiled.

"Oh!" exclaimed Kit. "You think I'm too cock-sure!"

"I was only wondering how you can be sure that your new methods are better than his old-fashioned ones. It must be so difficult to know. Sometimes people get better by themselves, don't they? How can you tell whether you're curing them—or just nature?"

He had to laugh at that. "You can't, of course," he said. "Some treatments are definitely proved and others are just hopeful expedients, but you've got to seem cock-sure or else you're useless. Even if your heart is in your boots and you don't know what the devil is going to happen next you've got to appear perfectly calm and confident."

She thought about that. "Yes," she said, "it must be difficult."

"It's extremely difficult sometimes, but you wouldn't be any use to your patient if you started panicking. You'd be worse than useless."

"Tell me about modern methods," she said, harking back to her previous question.

"They consist to a large extent in cleanliness, common sense and simplicity. We've abolished the elaborate and disgusting practices of the Middle Ages and returned to Hippocrates. His dictum was that nature effected her own cure and the doctor's job was to help her as much as he could."

"It sounds very sensible."

"It *is* sensible," he said, "and of course it's perfectly true that hundreds of cases get better without any aid from the doctor at all . . . but . . ."

"But what?" she asked.

He smiled at her, "But you've got to do something for people who ask your advice. . . ."

Kit's voice died away and a companionable silence ensued.

This was his second meeting with Mardie Rochester, but already he felt that he could say anything he liked to her and whatever he chose to say would be received with interest and sympathy. The most outstanding quality which he had found in her was her warm humanity, and there was also something maternal in her nature which drew Kit to her irresistibly. He had knocked about the world for years (had taken knocks and given them) and all the while he had been on his own, he had been on the defensive; but with her there was no need for defence, he could be himself; this woman was on his side of the barrier which he had erected against the world. Her mind compared with his was untrained, but he found her logical, reasonable and wise.

Kit thought about her on his way home, but it was not until he had put his car into the garage and was washing his hands for lunch that he was struck by a sudden and very disturbing idea. Good Lord! thought Kit, I believe I'm in love with her! He put the soap back on the tray and stared at it without

seeing it at all—was he or was he not in love with her? If he
were, it was quite a different sort of feeling from any he had
experienced before. The question was, *which was Love?*—that
other peculiar madness or this calm happy state in which he
now found himself—they couldn't both be Love. This is just
friendship, Kit told himself firmly. There's no earthly reason
why I shouldn't go on seeing her. I like her and she likes
me—we understand each other. Why shouldn't we be
friends?

He thought for a moment of the shadowy husband in the
background of her life; he had not thought of him before as
bearing any significance . . . but we're just friends, Kit told
himself again.

The gong rang before he had come to any conclusion in the
matter and he dried his hands hastily and ran downstairs to
lunch. All that day he thought about it off and on, and he lay
awake a long time after he had gone to bed, thinking about
it, and arguing with himself; but deep down inside himself
Kit knew that he must not go on seeing her, for, if this was
not love, it was something a good deal stronger than friendship,
something with an element of danger concealed behind its inno-
cent-seeming exterior. After a pretty severe struggle Kit decided
that it would be safer not to see her again and, having made up
his mind to that, he fell asleep.

Several days passed and Kit avoided the Lynchet; he saw
Mrs. Rochester twice in the village and, instead of stopping, he
waved to her and drove on. He had fought and won his battle
and was pleased with himself at his victory. He missed her of
course, and he missed the warm feeling that he had made a
friend, and the comfortable feeling that he could "drop in" to
tea at the Lynchet whenever he liked, but the knowledge that
he was doing the right thing buoyed him up and he went
about his day's work quite cheerfully.

It was at this juncture that fate took a hand in Kit's affairs and changed the course of events, but whether the influence of fate was malign or benignant it would be difficult to say. It happened that Mrs. Rochester's parlourmaid was so unfortunate as to upset a kettle of boiling water—part of it over her foot—and the cook, with the best intentions, immediately dressed the scald with rags soaked in oil. Poor Morton was of a Spartan breed; she went about her duties for some hours and it was not until her mistress noticed that she was lame that the matter was brought to light. Mrs. Rochester was horrified when she saw the injury and telephoned immediately to the doctor's house.

Thus it was that Kit returned from his morning round to find on the telephone pad a message which said tersely—"Axident at the linshit plees come amejetly its the made."

He was aware from the spelling that Jem had taken the message, a task which he thoroughly enjoyed; Jem was not really allowed to accept important messages, but Kit had noticed that it was rather strange how often Jem seemed to be the only person available when the telephone bell rang.

"You see, Grandfather," he would explain, "you see Tupman was out in the garage and May was changing her dress, and Aunt Ethel had gone to the village . . . it was lucky I was there, really," Jem would declare, his brow as candid as the brow of a two-year-old child, and his eyes fixed upon his grandfather's face.

Today Jem's spelling, which usually gave Kit a great deal of pleasure, failed in its appeal. Kit gazed at the message in dismay. (The Rochesters were on his list of patients, for, as Dr. Peabody had pointed out, they themselves had arranged that Kit should come to Minfield and were therefore entitled to his services whenever necessary.) What should he do?

Should he ask Dr. Peabody to take the case? Should he make some excuse?

"But I can't!" exclaimed Kit. "How can I? What could I say? What excuse could I make?"

He could find no excuse at all—none that would hold water —and it was obviously impossible to explain the real reason why he shrank from attending the Rochesters' maid. He crumpled up the piece of paper and threw it into the waste paper basket and set off for the Lynchet without more ado.

CHAPTER X

THE NEW PATIENT

MRS. ROCHESTER was at lunch when Kit arrived at the Lynchet—he was conducted up the stairs to his patient's bedroom and found her sitting on a chair with her foot propped up on another. He saw at once that she was in pain for her face was grey and drawn and her lips firmly compressed. The first thing to do was to remove the cook's septic dressings and to dress the injury in accordance with modern ideas, and Kit set to work with gentleness and despatch.

"How long shall I be off work?" enquired Morton anxiously.

"Until you're better," replied Dr. Stone, "and don't ask me how long that will be, because I don't know. If they hadn't infected your foot it would have healed in half the time."

"Infected it?" she enquired.

"Put oil on it," he explained, "they couldn't have done anything worse if they'd *tried.*"

He was aware as he spoke that it was no use being angry—but he *was* angry. It always enraged him when ignorance and stupidity begat unnecessary suffering. People ought to be taught the elements of first aid; school children should be instructed how to dress bruises and scalds; a few simple lessons in first aid would be far more use to the average citizen than a smattering of geometry and Latin.

He was still on his knees, putting the finishing touch to the bandage when he became aware that Mrs. Rochester had come into the room. He could feel that she was there, standing behind him . . . Kit hesitated for a moment and then rose.

"It was so good of you to come at once," she said. "I was worried about it."

"She must stay in bed and keep warm," replied Kit, "I'll come tomorrow morning."

"I'm sure there's no need for you to trouble," Morton said.

"That's what doctors are for," Kit told her. He gave some simple directions about diet and followed Mrs. Rochester downstairs.

Now that he saw her again he knew that he was lost . . . there was no doubt left in his mind. The turn of her head, the tones of her voice, the crinkling of her eyes when she smiled—all these things about her chimed in his heart like a peal of bells giving him happiness and deep content.

"I was just in the middle of lunch," she said, "will you come and join me?"

"Yes, thank you," said Kit—and why shouldn't I? he thought. Why should I deny myself the pleasure of seeing her? Seeing her is enough, it's all I want, just to see her and talk to her. What harm is there in that?

The condition of Morton's foot was sufficiently serious to make it necessary for Kit to visit the Lynchet daily. When he had seen his patient it was quite natural for him to see Mrs. Rochester and to report to her so he saw her every day, and every day she became more precious to him. He was aware that to her he was merely a friend, and that she thought of him as much younger than herself, but he did not mind how she thought of him so long as he could see her. Perhaps he realised that there was a certain safety in this thought of hers, a safety for her. Perhaps he realised that if she had not had this subconscious thought she might realise the danger and draw back. She had begun to call him "Kit" quite naturally and he, greatly daring, had contrived to call her "Mardie". This had surprised her a little, he could see, but she accepted it without comment . . . it meant so little nowadays.

Having accomplished so much Kit was further emboldened,

and asked her if "Mardie" was a contraction of Margaret, and she told him that it was not. Mardie was an old family name and its origin was uncertain, but in that particular branch of the Macfarlane family the eldest daughter was always called Mardie. There had been Mardie Macfarlanes for countless generations, but there would be no more, for she was an only child and the last of her line.

"It made my father very sad to think that he had no son to carry on the old family traditions," said Mardie regretfully, "and I often wished for his sake that I had been a boy; but he would never admit that I was a disappointment to him. We were great friends, you see."

Kit listened and sympathised, and grew to understand her even better than before. He was perfectly happy during this halcyon time: the sun shone, the birds sang, and he saw Mardie every day. They talked and laughed together, they walked round the garden and admired the flowers, and one day Kit took Jem to tea at the Lynchet and they all three played hide-and-seek.

Jem was on his best behaviour that day, and ate his bread and butter like a civilised being; he talked neither too much nor too little, and indeed he was almost too good to be true.

"I'm having my Easter holidays now," he told his hostess in answer to a question on the subject. "I like holidays best, of course, everybody does, but school's quite decent really—I only go in the morning, you see."

"I suppose you have lots of friends."

"Yes," said Jem gravely, "lots of friends at school, but I'm having a rest from them just now."

Kit met Mardie's eyes and turned aside to hide a smile. Jem was a lone wolf; he would not share his strange imaginative games with other children, for he had found that they were apt to make fun of him, and since he liked his own type of game best he was obliged to play by himself.

"Do you like cricket?" Mardie enquired.

"I like it for a bit, but it usually goes on too long," replied Jem thoughtfully.

Kit was horrified at this criticism, for he had always been a keen cricketer, but Mardie sided with Jem.

"Of course it does," she agreed. "Hundreds of people think the same about cricket only they daren't say so."

"But Mardie, you don't understand!" cried Kit.

They argued about it for a little, and Jem sat still and listened with interest. He enjoyed hearing grown up people talking for they used long words and unfamiliar phrases, and he could store them up in his capacious memory and employ them himself when occasion arose. After a while his attention wandered, and he remembered something he wanted to ask; it was something he had heard yesterday in church, and he had not been able to understand it. Jem waited for a lull in the conversation and then came out with his question:

"Kit, are we made of dust?" he enquired.

Kit was somewhat taken aback; he gazed at Jem in perplexity.

"Mr. Wigmore said we were," declared Jem. "He said we were made of dust, and to dust we would return, and I wondered about it. Why don't I get muddy inside when I drink— or do I, Kit?"

"No, you don't," replied Kit firmly.

"Well, am I made of dust?"

"No, you aren't—at least—well, it's a little difficult—"

Jem sighed, "I suppose it's another 'when-you're-older'," he said with resignation. "Everything you really want to know is a 'when-you're-older'. I wish I was old, I wish I was really very old, like Mrs. Rochester and you."

His aged companions roared with laughter at this—Kit had never seen Mardie laugh so heartily before—she laughed till the tears ran down her cheeks.

"Oh Jem!" she cried, "and we've been playing hide-and-seek with you the whole afternoon. I do think it's a little unkind!"

The days passed quickly (ten of them, and each one with its own particular happiness) and Morton's foot healed. Kit was not sorry to see it heal for he had been somewhat anxious about it, but the recovery of his patient left him without an excuse to visit the Lynchet. It was then he realised how much Mardie Rochester meant to him, how his whole life had become centred round her. He sought for ways of seeing her and sometimes he succeeded, and sometimes he dropped in for a cup of tea—as she had asked him to do—but it was not the same. Kit felt the difference very keenly; he had been perfectly happy while he was visiting the Lynchet professionally, for he was able to still the pangs of conscience by telling himself that he was doing his duty—and little more—but now it was obviously his duty to keep away from the Lynchet, and he could not keep away. It was not only when he went to her house that he met Mardie Rochester, he met her in the village, or in the road, exercising her dogs, and once he met her at a sherry party and found her surrounded by a horde of troublesome people. She looked quite different that day, dressed up in her best clothes with a silly hat hiding the shape of her dark head, but she saw him at once when he went in and sent him "the little look across the crowd". It was a look of candid intimacy, but it was no more—Kit knew that Mardie did not love him.

The days when he did not see her at all were wasted days, and, whenever his mind was free to wander, he thought about her and wondered what she was doing. He knew a great deal about her thoughts and feelings but she had been curiously reticent about her life . . . Kit would have liked to know what she did at every hour of the day so that he could imagine her doing it.

CHAPTER XI

MARDIE'S LIFE

IT WAS half past six. Mardie Rochester was sitting in front of the mirror in her bedroom brushing her hair; she brushed it vigorously until it stood out in a dark cloudy fuzz, and then she combed it and wound it round her fingers into a shiny roll. When she turned her head she could look out of the window and could see the garden, stretching down to the hedge, and beyond that the meadow, with quiet cows grazing. The ground sloped down steeper and steeper into the valley and rose again to low hills with fields and trees. She could see the little church amongst the trees and, beyond that, the chimneys of the village, but she could not see any of the new houses, for the building scheme lay round the corner out of sight. Mardie had always loved this view, she had loved it from the very first moment—three years ago—when she had come to the Lynchet as a bride, and for three years she had seen it nearly every day, had watched the seasons pass over it and change it . . . she had a strange thought that the land had been watching her change too.

Mardie had had a quiet day. She had wanted a quiet day for she had suddenly realised that she was being caught up in a round of engagements—there were so many people in Minfield now and people were so nice. People asked you to dine and then you asked them, but it didn't end there. They had sherry parties and bridge-parties, and then you had to have a sherry party . . . there was tennis, too, of course, but Mardie liked tennis, and the exercise was good. She decided that she would cut out bridge and go on playing tennis and perhaps she would take up some definite work. She thought, how lazy I've been! I've done nothing at all but amuse myself . . . and it doesn't amuse me. You've got to make up your mind whether you'll let things happen to you or whether you'll do something about it . . . I must do something. I'm getting nowhere except travelling towards old age.

She thought of Jem's remark, and smiled. There was no sign of old age in the face that looked back at her from the mirror. Mardie was twenty-nine today, but she did not look it . . . her cheeks had dimpled a little with the smile and one eyebrow rose a trifle whimsically. Twenty-nine today—it was a great age. Jack had not remembered her birthday this morning. She was much too sensible to mind, of course, and anyhow Jack had been late for breakfast and had had a rush to catch his train . . . but still . . .

She remembered that the first year they were married, Jack had given her a little brooch for her birthday—a dear little brooch with her initial in diamonds on it—he had had it made specially for her, and had been full of importance over it. The second year her present had been a new rug for the hall. This was the third year!

Mardie laughed to herself—she laughed at her reflection in the mirror—and the laugh was without any bitterness at all. What a fool you are! she told herself. You know Jack is worried!

Unfortunately she knew only too well that Jack was worried; but Jack was always worried now. It did not seem to matter whether he was making money or losing it, he worried just the same.

Mardie had thought a lot during this quiet day, indeed she had kept it free so that she could think things out. In the morning she had worked in the garden, and after lunch she had taken the dogs and gone for a walk on the common. It was Mardie's favourite walk for it reminded her a little of her own country. There was heather here, and there were rocks and stones and gorse and winding paths which led in all directions, and sometimes, in a small hollow, one came across a little pond, reflecting the skies. It was a wild deserted sort of place (except on Sundays and Bank Holidays) and it stretched for several miles from Minfield to Suppley, and one could walk here for quite a long way without seeing a house—or indeed any sign of man—but in spite of this Mardie could not feel that this common was really and truly wild. It had not the feeling of real wildness but seemed artificial like the scenery one sees on a stage. When she was walking there this afternoon she had remembered the conversation she had had with Kit on the subject of freedom, and she had thought, yes, that's what it is. The common is like a tame wild animal. It's like a lion, she decided, as she looked out over the heather, a caged lion, weary with the monotony of its days . . . and she thought that— like a captive lion—it looked better from a distance, for when you came too near you saw the mangy fur. There was an empty salmon tin behind a gorse bush and Mardie had scraped a hole with her stick and buried it, but she was aware that her action was done more from principle than because it was any use. The tin was a mere detail—a tiny blemish on the captive lion—if the lion had been free the blemish would not have mattered.

She had walked a long way, and had thought about all sorts of things but principally about her own life. She had stood aside and looked at her life and had realised how different it was from what she had expected. . . . No, that was wrong. Her life was what she had expected, it was her attitude towards it that had changed . . . her attitude towards Jack. She tried to see as honestly as she could where the fault lay, and she tried to see how she could improve matters.

Mardie was so busy with her thought that she did not hear the car drive in at the gates, and she was still sitting in front of her mirror when she saw the door behind her open suddenly and knew that Jack had returned. She swung round, and her eyes went anxiously to Jack's face, for his face would tell her what sort of a day he had had and whether the Stock Exchange had been "touchy" or "quiet" or "firm". Mardie had only a vague idea what these words meant but she knew their effects upon Jack.

She looked at him, and she saw that he was smiling. He was on top of the world.

"Prinking!" he cried, striding into the room like a conqueror. "Prinking and titivating—where are we going tonight?"

"Nowhere," said Mardie, smiling back at him.

"Somebody coming here?"

"No," said Mardie.

He stood still for a moment and she saw his face fall like the face of a disappointed child. "Nothing on?" he asked incredulously. "What's happened to everyone?"

"I thought it would be nice—" she began.

"But why didn't you fix up something?"

"I thought it would be rather nice to have a quiet evening— just you and me—"

He was not listening. "I know!" he cried, "we'll go up to town. We'll dine at the Savoy and go on to a show—"

"But Jack—"

"There's a good show on at His Majesty's; we ought to see it. . . ."

As a rule Mardie subscribed to his whims, for it was so much easier; but tonight she decided not to. They had been out to dinner last night, and the night before also . . . and Jack found it so difficult to get up in the morning. She was stiffened in her moral fibre by her long quiet day, stiffened to the point of obstinacy. "No," said Mardie firmly, "no, I don't feel like it, Jack."

He had turned away, believing the matter settled, but now

he spun round and gazed at her in amazement, "You don't feel like it!" he asked.

She shook her head.

"Are you ill?" he asked.

"No, I just don't want to go, that's all."

"But I do."

Mardie smiled. "But what about the morning?" she said. "You know how tired you were—"

"Damn the morning!"

"It's so bad for you, Jack. You ought to have your sleep."

"Why don't you want to go?" he demanded. "Why on earth . . . what do you *want*?"

"A quiet evening," Mardie said.

"But why?"

"I'm tired of rushing about—"

"Tired!" he cried. *"Tired!* What have you been doing? What do you do all day to get tired? You walk the dogs to the village and back . . . you go down to the vicarage to tea . . . and then you're too tired to go out with me when I come home! What about me? D'you think I'm not tired? What d'you think I've been doing? I've been rushing and tearing and shouting all day long and I'm so tired I could lie down and die . . ."

"That's just why—" she began, and then she stopped, for she knew it was useless to argue with him, or to reason. Her face hardened a little with the effort to keep quite calm. "I know," she said gently, "I know you're tired, Jack. We'll have a quiet evening together, Darby and Joan."

She saw him consider the idea and reject it. His thin nervous face was so full of expression that she was able to read his thoughts as clearly as if they had been in print.

"No," he cried, "no. Good Heavens, I can't sit still all the evening . . . and think . . . the only way to carry on is to keep on doing things."

"Please Jack," Mardie said persuasively, "we've been out so

much lately. It would do us both good. I've ordered such a nice dinner, and cook would be disappointed—"

He laughed harshly. "Cook!" he exclaimed. "We've got to stay at home because cook will be disappointed!"

Mardie did not answer. She turned back to her dressing-table and took up her comb. In spite of her efforts to keep calm she found that her hand was shaking.

"Hurry up," said Jack. "I'll telephone to the Savoy for a table. Ring your bell and we'll send a message to Bill to bring round the car—"

"No," said Mardie firmly, "no Jack, I'm not coming."

"Not coming!" he echoed, and she could see his face in the mirror, angry and incredulous. "Not coming! All right, then. I'll get somebody else."

"Yes, why don't you?" Mardie said.

Jack was somewhat taken aback at her calm acceptance of his suggestion. He had no wish to take a substitute, and had only proposed it to induce Mardie to come.

"Why don't you get somebody else?" repeated Mardie.

"Who could I get?" he said. "Besides it's much too late now . . . it's after seven. Do come, Mardie."

She shook her head. Already she was regretting her decision to oppose his plan, but the trivial thing had become an important issue between them. She had told him she did not want to go, and somehow or other she felt that she must stick to her guns.

"What's the matter with you?" he asked.

"We're rushing about too much. I want a little peace."

Jack seized upon the word, "Peace! Why on earth do you want peace? There will be plenty of time for peace when we get old. You're twenty-eight and—"

"Twenty-nine," said Mardie. She was sorry when she had said the words for she had not intended to remind him of her birthday.

"So that's the reason!" he exclaimed. "Because I forgot your birthday . . . you're paying me out like this. . . ."

"Jack!"

". . . refusing to come with me. How petty and small-minded! How like a woman!"

"It isn't—it wasn't that at all," cried Mardie.

"Don't you realize that I've got a thousand things on my mind . . . my brain is bursting with them, *bursting*."

She held out her hand, "Jack, it wasn't that. I know you're worried. It wasn't that. I never thought—"

"It was—it is. I can see the whole thing. Why couldn't you have reminded me about your birthday? How do you expect me to remember every date in the calendar? You don't understand how worried I am, you don't care. You sit here at home and brood, and rake up every silly little grievance. . . ."

Mardie shut her ears—or tried to. She had begun to form the habit of shutting her ears to Jack's voice. It went on and on pitched upon a whining note that drilled her nerves. She minded it less for herself than for him—it was so terribly degrading for any human being to behave like this. She knew that he did not mean half he said and he would have forgotten it in half an hour but she could not forget so easily. She was not used to people who talked and talked and did not mean half they said; she was used to quietness, to dignity, to reserve. She had been brought up to respect herself and others and to consider the feelings of her neighbours. Mardie shut her ears and thought of her father, and of her old home in Scotland— the big old-fashioned house which was so shabby and inconvenient but so full of peace. It had been sold when her father died (and the rich business man who had bought it had "gutted" it and brought it "up to date") but it was still very clear in Mardie's memory, and she found it easy to believe that it was still there—the same as ever. If she shut her eyes she could walk in through the wide door, which always stood open, and find herself in the big dark hall . . . the dogs would dash out of the shadows to welcome her. . . .

"Mardie!" cried Jack, "Mardie, do you hear what I'm saying? No, you aren't listening . . . you sit there with a silly smile on your face and don't listen to a word I say! What on earth's wrong with you these days? Why do you suddenly—suddenly go miles away?"

Mardie came back from her long journey and looked at him sorrowfully. "I try not to listen because it's the only way I can bear it," she said.

His face changed. It crumpled like the face of a child. "Oh Mardie!" he cried, "oh Mardie, I don't mean . . . I can't help it. Oh Mardie, I don't know what's the matter with me . . . and you're so patient . . ." he flung himself on his knees beside her and seized her hand, he pressed it to his lips. "I'm not worthy of you," he declared, "no wonder you've turned away from me—"

"But, I haven't," Mardie said, stroking his hair, "I haven't turned away from you, Jack."

"I don't mean it," he continued, in bitter despair. "I don't mean a word I say. . . ."

"Never mind. It doesn't matter."

"I love you, Mardie—I love you."

"I know," she said gently. "I know that. It's all right," but even as she said it she knew that it was not all right. She was sorry for him, terribly sorry, but she did not love him any more. The doors of her heart were shut to him—he had shut them himself—and Mardie could not open them. Fortunately it was easy to comfort him, to change his thoughts into a different channel. She had done it so often that she knew exactly what to say, and she was so sorry for Jack that she was able to say it with only the faintest feeling of distaste.

Soon he was striding about the room and talking confidently of all he intended to do. "You wait," he said, "and you won't have long to wait either—we're going to be rich, Mardie. I'm going to sell the old car and buy a Bentley. That'll make Minfield sit up, won't it?"

"Yes," agreed Mardie with a sigh.

"I'll buy you something tomorrow; something really decent for your birthday. You'd like that, wouldn't you?"

"Yes," said Mardie, trying her best to look pleased and grateful but not succeeding very well.

"I'll buy you—I'll buy you a string of pearls. Yes, that's the thing. You'd like a string of pearls, wouldn't you?"

Mardie did not want pearls, she only wanted peace. She only wanted Jack to be gentle and kind—as he used to be—and she thought that if he could be persuaded to leave this life of his which was wearing him to a shred, and they could settle down somewhere in a tiny house with a settled income everything might come right. A small house with one servant and a little garden—that was all she wanted. She knew that this sudden access of wealth would not last. In a few days, or a few weeks, Jack would have lost all the money he had made. He would return from town weighed down with despair and full of forebodings and would declare that they were ruined, that they must economize—drastically—that they might have to leave the Lynchet; he would have to sell the car, and Mardie must reduce her staff. She would agree, of course, and perhaps make up her mind to part with Morton, and Jack would say, "Well don't do anything just at once. Wait till next week," and Mardie would wait in fear and trembling and by next week the crisis would be past and Jack would laugh at her anxieties and tell her to go and buy a new frock. This had happened so often that Mardie should have got used to it, but somehow she never had; every time it happened she was frightened and miserable and thoroughly upset. She could have borne it more easily if she had understood about Jack's business, but, in spite of the fact that he talked about it unceasingly, he never made it clear to her. He never told her anything definite about his dealings on the Stock Exchange and, when she asked questions about it, trying to get some sort of grip upon it, he refused to answer sensibly; for it was his firm conviction that women did not understand business matters, they had not the brains. He talked to relieve his feelings, that was all, talked vaguely of mergers, and the market being narrow, or dull, talked of downward trend, and stock suffering from realisation. Mardie knew all these terms, but she had not the slightest idea what they meant, nor how they affected Jack.

"No, Jack, I don't want pearls," Mardie said.

"Not pearls!" he exclaimed, "what nonsense, Mardie. All women love pearls."

His habit of clumping "all women" together in one category still had the power to infuriate her (all women loved pearls, all women loved clothes, all women were irrational, unpunctual, full of fads and fancies) but she crushed down her irritation and managed to summon a smile. "I must be the exception, then," she said mildly.

"What do you want?" he asked.

"Security," she replied, "a quiet peaceful life, and security."

He did not understand. "But Mardie, how absurd! We're going to be rich. I can give you all you want—clothes, jewels, furs—we *are* secure. I don't know what you mean. . . ."

"I mean a settled income," said Mardie slowly. "A settled income so that we should know exactly where we were. So that we should know how much to spend, and what we could afford."

He laughed in a genial manner, "You'll be telling me that we ought to cut our coat according to our cloth!"

"Well, yes," she nodded. "That's sense."

"It's nonsense!" he cried. "Absolute nonsense—it just shows how little women understand about modern finance. I haven't any cloth at all one day, and a week later I have enough to cut seven coats."

"That seems wrong, somehow—"

"Spend what you've got when you've got it to spend," he cried. "Buy whatever you want. Make a splash."

"But why? Wouldn't it be better to save it—"

"No, it wouldn't. You want to impress people with the idea that you're rich; then you *are* rich. If people think you have money to burn they'll give you as much cloth as you want— cloth to cut a hundred coats. That's credit, Mardie. Modern finance couldn't function without credit."

"But Jack—"

"But Mardie," he mocked. "But Mardie you don't understand, that's all. Money is merely a counter, money doesn't mean anything at all. The important thing is credit. As long as people think you have plenty of money it doesn't matter whether you have any or not."

Jack had never spoken so frankly before, had never put his creed into such plain words. Mardie considered it carefully. To her the whole idea seemed not only dangerous but positively dishonest. You were to make a splash with money which you hadn't got to make people think you had it; you were to build your life upon a gigantic bluff.

"Well," he said, smiling down at her, "well, you don't understand, do you? Supposing you leave business to me . . . why should you bother your silly little head with business? Let's go down and eat this marvellous dinner you've ordered."

CHAPTER XII

MORE ABOUT MARDIE'S LIFE

THE Rochesters went downstairs together and ate their dinner—it was an excellent dinner, perfectly cooked and served—during the meal they talked about impersonal matters, and about people they knew.

"Why don't you ask young Stone to dinner?" Jack enquired. "We might have had him tonight. Stone was asking me if I'd seen anything of his brother and I had to say no. It looked rather queer."

"He's busy in the evenings," Mardie said.

"Busy? He can't see patients in the evenings."

"No, but Dr. Peabody likes him to be there—they discuss their cases after dinner."

Jack smiled. "You seem to know all about him!"

"Quite a lot," she replied, "he's been attending Morton, and he comes to tea sometimes. I told you, Jack."

"What is he like?"

"Nice," said Mardie promptly, "not like his brother at all, but very nice in his own way. I think you'd like him."

"Ask him to dinner," Jack said. "Surely old Peabody lets him out occasionally. He isn't a slave."

When they had finished dinner Mardie went into the drawing room and sat down. She was tired, not so much physically or mentally but spiritually tired. She had not thought of Kit all day but now she thought of him—it would have been nice to talk to Kit. It would be nice if he dropped in now at this very moment. There was something rather comforting about Kit—something soothing. You could say what you liked to him without thinking first and without any fear of being misunderstood. Mardie was glad that Kit had come to Min-field, and that he had become her friend. There were so few people who became real friends. Kit was a dear boy.

She sighed and looked round the room. Kit had liked the room, and it really was nice. She had taken a good deal of trouble over her colour scheme of greens and browns and now, after three years, the colours had faded a little and mellowed so that the room had a restful note.

When Jack came in Mardie smiled at him. "Would you like to read?" she asked.

He did not reply. He was standing in the middle of the room, balancing from his heels to his toes and back again.

"Come and sit down," said Mardie, patting the sofa invitingly.

"We ought to have gone up to town," he said. "There's nothing to do here . . . what about going down to the picture house at Minfield?"

"I don't think you'd like it much, and I'm sure I shouldn't."

"It would have been something to do," he said crossly. He went over to the wireless and fiddled with the knobs. "I suppose this thing is broken again," he said.

"You haven't turned on the switch," Mardie told him. She took out her work and began to embroider a rose.

"That's Prague," Jack said, as a rich contralto voice filled the room, "sounds like opera, doesn't it?"

"Yes, I like it."

"I'll get Radio Paris. They usually have something good."

Radio Paris was putting a play on the air. Jack listened to it for about a minute and then switched over to Berlin. They were broadcasting dance music from Berlin. "That's no good," said Jack.

"Prague was nice," suggested Mardie.

"We'll try Rome," Jack declared.

He tried every station he could get but none of them pleased him, there were snatches of talk, fragments of music, tantalising snippets of news.

"Why not leave it at Daventry?" Mardie said.

"We must get something decent," he replied. "I'll try Rome again. That's Rome . . . rotten, isn't it? I'll try Madrid."

Mardie's nerves, already frayed, were now almost at snapping point. "If only you would leave it at *something*," she said. "Please Jack, I can't bear it. . . ."

He turned it off. "I don't know what's the matter with you," he said.

There was a short silence. Jack came over to the table. He took up a book and flicked over the pages—"What awful tripe people write!" he said scornfully.

Mardie did not answer.

"Don't you agree?" he asked with an edge to his voice.

"Yes," said Mardie quietly, "I agree that some books are rubbish but that was well reviewed. It's a detective novel. I thought you might like it."

"Well, I don't like it," he said, tossing it on to a chair.

He waited for her to say something, but she said nothing. Her head was bent over her work.

"What's that you're making?" he asked.

"It's a cushion cover," Mardie told him, and she held it out for him to see.

"Rather pretty!" he said. "Is it for this room?"

"No, it's for your mother's birthday."

He was looking round the room now with a critical air. "This room's getting shabby," he said. "I know what we'll do, we'll refurnish the whole thing. I'll give it to you for a birthday present."

"But I like it!" Mardie cried.

"Modern furniture," said Jack thoughtfully. "I don't mean

steel tubes, of course, but plain wood—those plain modern things are rather effective—and black curtains and coloured cushions."

"No Jack—please," said Mardie.

"Why?"

"I've told you," she said, trying to speak calmly, "I've told you I like it as it is. I like it much better now than when it was new."

"It's shabby."

"No, not shabby. It's just restful and pleasant. Oh Jack, please don't alter it—"

"But Mardie—"

"You'll make it like a room in a hotel."

"Nonsense!"

"Jack, *please*. After all, I've got to sit in it."

"I don't understand you tonight," he said. "You're most extraordinary. You won't agree to anything I suggest. What on earth is the matter with you?" He walked over to the window and looked out. It was getting dark but the moon had risen, and was sailing in a clear cloudless sky.

Mardie could see his thin figure standing between the two lights—the yellow light of her electric lamp and the silvery light of the moon. He was very thin, and getting thinner, but what could you expect? He could not rest. It seemed to be impossible to him. The quiet evening had been a mistake— she saw that now—it would have been better to do as he had wanted, to go up to town with him, and dine and do a show.

"Who's that?" Jack asked suddenly. "Mardie, there's somebody in the garden—who is it?"

"It's Fraser, I suppose," she replied. "He always comes up at night to shut the frames."

"It isn't Fraser. Who is it?"

"Fraser's brother, perhaps."

"Fraser's brother!" cried Jack. "What on earth is he doing here?"

"He's staying with the Frasers for a few days. Fraser asked me if he could come. He's in the Navy."

"So you fixed it up behind my back!" cried Jack furiously. "You and Fraser between you—you never thought of asking me if the man could come and live in my cottage."

"Jack!" she cried, rising and going towards him, "Jack, I never thought—" She saw that his face had gone as white as a sheet and his eyes were glittering. She was quite frightened at his appearance, so frightened that her words died on her lips. "Fraser's brother!" he cried in a violent, rough sort of voice. "How do you know it's his brother? It isn't his brother at all —it's somebody else, somebody come to spy—Fraser's brother —that's a likely tale!" He turned to the window again and, standing behind the curtain, he peeped out round the edge of it. "He's still there . . ." he said in a breathless voice ". . . still there . . . standing there . . . looking at the house. Who is he, Mardie?"

Mardie's heart was beating so rapidly that it almost choked her. She put her hand on his arm. "Jack, what is the matter?" she asked. "It's Fraser's brother, that's all. Do come and sit down—you're frightening me."

"Frightening you?"

"Yes . . . terrifying me. What is the matter, Jack."

"Nothing," he said sullenly.

"But there must be—"

"No, nothing . . . pull the curtains, Mardie."

The rage, which had possessed him so suddenly, had died out of him and left him limp. Mardie pulled the curtains and took his arm and led him over to a chair. He came quite meekly, and sat down, and Mardie knelt down beside him and kept her hand on his arm—

"There," she said, patting him as if he were a child. "There,

Jack, it's all right. It was Fraser's brother, that's all. It wasn't
—it wasn't anybody else—"

He lay back and shut his eyes. "I'm tired," he said in a
slurred voice.

"Rest quietly," she said.

There was silence in the room. The ticking of the gilt clock
on the mantelpiece sounded very loud.

CHAPTER XIII

THE UNWELCOME RESEMBLANCE

ONE afternoon, when Kit had been at Minfield for a little over a month, he returned from his afternoon round to find a strange young woman in the library. She was sitting in the big leather chair which Kit always occupied and which, in his subconscious mind, had already become his own. The chair stood by the fire with its back to the door and the first thing Kit saw when he entered the room was a pair of legs in sheer silk stockings, cocked over the arm of the chair and therefore in full view. Kit was somewhat taken aback for the library was Dr. Peabody's sanctum—Miss Peabody and her friends used the drawing room upstairs—and for a moment he thought that this must be a patient who had strayed in here by mistake, but the idea vanished as quickly as it had come.

He saw at once that the legs were extremely well-shaped, they were long and slim and elegant, and the feet which finished them off were models of what feet should be. They were encased in brown suede shoes which fitted snugly round the heel and showed off the line of the high instep to perfection. He shut the door softly and came in and stood looking down at the rest of the person (he felt a little like one of the three bears who found Goldilocks in his bed, and the analogy was further heightened by the fact that the intruder had hair of purest gold which waved and curled round her fair rounded face). Her eyes were tightly shut, Kit noticed, so he had ample opportunity to study her features, and, as he made good use of his opportunity and studied them intently, he became aware that her features were somehow familiar to him. He had not seen the young woman before, he was certain of that, but she was like somebody that he knew quite well; she was a little like Miss Peabody.

Having made up his mind on this point Kit realised immediately that Goldilocks was none other than Mrs. Dorman, and that her right to the chair was therefore greater than his. He was about to tiptoe silently from the room when her eyes opened widely and looked at him.

"Hallo!" she said in a comfortable sort of voice, "Dr. Livingstone, I presume!"

Kit was struck dumb. He had thought that Goldilocks was asleep, and had stared at her unblushingly for several minutes, but it was quite obvious that she had not been asleep at all for she was in full possession of her wits.

"Have I made a mistake?" she said in a dreamy sort of voice. "Can it be that this is not Dr. Livingstone at all, but just another damned savage, not conversant with the speech of civilised man?"

Kit burst out laughing.

She watched him gravely but there was a twinkle of humour in her sky-blue eyes.

"Mr. Stanley," said Kit at last, "or should I say Mrs. Stanley?"

"Mr. Stanley, I think," she declared with composure.

"Mr. Stanley," said Kit obediently, "you are correct in your assumption that the person you see before you is a fellow countryman of your own. His excuse for his—er—his temporary loss of speech must be the astonishing youthfulness and—er comeliness of your appearance."

"I believe I ought to have a beard," she nodded in a thoughtful manner, and she stroked her smooth cheeks.

Kit laughed again and this time she joined in—

"Oh joy!" she cried, swinging her legs off the arm of the chair and jumping up. "Oh joy, you're human! I wondered what you'd be like . . . whether you'd be shy and stupid, or dull and prosy, or—or *learned,* or gushing, or smug and proper. . . ."

"You put me through a pretty severe test."

"Yes, I know," she said quite seriously, "it was most carefully thought out. If you had been a smug and proper young man you would have gone away when you opened the door and saw my legs."

"I suppose I should," said Kit thoughtfully, "but the fact is . . ." he paused uncertainly.

"Well?" she enquired with interest.

"The fact is I wanted to see the body belonging to them."

"Of course you did," she agreed, "and why shouldn't you? They're very nice legs—though I say it myself—quite one of my best assets . . ." she paused a moment and then added, "if you hadn't played up to my silly joke I shouldn't have bothered with you any more."

"Isn't that a little drastic?" enquired Kit, leaning against the mantelpiece and lighting his pipe.

"Of course it's drastic. I'm a drastic sort of person; there are no half and half measures about me. If I like a person I like them, and if I don't . . . well, I just don't bother with them any more."

"I see," said Kit doubtfully.

"It may sound a bit selfish, perhaps," she continued, watching his face, "but it isn't really selfish at all, because if I don't like a person there's no chance of them liking me—it works both ways."

Kit saw that this was true and, although he was not quite so sweeping in his method of separating the sheep and the goats, he subscribed to the same principle. "Yes," he said slowly, "yes, but one does it subconsciously."

"I don't," declared Mrs. Dorman frankly, "I do it consciously, and I do it directly I meet somebody for the first time. I say to myself, 'Is he (or she) any good to me—and am

I any good to him (or her)?' It's quite simple and there's no time wasted on either side. It's a waste of time pottering about and getting to know people slowly. You want to make friends at once or not at all. The Navy has taught me that."

"The Navy?"

"Yes," she nodded gravely, "because before you know where you are you're whizzed off to Malta or Invergordon or Hong Kong and the opportunity has gone."

"Oh I see," said Kit.

"So there you are," she said, smiling at him. "We're friends now—if you want to be friends—and you can call me Dolly —if you'd like to, of course."

Kit thought it would be easy and pleasant to be friends with her and call her Dolly, for she amused and interested him. There was a mixture of foolishness and common sense in her which he found intriguing and her absolute frankness reminded him of a sea wind. He had thought her like Miss Peabody, but it was only their features that were alike—and even their features were alike only in repose. Kit decided that if Dolly had been awake when he had first seen her (or at any rate had not been shamming sleep) he would not have thought she resembled her sister in the least. Their eyes were different and their expressions were different and their technique of social conduct was the most different of all.

Dr. Peabody showed no surprise when they met at dinner and his youngest daughter greeted his assistant like a life-long friend. Perhaps he knew her too well to be surprised at anything she did.

"So you two have met already!" he said, beaming upon them cheerfully. "Sit down, my dear, sit down," he added. "It's very pleasant to see you here again, in your usual place—isn't it, Ethel?"

Miss Peabody did not reply, and Kit, glancing at her, saw

that her mouth, which was a buttoned-up mouth at the best of times, wore its most forbidding expression.

"You're looking well," continued the old doctor affectionately. "Yes, I believe you've put on a little weight, and it suits you."

"I see no difference in her," Miss Peabody said.

"Don't you think I'm prettier?" enquired Dolly, turning to her sister with an innocent air.

"I've said that you look the same," replied Miss Peabody, "and perhaps if we could see ourselves as others see us we might be less pleased with our appearance."

"How lucky for you that we can't!" exclaimed Dolly, gazing at her sister with a horrified expression.

Miss Peabody answered grimly, "I should have less of a shock than some people for I have fewer illusions about myself. I can face the truth."

"Oh, so can I," agreed Dolly, "as a matter of fact I think absolute honesty is the quality I most admire. What do you think, Kit?"

Kit was unwilling to be drawn into the argument but he saw no escape. "I believe honesty is the best policy," he said lightly.

"Honesty with ourselves as well as with other people," Dolly added.

"That was what I said," Miss Peabody remarked, "but very few people can be honest with themselves. They are quite pleased with themselves but they would not care to know themselves if they could meet themselves in everyday life— they would shrink from all contact with themselves if they could obtain an outsider's view of their natures."

"You seem slightly muddled," Dolly told her.

"On the contrary, I am perfectly clear. I didn't expect you to understand what I meant."

"I understand perfectly, my pet. I've known you for years so your nature is an open book to me."

The conversation had been carried on in a low tone and Dr. Peabody had paid no attention to it. He never paid much attention to the conversation at mealtime (Kit had noticed this before); he concentrated on the business at hand and ate in a neat quick manner as if he cared very little what kind of food it was, but used it only to sustain his body and to give him the required amount of nourishment. Perhaps this habit had been formed of necessity rather than choice for his patients always chose his mealtimes to ring him up on the telephone, and scarcely a meal passed without his being called away. Kit was therefore somewhat surprised when he looked up from his pudding and remarked in a pleasant voice:

"Surely there is no need to start bickering the moment Dolly comes home."

"Ethel has had nobody to bicker with for nine months," replied Dolly smiling. "You're an impossible person to bicker with and Kit isn't much better."

"I don't agree that we were bickering," Ethel declared.

"Of course not, dear," replied Dolly promptly. "We were conversing pleasantly together as sisters should. Father should be charmed to hear the sound of our innocent prattle."

The doctor smiled. "You did not seem to be agreeing very well," he pointed out.

"People can't agree about everything—it would be dull if they did," said Dolly gravely.

"No doubt, no doubt," her father replied, "but you must consider Dr. Stone. It can't be very enjoyable for him to listen to you 'conversing pleasantly together' and he doesn't possess my advantage."

"Your advantage, Father?" enquired Dolly opening her blue eyes very wide.

"The advantage of being slightly deaf," explained Dr. Peabody promptly.

Dolly was a trifle squashed, but not for long. After a few moments' silence she remarked, "I wonder if you are as deaf as you seem, darling."

He replied with twinkling eyes, "I can't be expected to answer that, can I?"

"Why not?"

"Because I can't possibly tell how deaf I seem."

"Sometimes you seem slightly deaf," Dolly told him.

"Then you may take it that that is what I am."

"And at other times you seem to hear all you want."

"That, also, is a fact," he told her gravely.

"I never noticed that you were deaf at all, sir," declared Kit.

"There," said Dr. Peabody, smiling, "my argument is confirmed . . . and now perhaps you will leave me in peace to finish my dinner before the telephone rings again."

"Shut your ears, darling," said Dolly mischievously, "you can evidently do that when you like—then our conversation won't worry you."

There was silence for a few moments while Tupman cleared away the pudding plates and put the dessert on the table. Miss Peabody helped herself to an exceedingly green apple and began to peel it.

"What will you have, Kit?" enquired Dolly somewhat pointedly. "Do you share Ethel's peculiar taste for unripe fruit?"

"What about you?" returned Kit politely.

She smiled at him across the table. "Let's share a pear," she suggested. "You choose a ripe one and cut it in half. You like pears."

"How did you know?"

"I was making a shot in the dark."

"It was a good shot," said Kit.

"Dr. Stone might prefer a whole pear," suggested Miss Peabody somewhat acidly.

"He might," agreed Dolly readily, "but he wasn't offered a whole pear. Nobody seemed to think of offering him one . . . surely half a pear is better than no fruit."

"Dr. Stone knows that he can help himself to what he wants. He has made himself at home in this house, he isn't a stranger now."

"And I've made myself a stranger!" cried Dolly in mock dismay. "Kit, I apologise humbly . . . I didn't realise my position . . . I should have waited for you to offer me half a pear, but you see I never realised that marriage had made me a stranger here. You *do* understand, don't you?"

Kit did not know what to say, so very wisely he said nothing. He chose a pear and began to peel it carefully. He was not very fond of Ethel Peabody, and it grieved him not at all to see her teased and tantalised, but he had got to live in the same house with her—possibly for years—and he had no wish to make an enemy of her. Dolly was a little minx and she was determined to draw him into the fray . . . he would have to watch his step very carefully.

"You won't be a stranger for long," Miss Peabody was saying in a cutting sort of voice.

"That's my friendly nature," Dolly told her, "I'm a bright little sunbeam, aren't I, Kit?"

"I think you're more like a breeze," said Kit.

"A breeze," she repeated, considering the matter thoughtfully. "Well, perhaps I am. I rather like the idea, somehow."

"People's disadvantages are more easily borne by themselves than by others," remarked Ethel.

"Why, yes," Dolly agreed, "I see that too. When the breeze blows somebody's hat off and it goes scooting down the street it's the owner of the hat who suffers, not the breeze. The breeze is just enjoying itself in its own merry way, isn't it?"

Miss Peabody did not reply, and after a moment Dolly added, "Poor Ethel, why don't you sew on a piece of elastic? Your hat blows off too easily, my dear."

There was silence for a few moments, but Dolly could not be silent for long. She smiled at Kit and enquired in an innocent voice, "What is Ethel like? I'm sure she'd like to know."

"She hasn't said so," Kit pointed out.

"That's because she's shy," declared Dolly nodding gravely. "You mustn't worry about that. Just take a good look at her and make up your mind . . . or perhaps you've made up your mind about Ethel already. I keep on forgetting that you've known each other for more than a month."

Kit searched for something to say, but found nothing, and a somewhat uncomfortable silence ensued. It was broken by Dr. Peabody who had finished his dinner and had poured out the port.

"They're alike, aren't they?" he said, looking at his daughters with a pleasant smile. "I've always thought they were alike but I see the resemblance more clearly than ever tonight. Anybody would know they were sisters."

Kit could not deny it, of course, for he had proved the truth of it—the two fair faces were cast in the same mould—but he was uncomfortably aware that neither of the sisters would be pleased if he agreed with their father's statement.

"There's usually a slight resemblance between children of the same parents," said Kit with a judicial air, "but it's the difference, rather than the similarity which—"

"I've often seen it," interrupted Miss Peabody firmly.

"You think that we're alike!" cried Dolly incredulously.

"If you ever faced the truth you'd have seen it long ago."

"But Ethel—"

"I don't welcome the resemblance any more than you do,"

declared her sister, "make no mistake about that; but we have no choice in the matter. It's a thing that must be borne. . . ."

(Dolly seemed less able to bear it; her eyes were fixed upon her sister's countenance with ludicrous dismay.)

Ethel continued, "To look at you, and reflect that I wear the same doll-face gives me no pleasure at all. You're more fortunate, for your nature and your face match."

"Kit doesn't think we're alike," cried Dolly.

"Dr. Stone will see one resemblance, anyhow. He'll think we both take an undue interest in our appearance."

There was a short silence.

"Where is Commander Dorman, now?" enquired Kit somewhat desperately.

"On his way to Malta," replied his wife.

"I was there once," Kit declared. "It's a gay spot, there's lots of tennis and bathing. I suppose you'll be going out to join him."

"Not I," said Dolly with an impudent grin. "I think it's so silly for sailors' wives to rush after them all round the world."

"Dolly thought it would be pleasant to have a change from married life," explained her sister in a low even tone, "she has been married for nine months, you see. It's a long time, isn't it?"

"You don't understand," cried Dolly impetuously.

"No, I don't really," admitted Ethel. "Our natures are not alike, you see."

Kit gazed at his plate. He could feel the strain and bitterness which ran beneath the surface and he wished devoutly that something would happen to ease the tension or to give him an opportunity to escape from the room. If only the telephone bell would ring. . . .

"They are both like their mother," declared Dr. Peabody, turning to Kit and pointing to an oil painting which hung over the mantelpiece.

It was a fact, but it only added to Kit's discomfort. He rose
and examined the picture with elaborate interest. "It's beautifully painted," he remarked, "and the flesh tints are delightful.
What year was it painted, sir?"

"Let me see," said Dr. Peabody. "It was the year after we
were married—must have been nineteen hundred . . ." and to
Kit's delight he immediately launched forth into an account of
various circumstances connected with the picture which ef-
fectively changed the subject. His daughters looked bored—it
was obvious that they had heard the story before—and as they
had now finished their dessert they rose with one accord and
made for the door. Kit was just in time to open it for them
and to receive a mischievous grimace from Dolly as she followed her sister out of the room.

"You mustn't mind them, Stone," said Dr. Peabody, as the
clatter of their high heels on the polished boards died away
in the distance, "they're good girls in their way, and fond of
each other too, though you mightn't think it . . . their mother
died when they were very young."

(It was obvious that Dr. Peabody was not as deaf as they
thought.)

"They don't mean what they say, of course," Kit agreed,
smiling.

"Well, I wouldn't say that," replied Dr. Peabody thoughtfully. "They do mean it in a way—they've never got on very
well, those two—but they're really very fond of each other."

"Yes, of course," agreed Kit, somewhat doubtfully.

"They're too much alike to hit it off well," continued Dr.
Peabody. "They are both strong characters and neither of them
will give in to the other. Poor Ethel is a trifle embittered—there
was some trouble between them over Ralph Dorman. I never
quite understood the ins and outs of it to tell you the truth. If
their mother had been alive everything would have been quite
different. . . . Come," he added in a more cheerful tone,

"come along, Kit. We'll have our talk and join them in the drawing room. I must see as much as I can of Dolly while she's here."

Kit was quite willing to fall in with the old doctor's plan. (He had been very much annoyed with Dolly for the discomfort she had occasioned him, but annoyance was giving place to amusement. She was a mischievous kitten of a creature, and one could not be angry with a kitten for long), but the telephone bell rang and the doctor was obliged to go out, and Kit was left to go up to the drawing room alone.

When he opened the door and looked in he saw that Dolly was there by herself; she was lying on the sofa in a listless attitude and the standard lamp behind her shed a soft glow on her hair. Kit hesitated—the room looked different somehow, and it was a moment or two before he found the reason for its unfamiliar appearance. He was used to seeing the drawing room lighted by a harsh white glare from the ceiling, but to-night it was lighted only by the soft illumination of the lamp. The heavy Victorian furniture and the patterned carpet were mellowed by the change in lighting, and the room wore a peaceful, homey look.

"Hallo!" said Kit, going forward.

"Hallo," said Dolly in a casual voice.

He looked down at her and saw with surprise and dismay that her eyes were full of tears, and there were tears on her cheeks too, big crystal tears running down slowly.

"Dolly!" he said uncertainly.

"It's nothing," she declared, seizing her handkerchief and scrubbing her eyes almost savagely. "It's nothing. I'm silly, that's all. Sit down and talk to me, Kit."

He sat down beside her on a little stool and took her hand.

"Don't be nice to me," she warned him, drawing her hand away.

"All right, I won't," he said, "but you might tell me what's the matter. I thought we were friends."

"It's silliness," declared Dolly, pulling herself together with a determined effort, "just sheer silliness. I knew when I married Ralph that he'd have to go . . . wherever he was sent . . . but I always hoped . . . I'd be able to go too."

"Couldn't you?"

She shook her head.

"But why not?" asked Kit. "Why don't you go out to Malta? Lots of naval wives do."

"I'm going to have a baby," said Dolly in a very small voice.

There was a little silence, but it was a friendly sympathetic silence with no discomfort in it.

"You *are* a dear," said Dolly at last, and she slipped her hand into his. "You really are a pet. I believe you understand . . . I'm glad I've told you."

Kit was glad too. "Why don't you tell your sister?" he asked.

"Because I don't *want* to," said Dolly with more spirit. "Because she's so damned inquisitive, that's why. I'm not going to have her poking and prying into my affairs. Nobody knows about it—nobody except Ralph—and I don't *want* anyone to know."

Kit smiled at her. "All right," he said, "don't get so excited, I'm as safe as the bank."

"I suppose you think it's silly?"

"No, not really. Are you pleased about it?"

"No," she said quickly, and then she added, "yes, of course I am . . . but I wanted to go with Ralph. Oh, I don't know whether I'm pleased or not . . . I'm all muddled."

Kit pressed her hand. "I'm sorry," he said.

"I thought I told you not to be nice," she murmured, turning her face away.

CHAPTER XIV

THE BREAKFAST TABLE

ON THE morning following her arrival Dolly was late for breakfast, indeed the others were finishing their meal when the door opened and she walked in.

Jem sprang up and hugged her ecstatically, "Darling Aunt Dolly!" he cried. "Why *ever* didn't you come and see me in bed when you arrived?"

"I did see you," replied Dolly, kissing him fondly, "but you didn't see me. You had your eyes tight shut—horrid of you, I thought."

"I was asleep, I s'pose. Well, of course I must have been asleep."

"It seems fairly obvious," remarked Ethel Peabody dryly.

Dolly took no notice of this; she kissed her father on the top of his head, smiled at Kit, and helped herself to half a grape-fruit.

"Breakfast in this house is at half past eight," said Ethel in a pointed manner.

"It always was," agreed Dolly, "except on Sundays, of course. Do you still have it at nine on Sundays?"

"You seem to have it at nine on week days."

Dolly glanced at the clock, "Five minutes to nine is my hour," she declared. "It really is the ideal time for breakfast. Don't you agree, Kit?"

"Dr. Stone comes down at the proper time," said Ethel firmly.

"That doesn't mean that he likes it," Dolly pointed out. "It only means that you've imposed your will upon him."

Ethel returned to the attack, "If you had got up when the bell rang you would have been down in time."

Dolly agreed at once. "Of course I should have been," she said, "but I didn't want to get up when the bell rang, I wanted a nice little snooze. That's the effect it always has on me. I may wake quite early and be wide awake for hours, but the moment I hear the getting-up bell, I feel as sleepy and comfortable as a dormouse."

"You have no self-discipline," Ethel pointed out, "you ought to be firmer with yourself, you ought to *make* yourself get up."

"Why should I?"

"Because it's the right thing to do. This house isn't a hotel. You must show a little consideration for the servants."

Dr. Peabody looked up from his paper. "Dolly had a long journey yesterday," he said. "There is no need to discuss the subject further."

"As long as she doesn't make a habit of it," grumbled Ethel. "It puts the work of the house all wrong if Tupman can't get the table cleared." She rose as she spoke and stood there looking at them.

"There's no hurry," her father said, "Tupman can wait until we've finished."

"That's all very well," she retorted. "It's difficult enough to run this house without people being late unnecessarily. When you're late, or Dr. Stone, I know it can't be helped, but Dolly has no excuse. I do my best but nobody seems to appreciate what I do; I slave night and day and nobody gives me a word of thanks—"

"You slave night and day!" exclaimed her father in justifiable surprise. "My dear Ethel, you don't know what you're saying. If you can't run the house with Tupman and two maids—"

"You don't understand!" she cried. "It's *difficult* to run a house, and especially difficult when it's a doctor's house. I can manage it, of course, but why should Dolly make things more difficult? I don't know why she's here at all—"

"She's here because I like to have her," said the old doctor firmly.

Ethel realised that she was beaten. She hung about for a few moments and then she said in quite a different tone, "What are you doing this morning, Dolly? Nothing, I suppose."

"Quite right," replied Dolly agreeably, "nothing at all."

"Then perhaps, you could—"

"No, I couldn't possibly," interrupted Dolly in a pleasant easy voice. "When I say that I'm doing nothing I mean just exactly what I say, so it's no good asking me to do any of your nice little chores."

"Father, do you hear that?" cried Ethel furiously. "You must tell Dolly she's to help in the house while she's here. I do my best, but I can't be in two places at once."

Dr. Peabody had finished his breakfast now. He rose and surveyed his daughters with twinkling eyes but his voice was perfectly grave as he replied, "Even you must find that quite impossible."

"You must tell her, then," Ethel pointed out.

"Are you sure you want me to tell her? Are you sure you want her aid?"

Ethel was silent. She did not want Dolly's help but neither did she want Dolly to be perfectly free to amuse herself all day long.

"Think it over and let me know," said Dr. Peabody and he left the room.

"You might help to make the beds, anyhow," Ethel said in a grumbling voice.

"I'm a stranger here," explained Dolly, scooping away industriously at her grapefruit. "You said so yourself last night. Strangers never make the beds; nobody expects them to."

Jem chortled suddenly.

"There," said Ethel, "you might think of the child. He listens to everything."

"I can't help it," Jem declared. "How can you help listening when people are talking?"

He spoke so earnestly that it really seemed as if he were anxious for an answer to his question and Kit, also, would have liked an answer to it for he was in the same predicament. Kit had been brought up almost like an only child, for his brother was so much older than himself that there had been little or no companionship between them. He was therefore unused to family rows and it seemed very strange to him that the doctor's daughters could quarrel so fiercely and yet remain on comparatively easy terms. It seemed even more strange that they could quarrel with such freedom in public; the presence of an outsider did not seem to cramp their style in the least. Kit had been reflecting upon this queer phenomenon while he was finishing his breakfast and presently he came to a very sensible conclusion: if they don't mind why should I? After all I'm not invisible.

"Jem's just a baby," Dolly was saying in a fond indulgent voice. "He's grown a lot, of course, but he's just the same as ever and he hasn't forgotten his old married aunt—"

"A baby, indeed!" cried Ethel. "He's no more a baby than you are. It's high time he went to school and learned how to behave."

"I thought he went to school," Dolly said.

"Oh yes, he goes to Miss Elton's, but there isn't any discipline *there*. He ought to be sent away to a boarding school—everybody spoils him."

"But he isn't spoiled," Dolly pointed out. "Everybody spoils him—except you, of course—but he isn't spoiled. That's the main thing."

"He *is* spoiled," objected his elder aunt, "and you're very silly to talk about him like that before his face. He's bad enough as it is and you make him worse."

"Mais il est tel amusant," declared Dolly, smiling at Jem affectionately. "J'aime son petit visage angélique et son air si plein d'audace."

"Strange taste!" commented Ethel dryly.

Jem had been attending with interest to his aunts' ideas of his character and appearance and now, quite suddenly, he saw fit to enter the conversation. "Plain features, but a charming expression," he announced.

They all looked at him in surprise.

"That's me," he said, nodding at them gravely. "I heard Miss Sinclair say it 'plain features, of course, but a charming expression'."

He put so much feeling into the words and was so serious about it that Kit burst out laughing. He knew that he shouldn't laugh but he couldn't help it. Dolly joined in, and the two of them rocked helplessly with uncontrollable mirth.

"I see nothing funny in it," Ethel declared. "It just bears out what I said—the child listens to everything. Olive Sinclair and I were talking in *quite low voices* and I had forgotten that he was in the room."

"I don't like Miss Sinclair," said Jem with a thoughtful air. "She's got one of those faces . . . I mean her face is all close together in the middle and lots of emptiness all round . . . I mean. . . ."

"And she doesn't like your face," retorted his aunt furiously.

Kit had finished his breakfast now so he made his excuses and fled.

CHAPTER XV

THE TENNIS PARTY

IT WAS May now, and the country round Minfield was busily putting on its summer dress. Kit had not seen an English spring for years and it seemed to him that he was seeing it for the first time. He had seen nothing in other lands to compare with the beauty of the tender leaves and the delicate flowers of the English countryside, and he had felt nothing to equal the sparkling freshness of the air. Sometimes he would stop his car near a stream where golden king-cups grew—each flower bright as a newly minted sovereign amongst the lush green leaves—or he would stop in a side road and feast his eyes upon a wood where a carpet of bluebells lay spread beneath the trees. It was a season of heavy showers, of clouds which came up suddenly in the blue sky, and emptied themselves upon the land. They were inconvenient, of course, but Kit did not mind that, he did not even mind when the rain poured through the tattered hood of his old car and dripped onto his shoulders or his knees. He did not mind the showers because they were so beautiful—they were the most beautiful of all the beauties that he saw. He liked to stop and see the rain falling among the trees, washing them, and refreshing them; and then, when the shower passed and the sun shone out, every little drop of rain was like a diamond glittering upon the leaves, and the earth rejoiced and sent up a fragrance of growing things and of fertile soil, and the birds burst forth into song. He would listen to the thrushes' song and the blackbird's pipe, and it seemed to him that the bird music was spring itself expressed in sound. If he were happy the thrushes'

song sounded like a song of love and hope and if he were sad
the song seemed unearthly and heartless. He thought that
the earth was old, and yet there was this wonderful youth in
it. The sap rose from the old, old soil and became the tender
green of young leaves. Here was a mystery and a wonder
greater than the mystery of human birth, greater than the
wonder of human love. Kit had travelled in distant lands but
their beauties had not moved him. He had seen them and
appreciated them with his eyes but they had not touched his
heart nor stirred it to tenderness. But this was his own land
and its beauties belonged to him.

In a technical sense Kit did not own a foot of English soil
—the wood, the stream, the verdant meadows belonged to other
men—but because he was born and bred an Englishman all
England was his, and it was the more his because he loved it.

Kit thought about this and he saw in it an analogy with his
feelings for Mardie. Other women might be more beautiful
and more glamorous, but she belonged to him because he
loved her ... and he loved her because she belonged to him.

These ideas of Kit's made a background for the pattern of
his life. His work went on (and was not affected by them) and
his friendship with Jem, and his visits to the Fig and Thistle.
He had foreseen that the advent of Dolly Dorman would make
a difference in the doctor's household and his prophecy had
proved correct. Her presence made life a good deal less comfortable, but, on the other hand, it made life a good deal more
interesting. One could not feel dull in Dolly's vicinity for one
never knew what she would say next; she was as lively as a
kitten and as attractive and mischievous and irresponsible.
Mealtimes had become dangerous and exciting with sparks
flying in all directions, and Kit had less time to brood over his
private trouble, and less time to plan out ways and means of
seeing Mardie.

It was Kit's free afternoon and the Furnivals had asked him to tennis. Gilbert was not fit to play, of course, but he was well enough to take an interest in life and it was he who had arranged the party and invited the guests. A set was in progress when Kit arrived, but Mrs. Furnival was not playing. She rose when she saw Kit and came to meet him.

"We're sitting in the summer-house," she said, taking his arm, "come along, I'm so glad you've come. I was afraid some tiresome person might be ill, and send for you at the last minute. . . . Look at Gilbert, just look at him! It's all your doing, you know." ·

Gilbert certainly seemed in good form. He was umpiring for his guests and was waving his arms and talking in a loud cheerful voice and giving his opinion on some disputed point in the game.

"It's your doing," repeated Mrs. Furnival, pinching Kit's arm, "and when I look at him and think of what he was like six weeks ago . . . and of what we felt about him . . . the awful hopelessness of it . . . Alan and I feel . . . we feel we can't thank you enough. There simply aren't words to thank you."

"I haven't done much."

"Don't say that. You've made life worth living for three people. I'm not going to worry you any more but I had to say it once. If ever we could do anything for you it would make us happy . . . Alan feels the same as I do about it."

"It has made me happy to be able to help Gilbert."

"I know," she said, "I can understand that, but it doesn't make us less grateful. You've done more for Gilbert than treat him professionally—much more. I feel as if you had gone into a bog and pulled him out."

Kit thought that this was true. It was exactly what.he had done for Gilbert: he had gone into the bog and pulled him out.

"Oh well," he said uncomfortably, "I'm glad . . . I mean it's
been a great pleasure . . . and . . . and . . ."

"Come and sit down," said Mrs. Furnival in a different tone.
"The set will be over in a few minutes. You know Mrs.
Rochester of course."

Kit shook hands gravely with Mardie and with Cecil Wigmore, the Vicar's son, who was down from Oxford. He had
hoped that he might meet Mardie at the Furnivals' and was
delighted to find his hopes materialize; at the same time he
found that meeting Mardie like this in company with other
people was a mixed pleasure, for he wanted her whole attention, not just a little piece of it.

Mardie smiled at him very kindly and said, "Hallo, Kit!"
and went on talking to Cecil Wigmore about some mutual
friends who had left Minfield before Kit's arrival and had
gone to live near Oxford.

"I'm glad you looked them up," she declared. "Angela
doesn't know many people yet, and of course it's a little difficult for her to get about."

"Of course," agreed Wigmore, nodding, "she doesn't
make friends easily, but we're having a party in a couple of
weeks. . . ."

Kit could not think what Mardie saw in young Wigmore.
(Only a bounder would allow his hair to wave like that, or
would clip his moustache into such a silly little tuft.) Kit sat
down beside Mrs. Furnival and tried to talk to her, but in spite
of all he could do to keep his mind riveted on Mrs. Furnival's
conversation he found himself listening with one ear to the
conversation going on beside him, and very soon he became
so muddled between the two that he did not know what he
was saying. Mrs. Furnival was somewhat surprised to find
Dr. Stone so *distrait,* but fortunately she was very fond of him
and sincerely grateful, so she chattered on about her garden
and her servants and about the new car—which they had

bought for Gilbert—and left her companion to listen or not listen as he pleased.

The set went on rather longer than Mrs. Furnival had anticipated, but at last it was finished and Gilbert came over to the summer-house to arrange the next four.

"Are you going to play, Mother?" he enquired.

"Well, I don't know," said Mrs. Furnival vaguely.

Gilbert laughed. "I think you must be going to play," he told her, "otherwise you wouldn't have put on your tennis shoes."

"I'll play if I'm wanted," she said, smiling at him.

"All right, you can play now. There are four of you."

"I'm not very good, you know."

"That doesn't matter; you can play with Cecil against Mrs. Rochester and Kit—where's your racket?"

Kit's spirit went up with a bound as he walked onto the court with Mardie. He wanted to say all sorts of things to her. He wanted to say, "I haven't seen you for three days and it feels like three years." He wanted to say, "Darling, I adore you, and you're sweeter than ever in your short white frock." He wanted to say, "You *do* like me better than that bumptious young oaf with the wavy hair, don't you?"—but of course he could not say any of these things.

He swallowed twice and enquired in an unnaturally polite voice, "Which court do you prefer?"

"The left," said Mardie promptly.

"I haven't played for months," Kit told her.

"I'm frightfully off my service," said Mardie.

"Is he good?"

"He's amazing . . . he's astoundingly good. He'll probably smash us to bits, but it doesn't matter, does it?"

Kit thought it mattered a good deal for he wanted to win this set with Mardie as his partner. "I don't suppose Mrs. Furnival is much use," he said hopefully.

"No," agreed Mardie with a smile, "but that won't make any difference. Enid will stand meekly in the corner and Cecil will smash us singlehanded."

"Play!" cried Cecil Wigmore in commanding tones.

Kit saw very soon that Mardie was right in all she had said. Wigmore was a first class tennis player. He did what he liked with the ball and his opponents had no chance at all against him. Kit ran about the court, hitting and smashing to the best of his ability, and Mardie did her utmost to back him up, but Wigmore had them taped. . . . Wigmore seemed to be everywhere at once and was always ready and waiting for the ball no matter where it landed. Mrs. Furnival did little except return her opponent's services and serve, herself, when her turn came—it was all that Wigmore asked, or indeed desired of a female partner.

"This is frightful!" Kit said as he mopped his brow and gathered up the balls at the back net.

"Frightful," Mardie agreed.

"I'd like to get one game," he said, almost desperately, "it's love-five, you know."

"Perhaps we shall win this game—it's your service."

"Yes," said Kit. He said it almost fiercely, for he was absurdly anxious to win at least one game from Cecil Wigmore. I mustn't be angry, he told himself, I must keep quite cool and concentrate . . . I must win every point from Mrs. Furnival, and one point from Wigmore.

He served to Mrs. Furnival first, and she muffed it—"Fifteen love," declared Kit with satisfaction. They crossed over and he served to Wigmore who returned to Mardie, and Mardie produced one of her forehand drives. It was a good stroke and well-placed, but Wigmore was at the net by this time and smashed it into the corner of the court. . . . "Fifteen all." Kit collected the balls and served to Mrs. Furnival who dabbed at the ball wildly and hitting it on the wood returned it just over the net. Kit was too late in getting there and the point was lost. . . . "Fifteen thirty." He felt hopeless as he faced Wigmore again, but he pulled himself together and struck the ball well. Wigmore returned it down the side line and Mardie was too far forward to take it. There was still a faint hope—or so Kit tried to believe—he served a snorter to Mrs. Furnival, but it was a fault . . . and his second service was weaker. Mrs. Furnival returned the ball quite easily and Kit ran forward and tipped it back to her. He was aware that she was rather a slow starter and could never get to it in time, but, even as he hit it, Wigmore had crossed the court . . . Wigmore was waiting for the silly ball to bounce, and Kit had no idea at all what Wigmore intended to do with it. He hesitated, trying to make up his mind whether to advance or retire, and the ball slipped past like a flash of lightning and raised a cloud of white from the back line.

"Game and . . ." said Kit trying to smile and look pleased about it.

"Game and . . ." agreed Mardie, "and there's a ball somewhere in the hedge. . . ."

Kit was quite glad to poke about in the hedge for the missing ball, for he was ridiculously upset over the defeat. What's the matter with me, he wondered as he peered about in the hedge, why on earth can't I take a beating in the proper spirit?

"Here it is!" Mardie cried.

They walked over to the summer-house together, and as they went Kit put his feeling into words. "You don't seem to mind," he said.

"Mind!" she echoed in surprise. "Oh, you mean I don't seem to mind being beaten? No, why should I mind?"

"Oh, I don't know. . . ."

"Cecil plays every day," explained Mardie. "Cecil *lives* for tennis. If you gave up your whole life to tennis you could be as good a player as he is."

It was quite obvious that Mardie thought tennis a poor sort of life's work, and Kit was comforted. He was even more comforted by what ensued, for Cecil Wigmore was not a good winner and his victory seemed to evoke the unlovable side of his nature. Perhaps it is harder to be a good winner than a good loser at social tennis, but Kit did not think of this; he was in no mood to make allowances for the young man.

"Oh no," Wigmore was saying to Mrs. Furnival as they approached, "oh no, not the least hot, thank you. It takes more than that to warm me up, actually. I never got going—if you know what I mean."

"I'm afraid we didn't give you a game," said Mardie gravely.

Wigmore laughed. "Well, no," he said in a deprecating way, "one could hardly call it a game, actually. A love-set isn't what you could call a *game,* is it?"

Mrs. Furnival looked somewhat uncomfortable. "I thought they played up very well," she babbled. "I mean—after all— I mean the score doesn't always give you a proper idea of the play. Some of the games were quite close, weren't they? . . . Deuce and vantage over and over again."

"That was only in one game," declared her partner in a judicial manner. "It was the third game, and you were serving. You served three double faults."

"Oh, did I?" said Mrs. Furnival in a faint voice.

"Yes. Three doubles. It's a bit of a handicap, actually. I mean it's three points absolutely thrown away."

"Yes, of course," agreed the culprit meekly. "I'm—I'm afraid I'm rather off my service today."

Wigmore nodded. "You need practice," he said. "Take my advice and practice seriously. Come out with a bag-full of balls and try to place them—your placing is the worst feature of your game—an hour every morning would make a lot of difference to you."

Kit almost spluttered with laughter at the idea of Mrs.

Furnival repairing to the tennis court every morning with a bag-full of balls to practice her service. He glanced at her and saw that her eyes had widened with horror at the bare idea.

"But I haven't time," she bleated.

"One can always make time for anything one really wants to do," Wigmore told her earnestly. "I haven't much time myself, actually, but I *make* time to practice. I have to do that or my game would suffer."

"I see," said Mrs. Furnival in a bewildered manner. "But I really don't think my game is worth it."

"Oh, I don't know," replied Wigmore kindly, "you've got quite a nice forehand drive—and you'd be surprised how much you'd improve. Gilbert could stand in the court and tell you whether the ball was on the line. It would be something for him to do." He turned to Mardie and added complacently, "My service seemed to bother you a good deal!"

"Oh it *did*. I couldn't take it at all," agreed Mardie. She spoke very gravely, but there was a twinkle in her eye which Kit did not miss.

"I was talking to one of the Davis Cup fellows the other day," continued Wigmore in a loudish voice. "He said to me: 'Wigmore, I wish you'd tell me one thing'—actually he couldn't understand how I get the pace and the break at the same time."

"And how do you?" enquired Mardie.

"I can break the ball both ways," continued the unfortunate youth, swinging his racket over his head to illustrate his method. "Like this, you see . . . or else like this . . . I expect you noticed I could break it both ways."

"Oh yes, we did, didn't we Kit?" said Mardie.

"Yes, indeed we did," agreed Kit promptly. He was perfectly happy now for it was better than if they had won the set—to have lost it together and to see the victor making such an exhibition of himself.

"And my service," continued Wigmore earnestly. "Perhaps

you noticed that I put *more* pace into my second service, actually. It took me a long time to get that, and a tremendous amount of practice, but I find it pays. I have a very good eye, of course; you couldn't do it unless you had a very good eye. . . ."

"Shall we go in to tea?" enquired his hostess.

"In a minute," he declared, "I must just show them something . . . I must just explain. Most people imagine that if their first service is a fault they must hit the ball *less hard* for their second service. I daresay you thought that?"

"Yes," said Mardie meekly.

"But I merely change the angle," said Wigmore, "there's absolutely no need to hit the ball less hard if you change the angle. I was having a knock-up with Trimble the other day— I daresay you've heard of Trimble—and he said to me that the only possible way of taking my service was to take it at half volley."

Gilbert Furnival had been talking to one of his other guests but now he joined the group round the summer-house. "You wait," he said, smiling at Wigmore in a friendly way, "you just wait till I'm ready to take you on. I'll disarrange your permanent wave for you, my boy."

They all laughed at that, and Wigmore (who was not really such a bad soul, but only foolish) joined in and declared that he would hold himself at Gilbert's disposal.

"I'll let you know," said Gilbert seriously, "the moment my medical man gives me the word, and I'll play you for half a crown. Is it a go?"

Wigmore said it was.

Having settled this, Gilbert endeavoured to form another set, for if he could not play himself he was determined that his guests should have as much tennis as possible; but the four people who had been sitting out showed their reluctance too plainly and their hostess rescued them.

"We had better all have tea together," she said, "and then you can mix up the sets afterwards."

"It's such a waste of time when we have only one court ..." said Gilbert sadly, but nobody listened to him and the whole party strolled back to the house and partook of nourishment in the usual form.

Kit maneuvered for a seat next to Mardie but was foiled in his attempt by Cecil Wigmore who wanted to explain the correct method of holding the racket for a backhand. He had found Mrs. Rochester willing to take instruction and advice and was only too willing to give it to her. He demonstrated his method with the bread knife, and Mardie was obliged to listen, and although Kit could see that she was very bored it did him no good at all for he could not get near her.

They played again after tea but Gilbert mixed them up, as his mother had suggested, and Kit was put to play in a different set from Mardie. When she was playing he had to sit out and make conversation with a young woman, whom he had never seen before, and when Mardie was sitting out it was Kit's turn to play. He became so desperate that when Mardie rose to go he said he must go too and offered to take her home in his car.

"I think I'll walk home across the fields," said Mardie, smiling at him, "I'd rather walk home, really."

"I'll walk back with you part of the way," declared Kit boldly.

He was aware that the suggestion sounded odd, but he had become quite reckless for it was absolutely necessary for him to have Mardie to himself for a few minutes, to talk to her and to hear her voice.

They set off together and for a little while they walked along in silence; now that Kit had got his way, he could find nothing to say to Mardie. He was in no mood to discuss trivial matters, and his whole being was full of thoughts and feelings which he must not express. He realised that he had been very foolish to offer to accompany Mardie for she had not wanted him and the Furnivals were bound to think it rather queer. Kit had been so careful not to give Minfield any chance to gossip about his friendship with Mardie, and now, by one reckless move, he had betrayed himself. He glanced at Mardie sideways and saw that her expression was very thoughtful and sad. Was she angry with him, he wondered. He thought she had a right to be angry with him for he had presumed on their friendship.

"I'm sorry, Mardie," he said impulsively.

"Sorry!" she asked in surprise.

"I shouldn't have offered to come with you."

"But why?"

"Because you didn't want me."

"Nonsense," she said, holding out her hand and smiling at him.

"It isn't nonsense. I knew you didn't want me."

"I didn't want anybody," she replied, looking at him with her honest grey eyes. "Sometimes one has to be . . . alone. But now that you've come I like having you, and you can come as far as the gate."

He was aware that she meant exactly what she said, so he walked on beside her.

"It was nice of you to come," she continued, "but you mustn't expect me to be a cheery companion. I don't feel like it at the moment."

"You were very cheery at the party," Kit pointed out.

She nodded. "Perhaps that's the reason," she said thoughtfully. "You go out to parties and you talk and laugh and then you suddenly realise how silly it all is. We were rather unkind to Cecil, weren't we?"

"He deserved it, and as a matter of fact he had no idea we were being unkind—"

"That makes it almost worse."

They walked on for a bit and then Mardie said, "But it wasn't that, altogether. It was just that I had a sudden feeling that I couldn't bear it any more—that I must get away from them all, or I should scream—"

"Mardie, is there something the matter?"

"Not really," she replied in a doubtful voice, "only sometimes life is so difficult. You think you've escaped for a bit and then you remember that you haven't. It's waiting for you—"

"What is?" he asked in concern. "What do you want to escape from?"

"I can't explain," she replied. "It's just a feeling. Life seems to close in all around you until you can hardly breathe."

They had come to the gate by now and Mardie went through and shut it between them. She stood there with her hand on it and smiled at him sadly. It seemed to Kit that her action was symbolical—thus far and no further, she seemed to say—

"Mardie, I thought we were friends!" he exclaimed.

"Why of course we are," she said, "but even friends can only come as far as the gate. Everybody has got to bear life alone . . . everybody has got to go on . . . bearing whatever it is they have to bear . . . alone."

She smiled at him again and turned away and he watched her go up the path to the house between the high bushes of rhododendron. She stopped at a bend in the path and looked back and waved to him, and then she disappeared.

CHAPTER XVI

A SERIOUS CONVERSATION

KIT followed Dr. Peabody into the library and shut the door. It was the hour for their nightly conference, when they talked over their cases together and compared notes, and as a rule Kit enjoyed it, but tonight he was not looking forward to it at all.

"I've something to tell you," he said.

"You always have," chuckled the old doctor as he took up his pipe. "I never knew such a fellow for telling. Teaching your grandfather to suck eggs is your favorite form of employment. As a matter of fact I've got something to tell you tonight: you remember that case of bronchitis—old Mrs. Skipton down at Suppley—I was more than a little anxious about it. Well, it's clearing up, and the old dear will be on her legs again in no time. You can't teach me much about bronchitis, Kit," declared the old man, grinning at his assistant in a mischievous way. "You can't produce anything better than a poultice and a kettle. I'll take off my hat to the man who can. Hm—yes—take off my hat to him."

"It's serious," said Kit, who had waited impatiently for the doctor to finish. "I've got something *serious* to tell you."

"Not diphtheria!" exclaimed Dr. Peabody in alarm. "Don't tell me we're in for another bout of that devilish disease . . . down at Milestone Cottages, I'll be bound . . . that faulty drain . . . and the County Council won't do a ·thing about it . . . I'll. . . ."

"No," said Kit firmly, "no, it isn't anything like that. It's nothing to do with your patients, it's just. . . ."

"What is it?"

"I shall have to go."

"Go where?"

"Go away," said Kit desperately, "I've got to leave Minfield, that's all."

"Leave Minfield!" exclaimed Dr. Peabody in dismay.

"Yes," said Kit firmly.

"Nonsense. Perfect nonsense! Good Heavens, Kit, you can't leave me now."

"You can easily get someone else."

"Like hell I can! . . . What d'you mean? What's it all about?"

"It's just that I've got to go."

"Have you got something better? Going to put up your plate in Harley Street?"

"No," said Kit gravely.

"What's happened, then?"

"Nothing . . . so far."

"I won't let you go," declared Dr. Peabody, glaring at his assistant from beneath his bushy brows. "D'you hear that— I won't let you."

"You'll have to let me go. I mean it's really for your own sake . . . it will be better for you if I leave at once."

"For my own sake!" exclaimed the old doctor in bewilderment. "What on earth . . . look here, sit down and tell me about it. If it's a mistake you've made . . . well, we all make mistakes."

"It isn't a mistake," said Kit, and he added in a lower tone, "and I haven't made it yet."

"Leave off talking in riddles, can't you."

Kit came forward and sat down. He felt, quite suddenly, that he could tell the old man everything. He felt that Dr. Peabody deserved an explanation.

"It's like this—" he said, and then paused.

"Fill your pipe, Kit," said Dr. Peabody. "Fill your pipe and get down to it . . . now then."

Kit obeyed. "It's Mrs. Rochester," he said.

"Mrs. Rochester! What about her? What d'you mean?"

"I mean," said Kit. "Well, the fact is . . . well, I mean I love her."

The old man looked at him in dismay. "Good Heavens!" he cried, "but Kit, look here . . . what on earth. . . ."

"It just happened," said Kit helplessly.

"But it shouldn't have happened!"

"I suppose it shouldn't."

"But look here, Kit—"

"I couldn't help it," Kit told him. "I tried—I really did try very hard to avoid her and—"

"Now then, look here," said Dr. Peabody. "You and I—"

"No," said Kit, interrupting him firmly. "No, sir, if I'm to tell you anything at all I must tell you the whole thing and tell it in my own way."

There was a moment's silence. "Go on then," said Dr. Peabody. "I'll hear what you have to say."

"It's like this," said Kit, starting again. "I've knocked about all over the place and I've met hundreds of women and of course I've been in love once or twice—well, most people have been—but this isn't the same thing at all. It isn't a physical attraction. It goes much deeper." He struggled for words and then continued in a low tone. "We understand each other . . . we're friends . . . partners. We belong to each other. I knew it from the first moment I saw her. I knew we weren't strangers, and I believe she feels the bond between us in the same way only there is a crust of convention over her mind that won't let the knowledge through. I believe she—she feels it subconsciously, but she doesn't know it, she doesn't know that it's there." He sighed, "I wish I knew the *meaning* of it," he said, "I wish I knew whether we were really 'made for each other', as the saying is, and whether some freak of fate kept us apart and prevented us from finding each other sooner."

"Have you forgotten that she's married?"

"No, but my feeling for her is a fundamental thing. It's a primitive thing. I feel that out of all the millions of women in the world she's mine. I need her in the same way as I need air to breathe and water to drink. I need her companionship. It's a queer sort of feeling, really. If we had met before, if we had met anywhere—in the train, or in the street—I wouldn't have passed her by. I'd have known her at once for my woman. Queer, isn't it?"

Dr. Peabody did not answer, perhaps he could not.

"I never knew I needed anyone," Kit continued, "I never visualised—anyone—any girl or woman. If I had, it wouldn't have been anyone who looked like her. If you had asked me what type I admired I'd have thought of golden hair and blue eyes—I'm only telling you this to try and explain what I mean—it wasn't the outside of her that appealed to me. It was something else. Now that I know her, of course, she's all herself—every bit of her—complete—perfect."

Dr. Peabody cleared his throat. "Kit, I see—I see you must go," he said.

"Yes," said Kit nodding.

"I'm more sorry than I can say."

"So am I," replied Kit. "You've been so good to me, sir. And I hate the idea of parting from Jem."

"I feel for you very much," Dr. Peabody said, "but you'll get over it, you know. You won't believe this, of course, but you *will* get over it in time."

"No," replied Kit in a very low voice, "no, I shan't get over it. I'm not going to try. You don't understand."

"In time—"

"No," said Kit again, shaking his head, "I've been trying to tell you, to explain. I'm not going to give her up. I couldn't."

"What on earth d'you mean?"

"I'm going away because I don't want to harm you—that

would be a poor return for all your kindness—but I'm coming back."

Dr. Peabody gazed at him in dismay.

"I haven't done anything yet," Kit told him, "I haven't said a word to her."

"I should hope not!"

"I must be absolutely free. I must leave you and go away . . . then I can come back to her."

"I won't hear of it!" cried Dr. Peabody in a trembling voice. "I can't believe that you . . . that *you* would do a thing like that . . . no, I can't believe it."

"I can't help it," declared Kit.

"And even if you go away from here, even then I shall feel that what you do affects me. You met her when you were my assistant, you attended her professionally."

"I attended the maid," Kit amended.

"You went to the house in a professional capacity," declared Dr. Peabody, "but never mind that, it's a minor consideration. The point is . . . Kit, you haven't thought about it, have you? You haven't considered the matter sufficiently. You wouldn't try to take away another man's wife."

"I would take what was mine."

"But she isn't yours. She's Rochester's wife."

"She belongs to me because I understand her."

"It's a specious argument. Besides they're happy together. You've absolutely no right to interfere—no moral right."

Kit thought about that. "She isn't happy," he said slowly, "there's something wrong somewhere. I've got to find out what it is."

"They're happy," repeated Dr. Peabody. "I've seen them together and I know. You haven't seen them together, have you? No, I thought not."

"I've got to find out," said Kit earnestly. "That's why I want to leave soon; because, if I begin to talk to her seriously, I can't answer for the consequences. I want to be free to tell her that I love her—that's all."

"That's all!" exclaimed Dr. Peabody. "I should think it was quite enough! You have no right to break up their home. You're mad to think of it. You say that you must find out whether or not she's happy? Well, I can tell you this: if you managed to persuade her to leave Rochester and go off with you, she certainly would *not* be happy. She would feel that she had let him down. She would grieve over it. She would fret herself into her grave."

"But—"

"No, let me finish," said Dr. Peabody holding up his hand. "I don't believe for a moment that you would succeed in persuading her, because the woman's happily married, and because you've nothing to offer her. I suppose you think you'll drag her all over the world after you—"

"I've got to find out," said Kit, but he said it without much assurance.

"She would never be happy with you," said Dr. Peabody pressing home his point. "She would always remember that she had behaved badly to him, that she had broken her marriage vows. Some women could put that behind them and go forward freely, but she would carry her broken chains until the day she died."

"Don't," said Kit, putting up his hand as if to ward off a blow.

Dr. Peabody was silent. He believed he had said enough.

CHAPTER XVII

THE DINNER PARTY

DR. PEABODY'S words made a deep impression upon Kit, for he saw that there was a great deal of truth in them. He had been so full of his love for Mardie that he had not considered the various aspects of the case which Dr. Peabody had put forward. He had known, of course, that she was Rochester's wife in the eyes of the world, but he had felt—and he still felt—that she was his mate in the eyes of God. His feeling for her was so true and deep that he could not believe it was a wrong feeling. Kit was willing to sacrifice all he possessed for her sake —his career, his relations, everything—and he knew of a certainty that he would never look back and that he would want Mardie and nothing but Mardie all his life. If he had Mardie he would be rich beyond his wildest dreams, and if he had not Mardie he would be poorer than the meanest beggar. He had been willing to set aside his own selfish desires and content himself with Mardie's friendship, but she had given him a glimpse of her heart and he was sure that she was not happy. It was this certainty that had made him change his mind, for above all things he wanted Mardie's happiness, and he had felt that if she were not happy with Rochester she would be happy with him.

Dr. Peabody's words had destroyed this illusion, and had made Kit reconsider the whole thing, and he saw that it was far more complicated than it looked. Mardie was not bold and free—as he was—she was bound by chains of duty, she was gentle and kind, and above all she was home-loving. She had told him that she wanted to travel and see the world, but she had added that she was not a true nomad for she would always want to come back. This was deeply true of her nature—in fact it *was* her nature—there was something in her which bound her to her own land. It was like a chain, Kit thought, and because he understood Mardie so well he saw that this chain would bind her to the past. It would operate in Time as well as in Space.

Kit told himself that he would make it up to her, he would *make* her forget the past; he would take her round the world and show her all the wonders and beauties she had dreamed of; he told himself that he would spend his whole life making Mardie happy . . . but somehow or other he knew in the depths of his soul that he would not succeed.

It was Mardie's nature that was the stumbling block, and although he saw this clearly he would not have had her different. She was perfect as she was, and if she had been different she would not have been Mardie.

By this time Kit had decided that if Mardie was happy in her present life he would go away and never see her again. He was obliged to decide this, for Mardie's happiness came first. If Mardie was happier as Rochester's wife than she would be with him she must remain Rochester's wife. Kit loved her too truly to bring her sorrow. He thought about this for a long time, tossing from side to side of his bed, sleepless and miserable. Dr. Peabody had declared that the Rochesters were devoted to each other, and the old man was wise and honest. It was very unlikely that he could be mistaken, and he would not have lied. At the same time Kit was certain that there was something wrong in Mardie's life; what could it be?

Hitherto Kit had avoided a meeting with Rochester. (It had not been difficult, for the man was in town all day and he and Mardie often went away for weekends. Kit had been invited to dine at the Lynchet but had always refused the invitation, saying, with absolute truth, that Dr. Peabody liked him to be at home in the evening to discuss the day's arrangements.) But now Kit decided to put aside his disinclination, and to meet Rochester at the first opportunity. He was aware that it would be extremely trying to see them together—Mardie and the man to whom in law she belonged—but there was no other way. He must be *sure*, he must be absolutely certain that he was doing the right thing if he were going to give her up. It was in this spirit that Kit accepted an invitation to dine at the Lynchet on Saturday night.

Kit shaved and dressed and brushed his hair with more than average care, and Jem—who was sitting on the bed watching the proceedings—encouraged him with pleasant conversation.

"Of course you must look your best," Jem declared gravely, "because Mrs. Rochester is so pretty. You think she's pretty, don't you?"

"Yes," said Kit.

"Only just yes?"

"Yes, *yes*, YES," said Kit smiling at Jem in the mirror.

"That's better," said Jem. "That's what I think too."

"Why aren't you in bed?" enquired Kit.

"I like watching you," explained Jem, "and I wasn't told to go to bed. Aunt Ethel just said, 'It's bedtime. Go upstairs at once,' so I came upstairs."

"Well, she meant you were to go to bed."

"Well, she should have said so. Besides, it's good for me to watch you dressing—it's a lesson to me. I've got to learn how to dress myself when I grow up. I shall buy a little brush to brush my collar—like you do—and then my collar won't be all dusty and scurfy like Mr. Robinson's collar is."

"Mr. Robinson?"

"Oh, *you* know him," said Jem, "he sits in front of us at church."

"Oh yes," agreed Kit nodding.

There was a short pause.

"You know . . ." said Jem throwing himself back on the bed and gazing up at the ceiling. "You know, Kit, it's an *awfully* funny thing. Mr. Robinson has taught me how horrid it is not to brush your collar."

"Has he?"

"Yes. He doesn't know he's taught me that, of course. Perhaps he'd be surprised if he knew."

"He might be."

"It's funny, isn't it?"

"Most peculiar," Kit agreed, wrestling with his collar stud.

"Most peculiar!" echoed Jem, rolling over on to his stomach and hanging his head over the side of the bed and gazing at the floor.

There was a short silence.

"Kit," said Jem suddenly.

"Yes," said Kit.

"Kit, I've just discovered a funny thing."

"Have you?"

"Yes. Do you know if it wasn't for my body I couldn't tell which was the ceiling and which was the floor. My body tells me, because the bed presses on it so hard . . . if I was floating in the air I couldn't tell which was up and which was down."

"Couldn't you?"

"How could you?" enquired Jem anxiously.

Kit had a moment's impulse to explain the law of gravity to his small friend, but managed to refrain. There wasn't time. He was aware that, if he started to explain it, Jem would not desist from questions on the subject until he understood it thoroughly from beginning to end. Jem was like that.

"How could you, Kit?" Jem repeated.

"You couldn't," Kit declared.

"You couldn't," repeated Jem with a sigh of relief. "No, you couldn't possibly tell. . . . I'm pretending now that the floor

is the ceiling and the bed is a sort of balloon, pressing me down.
Do you ever pretend that?"

"Hardly ever," Kit declared.

"Well, do it," said Jem, "do it tomorrow morning, will you,
and tell me how it feels. Will you, Kit?"

"Yes," said Kit. It was not the first strange experiment which
he had undertaken at Jem's behest and he was pretty certain
it would not be the last . . . unless, of course, he was leaving
Minfield immediately. . . .

"Try hard, won't you?" said Jem in an earnest voice. "It's
very difficult, you know."

Kit seized up his coat and fled.

At dinner, Kit studied his host—or tried to study him—with
an open mind. It was extremely difficult for Kit to make himself realise that this was Mardie's husband. Mardie's husband
had always been a shadowy figure to Kit and now he had suddenly become flesh. Kit would have liked to think that the man
was a rotter, but he could not think it. The man was a pleasant host, considerate and courteous. The dinner was good and
the wine more than good. Kit had a few qualms about eating
Rochester's food but he reflected that he could not have met
Rochester in any other way, and it was to Rochester's advantage that Kit should meet him in his own house. Kit was really
giving Rochester a trial, giving him the opportunity of proving
himself a fit husband for Mardie. If Rochester passed the test
he was safe . . . and he was passing the test very well so far.

Kit ate and drank and took part in the conversation to the
best of his ability. There was no strain about it at all. Rochester
talked well—almost brilliantly—and Mardie filled in the gaps
. . . but presently Kit began to feel that there was something a
little odd about his host. The brilliant (or nearly brilliant) flow
of conversation was inconsecutive, and sometimes even Mardie
found the gaps too wide to bridge. Rochester passed from one

subject to another in a bewildering manner, he left frayed ends behind him as he went. He began a story and passed on to something else before he had finished it.

That's nothing, thought Kit. Lots of people do that. The man is a bit neurotic. Kit tried to make his mind a blank, tried to imagine that he was meeting this man in a perfectly ordinary way, and, having imagined that to the best of his ability, he tried to sum him up. Was there something a little odd about his manner, or wasn't there?

It was difficult for Kit to answer the question because he realised that it might easily be his own feelings which made him see oddness where there was no oddness at all. Was he looking at Rochester through the distorted spectacles of his own odd feelings? . . . for, of course, it was a very strange experience to sit here at this beautifully polished and well-appointed table with Mardie . . . and this stranger . . . who was not really a stranger at all.

Suddenly a very uncomfortable thought crossed Kit's mind: perhaps his host was not oblivious of the undercurrent. Perhaps he knew, or suspected, that everything was not quite what it seemed . . . but no, he couldn't guess, thought Kit. How could he guess? Even Mardie hasn't guessed my secret. It is locked up safely in my own heart.

The port was put on the table and Mardie rose to go.

"Don't be long," she said, and she laid her hand on her husband's shoulder as she passed, "don't be long, Jack."

"No, we shan't be very long," Rochester declared.

Kit had opened the door, and Mardie smiled at him as she went out, but he could not smile back—it was quite impossible —for she was passing out of his life.

It's my own feelings that are making everything seem queer, Kit decided.

CHAPTER XVIII

ANOTHER SERIOUS CONVERSATION

DR. PEABODY was still in the library when Kit came in. Kit found him there, sitting over a half dead fire, reading the papers.

"So you're back!" said Dr. Peabody, looking up and smiling. "Did you have a good dinner?"

"I don't know," said Kit, flinging his coat into a chair. "Yes, I suppose I had—" his voice died away and he stood there, silent, his head bent; his eyes on the floor.

Dr. Peabody's smile vanished. "Kit, where are you? What's happened?" he enquired.

"I don't know where I am," replied Kit. "I don't know whether—whether I'm standing on my head or my heels." He came over to the doctor's chair and looked down into the old man's up-turned face. "You know why I went there tonight," he said gravely. "You said I was to consider Rochester. I had to find out whether it was true that they were happy—you know that."

"Yes . . . at least I didn't really mean . . . I didn't mean you to constitute yourself a judge of—"

"I did it," Kit interrupted, "I went there on purpose to find out. I had decided that if they were happy I would—would give it up."

This seemed a very strange idea to the old doctor. Marriage was marriage to him whether it was happy or not. Of course, it was much better when marriage was happy, but even if it was not happy it was still binding. He tried to explain this point of view to his assistant but without much success.

"Her happiness is the most important thing in the world to

me," said Kit firmly. "I thought you agreed with me there. I thought your argument was based upon that; but anyhow that's what I think, and that's why I went . . . to see Rochester."

"He loves her," Dr. Peabody said.

"Yes," agreed Kit in a low voice, "yes, I believe he does—in a way."

"Well then," said Dr. Peabody.

"I discovered something else," Kit told him, "and . . . and I don't know what to do . . ." he flung himself into the chair and put his hands to his head. "I don't know what to do!" he repeated in despairing tones.

"Kit, what on earth is the matter now?"

"I've discovered a frightful thing," Kit said, "I've discovered something that—that upsets—everything. I can't—I don't know—I can hardly tell you." He paused for a moment and then added, almost in a whisper, "Rochester is insane."

"Insane!"

"Yes, there isn't any doubt of it. None whatever. I couldn't be mistaken. You see I've—seen it—before."

Dr. Peabody gazed at him in horror.

"It's true," said Kit. "It's perfectly true . . . I didn't . . . at first I couldn't believe my own eyes. . . ." He dropped his face in his hands and groaned aloud.

"Pull yourself together, Kit," said Dr. Peabody, recovering himself with an effort, "pull yourself together. We must face this. Something must be done . . . I suppose you're absolutely certain of what you say?"

"Absolutely certain," replied Kit in a restrained voice. "I couldn't be mistaken. He has all the symptoms of incipient insanity: sudden changes of mood, sudden and uncontrolled outbursts of temper . . . he starts to tell you something, and stops in the middle of a sentence and glances over his shoulder . . . and forgets . . . forgets what he was saying."

"Neurosis," suggested Dr. Peabody, "overwork . . . over-strain. . . ."

"No," said Kit, shaking his head.

The old man rose and began to pace the floor. "I haven't seen a case," he said. "I haven't had one in all my years of practice."

"You're lucky!"

"I know, I know. Tell me about it. Tell me more."

"It's the same," Kit said, "almost exactly the same as the other case—the one I told you about—that's why I'm so sure. Persecution mania . . . paranoia . . . super-evaluation of the ego."

"But what is the cause—the fundamental cause?"

"The man's nature," replied Kit in a tired flat voice. "An arrogant nature can't admit defeat . . . or at least not an ordinary defeat. In Rochester's case we have an arrogant nature trying to cope with life—with the ups and downs of the Stock Exchange. He isn't fitted for it. He can't take a reverse in the right spirit. He's so important to himself that he can't admit to being worsted. Presently he begins to imagine that the eyes of the world are focussed upon him. His smallest set-back is magnified out of all proportion and, since his nature can't admit defeat, or accept it, he begins to blame others for his ill fortune. He begins to think that the whole world is banded against him. This is the defence which his nature—his subconscious—puts up against the thought of defeat. He can't fight against the whole world and therefore the defeat is not his fault. He deludes himself into the belief that he's being hounded by the world, and immediately he perceives that he's being watched, followed, spied upon by enemies."

"Rochester thinks that?" enquired Dr. Peabody incredulously.

Kit nodded.

"How do you know?"

"Because he told me—he showed me. I could see—"

"Go on," Dr. Peabody said, "tell me the whole thing. When did you begin to suspect—all this?"

Kit drew his hand across his eyes. He felt as if his brain were drugged, doped. He was trying to see everything at once —all the implications of it—trying to work it out and discover how it would affect himself and Mardie.

"He was all right at dinner . . . or perhaps I should say he was almost normal," said Kit at last. "He was a little excitable and touchy and he talked a bit wildly but I—well, I put him down as neurotic, that's all. Then Mardie left us to have our port and the moment she had left the room he was like a different man (it was almost as if her influence had kept him normal) his very face seemed to change before my eyes . . . it became furtive . . . his eyes glittered. I don't know how it started but suddenly he was telling me how he was being followed and persecuted—the words poured out of him—they were trying to ruin him, they had secret understandings with each other, secret signals. They were working against him, bearing shares when they found out he had bought them—"

"Who were?" Dr. Peabody asked.

Kit made a helpless gesture with his hands.

"You mean he doesn't even know who his enemies are?"

"It's imagination," Kit said. "The whole thing is a delusion. People don't behave like that. Why should they? Stockbrokers have their own business to attend to."

"What happened next?"

"He was shouting," Kit said, "and suddenly the door opened and Mardie was there. It was over in a moment and he was talking of something else—talking quite reasonably. That was really the most significant symptom of all—that sudden return to normality—"

"What are we to do!" said Dr. Peabody in a low voice.

At midnight they were still discussing the situation. They

were surrounded by large medical tomes which were lying open on the table and on the chairs. Dr. Peabody had wanted to verify his knowledge of the law, to find some way of dealing with the case. He had known to start with that only two courses were open to them and he knew no more now. They could either certify the patient, or persuade him to sign a paper putting himself into competent hands for a course of treatment. Technically, of course, Rochester was not their patient for they had not been called in professionally, but that point could be overcome. They were agreed that something must be done immediately. An alienist must be called in to confirm Kit's diagnosis; but how was this to be accomplished?

"You'll have to see Mrs. Rochester and tell her," said Dr. Peabody at last.

"I can't do that," replied Kit. "It's bad enough for her as it is. How can I lay that burden on her? How could she go on— even for a day—if she knew that he was mad?"

"There's no other way."

"We must find another way," said Kit firmly. "We must think of some way of letting Ames see him. We must have the whole thing cut and dried before we tell her . . . don't you understand? We simply can't tell her now and let her go on living with him—it would be dangerous. It might lead to the most frightful consequences."

"You don't mean—"

"No," said Kit quickly. "No, I don't think he's dangerous— yet. I'm sure of it. D'you think I'd be sitting here talking to you if I thought there was the least chance? But you never know how soon . . . I mean it develops quickly . . . and changes. If he felt that she had turned from him; if he sensed the horror in her . . . the horror that she would feel . . . that anyone would feel . . . if there was any change in her, or in the relationship between them. . . ."

There was silence for a moment and then Kit reached for

a book which was lying on the table. "You see what Bevan Lewis says about paranoia."

"I know," Dr. Peabody said quickly. "I know—there's no need to go into it again. The difficulty is I've got to try to see the case from a professional angle—and I can't. I wish you hadn't told me about your—your—about Mrs. Rochester."

"I can't look at it professionally either," Kit pointed out. "The whole thing is like a nightmare to me. I feel as if I were going mad myself." He looked it too, for his face was as white as a sheet and his hair and clothes were disordered and his eyes were shadowed with weariness and sunken in their sockets.

Dr. Peabody patted his arm. "I know it's hard for you," he said, "devilish hard, but you and I have got to work together in this. You've got to put your feelings on one side—and so have I."

"How can I?" said Kit hopelessly.

"You've got to do it. You can't go on with this business of Mrs. Rochester now. Think of the man. He's got enough trouble without your adding to it. You said yourself she has a restraining influence upon him. It would be a cruel and inhuman thing to try and take her away."

"D'you think I haven't seen that?"

"You must wait," said Dr. Peabody, patting his arm again.

"Wait for what?" asked Kit in a hopeless voice. "Wait for him to recover . . . or die? They don't die, you know . . . and what about her? Is she to go on . . ."

"Wait," repeated the old doctor, "take one thing at a time. Take the first thing first."

"The first thing!" cried Kit. "Don't you see *she's* the first thing—the only thing that matters a tinker's curse to me. I want to go to the house and take her away and put her in a safe place. Then I could listen to you and discuss the whole thing with you reasonably."

"But you can't. You aren't a savage, Kit. You're a civilised man—a doctor."

Dr. Peabody had put his finger on the spot. Kit was a doctor and, as such, he was bound to consider the weak, the helpless, the diseased. He had been born and bred in a doctor's house and had seen his father struggle out of bed with a temperature to attend his patients, and all his training had served to establish and intensify in him the creed that a doctor's first duty is to succor the sick and alleviate their sufferings; to put their interests first and to sink his own desires and feelings. . . .

"Yes," he said, slowly, "yes, they've tied me again. I've always been tied . . . I thought . . . I thought for a little while that I was free."

"Nobody is free," Dr. Peabody said, "if you haven't got actual chains upon you . . . you bind yourself."

CHAPTER XIX

CROSS QUESTIONS AND CROOKED ANSWERS

"WE MUST go to bed," said Dr. Peabody at last, and he rose from his chair and stretched himself.

They had found no solution to their problem, but they had decided that Dr. Peabody must see Rochester at the earliest opportunity and form his own opinion upon the case. That was obviously the first step, and there was not much difficulty attached to it. Kit had been invited to go to tea at the Lynchet on Sunday (it was Sunday now, of course) and to take Jem with him to play in the garden. Dolly was going too.

"You can go instead of me," Kit said, as he put out the light and followed the old doctor upstairs. "It will be a good opportunity for you to see him, and we can't both go."

Dr. Peabody agreed to the plan with some reluctance for he preferred to drink his tea comfortably in his own house.

"It's a pity I couldn't see him professionally," he said with a sigh.

"But you can't," replied Kit.

Dr. Peabody nodded. "All right, I'll go," he said, "and then, somehow or other, we must get him to see Ames. We must have Ames down to look at him . . . though how we're to accomplish it is more than I can see."

They went to bed but Kit could not sleep. He felt as if he would never be able to sleep again. How could he sleep when he knew that Mardie was alone in that house with a madman? He had told Dr. Peabody that Rochester was not dangerous and he was assured of the fact because he had seen the influence which Mardie possessed over him and he had seen her calm him with a few words; but, although he was assured of this in his mind, he could not rest. His imagination began to get the upper hand of him. He pictured them lying side by side in the twin beds which he had seen in Mardie's room. Mardie would be asleep, of course, but Rochester would not be sleeping. Insomnia was one of the first and most significant symptoms of a derangement of the mind, and one of the worst to bear. Rochester would be awake; he would lie awake hour after hour brooding upon his troubles; the delusion that the whole world was banded together against him would grow stronger and more insupportable. He would raise himself upon one elbow and look at Mardie in the other bed . . . Mardie sleeping peacefully, her breast rising and falling gently as she breathed. . . .

"No, no!" cried Kit aloud, "no, no, I can't bear it! No. He wouldn't. He wouldn't . . . he loves her. She's precious to him!"

But Kit could not stop the working of his imagination—it was beyond his control. He knew too much about the strange delusions and hallucinations which afflict a mind diseased. Dr. Peabody's books were full of cases, terrible cases, which had developed suddenly in unexpected ways. All that men knew or had learnt about insanity, and it was not very much, served to show that when once the delicate mechanism of the brain became affected it was impossible to predict the course of the disease.

Kit rose and dressed. He went down through the quiet house and took out his car. He drove over to the Lynchet. It was a fine night, starry and still, but there was no moon. He parked the car in a lane and walked down to the house. The house was dark and very quiet, it loomed up before him, an oblong mass of masonry with gables cutting across the sky. Kit walked round to the back of the house, taking care to walk on the grass. He stood and looked up at Mardie's window . . . and listened. He could hear nothing at all—nothing except the sudden screech of an owl—a far away sound, eerie and forlorn.

He sat down on the seat beneath the apple tree and rested his elbows on his knees, and his chin upon his hands. It was dreadful to love Mardie like this . . . he loved her so dearly, so tenderly, and he was helpless. There was nothing he could do for her—nothing. He had no right to do anything for Mardie. He had not even the right to watch over her. He could not protect her body, far less her mind.

A greyness began to come in the sky, and Kit found that he could see objects which had been invisible a few minutes before. Dawn was coming. He was tired now, so tired that his feelings were blunted by weariness . . . even his feelings for Mardie. He wanted to sleep . . . he would have to go home, but what a nuisance it was to have to go home! What a lot of things he would have to do before he could crawl into bed and lay his head upon the pillow! All these things that he must do seemed beyond his power, he was so tired. He thought of all that he must do, thought them over one by one: he must walk to the car, he must start it up, he must drive home, put the car away, drag himself up the stairs and take off his clothes. If he had been a savage he could have lain down upon the ground and gone to sleep, here and now, but he was not a savage; he was a doctor. He gave a deep sigh and rose from the seat. There might be an urgent call for him and he would not be at his post to answer it. He was doing no good here, mooning about Mardie's garden like a love-sick Romeo. . . .

Kit looked up at the window again (but there was no sign of life, no sound at all) and then he went home. He was still tired when he crawled into bed, but all desire to sleep had vanished and he lay awake until the bell rang.

The afternoon was sunny and warm, the sky was pale blue and cloudless—it was like an inverted bowl of translucent porcelain over the land. Kit came out from the house to see the little party set forth to their tea-party at the Lynchet. Dolly was looking very pretty and cheerful in a blue silk frock and a straw hat with flowers on it which was cocked over one eye at a rakish angle. There were very few people who could have worn the hat without looking ridiculous but Dolly was one of the few; she looked charming and was happily aware of the fact.

Jem was in high spirits, and chattered unceasingly of all he was going to see and do in the Lynchet garden.

"There will be nests, you know," he said, as he skipped down the brick path. "Fraser said there would be nests in the hedge, and I shall look for them very carefully and peep in. There will be little birds in the nests but I won't frighten them."

"No, you mustn't do that," said Kit.

"I'm sorry you aren't coming, Kit, because it's more fun when you're there; but perhaps Grandfather will come and see the nests if I find any. It's nice for Grandfather to be going out to tea, isn't it?"

"Yes," said Kit, "and we can't both go. I've got to be on duty."

"He hasn't been out to tea for ages and ages," said Jem, "so it's really his turn; but I'm sorry you can't come with us and *she'll* be sorry too. Shall I give her your love?" He was climbing into his grandfather's car as he spoke.

"No," said Kit firmly, "you can give Mrs. Rochester my kind regards if you like."

Jem put his head out of the window and beckoned to Kit to come nearer. "I'll tell her to ask you another day," he whispered.

Dolly had taken the seat in front beside her father. She turned her head and smiled at Kit, "Good-bye, be good," she said, "you can have my share of cherry jam for tea—tell Ethel I said so!"

The car moved off and Kit stood on the pavement and

watched it out of sight. There was a sense of foreboding in his breast, a feeling of unease. He could not define it nor account for it in a reasonable way. There was no reason in it, of course, nothing would happen. Nothing was different from yesterday or the day before.

The house was very silent after the departure of his three friends; the silence seemed to close in upon Kit as he stood in the hall and wondered what he should do. Miss Peabody would be writing letters; she was always writing letters and Kit could not think what she could find to say in these letters . . . nor to whom she wrote at such length. He disliked letter-writing himself and only wrote when he was obliged to do so or had some definite information to impart. He thought about Miss Peabody deliberately with the intention of guiding his thoughts away from Mardie, and from that strangely significant tea-party which was taking place at the Lynchet.

He was still standing there when Miss Peabody came downstairs.

"Tea's ready," she said. "We had better go and have it."

He had not realised until now that he would be having tea alone with Miss Peabody; the idea did not please him, but, unless the telephone bell rang and he was called out, there was no escape.

"Father doesn't often go out to tea," she declared as they took their seats at the table.

"Doesn't he?" asked Kit.

"You know he doesn't . . . and it's your free afternoon."

"There's no hard and fast rule about it."

"I wonder why he went," Miss Peabody said.

Kit did not reply.

"It's so strange," she continued, speaking in an easy conversational tone, but with an undercurrent which was neither conversational nor easy. "It really is *very* strange. Father is such a creature of habit, isn't he?"

"Can doctors ever be creatures of habit?" enquired Kit lightly.

"You know what I mean. This isn't a professional visit—or perhaps it is?"

Kit helped himself to a bun and began to butter it carefully. "You had better ask Dr. Peabody," he said.

"You've been at the Rochesters' a good deal lately, haven't you?" she asked.

He wondered how she knew; he wondered how she managed to find out things like that. Her Secret Service was remarkably efficient.

"You have, haven't you?" urged Miss Peabody.

"Yes, I have," replied Kit in desperation. "The parlourmaid scalded her foot—but perhaps you know that already."

"How could I know it?" she enquired.

"Well, she did. She upset a kettle of boiling water over her foot and the cook plastered it with rancid oil which induced a septic condition."

"Very interesting!" remarked Miss Peabody with elaborate sarcasm.

"I thought you wanted to know," said Kit in an innocent tone.

She did not reply and indeed there was no necessity, for they were both aware that this was not what she wanted to know.

"Mrs. Rochester is very pretty, isn't she?" enquired Miss Peabody after a pause.

"I shouldn't call her pretty," replied Kit truthfully.

"Wouldn't you? What would you call her, then?"

Kit would have called her beautiful, peerless, adorable, and various other adjectives of the same nature, but he would not have called her any of these things to Miss Peabody.

"I think she has a very interesting face," he said.

"You've known her a long time, haven't you?"

"A long time!" Kit echoed in surprise.

"Did you know each other when you were children?"

"No, of course not. I never saw Mrs. Rochester until I came to Minfield."

Miss Peabody looked at him in amazement. "But I thought you were a great friend of hers!" she exclaimed, "I thought she recommended you to Father! I thought that was why you came!"

"Mr. Rochester is my brother's partner," replied Kit shortly.

"You didn't know her at all?"

"No."

She was silent for a few moments and there was an expression of chagrin upon her face. Somehow or other Kit became aware that this was the reason why she had been prejudiced against him from the very beginning—he had always wondered about it—perhaps, if she had not made this curious mistake, she would have been quite nice to him; they might even have become friends! But no, thought Kit, looking at her with distaste, no, I don't believe I could have been friends with her. . . .

"Why didn't you tell me?" said Ethel Peabody at last, "I thought you were her friend . . . she and Dolly were always against me. . . ."

"You were always against them," Kit pointed out, "you can't expect people to be friendly unless you meet them half way."

"I don't want to be friendly with *them,*" she cried, tossing her head.

Kit did not reply.

"What do you know about them?" she continued. "You like them because they smile and look pleasant. Men never look below the surface—men like to be amused and flattered—they lay little store on loyalty. It's loyalty that matters, loyalty and sincerity, not empty chatter and false smiles."

"If you're talking about Mrs. Rochester—" cried Kit goaded beyond endurance.

Ethel Peabody laughed bitterly. She had worked herself up

to such a pitch that she scarcely knew what she was saying. "Mrs. Rochester and Dolly," she cried. "Neither of them knows what loyalty means . . . yet they're both married! What fools men are! Ralph preferred Dolly to me—he was my friend first, but he preferred Dolly—and now, after nine months, she's tired of him; she doesn't want to be with him; she has let him go out to Malta alone. It would serve her right if he found another woman . . . but perhaps that's what she wants."

Kit had listened in horrified silence, but it was impossible to let this pass.

"Oh, Miss Peabody, you ought not to say such a thing," he told her. "You're wrong—you're completely wrong about Dolly. She's devoted to her husband."

"Then why hasn't she gone with him?" demanded Miss Peabody. "Why has she come back here instead? Perhaps you know the reason, do you?"

Kit hesitated a moment, but only for a moment. Dolly's secret was in jeopardy and he had promised faithfully that it would be safe with him. He saw that he would have to lie, for Miss Peabody could not be put off with half-truths; she was much too clever.

"Reason!" he said with a surprised inflection in his voice. "I know of no reason except that this is the worst season of the year in Malta. This is the time when everybody comes home. The climate is unhealthy and unpleasant. The sirocco makes life unbearable. It seems quite natural that Commander Dorman should decide not to let Dolly come out to Malta until September."

"Is she going out in September?" enquired Miss Peabody with interest.

"Of course she is," replied Kit firmly, and he looked his interlocutor straight in the face.

Her eyes fell before his—which was rather odd, all things

considered—and she busied herself with the teacups, moving them aimlessly about on the tray.

Kit rose and left the room. He went up to his bedroom and sat there waiting for the sound of the doctor's car.

CHAPTER XX

IN THE STABLE YARD

KIT had been sitting in his bedroom listening for the car for more than an hour, and he was beginning to imagine all sorts of disasters when at last he heard it. He ran downstairs at full speed, and down the brick path and opened the green door in the wall. The car had drawn up at the curb and Jem was getting out.

"Hallo," said Jem. "We had a lovely tea, Kit. I played at Indians in the garden. I didn't look for nests at all, but just played Indians the whole time. I was hiding in the bushes and I saw a real pale face—a real live one—so I stalked him very carefully. . . ."

But for once Kit could not listen to the child's chatter. His eyes went straight to Dr. Peabody's face and remained there, riveted.

"We'll have a talk," said the old man, nodding to show that he understood and sympathised with Kit's anxiety. "Run along, Jem. It's your bedtime, isn't it? I want to talk to Kit."

Jem went in at the door and disappeared, but the doctor did not move.

"You're tired, sir," Kit said in concern.

"Yes, I'm tired. Get in, Kit, and we'll drive round to the garage."

Kit obeyed. He realised suddenly that Dolly had not returned with her father, and he wondered more than ever what had happened. He would soon know, of course. Dr. Peabody would tell him everything, but would tell it in his own way. It was never the slightest use trying to hurry him.

They drove round the corner and through the big gates into

what had once been the stable-yard (Tupman was not there, for it was an unbreakable rule in the household that Tupman should have Sunday off duty). Kit got out, and opened the garage doors, and the doctor drove in. He climbed out of the car somewhat stiffly, and Kit shut the doors.

It was perfectly quiet in the yard. The sun was less hot now than it had been in the earlier part of the day but the yard was sheltered, and the stones of the wall were warm to the touch. Kit noticed it subconsciously—the whole of his conscious being was keyed up, waiting for the old doctor to speak.

"We'll sit down here," Dr. Peabody said, sitting down upon an old wooden bench near the hosetap. "It's pleasant here in the sun. Any messages for me?"

"None of any importance, sir."

"Well, you want to hear about it, of course. I left Dolly there. Mrs. Rochester seemed to want her . . . they're great friends . . . she's staying the night. I offered to send along her clothes and things but Mrs. Rochester said she would lend her everything she needed. They'll enjoy a chat, the two of them."

"Yes," said Kit.

"Dolly's no fool," declared her father.

"No," said Kit.

Dr. Peabody sighed. "At first I thought you were wrong," he declared. "Yes, I couldn't see anything the matter with the man. He was a bit restless, of course, and he didn't seem able to sit still, but what's that? It's a lost art nowadays—nobody can sit still. I tried to put aside your diagnosis and make my own, and I decided that the man was suffering from a pronounced form of neurasthenia."

"Well, perhaps—"

"Wait a minute," said the old doctor. "That was what I thought at first. I saw afterwards only too clearly that you were right. He isn't normal. Mind you, Kit, I haven't seen a case of this kind before. You've had experience of it."

"It was much worse," Kit said with a little shudder.

"But essentially the same?"

"Yes. It was in America. The man was a—"

"You needn't tell me about it now. We've got to consider Rochester's case."

Kit sat down beside him on the seat and immediately wished he had remained standing. Dr. Peabody had said that Rochester was restless—Kit was not less so. He found it almost impossible to control his limbs. . . .

"We had tea," Dr. Peabody said. "Jem chattered . . . and Dolly, of course. The two young women had plenty to say to each other. I noticed, however, that Mrs. Rochester kept an ear on what we were saying, Rochester and I, and she chipped in once or twice and turned the conversation . . . gave it a twist into a different channel. Perhaps that's the most significant symptom of the lot, for she isn't the kind of woman to push in her oar where it isn't wanted." He paused for a moment, but Kit said nothing.

"Oh well," he continued. "Let that be. There was worse to come. We finished tea and Jem ran off into the garden. Rochester invited me into his study and I fully expected that the two girls would vanish upstairs for I knew Dolly was anxious to get Mrs. Rochester to herself; but no, they followed us into the study and there they remained. I had hoped to get the man alone and have a quiet chat with him, but she wasn't going to have it. Odd, wasn't it?"

"It would have been odd if—"

"That's what I meant," interrupted the old man. "It would have been odd if everything had been perfectly normal. By this time I had made up my mind that something must be done. I hadn't made up my mind whether it was a case of neurasthenia or incipient insanity, but whatever it was there was no time to be lost. We talked a bit and I asked what he had been reading (he used to be a tremendous reader, and could talk about books by the hour). The moment I said the words his face changed and he lashed out into a violent tirade (there was nothing fit to read, that was the gist of it, but it went on and on, and he repeated himself and contradicted himself every few seconds). It was a most extraordinary exhibition, unreasonable, violent and completely uncontrolled. Dolly went as white as a sheet, but Mrs. Rochester was perfectly calm. She smoothed him down and turned the subject. It was obvious that she had done the same thing a hundred times."

"Oh heavens!" cried Kit, rising to his feet and beginning to pace up and down.

"You must face it," said the old man quietly. "It does no good hiding your head in the sand."

"She's got to face it. That's the hellish thing."

"She is facing it, and facing it staunchly," Dr. Peabody reminded him.

There was a short silence and then the old doctor continued his tale. "The storm blew over in a few moments and he was perfectly calm and friendly again. Perhaps I should have left it like that. Perhaps I should have come away and left it, and we should have got hold of Mrs. Rochester and put the case before her. I don't know, of course . . . she might not have been able to . . . at any rate the harm's done, if harm there is. I began to ask him about his health and I told him he was losing weight and that he obviously needed a rest. Mrs. Rochester kept looking at me as if she wanted to shut me up, but I took no notice. 'You need a complete rest,' I told him. He laughed bitterly and said he supposed I wanted half a guinea. Couldn't I come to tea without turning it into a professional visit? Mrs. Rochester tried to stop him, but I pretended that it was a joke. 'I'm giving you the advice in exchange for my tea,' I told him . . . and then I went a bit further and said that if he didn't take the advice he would be ill. I had half-expected a flare up, but he accepted it quite quietly. He sat there for a moment or two with a queer sly brooding look on his face, and then he said, 'How do you think I could rest? Do you think I could lie still in bed?' I told him that people did, and that if he were ill he would have to. Wouldn't it be better to have the rest now, and avert an illness? . . . 'I couldn't,' he said. So then I laughed and told him that the best thing that could happen to him would be a broken leg. 'A broken leg!' he said. 'Are you wishing that on me, you old wizard?' I laughed again and said that I was wishing it on him for his own good. It had all been said quite lightly and pleasantly but there was a queer sort of strain in the air. The girls had stopped talking and were sitting there listening to every word. In spite of the strained feeling I was rather pleased with the way he had taken it—I had broken the ice, as it were—I had put the idea into his head, d'you see. I felt that was all to the good . . . and then suddenly he leaned forward and said, 'You want to shut me up.'

"It was exactly what I'd been thinking, and I was so taken aback that I couldn't speak. There was a most extraordinary pause and it seemed to last a most unconscionable time. It was Dolly who broke the silence—the girl's no fool—she began to chatter like a magpie. 'Doctors always want to do that,' she declared. 'They like to dump you into bed and keep you there and have you at their mercy, and Father is no exception to the rule. Father likes to see his patients lying in bed but he isn't keen on lying in bed himself—' she prattled on talking nonsense and the tension gradually relaxed. Mrs. Rochester began to prattle too. We laughed over it . . . even Rochester managed a half-hearted sort of smile. Then he got up and excused himself—he had to put through a business call to the United States. He went away to do it. We talked more freely when he had gone and I told Mrs. Rochester that he was neurotic and underweight and that I would like a friend of mine to have a look at him—I was paving the way for Ames to see him of course

—and she accepted that. I could see she'd been worrying about him, and I had the feeling that she was glad I'd spoken, that she was glad to shift a bit of the burden onto me. 'You think he's *ill*?' she said, and there was relief in her tone. She was glad to have that explanation of his abnormal behaviour. I told her I was sure he was ill, that he must have complete rest and proper treatment, and that I would make enquiries and find a quiet nursing home somewhere in the country, and she must persuade him to fall in with the plan. 'It will be difficult,' she said, 'couldn't he rest here?' I asked her whether she thought it would be possible to make him rest at home, and after a little thought she agreed that it would not be possible. 'He's so restless,' she said, 'and he can't sleep. Couldn't you give him something to make him sleep?' I said of course I could . . . we must send up some luminol tonight, Kit."

Kit nodded. "I think you've done splendidly," he said, "better than I had hoped—much better."

"Well, I don't know," Dr. Peabody said doubtfully, "I did my best, but I'm not sure . . ." he paused for a moment and then continued in a different tone, "it was getting late and I thought it time to make a move, but it was a good half hour before we got under way. First there was a discussion about Dolly staying the night—she suggested it herself, but I could see that Mrs. Rochester was pleased—and then Rochester had to be found. Mrs. Rochester went to look for him, for she seemed to think that he ought to come and say good-bye to me . . . but she couldn't find him. She was full of apologies, but I told her not to worry. As a matter of fact I'm pretty certain he'd forgotten that I was there."

"You noticed that," Kit asked, "you noticed his inability to retain an impression?"

"Of course. I couldn't help noticing it . . . and then, when I was on the point of departure, I suddenly remembered Jem. He'd been playing in the garden and we had to find him and bundle him into the car. He was filthy, of course, and wanted to wash before Ethel saw him, but I couldn't wait for that."

There was a short silence. Dr. Peabody heaved a sigh and rose. "We must go in," he said. "It's getting cold . . . I don't know when I've felt so tired," he added in a surprised tone.

They went in together and parted in the hall. Kit was half way upstairs when he heard the old man's voice calling him.

"Kit," said Dr. Peabody. "I'd nearly forgotten . . . it was a thing that came into my mind as I was driving home. He's your brother's partner, isn't he?"

It was dim in the hall and Kit could not see the doctor's face, but he sensed the urgency underlying the words. It was not a question—for Dr. Peabody knew the connection between Rochester and Henry Stone as well as Kit, himself—it was a reminder. Rochester was Henry's partner and he was insane.

"But we can't—" cried Kit in dismay.

"No," agreed the old man doubtfully. "No, of course we can't—but still—"

Kit was considering the matter in all its aspects, and was changing his mind. "But we must—" he cried. "Great heavens, we can't just sit back and do nothing!"

"Wait till tomorrow," Dr. Peabody said slowly, "by that time we may have been able to . . . and anyhow one day can't make much difference."

CHAPTER XXI

"WHAT DO YOU THINK HAS HAPPENED?"

THE Peabodys had a cold supper on Sunday nights, and they waited on themselves and helped each other from the dishes on the sideboard. Kit handed round the plates and the salad while Miss Peabody carved—this was the usual procedure. Dr. Peabody was even more silent than usual, for he never considered it his duty to make polite conversation. It was extremely dull without Dolly, there were no fireworks, nothing to break the monotony of the meal.

"You are not a very lively companion, Dr. Stone," said Ethel Peabody at last with a little laugh.

Kit was about to apologise for his sin but the old doctor was before him—

"Neither of us feels inclined for bright conversation tonight," he declared in a downright manner.

Ethel relapsed into silence and Kit saw that she scented a mystery and was doing her best to unravel it. It had often amused him to see her trying to pump the old doctor. Sometimes she managed to squeeze a few drops of information out of him and sometimes he discovered her purpose and withdrew from her clutches saying, "That will do, Ethel," or "I have a troublesome case on my mind." His family accepted these phrases without demur for they had been trained from their infancy to accept them, but tonight Dr. Peabody had used different phraseology and Ethel was obviously wondering whether the words had the same underlying meaning.

After a little she leaned forward and enquired of Kit in a low voice, "Is it a troublesome case?"

"Yes," replied Kit, reflecting with some amusement that, if the words were not strictly accurate in the sense which Ethel understood them, they were more than true in a literal sense.

She was silenced again for a few minutes, but presently she had another question prepared. "Is it Mrs. Rochester or Mr. Rochester who is ill? Is that why Dolly is staying at the Lynchet?"

"No," said Dr. Peabody firmly, "the Rochesters are perfectly well. Dolly is staying there because she was asked to stay and wished to do so. There is no illness at the Lynchet."

Kit was somewhat taken aback by the bare-faced lie, but after a moment's thought he perceived that no other course was open to the doctor. He thought it was rather curious that both he and Dr. Peabody should have been obliged to lie to Ethel. By nature they were honest and truthful but Ethel Peabody had forced them to behave like Ananias and they had both been able to lie with absolute conviction.

"Then who is ill?" enquired Ethel, her curiosity getting the better of her, "and how do you know about it? There haven't been any telephone messages as far as I know."

"That will do, Ethel," said her father firmly.

He had hardly spoken when the telephone bell shrilled loudly and Kit, whose nerves were on edge, leaped to his feet to answer it. He leaped up so quickly that his wine glass was knocked over and a stream of claret, red as blood, ran across the polished table and dripped onto the floor.

"Oh goodness!" cried Kit, gazing at it in dismay.

"Never mind it, never mind it," said the old doctor testily. "Run and answer the telephone . . . Ethel will see to it. . . ."

Kit murmured apologies and ran. He picked up the receiver with a hand that trembled slightly in spite of all that he could do to steady it.

"Dr. Stone speaking," he said quickly.

"It's Dolly," said Dolly's voice in his ear, "I'm glad it's you, Kit. We don't know what to do. . . . Mr. Rochester hasn't come back."

"Hasn't come back from where?"

"We don't know where he's gone. He left when Father was here—soon after tea—did Father tell you?"

"Yes."

"Well, he hasn't come back at all and Mardie is rather fussed about him. What do you think we should do?"

Kit had not the slightest idea what they should do. On the one hand the man might have gone out for a walk and have been delayed (he might turn up at any moment) but on the other hand. . . .

"Hold on," said Kit, "I'll get the doctor to speak to you."

He put down the receiver and returned to the dining room —"Somebody to speak to you, sir," he said. "It's rather—er—important. Perhaps you wouldn't mind—"

Dr. Peabody looked at Kit's face, laid down his table-napkin and went to the telephone without a word.

"I think you had better go over to the Lynchet, Kit," said Dr. Peabody. "It's rather hard on the girls . . . you could stay there for the night if you found it necessary. I'll move the night-bell to my room."

"Then you think—"

"I don't know what to think."

"Did he take the car?" Kit wondered.

"You can find out. Make enquiries as tactfully as you can. We don't want to go to the police unless we're obliged to do so."

"The police!" exclaimed Kit.

"We may have to. We *shall* have to unless he turns up pretty soon. I'm remembering what he said, and the look on his face when he said it: 'You want to shut me up,' that's what he said. Perhaps the poor devil knew what I was thinking and decided to—to do away with himself."

"Great heavens!"

"That's the worst, of course, but we've got to face it . . . there are a good many other possible explanations."

"Yes, of course," said Kit, and he tried to think what other explanations would fit the facts.

The clock in the hall chimed nine as Kit was shown into the drawing room at the Lynchet. He found Mardie and Dolly sitting together on the sofa.

"Oh Kit!" cried Dolly. "How nice of you to come!—but of course it isn't for me to say it."

"You said it for me," said Mardie with a faint smile, "I only thought it."

"Don't move," said Kit, quickly.

"We weren't going to," declared Dolly with an impudent little grimace, "at least I wasn't going to move—I'm far too comfortable—and Mardie did not seem to be making any attempt to leap to her feet and greet you."

They laughed, though perhaps not very heartily.

Dolly was obviously trying to make light of the situation, and it was a wise thing to do, but Kit wanted to find out what had been done so he was obliged to question them on the subject. He accepted a cigarette and lit it with elaborate care before he spoke.

"I suppose the servants don't know anything," he said.

"No," said Mardie. "It's Sunday you see, and Morton's out. The housemaid is rather a fool."

"And what about the gardener?"

"Dolly and I went round the garden. Fraser and his wife are both out—" her voice broke a little and she added, "Oh Kit, what do you think has happened?"

"We can't tell whether anything has happened," said Kit

gently, "I want to find out all I can—whether anyone saw him —did you ask the chauffeur?"

"He's out too," said Mardie in a flat voice. "Everyone seems to be out . . . well, of course it's Sunday . . . Dolly and I went down to Fraser's cottage and we found it shut up. You see the chauffeur is quite young, just a boy, really, and he lodges with the Frasers. It works quite well. He isn't a real chauffeur," added Mardie with a little smile, "he cleans the car and does odd jobs. Jack nearly always drives himself."

"Did Mr. Rochester take the car?"

"No," said Mardie, "the garage is locked and we know that the car hasn't been out because the drive was raked this morning and there are no wheelmarks."

"Boy Scoutish of us, wasn't it?" put in Dolly.

"Very Boy Scoutish," agreed Kit. He thought for a few moments and then added, "So he can't have gone far."

"Unless he took a bus," suggested Dolly.

"No, he wouldn't do that," Mardie said. "He simply hates busses. He wouldn't dream of going in a bus."

"Then he can't have *meant* to go far," said Kit.

Mardie leaned forward. "Kit," she said earnestly, "Kit, you *must* tell what you think. I've tried and tried to think of all the things that could have happened to him. . . ."

Kit paused before answering. "But I don't know any more than you do—not as much really. You know him so much better than I do. You know his habits. Has he ever done anything like this before?"

"Never," declared Mardie. "He might go for a walk, of course, but he would come back for dinner. It wasn't until dinner time that I began to worry about him."

"Don't worry too much," Kit advised. "He might have gone for a walk and have been delayed . . . he might come back at any moment."

"Of course he might," agreed Dolly.

Mardie said nothing. It was easy to see that she did not believe in this optimistic suggestion.

"Is there anywhere he could go?" enquired Kit, "any friends or relations who live near?"

"He wouldn't do that," said Mardie confidently, "I mean he would have to explain . . . he doesn't know anybody well enough to walk in to dinner without fixing it up beforehand. The Furnivals haven't seen him . . . I rang them up. His mother lives at Rye, but she isn't at all well and I don't want to worry her until . . . unless. . . ."

There was a little silence.

"You seem to have thought of everything," said Kit at last, "but I might go down to Fraser's cottage and speak to him. Perhaps they'll be back by now." He rose as he spoke. "I'll be back soon," he added, and went out through the French windows.

It was getting dark now, and the white roses in Mardie's rose-garden were like little white faces, peering out from their background of polished leaves. All the white flowers seemed to shine in the gloom as if with their own light—the white stock, the pinks, and rhododendrons. Kit saw that there were lights in the windows of the gardener's cottage and as he approached he heard voices so he knew that Fraser and his wife had returned. He knocked on the door, and it was opened almost immediately by a plump pleasant-faced woman in a white apron.

"May I speak to Fraser for a moment?" he enquired.

"Why, yes, of course," she said. "Come in, sir. It's Dr. Stone, isn't it? We've just got home—Fraser and me—we've been at church, and then we had a bite of supper with my sister. . . ."

Kit followed her into the little parlour.

"Here's the young doctor," she announced.

Kit knew Fraser, for he had spoken to him several times in the garden. He knew that Fraser came from Mardie's old home.

The man was a typical Scot, sturdy and honest, and well-spoken, his face was wrinkled and weather-beaten and his eyes were very blue. The young chauffeur was a stranger to Kit—he was really just a boy as Mardie had said—he had a heavy sort of face, rather stupid and expressionless.

"It's about Mr. Rochester," explained Kit, addressing his audience of three impartially. "He went out soon after tea and hasn't returned and Mrs. Rochester wondered if any of you had seen him."

"No, we haven't," said Fraser. "To tell the truth we've been talking about it. None of us have seen him."

"Cook told me he'd been out and hadn't come back," explained Mrs. Fraser, "but we've been out since dinner time—it's Fraser's Sunday off."

"You haven't seen Mr. Rochester, have you?" enquired Kit, turning to the boy.

"I bin out too, sir," he replied. "Mr. Rochester told me at dinner time he didn't want the car . . . so I took the opportunity of . . . well, I went out . . ."

"Bill's got a young lady," explained Mrs. Fraser smiling at him in a knowing way.

The boy blushed to the roots of his hair.

"Never you mind, Bill," said Fraser, clapping him on the back, "she's a very nice young lady—nothing to be ashamed of."

It was obvious that they could not help to elucidate the mystery of Rochester's disappearance, so, after a few moments' chat, Kit left them and went out. Fraser followed him and accompanied him up the path for he had to shut his frames and stoke the furnace in the conservatory.

"Is there anything I can do?" he enquired anxiously.

Kit shook his head. "We don't know what to do. It wouldn't be so bad if it weren't for the fact that Rochester is not very well . . . he is in a very—er—nervous condition," explained

Kit, using an expression which he disliked in the belief that it would convey the required meaning to his companion's mind.

"Nervous!" said Fraser. "Aye, he was as nervous as a cat—and short-tempered as well. There was trouble over my brother staying here. He said my brother was following him about. It was a queer thing altogether."

"Following him about?"

"It was imagination," declared Fraser, "sheer imagination. My brother wouldn't have thought of it—not for a moment." Fraser chuckled involuntarily and then continued, "He's a sailor, you see, my brother is. Well, if it had been a pretty girl he was following I wouldn't have put it past him. You know what sailors are."

Kit agreed that sailors usually had a soft spot in their hearts for the fair sex, and they walked on.

"What do you think has happened to him?" said Fraser suddenly.

It was Mardie's question and once again Kit paused before answering . . . he answered it differently this time.

"Well, Fraser," he said, "it's rather difficult to know. There may be some simple explanation and he may turn up at any moment; but on the other hand something may have happened to him—something serious. We know he was in this neurotic —er nervous condition."

"Maybe he's lost his memory," suggested Fraser. "Did you think of that? It's on the wireless sometimes: 'Missing from his home' and then it goes on and says the person has most likely lost his memory and it tells you what he's dressed in and so forth."

"It's possible," replied Kit.

They were now standing on the path outside the drawing-room windows and had lowered their voices instinctively. Fraser looked up at the sky.

"Well anyway, it's a fine night," he said.

Somehow Kit understood what he was thinking: they should be glad of that at least, for Rochester might be wandering about the country unable to find his way home, unable to remember the well-known landmarks, unable to recall his own name. For the first time Kit envisaged the man's plight and was ashamed that he had not thought of it before. It had needed Fraser to show him the situation from Rochester's angle.

"It's awful, isn't it?" Kit said.

"Aye, it's a bad business," Fraser agreed. "I'd be easier in my mind if something could be done; if we could organise a search for him the way we do in Scotland when a man's lost on the hillside, but I see your difficulty. He'd not be the best pleased if there was a fuss made."

"That's exactly the position."

Fraser nodded. "Och well, we can't do anything tonight. I'll keep a look-out . . . maybe I'll take a cast round before I go to my bed."

CHAPTER XXII

AN EERIE VIGIL

AFTER some little discussion it was agreed that Kit should spend the night at the Lynchet. He refused Mardie's offer of a bed and declared that he would be perfectly comfortable upon the drawing-room sofa. He had decided to keep the light burning in the room, and the French windows wide open for he thought there was a chance that Rochester might be wandering about in the vicinity and might see the light and walk in. A tray of biscuits and sandwiches and liquid refreshment was disposed upon a side-table in case he should feel hungry during the night.

The two girls went up to bed, and for a little while Kit stood at the window and gazed up at the stars. Then he rolled himself up in a blanket and lay down. The sofa was comfortable—it was a great deal more comfortable than many a bed which Kit had slept in during his travels—but he did not feel like sleep. The thought that Rochester might walk in at any moment was not inducive to slumber.

Kit had spent many strange nights in strange places but this was the strangest of all—it was the most eerie vigil he had ever kept. He lay and looked at the light and thought of many things. First of all he tried to make up his mind what could have happened to Rochester. He thought of all the theories which had been advanced and tried to see which was the most likely to be true. At one end of the scale was Dr. Peabody's theory that Rochester had sensed the fact that they wanted to "shut him up" and had rushed away and committed suicide, and at the other end of the scale was the theory that his absence was due to some simple accident. Between these two theories there were several others which were equally tenable: he might have been run over in the road and injured, or even killed; he might have lost his memory; he might have taken offence at the old doctor's words and have staged the whole affair to cause inconvenience and distress.

On thinking it over Kit inclined to the last of these theories for it fitted in very well with what he knew of Rochester's condition. It was the sort of idea which might easily take root in an unbalanced brain, a diseased imagination. Supposing Rochester had taken offence, and had said to himself, "All right then, I'll give you something to worry about, I'll cause a bit of trouble for you all. . . ."

This might be the explanation, or it might not. Rochester might be found, alive and well, or he might not be found at all.

Kit turned over on the sofa and drew the blanket round his shoulders; it was much colder now, and his thoughts took a different turn. Only last night he had been sitting outside in Mardie's garden looking up at her window and thinking about her and wishing he could do something to help her, and now he had got his wish. Now he was inside the house, an accredited guardian of her slumbers, and Rochester was outside, wandering about in the dark. Life is queer, thought Kit, it's damned queer! Who would ever have thought that *this* could have happened? . . . and yet it has all happened so naturally . . . one thing leading to another . . . that I don't feel a bit surprised.

There was a certain comfort in the fact that for tonight at least Mardie was safe. She had Dolly sleeping beside her and this was a pleasant thought. If Rochester returned safely perhaps they would be able to certify him and send him away for treatment, and if Rochester did not return safely . . . but I must not think of that, decided Kit. I must not allow myself to think of it.

The night wore on and presently Kit dropped off to sleep,

but he did not sleep very deeply. He was awakened by a crunching sound, the sound of a man's shoes on the gravel path outside the window. In a moment Kit was wide awake, in another he had flung off the blanket and leaped to his feet. A dozen thoughts swept through his mind: What should he say? What should he do? Would Rochester be furious at finding him here? Would Rochester be sane—or mad? Should he try to reason with him, or seize him forcibly?

Kit caught up the blanket . . . it was as good a method as any he knew . . . a blanket thrown over a man's head and held down tightly over a man's arms. . . .

There was a dark figure standing outside the window, peering into the lighted room, and Kit thought there was something furtive about the figure. He tried to make up his mind on a course of action, for it was so important not to blunder. He must not show himself too soon and perhaps frighten Rochester away, but on the other hand he must not let him escape.

The man came nearer to the window, and put his foot upon the step, and the light shone on his face . . . it was not Rochester.

"Fraser!" cried Kit, "Great heavens, what a fright you gave me!"

"A fright!" exclaimed Fraser.

"I thought you were Mr. Rochester."

"There's been no signs of him, then?" Fraser enquired.

"No."

"I didn't know you were here," explained the man in a low voice, "I saw the light, and I wondered what was doing. I've been having a walk around the place. I couldn't get it out of my head, couldn't get to sleep for thinking about it. I'm sorry I frightened you, sir."

"It doesn't matter," said Kit smiling, "I'll survive it all right."

Fraser smiled too, "You don't look to me like a man that's easily frightened," he declared.

Kit laughed. "Perhaps not," he said, "but the fact is I didn't know what to do. It's funny how things flash through your mind all in a moment. I wondered whether I should try to find some excuse for my presence here at this unearthly hour—"

"But he must know that we would be worrying about him," Fraser pointed out. "He must know that Mrs. Rochester would be terribly put out. That's the thing I can't understand, him going off like that and not saying where he was going. It's a thing no man in his sane senses would do—go off like that and never a word to his wife. I wouldn't: I know that," he laughed. "I'd get my head in my hands if I started that sort of carry on."

"Yes," agreed Kit. It was strange how terms of speech, debased by common use, sometimes assumed their own original importance; Fraser had used the expression, "No man in his sane senses," and had used it without a thought of the real implication of the words. No man in his sane senses would go off like that, but Rochester was not in his sane senses. . . .

"Come in and have a drink," said Kit hospitably.

"Well, I don't mind if I do," agreed Fraser, and he wiped his feet on the mat and came in.

Kit slept more comfortably after his chat with Fraser, but he woke early and went out into the garden. It was a glorious morning, everything was fresh and bright. The birds were singing madly. He stood for a few moments, stretching himself and breathing in the cool fresh air . . . and then he saw Mardie.

Mardie was in the rock garden; she was walking round very slowly with the heavy step of an old woman; her shoulders were bent as if she carried a burden upon them. She heard his step on the path and turned slowly and said, "Look at the forget-me-nots—so blue—and the dew on each tiny flower, like tears."

Kit could not find anything to say.

"I failed him," Mardie said.

"No, Mardie."

"Yes, I failed him. I didn't realise that he was ill. I see now that he has been ill for a long time. Why didn't I realise that he was ill? Oh Kit, where is he? What has happened to him?"

"We shall find out soon."

She shook her head, "You know something," she said. "There's something that you haven't told me."

"Mardie, you mustn't think—"

"I have a feeling that you're keeping something back," she continued. "I am sure of it. You've no right to do that, Kit."

It was true, of course. They had no right to keep anything from Mardie, but he felt that it would be impossible to tell her that Rochester was insane. He had no words to tell her, he could not even begin.

"I thought," said Kit at last, picking his way very carefully, "I thought Mr. Rochester was very much below par, and Dr. Peabody agreed with me. We are of the opinion that he requires a complete rest and suitable treatment."

She nodded, watching his face.

"That's all," said Kit.

"No, that isn't all," she said in a strained voice. "You must tell me more. You must tell me exactly what you thought of him—and what Dr. Peabody thought."

"We want another opinion," said Kit uncomfortably.

"The opinion of a neurologist?"

There was a choking feeling in Kit's throat. He said, "Dr. Peabody knows a specialist in London—he wants him to see Mr. Rochester."

"What is his name?"

"Ames, I think," said Kit reluctantly.

"Sir Horace Ames!" cried Mardie, "but he—he is a . . . oh Kit, then it's true! It's Jack's mind . . . his brain . . ."

Kit did not speak. There was nothing to say.

". . . I believe I knew it all along," cried Mardie, twisting her hands in her distress. "I believe I knew it in my heart . . . he was so changed. Changed in himself . . . and changed to me . . . he wasn't . . . Jack . . . any more. . . ."

Suddenly her eyes were filled with tears which overflowed and ran down her cheeks; she bowed her head in her hands and her body was shaken with sobbing.

Kit put his arm round her and led her to the seat beneath the apple tree. He did not try to calm her, for he knew that it was better for nature to take its course, but he watched her, and suffered with her, and his heart was wrung with pity and love. After a little while her sobs grew less, and she was quiet. Her hand was still clasped in his and she left it there like a trusting child; perhaps she could feel the strength and comfort flowing into her through that human contact . . . Kit hoped that she could.

At last she raised her head and faced the world again; it looked desolate enough, but she knew the worst, and had accepted it. She understood many things that had bewildered her.

"We must find him," she said in a voice that trembled a little.

"We'll find him," Kit said, ". . . and you mustn't feel hopeless, Mardie. It isn't incurable, you know. I'm absolutely certain that it was just the stress of business life. He must never go back to that."

"No, never."

"He isn't fitted for it," continued Kit. "He can't stand the prolonged strain. He must find some other kind of work, something peaceful. . . ."

Kit was speaking in this hopeful way on purpose to turn her thoughts, and he was successful, or partially successful in his attempt. She dried her eyes and straightened her shoulders . . . Jack would get well, and they would be happy together again. She had always wanted a peaceful, secure life, and Jack would have to give in to her now. He would get well and they would be happy—as they had been when they were first married.

Mardie repeated these comfortable words to herself several times, but strangely enough she found very little comfort in them.

CHAPTER XXIII

THE STONE BROTHERS AGAIN

THE permanence of routine, and above all the recurrence of meal-times is the last defence of civilized man against the vicissitudes of life. Lunch at the Lynchet was always at half past one and on the day following Rochester's disappearance Mardie and Dolly and Kit sat down at the table and unfolded their table napkins and made play with their knives and forks in the usual manner. Kit had accomplished his morning round of visits, and had returned to the Lynchet to see if there was any news, but there was none at all.

It seemed very odd to Kit—and he was sure his two companions must feel the same—that they were sitting here eating Rochester's food and drinking his wine, while he . . . and it seemed odd that everything in the room was the same as the night he had dined here and had seen Rochester for the first time. This was the same table, and the same silver; even the flowers were the same, for they were slightly wilted, and Mardie, looking at them with leaden eyes, remarked, "I must remind Morton to get some fresh flowers for the—" and then broke off suddenly, remembering that it did not matter about the flowers. It was Jack who always criticized the flowers, and was annoyed if they showed the least sign of fading. . . .

After lunch Kit persuaded the girls to rest, for neither of them had slept much the night before, and, as he himself had slept even less, and Dr. Peabody did not require him, he decided to take a little snooze in Rochester's study. He was dozing quietly in one of the big chairs with his feet supported upon the padded fender when Morton opened the door and looked in.

"It's Mr. Stone," she said in a conspiratorial voice. "Will you see him, sir, or shall I wake Mrs. Rochester up?"

"Mr. Stone!" exclaimed Kit in surprise.

Henry pushed past Morton and walked in. "I must see somebody," he declared irritably. "What are you doing here, Kit? Has everybody gone mad?"

"Henry!" cried Kit. "What on earth—" and then he broke off and waved to Morton. "All right, Morton," he said.

Morton withdrew somewhat reluctantly and the brothers were alone.

"Well!" said Henry, "you seem to be making yourself at home . . . you seem pretty comfortable. What are you supposed to be doing here?"

"I'm supposed to be sleeping," replied Kit. He was aware that everything would have to be explained to Henry but he wanted to put off the explanations. He was so tired, both physically and mentally, that he felt as if he could not face it.

"Sleeping!" cried Henry in disgust. "Is this the time for sleeping?"

"It's as good as any other time," said Kit, "and as a matter of fact I can usually sleep when I get the chance at any time, or in practically any place, and Mr. Rochester's chair is fairly comfortable."

"I'm sure he would be delighted to have your opinion on the subject," declared Henry sarcastically.

"I'll tell him the next time I see him," promised Kit, "but sit down, old fellow, make yourself at home. Don't stand on ceremony."

"Thank you, I will."

"Have a cigarette?"

Henry accepted a cigarette. He eyed his brother thoughtfully and then he burst out "What's the meaning of it—eh?"

"What's the meaning of what?"

"What's happened? That's what I want to know."

"How d'you know that anything has happened?"

"How do I know? Because it's all over London—the most extraordinary tale. A man came up to me this morning and said, 'I hear your partner has disappeared' . . . he said it just like that," declared Henry, putting a casual conversational tone to render the phrase. "He said, 'I hear your partner has disappeared' . . . Great Cæsar's ghost, you could have knocked me down with a feather!"

"What did you say?" enquired Kit with interest.

"What could I say?" retorted Henry. "I laughed of course —a hollow sort of laugh I daresay—and I said 'Disappeared! The fellow's in a Nursing Home having his appendix out. If you call that disappearing he's certainly disappeared'."

"Pretty smart of you, Henry," declared his younger brother, looking at him with respect.

"Not bad, considering," agreed Henry. "As a matter of fact I'd just been talking to a fellow whose partner had been whisked off to a Nursing Home in the middle of the night to have his appendix out; that gave me the idea."

"I see," said Kit, "but it was pretty smart of you, all the same. You mustn't be too modest, you know . . . and what did your friend say to that?"

"My friend? Oh, I see what you mean. The fellow swallowed it all right, but he'd probably spoken to at least half a dozen other fellows before I scotched the story. He lives near here, and he'd got the story from his wife, who had heard it from the cook, who had heard it from the milkman, who had heard it from some damn fool of a girl in this very house—the kitchen maid, I suppose."

"African Drums," murmured Kit. "Underground Telegraph in Twentieth Century England."

"What?" asked Henry, pricking up his ears.

"Nothing—go on."

"That's how idiotic stories spread," declared Henry. "It's

perfectly damnable, that's what it is. Of course I knew there was some simple explanation of the thing—it's the garbling of the thing that gets my goat. These damn fool people get hold of some perfectly simple thing and garble it until it's unrecognisable. Heaven alone knows how many people have got hold of the tale . . . it's probably spreading now," declared Henry, "people are discussing the thing at this very moment—over their blinking tea-tables—that's why I've got to get hold of Rochester at once. Where is he, eh?"

"He's disappeared," said Kit wearily.

"What!" cried Henry in a sort of squeak.

"I said he's disappeared."

"But where is he?"

"I don't know. Nobody knows."

"But Great Scott, he *can't* disappear," cried Henry in the most frightful dismay. "The man's got to show up and scotch this story. What's happened to him?"

"I don't know. He just walked out of the house and vanished."

"But when . . . and why . . . Kit, for heaven's sake! Don't you understand what it means to the firm? Don't you realise what people will say? It's absolutely ruination . . . it's worse."

Once more Kit explained the whole affair—he had begun to get very tired of explaining it but of course Henry had a right to know. He told Henry everything except the most important fact of all for, until his own diagnosis of Rochester's condition was confirmed, he had no intention of telling anyone that the man was insane. He was aware that you could get into the most appalling mess over the diagnosis of insanity and he intended to keep clear of that danger.

"Rochester was suffering from neurosis in an advanced form," said Kit with an air of grave conviction, and Henry accepted the statement without demur (it was really rather remarkable what you could put across a layman, so Kit reflected. You could make practically any statement you liked, and provided you made it with deliberation, they were prepared to swallow it whole).

"Neurosis—that's nerves of course," agreed Henry. "As a matter of fact I thought Rochester was a bit nervy, myself, and his secretary spoke to me the other day about it. We all thought he needed a holiday."

"He's been overworking, I expect."

"Well, it isn't so much that," explained Henry. "It's more that he's been worried and anxious. He was plunging pretty heavily. I happened to find that out."

"Was it your—I mean the firm's money?" enquired Kit.

"Good heavens, no. It was his own money. You couldn't run a stockbroking business on communal lines. But Godfrey and I weren't keen on being associated with a man who was beginning to be pointed out as a speculator. Our firm's always been—well, a reliable safe sort of firm, and we felt Rochester wasn't doing us any good. We talked it over and . . . well, it was only last night that we came to a decision. Mabel and I were dining with the Godfreys and after dinner Godfrey and I got down to it and discussed it thoroughly. We decided to give Rochester a sort of ultimatum: he must either draw in his horns or leave the firm. It wasn't pleasant to have to do it, especially as we like Rochester. Both of us like him. He's an amusing beggar . . . good company, and always plenty to say . . . but business is business."

"Did you speak to him?"

"No, we were going to do it this afternoon, and as tactfully as we could, but quite firmly. Speculation is a thing that grows on a man—it's exciting, and dangerous." Henry paused for a moment and suddenly his face changed, "Good heavens!" he cried. "It couldn't be—it couldn't be that!"

"Couldn't be what?"

"Couldn't be . . . I mean . . . I mean he couldn't have. . . ."

"Bust," Kit suggested helpfully.

"Shut up!" cried Henry, leaping to his feet and, shaking his fist at his irresponsible brother. "For heaven's sake shut up . . . you don't know what you're talking about. People don't talk like that. I must go. You don't understand what you're saying . . . I must go straight back to the office—or wait, where's the phone? I might get Godfrey on the phone. Where's the phone? Where's the damned thing?"

"There's a phone behind you on the table. Shall I leave you to discuss your affairs in private?"

"Yes . . . no . . . it doesn't matter a curse," declared Henry, clutching the instrument as a drowning man clutches at a straw.

Kit was comfortable where he was so he did not move and, in spite of the gravity of the situation, he could not help being considerably amused by Henry's telephone conversation with his senior partner. Kit had explained the matter so often himself that it was a relief to hear somebody else trying to explain it, and Henry was so extremely guarded in what he said, so careful to mention no names and to state no definite facts, that an expert cryptographer might have had some difficulty in understanding his story.

"It's Henry speaking," declared Henry earnestly. "Something rather important, old boy . . . what? . . . oh, I see; well, put me through to Mr. Godfrey, will you? . . . Hallo . . . Hallo . . . oh, there you are. Henry speaking . . . no, look here, I'm not in the office. . . . No, I'm here at *his* house. . . . No, I'm speaking from the house of the person we were talking about last night. No names, please . . . yes, but he isn't here, that's just the trouble. . . . What? . . . No, he isn't well, in fact he's very far from well. . . . No, it isn't flu; I wish to heaven it was . . . no, it isn't bubonic plague either, it's *serious,* John. . . . What? . . . Oh, yes, I know, but I mean it's no joke, it's really urgent. Something will have to be done. Well, as a matter of fact he isn't here. . . . Well, that's just the trouble, he hasn't *left* any address. . . . I said he's gone away and left no address. . . . But we can't get hold of him. . . . Yes, I know . . . yes . . . yes, of course. . . . Good heavens, I know that as well as you do, but we *can't* get hold of him. . . . No, she hasn't the least idea. . . . No. . . . Yes, very odd . . . well, I don't want to say too much, but I'll explain everything when I get back. . . . Yes, all right. . . . Yes, I'm coming straight back now . . . yes, but I thought you ought to know at once. . . . What? . . . Oh well, I thought you could look into things, understand? . . . That's what I meant . . . well, you'd better get hold of Staines before he leaves the office, he's the only person who knows what Roch—I mean he knows what our friend was doing. . . . Yes . . . yes, well hang onto him till I come . . . yes . . . yes, that's what I meant. . . . Still falling, are they? . . . I said *are they still falling?* . . . Good Lord, well, I happen to know he's up to his neck in them. . . . No, I don't suppose we can do anything at all . . . cheerful, isn't it? . . . What . . . I said it's a cheerful outlook . . . all right, so long."

Henry clapped on the receiver and turned to Kit. "What the hell are you grinning at?" he enquired.

"A telephone conversation can be very funny," said Kit apologetically.

"Funny! Is this your idea of fun?"

"No," said Kit, shaking his head, "as a matter of fact I'm . . . it's simply horrible, it's fantastic, ghastly. The only way I can bear it at all is by managing to see a glint of humour in it."

"You'd see humour in the situation if you were going to be hanged."

"I might," agreed Kit. "I don't know how people can bear things without an occasional lightening of the gloom. I can't."

"It may ruin the firm," said Henry heavily.

Kit rose from the chair. "I shouldn't worry too much," he

said quite seriously. "I think you'll find—well, I mean I don't believe he's—er—in financial difficulties. I think it's something else—something quite different."

"You know something you haven't told me," said Henry accusingly.

"I know he's in very bad health."

"Neurosis," Henry said. "But that wouldn't account for it, would it?"

"It might," replied Kit. "You see, people suffering from neurosis are often rather irresponsible. They're apt to fly off the handle."

"Good heavens!" cried Henry in dismay. "Do you think that's a good reason why I shouldn't worry? You tell me that my partner isn't responsible for his actions, and in the same breath you say I needn't worry!"

"Come and have some tea," Kit suggested. "You'll feel like a different man after a cup of tea. It'll be ready now in the drawing room."

"Tea!" cried Henry in disgust. "Tea in the drawing room! You must be raving mad. I've got to get back and see John Godfrey and try and clear up the mess. . . ." He rushed out, seized his coat and hat and disappeared. Kit heard the sound of his car starting and shooting off up the drive.

The disappearance of Rochester affected everybody connected with him in one way or another, thought Kit, as he strolled into the drawing room for tea. We were all cogs in the wheel of life and if one cog dropped out, or failed to function properly, it sent the whole wheel askew. Rochester's doings were—in a way—his own business, but in another way they were everybody's business. A man could not shirk his responsibilities when once he had shouldered them. A man was not his own master—none of us were.

CHAPTER XXIV

"MISSING FROM HIS HOME"

THAT day was the last quiet day at the Lynchet, and afterwards Kit looked back upon it with something like affection. On Tuesday morning there was still no sign of Rochester and no message from him, and in view of the various circumstances connected with his disappearance it was decided that the police should be informed. Kit telephoned to Henry and told him what was being done and Henry bleated for "more time" but the responsibility of concealing the facts was too great and Henry's objections were overborne. The police were called in and made exhaustive enquiries, and searched the neighbourhood without avail. Hospitals were searched. Hotels were searched. The B.B.C. broadcasted a description of him: "Missing from his home at the Lynchet, Minfield . . . John Oswald Rochester, aged thirty-three . . . five feet ten and a half inches . . . very slight figure . . . brown hair and brown eyes . . . thin face, very pale with delicate features . . . small brown moustache . . . was wearing a navy blue suit in good condition, a pale blue shirt, blue tie, blue socks and black oxford shoes . . . may be suffering from loss of memory. Will any person who has any information about him communicate with the Minfield Police Office, telephone number Minfield 8, or any local constabulary."

Kit happened to be at the Furnivals' house at six o'clock that day, and as he was anxious to hear the broadcast he asked them to turn on the wireless. They sat and listened to it in silence.

"I wonder if it will do any good," said Mrs. Furnival as she switched it off. "I can't believe it will, somehow. It's quite a good description of Jack, of course, but it would fit hundreds of other people just as well. Look at Gilbert, for instance."

They all looked at Gilbert.

"Not guilty," he declared, smiling, "I'm only five feet nine—there's an inch and a half difference between us—and I shan't be thirty-three for seven years."

"You fit the description in every other way," his mother declared, "age and height are difficult things to judge. It's funny, really, because you aren't a bit like Jack."

"Yes," agreed Kit. "The fact is you can't describe a person so that other people can recognise them. You might give a detailed list of every feature with measurements, and yet you couldn't make a picture of the person in other people's minds. . . ."

"I don't believe he'll ever be found," declared Mrs. Furnival thoughtfully.

It was the first time Kit had heard anyone voice this conviction and his whole being rose up to refute the idea. Rochester must be found, dead or alive, for there was no possibility of freeing Mardie until they knew what had happened to her husband. Kit considered the matter as he drove home, and he saw that Rochester had become an even greater obstacle than before. He had vanished into thin air, but Mardie was bound to him. It was absolutely impossible to set Mardie free until Rochester was found—dead or alive.

He drove on, considering the problem, and, as he was passing the small lake which lay at the bottom of the hill, he noticed a group of policemen standing under the trees. He stopped his car and walked down over the short turf and the police inspector looked up and saw him and came forward to meet him.

"We're dragging the lake, sir," explained the Inspector gravely, and then he added, "I didn't mention it to Mrs. Rochester!"

"No," said Kit, "much better not." He could not say more, for the horrible implications of the move sealed his lips. He looked out over the peaceful sunlit water and saw the boats, and the men busy with their gruesome task. They were calling to each other and shouting directions.

"It's a routine job, really," said the Inspector. "We mustn't leave a stone unturned, you see. Would you say he was likely to be of the suicide type?"

"He—he might be," said Kit, "it's difficult to say. It's difficult to know what any man might do."

"You doctors are pretty careful, aren't you?" said the Inspector with the suspicion of a smile. "You don't give anything away. I'd like to know what you think—"

"I don't know what I think," declared Kit, "I wish to heaven I did know what I thought. Isn't it a very unusual and extraordinary thing for a man to vanish into thin air like that?"

"Unusual, yes . . . but there have been cases. It isn't unprecedented. Now tell me this, sir. Was there anything queer about Mr. Rochester? There's queer stories going about the village . . . a bit unbalanced, wasn't he?"

"Er—yes, he was rather," said Kit.

(Suddenly he discovered that they were both talking of Rochester in the past tense—as if he were dead—it was the Inspector who had started it.)

"What do *you* think has happened to him?" Kit asked.

"Well, I think he's dead," the man replied. "We'd have had some word of him if he'd been alive. We'll find his body; it may take time, but we'll find it."

Several days passed. They were long days, as days of waiting always are. Dolly remained at the Lynchet, and Kit looked in whenever he had a free moment; and every time he called at the house he expected—or half expected—that there would be news of Rochester, but no news came. Mardie moved through life with a set, pale face and ordered her household as if she were in a dream. Policemen came and asked questions and went away. The telephone rang and everyone rushed to answer it.

At the doctor's house life moved on at its usual quiet tempo, for the doctor's house, though touched by the tragedy, was on the outside of the orbit. Miss Peabody had been made acquainted with the facts and indeed it was impossible to hide them, for everybody in Minfield knew that Mr. Rochester had disappeared. Kit thought that Jem must be the only person in Minfield who did not know what had happened, and was neither worried nor pleasantly excited by the occurrence. Dr. Peabody had decreed that Jem was not to know, and that the subject was not to be discussed at meals. If Jem had been a sociable child and had played with other children he would probably have heard of the matter from outside sources, but as he preferred to play by himself he remained in ignorance.

"Leave him alone," Dr. Peabody said. "There's plenty of time for Jem to worry about other people's troubles, and it will do us all good to refrain from talking about it when he's in the room."

One day, about a fortnight after Rochester's disappearance Kit had started to write a letter to Henry for his birthday. Kit had always made a point of writing to Henry for his birthday, and he saw no reason to break the time-honoured custom. It was true, of course, that he saw Henry fairly frequently nowadays (he had gone up to town and seen him only last week) and therefore the letter would not be very interesting nor exciting, but Kit had decided that Henry should have his birthday letter just the same. Last year Kit had been in China, and had written Henry's birthday letter from there. He had gone to China in the hope of seeing something of the war, and had actually seen a good deal more of the war than he appreciated. At Hun Hai a woman and a baby who were standing in the market place had been killed by a shell-splinter, and Kit had been so near them at the time that he had been spattered by their blood . . . he had seen plenty of human blood, spattered about in operating theatres but this was different, this was incredible and fantastic. Kit had almost fainted, and had only recovered himself when he had found that, although the woman and the baby were beyond his aid, there were several other injured people who needed attention. He had busied himself binding up the wounds of these strange stoical people and the horrible nausea had passed. It was difficult, now, sitting in this quiet pleasant room in this quiet law-abiding land, to believe that the ghastly thing had ever happened and that it was not merely a peculiarly vivid dream.

Of course there had been plenty of interesting things to tell Henry in last year's birthday letter. He had not mentioned the shell which had wrecked the market place but he had told Henry other things about his experiences in China and had sent him some photographs of pagodas and Chinese women— the usual tourist stuff. Today Kit could find nothing to say to Henry. He had written . . .

"My dear Henry,

"Once again I am writing to wish you many happy returns of the day—"

. . . and there he had stopped. The words stared up at him from the paper and seemed to mock him because he could not add to them. Kit wrote letters so seldom that unless he had some definite news to impart it was almost impossible for him to fill half a sheet. He considered the desperate expedient of signing his name and letting it go at that, but rejected it as foolish.

It was raining heavily now and Jem had come in from the garden and was playing about the room; he was playing one of his "special" games, and Kit turned slightly in his chair to watch what he was doing. There was no hurry about the letter, it would have to wait.

Jem was too engrossed in his game to know that he was being watched, he was playing with all his attention and his actions were so precise that Kit could follow them easily. . . .

He flung open two imaginary doors and fixed them back, then he walked forward and climbed into his grandfather's big leather chair and started up his car.

"You haven't cranked your car," said Kit, smiling at him. "Good motorists always give their engine a few turns before they start them up."

Jem came back to earth with a start. "But he didn't, you see," said Jem. "He just got in and started off. I expect his garage was heated."

Kit laughed at the plausible excuse, "It must have been," he agreed.

The game was continuing now; Jem had backed his car out of the garage and was talking to somebody—obviously his chauffeur—in a lordly way. The imaginary chauffeur got in beside his master and the car moved off; but it did not move far. It stopped suddenly with a grinding of brakes (Jem produced an appalling shriek for this) and Jem got out and ran back.

So far Kit had followed the whole thing with the greatest of ease, for Jem's acting was so intense that his audience was caught up with him into the illusion. The chair became a car to Jem—he did not merely pretend that it was a car—and, for the time being, it had become a car to Kit. But now Kit was lost, he had not the slightest idea what Jem was supposed to be doing; he was moving his body and arms backwards and forwards in a most mysterious manner and hissing between his teeth.

"What on earth are you doing now?" Kit enquired.

"Raking the gravel, of course. I want to leave it all smooth and tidy, you see. At least I expect I do."

"Who are you?" asked Kit, chuckling appreciatively.

"I'm Mr. Rochester," said Jem, and so saying he tossed his imaginary rake away, ran after his car and jumped in, "Brr—brrr—brrrr—" growled Jem, revving up, and letting in his clutch . . . and his head jerked backwards with the suddenness of his start.

"Mr. Rochester?" asked Kit, in an incredulous tone, "but Jem . . . Jem, look here. How do you know that Mr. Rochester did—did all that?"

"I saw him, of course," replied Jem promptly. "I saw him do it. You know quite well I have to see people before I can act them. You know that, Kit."

"Come here, Jem," Kit said.

The child came over and stood beside the chair and Kit put his arm round him. Their faces were on a level, and Kit could look straight into the clear candid eyes.

"Tell me about it, old chap," said Kit gravely, "I'd like to know exactly what happened."

"You saw me do it!"

"I know, but I want to hear as well. Start from the time you went out into the garden. It was after tea, wasn't it?"

"I was playing Indians," said Jem. "Stalking palefaces, you know—stalking them in the bushes like real Indians do. It's a good garden for Indians because the bushes are nice and thick. Well, then . . . *then* I suddenly saw a real live paleface! It was awfully exciting. . . . Well, of course, I knew it was only Mr. Rochester but I pretended it was a real live paleface."

"What did he do?" asked Kit, trying to speak in a calm, ordinary sort of voice.

"He came out of the house," said Jem. "He had a suitcase—

quite a small one—and a stick, and he ran along the path to the garage. He ran quite fast and then he stopped and stood still and looked round first on one side and then on the other. He was looking and listening to see if the Indians were after him—just like any paleface would do."

Jem had started to act it again and Kit unclasped his arm and set him free.

". . . like this," Jem said, running and stopping and glancing over his shoulder in a way that was horribly suggestive of a hunted—or was it a haunted—man.

". . . and then," continued Jem, "and then he put his suitcase on the ground, and took the key out of his pocket, and unlocked the doors, and opened them, and fixed them back" (Jem acted each motion as he spoke) "and then he took his suitcase and heaved it into the car—and his stick too—and then he got in and started."

Jem was sitting in the chair now, and the chair was a car. He backed it out of the garage, leaning over the side as a man would do to see that his wing was clear of the doorpost ". . . like that," said Jem.

"I see," nodded Kit.

"Then a man came," said Jem. "It was the chauffeur and his name was Bill, and he said, 'I didn't know you wanted the car sir,'—and he said it in a grumpy sort of voice—and Mr. Rochester said, 'Well, I do want it, and I'll want you to bring the car back. Lock the doors, Bill, and nip in. Don't bother about your uniform. I'm in a hurry.' "

"Is that all he said?"

"It's all I could hear," replied Jem, "they talked when they were both sitting in the car, but I couldn't hear. They went on a little and then they stopped and Mr. Rochester came back and raked the gravel." Jem paused for a moment and then added, "It was tidy of him, wasn't it . . . when he was in such a hurry, too!"

"Very tidy," agreed Kit. He rose and put his hand on Jem's head. "Good-bye, old chap," he said. "I've got to go out . . . play something else, now."

"I'll play Tupman cleaning the car," agreed Jem.

CHAPTER XXV

THE SEARCH

KIT seized his cap and ran. He scarcely knew what he was going to do, but he must do something. He backed his car out of the garage and set off for the Lynchet at top speed and, as he drove, his brain worked rapidly over all that Jem had seen and heard. The chauffeur had lied, of course, but why had he lied? Rochester must have bribed the boy to lie. Rochester had carried out his plan of escape with amazing cunning but Kit was aware that cunning of this kind was by no means incompatible with a disordered brain. I must see the boy first, Kit decided. I must put the fear of death into him. . . .

Bill was in the garage, fiddling about with the engine of his master's car, and he started somewhat guiltily when he saw Kit.

"I wasn't doing nothing," he declared. "Just cleaning up the plugs, and that."

"So you aren't allowed to touch the engine!" remarked Kit.

"Mr. Rochester wouldn't mind."

"Oh, wouldn't he? Why don't you ask him?"

"How can I?" enquired Bill in amazement.

"You know where he is," Kit pointed out.

The spanner clattered onto the floor. "Me! 'Ow could I know where 'e was!" exclaimed the boy, his aitches, which were usually carefully articulated, suddenly deserting him.

"You *do* know," said Kit firmly, "or at least you know where he went that Sunday afternoon, because you went with him, and you brought the car back."

"Me! I was out."

"You were out with Mr. Rochester. It was very disappointing for you when he had told you that he didn't want the car, and then you found that not only did he want the car, but he wanted you as well. Very disappointing. However, I daresay he made it up to you—"

"You're crazy!"

"What was it he said? . . . 'Lock the doors, Bill, and nip in. I shall want you to bring the car back. Don't bother about your uniform, I'm in a hurry.' "

Bill's eyes goggled with amazement.

"And then," continued Kit calmly, "and then you went on a little, and stopped, and Mr. Rochester came back and raked the gravel."

"Well!" exclaimed Bill. "Well, it beats me! 'Ow do you know that?"

"Where did you go?" asked Kit, suddenly becoming grave and stern, "where did you go that afternoon? Where did you leave Mr. Rochester?"

"So you don't know that!"

"I'm going to find out."

" 'Ow are you going to find out?"

"Through you, of course," said Kit patiently, "and the sooner you come clean the better."

"I won't say," Bill declared, bursting out suddenly into rapid speech. "No, I won't say a word. 'E didn't want people follerin' 'im, and I don't blame 'im. Why should 'e be follered and pestered out of 'is wits—'e ain't done no 'arm. A little peace—that's all 'e wants and I said I wouldn't let on where 'e'd gorn and I won't."

"How much did he give you to hold your tongue?"

"What's that to do with you?" enquired Bill truculently. "Nosey, that's what you are. Well, 'e did give me something— 'e's a fine generous gentleman. A real gentleman, that's what 'e is. Five quid 'e give me to 'old my tongue and I'm 'olding it, see? Five quid, and I went and bought a ring for my girl friend, see? Anythin' else you want to know?"

"Quite a lot," replied Kit calmly, "but first of all I want to tell you something. You aren't doing Mr. Rochester any good by holding your tongue. You're doing him harm. Mr. Rochester was ill and his friends wanted to help him. He ought to be in bed. That's the reason why he must be found. We want to find him and put him to bed and take care of him until he's better."

"They didn't ought to 'ave follered 'im," declared Bill. "It was that follerin' business got 'im down."

"It was a delusion—"

"What?"

"It wasn't true," explained Kit patiently. "Nobody was following him. Why should they? People who are ill often imagine things—you know that, don't you? They imagine all sorts of things that aren't true at all. We must find him, Bill. He may be lying ill somewhere with nobody belonging to him to take care of him. He may have lost his memory and not even know who he is."

There was a short silence.

"Is that straight?" enquired Bill in a different tone. "You ain't kidding me—leading me up the garden?"

"It's perfectly straight. I give you my word that it's true. Dr. Peabody would tell you the same."

"Well . . . 'e was odd," admitted Bill thoughtfully, "I'll give you that, Doctor. 'E was excited-like . . . talkin' nonsense, *you* know . . . like as if 'e didn't know what 'e was sayin'."

Kit waited patiently. He was aware that if Bill would not answer his questions he could hand him over to the police and they would make him talk, but he believed that he could get more out of the boy himself. Bill was stupid, and if the police frightened him he would probably become even more stupid than Nature had made him.

"Well . . ." said Bill after a long pause, "well . . . I dunno. It's difficult, ain't it? I promised him, you see. You'll be foller-in' 'im if I tell you where 'e's gorn—and that's what 'e didn't want."

"He didn't know what he wanted," declared Kit in exaspera-tion. "The man was ill. He's probably a great deal worse by this time. Don't you understand, he may be lying ill in hos-pital somewhere—ill and miserable—he may be dying."

"Dying?" exclaimed Bill in horrified tones.

"He *may* be for all we know. I wouldn't let a dog stray off like that and disappear into the blue without making any attempt to find it."

"Nor wouldn't I," replied Bill with spirit, "a dog can't look after itself like a man."

"A man can't look after himself when he's ill."

Bill considered that, and it seemed to convince him. "I dunno," he said slowly, "I dunno if I'm doin' right or wrong. You've got me all muddled, that's what, but I'll tell you where we went—it was Canterbury, see? 'E never said where we was goin' and I never asked. Well, 'e was driving. Yes, 'e drove, and it fair made my 'air curl the way 'e drove . . . shaved past other cars with 'ardly a inch to spare . . . and laughed! I don't want another drive like that . . . sweating all over, I was."

"You went to Canterbury?"

"Yes, and on beyond. It was the Deal road we took. I don't know that part and I was too scared to mind where we went but it was the Deal road, right enough. 'E stopped the car when we got to the top of an 'ill and 'e says 'Can you smell the sea?' 'e says. There was a kind of fresh smell and I said I could, and then 'e got out, and 'e says 'turn the car and go 'ome, lickety split', and 'e give me the five quid."

"What happened after that?"

"Nothing didn't 'appen. 'E just walked off, and I 'ad a job

finding my way back. I dunno where I went . . . it was nine o'clock before I got back . . . nine o'clock! 'Alf dead, I was. You were just in front of me."

"I was!" exclaimed Kit in surprise.

Bill nodded. "Your car turned in at the gates and I waited a bit and then I drove down to the garage and put the car away like 'e said I was to."

"And raked the gravel again?"

" 'E said I was to," said Bill reproachfully. "I didn't do nothing except what 'e said I was to . . . I did what 'e said all through . . . 'e was my master, wasn't 'e?"

"Run out the car," said Kit.

"What?"

"Run out the car. We're going to Canterbury, you and I, and we'll find your blasted hill and start from there. We've got to find him."

"I don't 'ave to take orders from you," said Bill sulkily.

"Very well, you can take them from Mrs. Rochester. You can come up to the house *now*. Come on."

With the greatest reluctance Bill washed his hands at the tap, put on his jacket and followed the young doctor to the house. He was sorry now that he had spoken. The young doctor had screwed it out of him, and Bill saw a good many rocks ahead. Bill felt aggrieved; he felt that he had been caught up in the machinery. He had been *used,* first by Rochester and then by the young doctor, and, although he did not see clearly how he had been used or why, he was pretty sore about it. The young doctor was a meddler and no mistake, he had stirred things up just as they were settling down. How on earth had the young doctor found out what Mr. Rochester had said? He had repeated the exact words—"Lock the doors, Bill, and nip in. Don't bother about your uniform, I'm in a hurry"—how had he known that Mr. Rochester had said that? . . . And how had he known about raking the gravel?

Bill had been as nervous as a cat for a day or two after Mr. Rochester had gone and had wondered several times whether he would be put in prison if his part in the affair were discovered by the police, but nothing had happened, and everyone had accepted his assurances that he had been out (well, so I *was* out, thought Bill) and now, just when he was beginning to feel quite comfortable about it, the young doctor had stirred it all up.

Bill was even more sorry for himself after his interview with Mrs. Rochester. She was quite friendly and pleasant and said that she knew Bill had thought he was acting for the best, but she put Bill completely at the young doctor's disposal and, Dr. Peabody's permission having been obtained, the two of them went to Deal and put up at an Inn and ranged the countryside searching for traces of the fugitive. Bill did not like Dr. Stone, but he was forced to respect him, for, although he did not spare Bill, he did not spare himself either. They were out all day long talking to people and questioning them; it was a weary job.

Kit worked in collaboration with the police, but he worked on his own account as well. He was determined to find Rochester. It seemed to him that Rochester must have been making for the sea, and Kit started his search by talking to the fishermen, and the men on the waterside. He went into the little public-houses and pursued his enquiries there. Everyone was extremely kind and patient, and everyone tried his best to help. It was extraordinary how kind everyone was. Having drawn a complete blank in Deal, itself, Kit enlarged the scope of his activities; and he and Bill patrolled the roads and spoke to stone-cutters and tramps, and frequented public-houses where drivers and road-men congregated, and visited farmhouses and village shops, and talked to bicyclists and hikers. Here again, Kit found interest and sympathy but absolutely no definite information. On one occasion they returned to the

Inn (which Kit had made his headquarters) exhausted after a long day's search and found a message waiting for them asking them to come over to Dover and interview a tramp who thought he had seen somebody answering to Rochester's description. On another occasion they were called out to identify a body in a morgue, and one night the telephone rang, and Kit was informed by one of the friendly fishermen that a man's body had been washed up at Hythe, and he roused Bill and they rushed off to Hythe and discovered that the body was that of a man of seventy, with straggly snow-white hair.

It was impossible to spend his whole summer searching for Rochester, and indeed it was unfair to Dr. Peabody to leave him to battle with the practice alone, so after a fortnight's intensive search Kit returned to Minfield and admitted defeat. He found that things had settled down into a temporary lull and Rochester's disappearance, which had been a nine days' wonder, had been forgotten by everyone except his immediate circle. The man had dropped out of life, and the waters of oblivion had closed over his head.

On the night of Kit's return he had a long talk with Dr. Peabody in the library.

"You've done your best," the old man pointed out. "You can't do anything now except wait. The police won't forget about him; they'll let us know if anything turns up."

"It won't," declared Kit, who knew how thoroughly he had combed the neighborhood. "The man has vanished into thin air. What's to be done, that's the question."

"But you can't do anything."

"How long have we got to wait before we can presume his death?"

Dr. Peabody did not know. "Years, I'm afraid," he said vaguely.

"And what about Mardie?" demanded Kit. "Have I got to

wait years and years . . . until the Law chooses to presume the man dead. . . ."

"I'm afraid so," said Dr. Peabody.

"But good heavens—"

"I've thought about it," interrupted the old doctor. "I haven't forgotten what you told me. You could take a lawyer's opinion, of course, and I think you should—later on—but it isn't the least use doing anything at present. You must have patience, Kit."

"Patience!" groaned Kit.

"Yes, it's a difficult virtue to cultivate . . . but apart from any legal considerations you must remember that Mrs. Rochester has sustained a severe shock. Give her time to recover before you say anything at all. That's my advice."

It was good advice, and Kit decided to take it. He would give Mardie the whole summer and then he would go to her and tell her that he loved her. Once he had the assurance that she loved him he could wait in patience for the day when she would be free. Rochester was dead—Kit was certain of it—and Mardie could not be bound forever to a dead man. Somehow or other she must be set free; the law could not be so foolish, nor so cruel as to keep her bound for ever. He longed to speak to her, to take her in his arms and comfort her, but he knew that it would be folly. Dr. Peabody was right. Mardie was not ready yet, she must be given time to forget and to recover.

A few days after Kit's return Henry Stone came down from London to see Mrs. Rochester. He arrived unexpectedly one afternoon, bringing with him a small case full of papers, and enquired if he might see Mrs. Rochester on business.

They sat in the study, one on each side of the large solid table, which Rochester had always used for his correspondence, and Henry proceeded to explain the state of Rochester's affairs

—or at least to try to explain it. Poor Henry found the job extremely distasteful; there were so many things which must be said, and he scarcely knew how to begin. He gazed at Mrs. Rochester with an agonized expression and cleared his throat several times.

"You must just tell me," said Mardie helpfully. "I expect Jack's money is all lost. That's it, isn't it?"

"No!" cried Henry in horrified accents. "Good heavens, what a frightful idea! Of course his capital has depreciated considerably because he ought to have sold out various stocks which he was holding . . . and he would have sold out if he had been there. We couldn't do anything about it because the stock was held in his name."

Mardie understood that quite easily. She understood all that Henry told her. In about half an hour Henry had made everything perfectly clear to her and she had learned more about business matters, and about stocks and shares, than she had ever known before. It was obviously impossible to wind up Jack Rochester's estate and Mardie could not even claim the income from his securities. Henry explained this somewhat diffidently—he felt it was extremely hard—but Mardie assured him that she would not starve, for she had a very small income of her own, and a house in Scotland, and this raised his spirits a good deal. She was quite touched by Henry's interest in her affairs, and very grateful to him for the trouble he was taking. It was especially good of him in view of the fact that Jack's sudden departure had caused the firm a considerable amount of inconvenience.

"You're a good business woman," said Henry as he collected his papers prior to departure, "you've got an excellent head on your shoulders . . . so has Mabel, you know. Mabel often helps me, she has an instinct for the market and she enjoys a little flutter occasionally."

This speech showed such a different point of view from

the point of view to which Mardie had been accustomed that she found herself unable to reply, or to make any remark whatever. She followed Henry to the front door and watched him get into his car, and it was not until he held out his hand to say good-bye that she suddenly found her tongue.

"I must give up the Lynchet," she said, as she took his hand. "I can't afford to stay on here, can I?"

"I'm afraid you can't," agreed Henry, fiddling with the gadgets on his dash board. "I'm afraid it—it wouldn't be possible."

After this momentous interview events began to move with feverish activity. The Lynchet was an attractive house and no sooner had it been put into an agent's hands to sub-let than a stream of would-be tenants appeared to look over it. Mardie had no "feeling" about the Lynchet, or at least no feeling comparable with her love for her old home at Kilnocky, but she felt that in giving up this house she was giving up her whole married life. It was putting Jack further away than ever, it was banishing him from her life . . . but Mardie had no choice in the matter and after all it was Jack's own doing that the place must be given up. She comforted herself with that as best she could and went about the necessary preparations with energy and determination.

There were no preparations necessary at the other end, for Mrs. Colquhoun was always ready to receive Mardie. The little house was kept from one month's end to another, swept and garnished so that its mistress could walk in at any moment and take up her abode. Mardie was aware of this, but she wrote to her faithful old servant all the same. She wrote and told Mrs. Colquhoun all that had happened; for it was easier to write than to tell, and she warned Mrs. Colquhoun that she was not coming to Hillside House alone; Mrs. Dorman was coming with her for a long visit, and it might be necessary to get a girl in from the village to help in the house.

CHAPTER XXVI

MISS PEABODY'S HAT

THE relations between Miss Peabody and Kit had not been improved by their heart-to-heart talk on the evening of Mr. Rochester's disappearance. There was no longer any mystery as to why Ethel Peabody disliked Kit and, although he was sorry for the woman, the bitterness and jealousy which had been poisoning her mind disgusted him. He was aware that she disliked him more than ever and he decided that this was because he had spoken plainly and had refused to listen to her diatribes against Dolly and Mardie, but Ethel's feelings were more complex—far too complex for Kit to understand. From the very beginning Ethel had made up her mind to have nothing to do with her father's assistant and she had stuck to her plan through thick and thin. It had been difficult at times because Dr. Stone was pleasant and amusing, but whenever Ethel had found herself relenting towards him she had reminded herself that he was Mrs. Rochester's friend—and therefore Dolly's—and had hardened her heart. It was extremely galling to discover that she had been quite mistaken and that Dr. Stone had never met Mrs. Rochester until he came to Minfield! Ethel, herself, had met Dr. Stone first and, if she had been pleasant and agreeable and had taken a little trouble to cultivate him, he might have become *her* friend. He had been driven over into the enemy camp, and Ethel had done it herself—no wonder she was furious.

Ethel was in a very unenviable frame of mind for she was angry with herself and with Dr. Stone, and she was angry with her father also. Dr. Peabody had not told her a word about Mr. Rochester's disappearance until the matter was common knowledge in Minfield. In fact Ethel had heard the news from an outside source, and had been obliged to admit complete ignorance on the subject.

"Why didn't you tell me?" she demanded of her father. "Olive thought it most extraordinary that I didn't know about it."

"What is extraordinary about that?" enquired the doctor calmly.

"You're their doctor," Ethel pointed out. "It looks as if you didn't trust me—and as a matter of fact you actually told me a deliberate lie about the Rochesters. Why should Dolly know all about it from the very beginning and not I?"

"Dolly was there when it happened," replied Dr. Peabody shortly.

"That doesn't explain why you lied to me—or excuse it."

"I don't need any excuse. You asked me a question which you had no right to ask and I had no right to answer. That will do, Ethel."

Ethel said no more but she brooded over the injustice of Fate, and life was a good deal less comfortable for everyone in the house. Even Jem, who was innocent of offence, came in for the back-lash of his aunt's ill-humour. The weather was sultry, and the equilibrium of life was upset and although Jem was not aware that anything untoward had occurred, he felt the strain subconsciously and was affected by it. His grandfather was irritable and unapproachable, his Aunt Dolly was at the Lynchet, and his beloved Kit was not so "listeny" as usual. Fortunately for Jem he had his own escape from the vicissitudes of life and used it to the full. He played his game from early morning to late at night, and indeed he became so wrapped up in his various rôles that he scarcely heard what was said to him. Having started history at school he had found a new store of characters to draw upon and he mixed them up with characters from real life in a most bewildering manner. "Who are you?" Kit would enquire, as he passed Jem on the stairs on his way in or out, and Jem would reply, "I'm Tupman polishing the brasses" or "I'm King Alfred burning the cakes" or, "I'm Aunt Ethel talking to cook" or, "I'm Richard the Lion-Hearted in prison."

Jem had always insisted that he could not "act people" unless he had seen them, but apparently he had overcome this disability now, and Kit was not sure that it was a good sign. As a matter of fact Kit was somewhat worried about Jem for the child seemed to be living in a world of his own. He was overdoing his imaginative games. But, unless he could be provided with some other outlet, it would be useless to try to stop him.

The atmosphere of the doctor's house was like tinder, needing but a spark to cause a major conflagration, and the spark fell one evening when Dr. Peabody was out on an urgent case. Jem had been playing that he was Miss Sinclair—Aunt Ethel's especial friend—and he had borrowed Aunt Ethel's best hat for the purpose. He was in the middle of his game, with the hat perched coquettishly over one eye and the dining-room tablecloth draped around his body, when Nemesis in the person of Aunt Ethel descended upon him and ordered him to bed without any supper.

As a rule Jem did not argue with Aunt Ethel, for he knew it was a useless expenditure of breath but tonight he stood his ground and tried to reason with her.

"I didn't mean any harm," he assured her. "I haven't done your hat any harm, either. I just borrowed it for a little and I was going to put it back. I needed it for my game because I'm Miss Sinclair, you see, so I have to have a hat. Grandfather doesn't mind me borrowing his hat and Kit doesn't either."

"You know perfectly well you aren't allowed to take my things," declared Aunt Ethel, snatching the hat off his head.

"I didn't know," said Jem earnestly, "and I haven't done it

any harm—just look at it and you'll see—I was very very careful with it."

"I've told you not to poke about in my room."

"I didn't poke. It was lying on the bed. It was lying on the bed and the door was open. Honestly, Aunt Ethel—I saw it lying on the bed—"

"That will do," said his aunt, borrowing the doctor's pet phrase, "that will do, Jem. Go straight to bed."

Jem looked at Kit in an appealing manner.

"He really *is* very careful," said Kit, "and I'm sure he didn't mean to do wrong; now that he knows that you don't like him taking your things—"

"It isn't only that," cried Ethel Peabody, "it's—it's that stupid game . . . making fun of everybody . . . imitating people behind their backs. . . ."

"It isn't a stupid game!" declared Jem, furiously.

"It is, and you ought to be ashamed of yourself—a boy of seven years old—to play such babyish games."

Kit felt impelled to take a hand. "But Miss Peabody," he began, "look here, I think you're wrong. Jem doesn't make fun of people behind their backs—"

"Of course I don't," cried Jem, "I just act them as they are."

"Well, you shouldn't," declared Miss Peabody firmly. "I shall speak to your Grandfather about it. You must learn to play games like other children, do you hear me?"

"No," cried Jem, stamping his foot, "no, I won't. You can't make me."

Kit intervened again—he was aware that it was unwise but he could not help it. "Hold on, Jem," he said, "you mustn't speak like that. Aunt Ethel only means—"

Miss Peabody turned on him, "I can explain what I mean without your assistance, Dr. Stone," she said, throwing up her head and speaking in a voice of restrained fury, "you interfere far too much. Jem has been even more difficult to manage

than usual since you came—you spoil him. I've told him to
go to bed without any supper and he takes no notice at all.
It's your fault—"

It was untrue, of course, and Kit was angry; he felt inclined
to reply in the same tone but he refrained for the sake of the
child. It would only make things more difficult for Jem, and
they were difficult enough already. Jem was standing there,
waiting for the verdict of his elders, looking from one to the
other in bewilderment.

Kit nodded to him and said in a quiet voice, "Better nip up
to bed, old chap."

He turned at once and went off to bed; a small drooping
figure stumbling over the tablecloth in which it was still
enfolded.

There was a little silence when the door had shut behind
him—and it was not a comfortable silence—Kit knew that
if he started to speak, and to tell this extraordinary woman
what he thought of her, he would not be able to stop. There
were many things he would like to tell Miss Peabody and
they were all definitely unpleasant. He took up a book and sat
down and tried to compose himself, but before he was settled
the telephone bell rang and he was called out to a case.

Eleven o'clock had struck when Kit returned to the doctor's
house. He was very tired, but considerably elated, and he
quickened his step when he saw that the light was still shining in the library window, for he wanted someone to talk to.

"See the Conquering Hero Come!" exclaimed Dr. Peabody,
looking up from the *Evening Standard* with a little smile.

Kit laughed, "What a wizard you are! How did you know
I was particularly pleased with myself?"

"I heard you come in. I heard your ringing step on the path.
You were whistling under your breath as you passed the
window."

"And what was your deduction?" enquired Kit.

"Mrs. Faulkner," replied Dr. Peabody promptly.

"Yes," said Kit, sinking into a chair, "yes, Mrs. Faulkner—thank heaven it's over. I've been dreading this case for weeks. I knew it would be a battle—and it *was*. Fortunately the nurse was a capable sort of creature."

"Nurse Winterton, wasn't it?"

"Yes," said Kit. "She's extremely capable. I was just thinking that it mightn't be a bad plan to engage her for. . . ."

Dr. Peabody waited, and then he looked up. "For whom?" he enquired.

"Oh, just for any case . . . any case we were anxious about or . . . particularly interested in," replied Kit with elaborate carelessness.

"Quite," said Dr. Peabody. "Oh, quite. You weren't thinking of any one in particular?"

"She'll have to remain where she is for a couple of months," said Kit, changing the subject. "She won't be available . . . I mean Mrs. Faulkner was pretty bad. I was scared to death in the middle and tried to get hold of you . . . they said you were out."

"Yes, it was Mrs. Wilmot," explained Dr. Peabody, smiling. "It's a funny thing, Kit, but troubles never come singly and babies have the same propensity . . . I've noticed it time and again in my own practice. Sometimes I don't have a confinement case for months, and then I have a run of them. It was a perfect nightmare when I was working alone . . . but what's all this about Jem?"

"All this about Jem?" exclaimed Kit in surprise.

"Ethel says these games of his must be stopped. What's your opinion?"

"You can't stop him," cried Kit, who had suddenly remembered all that had happened. "You mustn't try to stop him; it would be the height of folly to interfere. These games of his are the natural expression of the child's mind. If you try to stifle this, if you stop up this safety valve, I shouldn't like to answer for the consequences. Jem is the imaginative type, he—"

"All right, all right," cried Dr. Peabody, waving his hand, "don't excite yourself about it. I only wanted to know what you thought. My opinion coincides with yours in every particular and I've told Ethel to leave him alone." He sighed and added, "I wish *she* would leave him alone; she doesn't understand him. . . ."

"And he's so easy to understand," Kit interpolated softly.

". . . it's a constant battle between us," continued the old man. "It's 'Pull devil, pull baker' from morning to night, and the child suffers."

"But it doesn't seem to do him any harm. He's very good and sweet and reasonable," Kit pointed out. "If it were going to harm him it would have shown its effects before now. Jem's all right, sir."

"I see you've given the subject careful consideration," said Dr. Peabody smiling. "You've sized us all up: the doting grandfather, and the stern aunt?"

"Yes," agreed Kit. "And, most important of all, the intelligent and peculiarly perspicacious child. Jem understands life. He understands people. It would be very bad for Jem if he didn't understand what was going on, and was bewildered and perplexed at the different ways he was treated, but Jem understands the situation and accepts it philosophically. . . . You know," said Kit thoughtfully, as he leaned back in his chair and crossed his legs, "you know, sir, I don't believe in keeping children wrapped in cotton wool. They've got to go out into the world, later, and meet all sorts of people. It's just as well to start their education in the vagaries of human nature when they're young."

Dr. Peabody was amused at the grandfatherly air of his

young assistant, but he saw that there might be a good deal of truth in his words. He reflected that Ethel was certainly a study in complex psychology but he did not say so. After a short pause he rose and knocked out his pipe; it was the signal that he was ready for bed.

They went up the stairs together and parted on the landing.

"Good night, Kit," Dr. Peabody said, "I'll just have a look at Jem—"

"Good night, sir," replied Kit, and he walked along the passage to his own room. He opened the door and was about to put on the light when he heard the old doctor hastening after him.

"Kit, the child isn't there . . . he isn't in bed!"

"Not in bed!" exclaimed Kit.

"What can have happened to him? Where can he have gone?" cried the old man in distress.

By this time they were both just inside the door of Kit's room and he switched on the light. His eyes took in the room at a glance and suddenly he became aware that there was a small hump in the bed. . . .

"Look!" he cried, taking hold of the doctor's arm and pointing.

They went forward together and saw that the small hump was indeed the truant. He was curled up very comfortably in the big bed, and was fast asleep: one arm, in a pink pyjama sleeve, was lying outside the coverlet, and the other was tucked beneath his cheek. He looked pale and fragile and angelic; his brown eyelashes were spread out upon his cheeks and his mouth was curved in a little smile as though he were dreaming of paradise.

"The young rogue!" exclaimed his grandfather, "the young villain! Great heavens, what a fright I got!"

"Don't wake him," Kit whispered.

They bent over him and looked at him, and he was so young

and sweet and so pathetic in his helplessness that both their hearts were stirred with tenderness.

"His face is thinner . . . and pale," said Dr. Peabody at last in a low voice. "He's—he's quite *well,* Kit, isn't he?"

"It's the heat," replied Kit in the same low tone. "It has been very stuffy lately. You wouldn't think of letting him go to Scotland with Dolly and Mardie?"

"Go to Scotland!"

"They would like to take him, I know. Mardie suggested it the other day, but Dolly thought you would miss him."

"Of course I should miss him, but that doesn't mean I wouldn't let him go. I think it's a good plan," said Dr. Peabody thoughtfully. "I think it's a very good plan indeed . . . for various reasons. When do they actually leave?"

"Next week . . . on the first of August."

"Fix it up," said the doctor in a decisive tone. "Speak to Jem about it and see what he wants to do. He could go for three weeks or a month. It would do him a world of good."

There was a little pause and then Dr. Peabody sighed. "Well," he said, "well, we'd better carry him back to his own bed."

"No, it would wake him," Kit said quietly. "Just leave him where he is; there's plenty of room."

Kit undressed and crept into bed. He noticed that Jem was lying well over to one side, and he smiled to himself as he clicked out the light. Jem was a thoughtful person, and very considerate of others. It was rather pleasant to have Jem there, and to feel the gentle warmth which emanated from the small body. It was also pleasant to know that Jem had felt the need of his companionship . . . had wanted him and trusted him. The child had been unhappy and had come to him for comfort . . . that was a very pleasant thought. He understood Jem so well. They were friends. He valued Jem's friendship. He would never fail Jem. . . .

Kit had been sleeping very badly, lying awake for hours and worrying over his problem, trying to find a way out for himself and Mardie, but tonight he slept like a top and did not wake until the morning sun was streaming in at the window.

"I didn't wake you," said a small voice close to Kit's ear. "I didn't, honestly. You woke all by yourself."

"I know," said Kit sleepily.

"I lay as still as still," the voice continued. "I thought about all sorts of things . . . about all sorts of new games to play."

"Did you?"

"Yes. I say Kit, do you think . . ." (the voice was suddenly a very anxious voice) "do you think Grandfather will say I'm not to play my games any more?"

"No," said Kit, stretching himself and smiling up at the small face which was bending over him. "No, Grandfather isn't going to stop you. It's perfectly all right."

"Good," said Jem with a sigh of relief. "Oh goody, goody, good. I don't believe I *could* have stopped, somehow."

"No, I don't believe you could," agreed Kit.

There was silence for a few moments.

"Shall I tell you about the new games I've thought of?" enquired Jem at last.

"Yes."

"Shall I really tell you? Are you in a listeny sort of mood? . . . I mean you aren't tired, are you? It isn't really *very* early."

"Go ahead," said Kit.

"I'm going to play Grandfather," began Jem, snuggling down happily and comfortably against Kit's back. "I'm going to be Grandfather starting off in the morning and he forgets to take his case . . . you know how forgettish he is, Kit?"

"Yes."

"Well then, he goes to see a patient with a murmur in their heart and he—"

"How do you know about people having murmurs in their hearts?" enquired Kit in amazement.

"I've known about it for years," replied Jem reproachfully. "Years and years and years. What does it mean exactly?"

"It means that their heart doesn't beat in quite the same way as other people's hearts," said Kit, who always answered Jem's questions to the best of his ability.

"Yes, but how?"

There was a little silence.

"Is it another 'when-you're-older'?" asked Jem.

"Yes, I'm afraid it is."

"Oh bother! . . . Well, I'll go on about my game . . . well, Grandfather wants to listen to the murmur in this patient's heart, you see, and of course he can't because he's forgotten his case with his steffy-scope, you see. . . ."

Kit lay back and listened with half an ear and thought about Mardie. She was leaving Minfield next week so there were only five more days when he would be able to see her and after that he would not see her for months. He would not even be able to look at the house—the white house with its red gables shining amongst the trees—and think that she was there. Kit did not know how he was going to bear it.

CHAPTER XXVII

GOOD-BYE

IT WAS arranged that Jem should go to Kilnocky with Mrs. Rochester and his aunt. He was wildly excited at the prospect. The only person who was displeased with the arrangement was Miss Peabody (and this was strange, considering the fact that she was forever complaining about the trouble Jem caused in the house). First she declared that Dolly would not look after him properly, that she would allow him to get overheated, or would forget to send him to bed at the right hour, and, when these objections were countered, she raised a further objection and declared that Jem had no clothes.

"You can buy him some," said Dr. Peabody.

"There isn't time," his daughter replied.

Mardie Rochester happened to be present, for she had called in at the doctor's house to see Ethel and find out from her what Jem liked to eat, and other important matters connected with his welfare. She had listened to the argument between Jem's grandfather and Jem's aunt with some anxiety, for she wanted Jem. She wanted to take Jem with her to Kilnocky, and give him a good time.

"But he doesn't need clothes," declared Mardie with conviction. "He won't need anything except a jersey and a pair of shorts. Kilnocky is in the country, it's in the wilds. He'll just run about on the hills all day long and get as brown as a berry."

"You can't let him go out by himself!" exclaimed Ethel in horrified tones.

"Why not?"

"He might fall over a precipice . . . or into a bog . . . and . . . and aren't there wolves in—"

A burst of laughter from her companions cut short the category of dangers which Ethel Peabody was compiling. She blushed to the roots of her hair and glared at the floor. "Well, how was I to know that there aren't wolves?" she enquired angrily. "You said the place was in the wilds. . . ."

"I'm sorry," said Mardie, "I couldn't help laughing, really . . . it isn't as wild as all that, and I promise to take good care of Jem."

The night before the expedition was due to start for the wilds of Scotland Kit went over to the Lynchet to say goodbye. The house was all topsy-turvy for the furniture was being removed into storage, but he found the two girls sitting on the verandah on a couple of wicker chairs, and after the usual greetings he sat down near them on the steps. For a little while they talked of impersonal matters, and Mardie spoke of her cottage at Kilnocky and of her pleasure at the prospect of having Dolly and Jem to stay with her there, and Dolly remarked that she had never been to Scotland and was looking forward to it immensely. It was the sort of conversation which often takes place before the parting of good friends, when there is so much to say and nobody says it, when the surface is smooth and light and the undercurrent is painful. It was dark on the verandah and the three figures were barely visible to each other's eyes. The quiet voices seemed part of the quietness and stillness of the sleeping garden.

"Father will miss Jem," said Dolly at last with a little sigh.

"He's going away for a holiday himself," replied Kit. "I meant to tell you that piece of news. He's going to Wales to stay with an old friend and have some fishing and I've managed to persuade him to take a fortnight."

"Marvellous!" declared Dolly. "Father hasn't taken a holiday in the memory of man—or perhaps I should say in the memory of woman for of course I mean that I never remember his taking one. How did you persuade him, Kit . . . and oh, Kit," she added, before he had time to reply, "oh, goodness gracious, Kit, you'll be left alone with Ethel! How lovely for you!"

"I don't think I shall have that pleasure," said Kit, smiling a little under cover of the darkness, "I believe Miss Peabody has arranged to go and stay with Miss Sinclair—"

"She's afraid you'll take advantage of her," Dolly declared. "She's afraid of being deflowered."

"Really Dolly!" exclaimed Mardie.

Dolly giggled mischievously. "It's true," she said. "Ethel is that sort of person. She labours under the delusion that every man she meets is a Lothario in disguise and is only awaiting a favourable opportunity to tamper with her virtue . . . but I've never been able to make out whether her attitude is one of hope or fear."

Kit chuckled involuntarily—Dolly was a little devil. He reflected that Ethel Peabody had little to fear from him, or to hope for, either.

"Well, my children," continued Dolly's voice. "Well, my dear children, I must now leave you and go to bed . . . I've been working like a slave all day, and I've got a long journey before me. . . ." Her chair creaked as she moved and Kit felt her hand on his shoulder, patting it, "Good-bye Kit," she said softly.

He took the hand, and turning his head, he kissed the fingertips. "Good-bye, little Dolly," he replied, "take care of yourself, won't you? Don't do anything . . . silly."

"Mardie knows. Mardie will take care of me," she said, "and I'll take care of her—for you."

The last two words were murmured very softly in his ear, and the next moment—with a little whisper of her frock and a little clatter of her heels upon the tiled floor—Dolly had gone.

There was silence after that, and Kit heard the "cheep cheep" of a sleepy bird in the garden, and the gentle rustle of air in the heavy foliage of the trees. He knew that Dolly had left them so that he could have Mardie to himself to say good-bye,

(Dolly had guessed . . . Dolly was on his side) but he had decided not to speak to Mardie yet. He had decided to give her time. Should he speak to her now and tell her what was in his heart . . . or should he wait?

Mardie's chair creaked. "Kit," she said, "Kit, I wanted to talk to you—I think Dolly knew—I wanted to thank you for all your goodness to me, Kit. . . ."

"Oh, Mardie, but—"

". . . but Kit, I don't want you to—to go on thinking about me and being sorry for me."

"Mardie, don't you see—"

"Please, Kit, I want to say this, and it's so difficult to say. I've thought about it such a lot, and I must say it. I don't want you to be tangled up in my troubles."

He burst out, "Mardie, darling, I—"

"No," she cried, "no, Kit. This was what I wanted to avoid. I wanted to make you understand. Oh Kit, you must try to understand what I mean."

"But you must try to understand, too."

"Perhaps I do," she said very softly. "Perhaps I do understand, but it isn't any good, Kit. You can't help me—nobody can. I must just go on alone . . . and wait."

"Wait for what?" he asked in a voice that trembled a little.

"For Jack to come back," she replied in a low tone.

Kit was afraid to say any more, for there was so much he wanted to say. His whole mind and heart and soul were bursting with all he wanted to say to Mardie. He wanted to tell her that Jack would never come back, and that even if he did come back she could not accept him and take him back into her life on the old terms. He wanted to tell her that Jack had deserted her basely and meanly and had forfeited all right to consideration or respect. Last but not least he wanted to tell her that he loved her, and would wait for her all his life, or die for her if need be.

There was a long silence between them, a silence that vibrated with all the things which were left unsaid, and at last Kit rose to go. He took Mardie's hand and held it for a few moments and then turned and went out into the darkness without another word.

Kit was alone in the big old-fashioned house. They had all gone, and were scattered to the different points of the compass. Even the Furnivals had left Minfield and had gone to Cromer for a month's holiday, to complete Gilbert's convalescence by giving him a change of air. Minfield was dull. Minfield was a desert without a single oasis to break the monotony of its arid plain. There was not even enough work to keep Kit occupied; for many of the inhabitants had departed to the seaside or to the moors, and those that remained seemed to be enjoying a prolonged spell of excellent health. Beyond a few chronic cases, and elderly hypochondriacs who required an occasional visit from a medical practitioner to keep them happy, and one or two cases of gastric trouble among children—due to an excess of ice-cream or fruit—Kit had nothing at all in his case-book and therefore nothing at all to occupy his mind. He avoided passing the Lynchet whenever possible for it was horrible to think of other people in that almost sacred house. If he were obliged to pass the gate on his daily round he kept his eyes fixed upon the road so that he should not have the pain of seeing other people's curtains in the windows or other people's cars standing in the drive. He was aware that the house had been sublet to a couple with several children (Henry knew the man in the city; his name was Victor Breeze); but, despite Henry's assurances that they were very nice people, and his advice to call on them at the first opportunity, Kit intended to avoid them like the plague. He *intended* to avoid them, but his intention was frustrated by the direct intervention of Providence in his affairs, for one afternoon when Kit was partaking of a lonely tea in the library, and was trying to beguile his loneliness with a detective novel, a message came through that he was wanted at the Lynchet at once.

"It's an accident," said Tupman, who had taken the message on the phone. "She didn't say what 'ad 'appened but just to come at once. A fine fizz she was in."

Kit gulped down his tea and picked up his bag and ran out to get his car.

The house looked exactly the same from the outside—he could almost imagine that Mardie was there—but the moment the door was opened he saw that the inside of the house was completely different. The carefully chosen and beautifully polished furniture had given place to a shabby and heterogeneous collection of pieces which looked as if they had been bought for use rather than ornament and had been bought at different times without the slightest relation to each other. The delicately coloured rugs had been replaced by worn carpets . . . there was a child's bicycle in the porch, and a perambulator in the hall, and a couple of golf bags and some tennis rackets were piled against the wall in the corner. But it was the atmosphere of the house which had changed the most; the quiet leisurely peacefulness of Mardie's reign had gone and the whole house seemed full of children's voices and the scampering of small feet.

Kit was glad that the house was so different, for he felt it was a different house, and there was something rather pleasant about it in spite of the ugly furniture and shabby carpets. As he stood in the hall and waited for Mrs. Breeze to come, he thought that Henry had been right about these people. He was sure that they were nice.

Mrs. Breeze was an attractive woman, very small and neat with dark brown curls and a pretty complexion.

"Oh, Dr. Stone!" she cried, running lightly down the stairs to meet him, "oh, thank goodness you've come! It's his head,

I think . . . I'm so terribly worried . . . and his arm, of
course . . . but that doesn't matter so much, does it?"

"Possibly not," replied Kit somewhat cautiously, "I can't tell,
of course, until—"

"I'm always so frightened of anything to do with heads,"
declared Mrs. Breeze, her eyes large with distress, "you never
know with heads, do you? Arms are bound to mend in time
even if they are broken."

"Yes, but heads mend, too," said Kit, who was less bewildered
by Mrs. Breeze's peculiar logic because he had encountered so
much peculiar logic in his medical career. "Is it your husband?"
he added enquiringly, in a praiseworthy attempt to get at the
root of the matter without loss of time.

"Oh goodness, no!" cried Mrs. Breeze. "That would be frightful . . . well, of course it's frightful enough as it is . . . but I
mean grown-ups fall so much more *heavily*, don't they? It's
Philip, really . . . I must say he's been very brave, but all the
same he knows perfectly well that he shouldn't have been on
the roof at all—"

"On the roof!" cried Kit in alarm. "You don't mean he fell
off the roof, surely!"

"Yes, he did!" declared Mrs. Breeze. "He was playing on the
tool-shed roof and—"

"Oh, the *tool-shed* roof!"

"Yes, didn't I say that? I'm sorry. I thought you knew."

"How old is he?" enquired Kit, as he followed her up the
stairs.

"Ten," said his mother. "It's a frightful age. They're so reckless at ten and they haven't learned sense. Norman was just
the same when he was ten . . . he had a concussion twice from
falling out of trees . . . and now Philip is starting the same
sort of thing. Do you think Philip has got a concussion, Dr.
Stone?"

This was the sort of foolish question that people asked. They were so anxious to know what was the matter that they wanted a diagnosis before you had seen the patient at all. Fortunately Kit understood their anxiety and sympathised with it, so he was able to make allowances for them.

"We'll soon see what's the matter," he said comfortingly.

"It's such a high roof, and the path is so hard. He may have bumped his head on a stone. If only he had fallen over the *other* side into the flower bed—"

"Most unfortunate," Kit agreed.

"It's a lovely garden for them to play in of course, but—"

"Do they play Indians?" enquired Kit.

She stopped with her hand on the door-handle and looked at him in surprise. "Indians!" she said, "yes, of course they do. All children play Indians . . ." then she opened the bedroom door and they went in.

Philip had incurred a fairly serious concussion and a broken collar bone, and before Kit had finished with his patient (and passed him as perfectly fit to resume his usual holiday activities) he had become quite accustomed to seeing the Lynchet under its new régime. He had also become a friend of the whole family; the children adored him and Mr. and Mrs. Breeze gave him a standing invitation to drop in whenever he felt inclined. Kit made use of this invitation for he was lonely and he was aware that the Breezes, being newcomers, had very few friends in Minfield. They would make friends, of course, for they were the sort of happy-go-lucky people who make friends very easily, but just at the moment they were finding Minfield dull. Mr. Breeze liked a game of tennis when he returned from the city and Kit was quite pleased to oblige. He soon formed a habit of dropping in several times a week for a few hard singles at the Lynchet.

CHAPTER XXVIII

DOLLY'S ADVENTURES

"OH DOLLY—Dolly, look!"

These words roused Dolly from a deep sleep and she awakened to the jolting of the train and the long slow rumble of the iron wheels upon the metals. It took her a few moments to gather her thoughts for she had been dreaming about Ralph . . . she was with Ralph at Malta, sitting on a white shiny beach looking out over the blue, blue waters of the Mediterranean . . . then she saw Mardie leaning out of the window and everything came back to her in a flash. She remembered the rush of packing, the early start from the Lynchet; she remembered calling for Jem at the doctor's house, and then the bustle and confusion of the big station and the peaceful feeling which had come to her as the train slid quietly away from the platform, bearing her into the unknown. Dolly had been very tired for she had insisted on helping Mardie, and had run about the house doing a hundred and one small jobs for her friend, but today in the train she had slept peacefully most of the way and she was rested and refreshed. Jem had slept too, for the rumble of the train had lulled him, and Mardie had wrapped a rug round his small body with gentle hands and had sat back in her corner and watched the fields and meadows and towns and villages whirl by. At first her thoughts had been sad, but, as the well remembered landmarks appeared and flashed past, she began to feel a rising excitement, and at last, when the train left the lower levels and began to ascend Beattock, she could contain herself no longer.

"Oh Dolly—Dolly, look!"

Mardie was leaning far out of the window with a wrapt ex-

229

pression upon her face, and a cool wine-like air was blowing in from the wide uplands rustling the papers which were lying upon the seat.

"What is it?" enquired Dolly sleepily.

"Look . . . my hills . . . how wide and free and still they are! Oh, Dolly, I can breathe now. Why didn't I come home before? Listen, Dolly, do you hear that? It was a whaup—a curlew—yes, there it is again. Oh Dolly, why did I stay away so long?"

Dolly looked at her in surprise for she had never seen Mardie in this sort of mood, and there did not seem to be much to account for her excitement. She looked out of the window and saw bleak hills covered with yellowish green grass, and a few patches of heather. (The heather was not yet at its best and Dolly was a little disappointed for she had expected to see mountains covered with purple, like the robes of an Emperor.) Here and there a stone dyke climbed laboriously to the shoulder of a hill and disappeared. Here and there on the lower slopes there were forests of dark conifers. The sides of the hills were scored with little streams, brown and flecked with foam. A soft drizzle was falling, and upon the rounded top of one of the higher hills a cloud rested, soft and nebulous as a baby's breath.

"The air is certainly very bracing," said Dolly, trying to make her voice sound as appreciative as she could, and she added, as she pulled her coat more closely round her, "it's awfully cold, Mardie, don't get a chill leaning out like that . . . and your hat is getting wet."

Mardie laughed ringingly, and there was an unwonted brightness in her eyes as she turned to look at her shivering companion. "My poor Dolly!" she exclaimed, "you'll have to forgive me. The air has gone to my head. I was forgetting that you can't be expected to love these bleak hills as I do."

Dolly looked again, and tried to capture a little of her

friend's enthusiasm. "They are very wild, and very lonely," she said, "and somehow they look as if they hadn't changed much in the last thousand years. I thought they would be higher and rockier and—and grander."

"The craggy sort of mountains are farther north," Mardie told her. "Perhaps they *are* grander and more spectacular, but there's something very fine about these rounded hills when you get to know them. You should see them in the depths of winter, all black and white, deserted by man and beast, so deep in untrodden snow that nearly every landmark has vanished and even the shepherds who know them well are chary of crossing them. The wind blows, and piles the snow into deep drifts— Oh Dolly," she cried, interrupting herself suddenly, "look at that little farm upon the hillside with its whitewashed walls and grey slated roof. That little farm-house is typical of the country."

Dolly looked and saw the tiny house cowering amongst a few stunted trees with desolation on every side. "How terribly lonely," she said, with a little shudder. "What on earth do they do with themselves all winter? I suppose they're completely cut off from the outside world."

"Oh, they read, and play cards and they have plenty of work to do, looking after the sheep and rescuing them from drifts. Look, there are some sheep on the shoulder of the hill! Can you see their dear funny black faces?"

"How small they are!" exclaimed Dolly, "not big and clumsy like English sheep. I suppose they have to be nimble if they live on hills like that . . . and there's a shepherd with his collie!"

They had reached the summit by now and they stopped for a few moments while a man came along to test the wheels. Mardie spoke to him out of the window and there was a queer unfamiliar lilt in her voice.

"Are we running up to time?" she enquired.

"Aye, ye're nae daein' sae bahd," the man replied, consulting a large silver watch. "Ye should be in at the back o' sax."

"What on earth did he say?" Dolly demanded.

Mardie laughed delightedly. "Oh, my dear Dolly, your education has been sadly neglected! You must set about learning the language without delay!"

"But what *did* he say?" enquired Jem who had been awakened by the stopping of the train and had awakened, as all children do, in full possession of his faculties. "I don't mind much if we *are* late," he added, "I like travelling in a train."

Hillside House was situated on the side of a hill about half a mile from the village of Kilnocky. It was little more than a cottage in size but there was a certain dignity about it which seemed to give it the right to the more important designation. It was over a hundred years old and was made of solid grey stone and dowered with diamond paned windows and a slated roof. The garden consisted of an acre of steeply sloping ground and was, for the most part, in a wild uncultivated state; there were fir trees and heather and a small burn which leapt blithely from rock to rock and incidentally supplied the house with water. There was little attempt at flower cultivation (for Mrs. Colquhoun was a matter-of-fact sort of person) but a small rectangular plot was planted with vegetables and potatoes in neat rows. A path wound up to the house between the fir trees and it was scored and rutted by torrents of winter rain. At the back of the house the hill became even steeper and more rocky and Mardie's garden merged imperceptibly into the true wildness of the moor. The house stood high, and the view from its windows was wide and free. It looked across the valley, where the little village lay, towards woods of pine and larch, and, beyond that, rolled more hills in ever ascending height to the horizon.

In spite of the wheel-tester's optimism the north-bound train was late and it was dark when Mardie and her two guests drove up to the gate of Hillside House. So dark that Dolly could see nothing of the hills and trees and was glad to cling to Mardie's arm as she stumbled up the rough path. The door was open and a gleam of mellow light streamed out to meet the travellers, and in the doorway a big motherly looking woman was awaiting them, her face one large smile of welcome.

"Eh, Miss Mardie!" she cried, as she hugged the slight figure of her mistress, "I should be saying Mrs. Rochester but the other comes more easy to my tongue . . . you're no a day older! Nay, let your old Hoony look at ye," she continued, holding Mardie at arms' length for a moment while she studied the tired face with loving solicitude, "aye, you're a bit peaky-looking now that I see ye in the light, but no sae bad as I expected after all these years in England. Aye, it does me good . . . you're a sight for sair e'en, that ye are, Miss Mardie!"

Mardie was very touched. "Dear Hoony!" she said, patting the old woman's arm, "what a nice welcome!"

"It's been waiting on ye these three years," Mrs. Colquhoun replied. "You'll aye get a warm greeting in your ain hoose so long as old Hoony is alive tae give it ye."

So saying Mrs. Colquhoun led the way into the little sitting-room where a bright fire was burning and the table was laid for supper. The room was quite a good size, and because of the thickness of the old walls each little window was set in an alcove and in every alcove there was a brown pottery bowl full of cottage-garden flowers.

"How pretty the flowers are!" Dolly exclaimed.

"They're naught but rubbish," declared the old woman, smiling with delight to find her efforts appreciated, "and a fine mess they make too, with petals falling off and staining everything."

"This is my friend, Mrs. Dorman," Mardie said, "and this is Jem . . . I told you about them in my letter, didn't I?"

"Ye did so, and I'm real glad tae see any freends o' yours," declared Mrs. Colquhoun in cordial tones, and she wiped her hand on her apron—quite unnecessarily—and shook hands with them both.

Dolly looked at the old woman with a good deal of interest for she had never seen anyone quite like her before. She was tall and big-boned with large well-shaped hands coarsened by a lifetime of hard work. Her skin was a trifle sallow and she had brown eyes and high cheekbones. Her hair was dark with a few threads of white amongst it, and it was drawn back smoothly from her forehead and ears into a large plaited "bun". But the chief thing that struck Dolly about her was her well-shaped head; it was set well back upon her shoulders and was carried with a proud air, as if she had weathered many storms in this cold bleak northern land to which she was bred.

"The supper's ready," declared Mrs. Colquhoun. "The wee laddie will be fair famished, I doot. His bed's all ready for him when he's ready for it. . . . Now, bide a wee till I tell John Anderson which rooms tae put the kists . . . and I'll fetch the broth in from the kitchen. I made some broth. Ye were aye fond of broth, Miss Mardie."

"You haven't forgotten," Mardie said smiling.

"Forgotten!" cried the old woman reproachfully, and then she added, "you'll no have got broth in England, I'm thinking!"

The tone of her voice indicated her opinion of the last mentioned country, and Mardie smiled at Dolly as she bustled away.

"You mustn't mind, Dolly. She's such a good, kind creature and I do want you to like her."

"But I like her already," Dolly declared. "She's so—so different from anyone else. I like the way she talks to you. She's friendly, but not a bit disrespectful."

"Scottish servants are like that," Mardie told her. "You can allow them more latitude because they know just how far to go. Hoony's type is dying out now, I'm afraid."

"Why d'you call her Hoony?" enquired Jem, who had sat down at the table and begun to eat some bread.

"I called her Hoony when I was a child," Mardie replied. "It's short for Mrs. Colquhoun, and I'm sure she would be quite pleased if you called her Hoony, too."

"I shall ask her," Jem declared, "it's a nice name."

Mrs. Colquhoun brought in the broth and put it on the table. "There it's," she said, "now set to work and finish it up . . . maybe you'll want a wee pick of pepper in it. I spared the pepper for the laddie's sake."

"It's lovely," Dolly said.

"Ye wouldn't get broth like yon in England?"

Dolly shook her head and declared that she had never tasted anything so good before.

"Och well!" said the old woman dryly, "England's a guid enough place for them that likes it," and she went away.

"I expect you'll find it all very strange at first," said Mardie, somewhat apologetically.

"Oh, it is," agreed Dolly, "but that's part of the fun. It's like a foreign country . . . the air, the whole atmosphere is strange . . . I had no idea it would be so different. And how funnily they speak! Mrs. Colquhoun is easy enough to understand, but the man who drove us here in the taxi from the station was completely unintelligible—I suppose he was speaking Gaelic, was he?"

Mardie smiled, "No, indeed he was not, nobody in this part of the country speaks Gaelic. You'll be asking next why he wasn't wearing a kilt!"

Dolly wondered why that should be considered a foolish question, for she had always imagined that the kilt was the national costume of the Scot. She hid her ignorance rather skilfully by remarking, "It would be rather an uncomfortable garment for driving a taxi," and joined in the laughter at her own expense.

CHAPTER XXIX

MORE ADVENTURES AT KILNOCKY

MARDIE was nearly ready for bed, she had been in to look at Jem and had tucked him up securely for the night, and she saw Dolly off to bed and said good night to her, and then she had dawdled a little and unpacked her things and stowed them away in the capacious drawers of the big armoire which had stood in the night nursery of her old home. It was pleasant to be back here again and to be surrounded with her own things—furniture and carpets and pictures which she remembered from her infancy. I shall live here *always,* she thought, and if Jack comes back perhaps he will settle down here. . . .

Suddenly there was a loud knock at the door of her room, loud and startling in the stillness of the night, and Mardie's heart began to beat unevenly.

"Who's there?" she asked.

"It's just me," was the reply, and although the words were not informative Mardie recognised the voice at once.

"Come in, Hoony, what a fright you gave me!" she said.

The door opened and Mrs. Colquhoun appeared, attired in a crimson flannel dressing-gown with her long hair in two plaits, "I couldna' rest," she announced, "ma bed was a torment to me, and I just said tae masel'—wumman go and tell her and get it off yer chest."

"Come and sit down," said Mardie kindly. "Come and tell me about it, Hoony. What's the matter?"

"It's wee Wattie, that's all," she replied and she said the words in a final tone as if they contained the full and complete explanation of her trouble.

"Who is wee Wattie?" Mardie enquired.

"Och, just a bairn—imphm—no any different tae any other bairn."

"But why are you troubled about him? Is he ill or—or anything?"

"He's no ill, he's a well-set-up bairn, and I dinna' find him any trouble at all. But if he's tae be a trouble he maun be sent away . . . only where will I send him? Ye see, Miss Mardie, his mither's deid."

Light was beginning to dawn upon Mardie. "I see," she said. "You've got the child here. Well I'm sure he won't be any bother to us. Is he your sister's child?"

"Land sakes, Miss Mardie, how would he be that, with Lizzie in her grave these twelve years and the bairn not nine? Na, na, Wattie's a kind o' cousin tae me . . . just a kind o' cousin."

"Well, you mustn't think of sending him away. He can play with Jem—it will be nice for Jem to have another child to play with—"

"It's good of ye," Hoony declared, "but you've tae say if he troubles ye, Miss Mardie. He's like other bairns, ye ken, whiles he's good and whiles he's bad. I'm right glad I've told ye," she added, gathering her dressing-gown round her and preparing to depart. "I'll win tae sleep noo, with wee Wattie off ma chest."

Mardie awoke next morning to the twittering of birds. The sun was shining brightly. She got up at once and leaned out of the open window drinking in the keen sweet air which blew off the hills.

"It smells of freedom," Mardie thought, and was amused to find she had said the words aloud.

The sky was a pale bright blue—very clean and newly-washed by the previous day's rain—and a few fleecy white clouds scampered across it in obedience to the steady hill breeze.

Breakfast was in the sitting-room, for there was no dining-

room in the little house. It was a most attractive meal—porridge
and cream and grilled trout fresh from the loch, and scones
and bannocks of various kinds—Mrs. Colquhoun was an excellent cook and had put her best foot forward partly for Mardie's
benefit and partly to impress the visitors from England. The
sun shone in through the diamond-paned windows and everything in the room glittered with polished cleanliness, even the
china dogs on the mantelpiece seemed to wink their red eyes
as the sunbeams fell upon them.

"I love this little house," declared Jem, as he handed in his
plate for a second helping of trout. "I love everything about
it, don't you, Aunt Dolly? Don't you think it's sort of cosy, and
happy. I think this little house is happy in its own self—that's
what I think."

"There's another little boy in this house," said Mardie smiling at her younger guest, "perhaps you'd like to play with him."

"Perhaps," said Jem doubtfully.

"Who is he?" asked Dolly with interest.

Mardie told the story of Mrs. Colquhoun's midnight visit
with a good deal of humour, and they laughed heartily over it.

"When are we to see Wattie?" Dolly enquired.

"As soon as Wattie can escape from Hoony's custody, I expect," Mardie replied smiling.

Presently Hoony appeared at the door and surveyed them
with an indulgent smile. For a moment or two she did not
speak, and then she threw her head back and crossed her big
arms on her breast and began.

"There's some folks that never kens when they're not
wanted. . . ." she declared.

(Dolly felt quite alarmed and wondered whether it was herself and Jem to whom the old woman was referring; she
glanced at Mardie and was relieved to find that Mardie was
regarding Hoony with a twinkle in her eyes.)

"Aye," continued the old woman, "there's some folks that

would push their ways in where angels fear to tread—though the twa Miss Johnstones are unco queer angels. Mind you I've nothing against the puir critters, but they dinna ken their place to come wamblin' roond to disturb their betters at this untimely 'oor. Could they not bide in peace till a body had time to red up the breakfast before 'payin' their respects'—whatever that might mean."

"Well, seeing that they are here," said Mardie quite gravely, "seeing that they've come all this way I think you had better ask them in."

"I will, that," declared Hoony, and she bustled away as if there was no time to be lost.

The visitors had been left to wait on the doorstep, and Hoony could now be heard inviting them to come in, but not without pointed remarks anent the inconvenient hour which they had chosen for their call.

"Who are they?" Dolly whispered, but Mardie had no time to reply, for the door was thrown open and the ladies were ushered in. Bereft of their escort in the doorway, they halted, a little dazzled by the bright sunshine which filled the room and a little doubtful as to whether, after all, they had been right to come so soon.

Mardie did her best to put them at their ease, and replied to their duet of apologies and explanations by assuring them that it was very neighbourly of them to call. Meanwhile Dolly watched these guests with interest and amusement. She found herself quite unable to place them (in the social sense of the word) for although their clothes were odd to the point of lunacy there was a natural dignity about them. She soon discovered that there was a pathetic side to the Misses Johnstone as well as a ridiculous side, for they were neither fish nor flesh, and life had passed them by leaving them stranded on the desert island of advanced middle age with no friends and few memories and nothing save the meagre solace of their mediocre accomplishments to while away their time. The thin Miss Johnstone was younger than her sister; she wore a muslin blouse, open at the neck, and a grey tweed skirt, and her hat was made of blue silk and trimmed with pink rose-buds. She also wore an air of youthful innocence which contrasted strangely with her elderly face. It was this artificial youthfulness which made the younger Miss Johnstone a pathetic figure in Dolly's eyes, for it *was* pathetic that any woman should have so little in life that she was forced to cling to her youth long after it had vanished. The elder Miss Johnstone had accepted the inevitable and was round and rosy and placid. She wore a wide skirt, which swept the floor, and a tight woollen coat, a most unbecoming garment for a woman of such a pronounced figure. She was under the thumb of her young and innocent sister.

"Kitty said to me we really must go and see Mrs. Rochester," she announced, when the introductions were over and they were all comfortably seated.

"You mean you said that to me," Kitty reminded her archly.

"Of course I did!" the elder lady cried, becoming more rosy than before, "how stupid of me!"

"And I said, 'But Mrs. Rochester won't want to see us'," declared Kitty, with a little simper.

"Yes," agreed Miss Johnstone, slightly out of her depth and obviously afraid of blundering further. "Yes, Kitty said—said that, and I said I was sure you would want to see us," she concluded, her face all smiles again at having found this heavensent inspiration.

"Of course . . . I'm delighted," murmured Mardie.

"We are all so pleased to see you back at Kilnocky," continued Miss Johnstone, smiling a really lovable and friendly smile. "We are so pleased to have you, even though you're not in your rightful place."

"But the Hall isn't my rightful place any more," said Mardie, shaking her head.

"We think it is . . . Kilnocky thinks it is," replied Miss Johnstone earnestly. "The new people are all very well in their way, quite kind and nice, you know, but it's very difficult to accept new people at Kilnocky Hall. . . . And by the way I hope you will both come to the Village Dance, it's on the first of September."

"That's very kind," Mardie said. "I'm sure we'd love to, wouldn't we, Dolly?"

Dolly agreed that it would be delightful.

"They'll all be so pleased," Miss Johnstone said.

"They like us to go to it," added Miss Kitty, "and they like us to wear our prettiest frocks . . . it's rather pathetic, really."

"You'll see them dancing reels," said Miss Johnstone to Dolly.

It was obvious that the Village Dance was an important event in the uneventful lives of the Misses Johnstone, and Dolly thought that they themselves were a good deal more "pathetic" than the villagers. They talked about the dance for a little and then Miss Johnstone turned once more to her hostess.

"I fear you will find many sad changes," she declared, "but the village people are much the same, except of course that they are a wee bit older."

"We all are," declared Mardie, who felt that she had aged considerably in three years.

"Oh no!" cried Miss Kitty in distress. "You look just the same and I am sure you will agree that the village people grow older far more quickly than we do. They have not the same interests, have they? So they are bound to grow old and dull—"

"You must come and see Kitty's book of poems," said her sister proudly, "so full of charming thoughts about birds and flowers. I don't know how she thinks of all the beautiful ideas."

"And you must hear Mary play the harp," put in Miss Kitty eagerly.

Mardie and Dolly accepted the invitation politely, but were able to avoid fixing a date.

"We have so much to do, you see," declared Mardie vaguely.

"And how is Mr. Rochester?" Miss Johnstone enquired. "Will he be coming to Kilnocky soon?"

Mardie had been expecting this question so she was ready with her answer. "Jack has gone away for a long holiday," she said. "He wasn't very well. He had been overworking, and the doctor said he needed a complete change."

Each of these statements was perfectly true in itself, but together they were really a lie and Mardie hated deceit in any form. She would much rather have told the truth but it would not be fair to Jack—everybody in Kilnocky would hear whatever was told to the Misses Johnstone, they would report the whole conversation with faithful accuracy.

"Has he gone on a cruise?" enquired Miss Kitty eagerly.

"My husband is away, too," declared Dolly, smiling at the visitors in a friendly manner. "That's why I'm here with Mardie—we're keeping each other company, you see. My husband is a sailor and his ship is at Malta just now. It's the *Terrible* you know, one of our biggest cruisers. Ralph is a Lieutenant-Commander and he's hoping for promotion in the next list. I shall be going out to Malta to join him later on—perhaps in October."

The ladies received this spate of information politely, but without real interest for it was Mrs. Rochester's husband, and not Mrs. Dorman's, whose doings were of importance to Kilnocky. They were about to pursue their enquiries regarding Mr. Rochester's present situation and future plans when Dolly suggested that they might like to see the garden. Mardie heaved a sigh of relief and rose at once—she was aware that Hoony was waiting for an opportunity to clear away the remains of breakfast.

They went out and Jem followed. He had been remarkably quiet during the conversation, but he had not been bored for he had found two new characters to study, characters which would obviously give plenty of scope for his imitative powers.

There was a cold east wind blowing and Dolly was so sorry for Miss Kitty in her muslin blouse that she offered to go and fetch a scarf for her to wear but the offer was refused.

"Oh, thank you so much, but I never wrap up my neck," declared Miss Kitty virtuously.

"Kitty never wraps up her neck," echoed her sister with a complacent air.

It was a legend in the Johnstone family that Kitty "did not feel the cold" and, like many another, the poor lady was a martyr to her reputation.

The four ladies and the small boy walked along the garden path in an uncomfortable silence. Mardie found it difficult to make conversation with her guests and Dolly had even less idea what to say, so they were both pleased when they came across another small boy (clad in a red jersey and grey tweed shorts) who was busily sawing up wood.

"Why, this must be Wattie!" Dolly exclaimed.

"Yes," replied the Misses Johnstone in unison, "it is."

"We must speak to him," said Mardie, making a step forward.

Miss Kitty laid a hand on her hostess' arm. "I suppose you know who he is . . ." she said meaningly.

"Of course," declared Mardie, and she beckoned to the boy to come.

He put down his saw and came forward, a little shyly, and stood looking round the circle of faces as if he were taking them all in.

"You're very busy, Wattie," Mardie said.

"Aye," agreed Wattie, "but if I'm wanted I can leave the wood. She said I could leave it if I was wanted. Are ye wanting me to take him on the hill?"

It was obvious from his eager eyes that he hoped for an

answer in the affirmative. It would be much more amusing to go out on the hill with "him" than to continue his present monotonous job. The boys were eyeing each other now, sizing. each other up and each was wondering what sort of stuff the other was made of.

"There's a cave on the hill," continued Wattie, after a moment's silence, "and I'll show him a wee burn where there's trout."

"I'd like to go with him," Jem declared with conviction.

Mardie looked at Wattie and she liked his face. It was a pleasant open face and the eyes met hers honestly and fearlessly. "You'll have to take good care of him," she said. "He doesn't know the hills. Can I trust you to take care of him and bring him home safely?"

"I'll do that," replied Wattie earnestly. "Aye, ye can trust me."

"Off you go, then."

They were off like the wind, tearing up the hill together, two small lithe figures, one in a red jersey and the other in a green. Mardie watched them, and she saw that red jersey was well ahead, but after a few moments red jersey stopped and waited, and the two went on together at a more reasonable pace.

"It's all right," she said with a sigh of relief.

The Misses Johnstone had watched the proceedings in silence but now Miss Kitty could be silent no longer. "Mrs. Rochester, I wonder at you letting him go with that boy!" she cried. "I'm sure you can't know who he is."

"He's Mrs. Colquhoun's cousin!" Mardie said in surprise.

"Cousin!" cried the Misses Johnstone together, and they looked at each other meaningly.

"It doesn't matter who he is," declared Mardie. "The only thing that matters is whether he will take good care of Jem . . . and I'm sure he will."

"But who is he?" enquired Dolly, when the visitors had gone, and the two friends were sitting together on the sheltered side of the house. "Who is he, Mardie? It's most mysterious, isn't it? Everything here gives me the feeling that I'm living in a fairy tale . . . those two poor funny old ladies . . . and the nice-looking boy of unknown origin . . . perhaps he's a duke in disguise."

Mardie smiled. "I'm afraid it isn't quite so romantic," she replied. "I don't really know who he is but I have my suspicions. I think he's Hoony's grandson . . . illegitimate of course, or she would not have disowned him."

"Tell me about it."

"Hoony was my nurse—you knew that, of course—but before that she was the wife of the Head Gamekeeper. It was when he died that she came to the Hall as nurse to me. She had one small boy and he was sent to board with her sister's children and grew up with them and went to school. Unfortunately he wasn't very satisfactory, he got into bad company and caused Hoony a great deal of trouble and anxiety. It is rather strange when you think of his parentage for his father was a fine man and Hoony is one of the world's elect."

"Then you think that Wattie—"

"Yes, I think he must be," said Mardie, nodding. "I don't know of course, but putting two and two together it seems a possible four. Hoony told me that Wattie's mother was dead and it would be just like her to accept the responsibility of the child."

CHAPTER XXX

LIFE AT KILNOCKY

IT WAS a very peaceful life at Kilnocky, and Dolly soon felt
as if she had been living at Hillside House for years. They fell
quite naturally into a pleasant routine and the days passed like
golden beads threaded upon a string. Jem and Wattie were
out together on the hills from morning to night, and Jem's small
face grew brown and rosy and his legs became firm and hard.
Soon there was no need for Wattie to moderate his pace or to
hold out a helping hand over the rough places. Mardie and
Dolly spent their mornings shopping in the village; they
bought their own bread and meat and vegetables and carried
it all home in a big basket with a double lid. Dolly enjoyed
this thoroughly, for it was fun to play at housekeeping, and a
chop chosen from the side of a sheep in the butcher's shop,
cut off in front of your eyes and carried home by yourself, was
somehow much more interesting than a chop ordered by telephone and appearing before you for the first time in its "ready-
to-eat" condition. There was no telephone in Mardie's little
house, and no gas nor electric light, and somehow or other the
absence of these products of civilization made life more peaceful and restful.

Kilnocky village was a little backwater and retained its
almost feudal atmosphere. The shopkeepers had all known
Mardie Macfarlane as a wild girl, full of fun and spirits, and
they received Mardie Rochester like a wanderer returned from
foreign lands. Among these simple folk Mardie was in her
element; she knew how to speak to them and draw them out,
and it seemed rather strange to Dolly that she could crack a

246

joke with any of them and still retain the dignity which was one of her chief charms. To Dolly these people were invariably polite, and, like the well-bred Frenchman, they never laughed at her "foreign ways" nor at her abysmal ignorance of local customs.

All sorts of queer purchases went into the big "message basket" for Mardie felt obliged to buy something from each of her friends—

"Eh my, Miss Mardie!" Hoony would cry, holding up her hands in horror when the contents of the basket were emptied out onto the kitchen table. "Eh my, what a lot of rubbish! Ye'll ruin yerself buying things ye can never use. What ailed ye to buy a wean's semmit?" she enquired, holding up the despised garment as she spoke.

"Well, you see, Hoony, I felt I had to buy something from poor old Mrs. Walker," replied Mardie apologetically.

"And what will ye dae with it, may I ask?"

"You take it, Hoony."

"Me!" cried Hoony. "What guid will I get out of it?"

"Perhaps it would do for Wattie," suggested Mardie humbly.

"Wattie! It would fit on his great toe! . . . Did ye get the fish for yer dinners?" she continued, burrowing about amongst the parcels which littered the table, in a vain attempt to find the one she required.

"Oh, Hoony, I'm afraid—"

"Imphm, I thought as much . . . well then, will ye take the semmit stewed or boiled?"

At this point Dolly and Mardie both collapsed, and laughed until the tears rolled down their cheeks, and even Hoony's austere features relaxed into a broad smile.

One morning Dolly went shopping by herself, leaving her friend to write some letters. The sun was shining brightly as she walked down the road to the village, and Dolly felt the pleasant warmth on her back and hummed cheerfully under her breath as she went along. By this time she had grown used to the spacious scenery (the wide rolling hills which dwarfed the little village and made it look like a handful of toy houses) and she did not feel as if she herself were dwarfed to the dimensions of a fly on the wall. Dolly's first stop was at the greengrocer's, which was kept by a certain Mrs. Leith. This woman always amused Dolly for she had a face like one of her own turnips, and her little round nose looked as though it had been stuck on as an afterthought without regard to the rest of her features. Her iron grey hair was scraped back so tightly into a small nob at the back of her head that the marks of the comb could be seen in it like cart-tracks in the heather. Mrs. Leith was remarkably agile for her age, and she whisked about her narrow shop like a whirlwind, scattering baskets of parsley and loose pieces of paper in her wake. To help her in the shop Mrs. Leith had a small boy, of a tidy and businesslike nature; he kept the shop tidy and sold the vegetables while Mrs. Leith whisked about and talked. On the morning of Dolly's solitary expedition, however, the small boy was not there and Dolly had to give her order to Mrs. Leith in person, and this was all the more unfortunate because Mrs. Leith had a habit of beginning a conversation in the middle without any preliminary explanations—a somewhat bewildering habit when one was not accustomed to the language and was trying to order vegetables.

"Aye," she began, "it's queer tae think you've never been in Scotland before and I've never been oot of it, and will ye tell Mistress Rochester the neeps is no just as nice, but the tatties are real guid."

"The—the neeps?" asked Dolly.

"Imphm, the neeps . . . but, mind, when I say I've never been oot of Scotland I'm not meaning that I've never been in a boat. It was Jamie Forres took me the day we went to Portobello. Would that be oot of Scotland, eh?"

"I suppose it would," said Dolly to whom the effort of following Mrs. Leith was a decided strain.

"Imphm, I suppose it would," echoed Mrs. Leith. "It would
be the North Sea, ye ken. Aye, and I mind when I was at
school we was learned tae call it the German Ocean—German
Ocean, indeed!" This with inconceivable scorn. "Take partons
noo," she continued. "Do ye like partons, Mistress Dorman?
I'm very partial to them masel', but there's aye a wee lingering
doubt at the back o' my mind as to whether they're wholesome.
It was when I was at Portobello, that I saw what like partons
were in their natural state—imphm—it gave me a kind o' scun-
ner at them. . . ."

Mrs. Leith could, and did, go on by the hour when once she
had started. One subject led to another and each produced an
original thought which she cast before her hearer (as pearls
before swine) without realising the humour of it. But Dolly
had no time to stop and listen—and indeed, owing to her difficulty in following the rapid flow, much of the humour was
lost upon her. She escaped at last and completed her purchases
quickly, for it had been decided to lunch early and go for a
picnic on the moors, and there was therefore no time to waste.
As Dolly came out of the baker's with a large loaf wrapped in
paper under one arm she ran into the Misses Johnstone who
were also shopping, but in a more leisurely and genteel manner
than the heedless Dolly. They had been waiting for her and
were primed with questions which they fired off at Dolly like
two machine guns as they walked along, one on each side of
her, up the High Street:

How long had she known Mrs. Rochester? Had she ever
met Mrs. Rochester's husband? What was he like? What was
the matter with him? Where was he? When was he coming
to Kilnocky? What time did Mrs. Rochester have tea? Did she
have dinner in the evening, or just supper?

These were but a few of the many questions which Dolly

was called upon to answer but they were put to her in such a naïve childish manner that Dolly could not feel they were impertinent. She saw that the poor dears had so little to think of that Mardie's return to Kilnocky was of the greatest moment to them and that they wanted to know everything about her simply because their minds were starved. Dolly smiled to herself and proceeded to feed their minds in a capable and business-like but not altogether truthful manner.

Although their life at Kilnocky was so full of small and amusing incidents it was merely their surface life, and neither Dolly nor Mardie was completely happy and contented. Dolly still yearned for Ralph and wrote and received long letters from him by every mail, and Mardie thought about her troubles and sought vainly for a way out of them. Dolly was aware that Mardie's troubles were a good deal harder to bear than her own, for her troubles were only temporary and after October—when her baby was due to arrive—she would be able to go to Malta and join Ralph. Mardie's troubles were far graver and more complicated.

Dolly had found Mardie sitting in the garden with a letter open in her lap, and an expression of tragic sadness upon her face. Dolly was aware that the letter was from Kit, and she sat down beside her friend without saying a word.

If only—, thought Dolly (and by no means for the first time) if only we could hear that the wretched Jack was dead! . . . Mardie and Kit are just made for each other . . . what is to happen to them!

She knew that Mardie had had several letters from Kit, for Mardie had shown them to her. They were friendly letters without a word in them which could not have been shouted from the housetops, and Mardie (she was pretty sure) had replied in the same friendly tone, but Dolly knew that Kit loved Mardie, she had seen it from the first, and now she was certain that Mardie loved Kit.

Jem talked of Kit unceasingly, for even in his new and tremendously exciting life he had not forgotten his friend. "I wish Kit was here," Jem would remark with a sigh, as he took up his spoon and prepared to eat his porridge. "Kit would like fishing in the burn. He would go with us on the hill. I'd like to show Kit the cave and everything." Or else some subject would crop up at mealtimes and Jem would declare: "If Kit was here he could tell us all about it. Kit can explain things so nicely. You can always understand a thing when Kit explains it." Or perhaps there would be some heavy piece of furniture to be moved, or a window would stick and nobody would be able to open it, and Jem would heave a deep sigh and say, "Of course, if Kit was here—Kit's so strong, you know. You should see the muscles in his arms—" Dolly was very fond of Kit but even she became a little tired of hearing his perfections enumerated and extolled; she noticed, however, that Mardie never tired of this. Mardie encouraged Jem to talk about Kit, and sat and listened to him with rapt attention.

That's how I felt about Ralph, thought Dolly, smiling to herself a little, I could sit and listen by the hour—in fact I did sit and listen for hours and hours when I went and saw his mother and she talked about him. And I could still sit and listen quite happily if only somebody would talk about Ralph. I love him quite as much as ever, if not more.

CHAPTER XXXI

JEM AND WATTIE

THE friendship between Jem and Wattie developed rapidly; the two boys were quite different from each other, of course, for Jem was highly strung and imaginative and Wattie was somewhat stolid and matter-of-fact. Wattie could not take part in the imaginative games which were Jem's chief delight, for he could not understand them, but there were so many new things to see that Jem was contented and satisfied, and his imaginative games were shelved for the time being. At first Wattie's superior strength and his familiarity with local conditions gave him the ascendancy; he could out-distance Jem on the hill, he could guddle for trout in the burn, he knew all the sheep-paths, and knew where the beautiful cool springs were hidden amongst the heather, where pure water gushed out of the ground to slake one's thirst; but Jem was quick to learn, and the quality of leadership, which was dormant in his nature, began to assert itself so that before long the ascendancy passed to Jem, and Wattie was his faithful slave. Neither of the boys was aware that any change took place in their relationship but Mardie and Dolly noticed the change and remarked upon it to each other.

"He admired Wattie tremendously at first," Dolly pointed out, "and did whatever Wattie told him, but now he tells Wattie what to do . . . it's rather queer!"

Mardie smiled. "Jem's a born leader, and Wattie's a born follower. It's just the way they're made, that's all."

"I hope he won't boss Wattie too much," said Dolly anxiously.

"I shouldn't worry. If Jem's hand is too heavy Wattie will rebel, but I think that Wattie enjoys it."

"Jem doesn't play those games of his now."

"I know, and I'm glad of that. It's a good thing for him to have a rest from those games. Kit was a bit worried about it, you know. He thought Jem was overdoing it. As a matter of fact Wattie is extremely good for Jem . . . it's lucky he's here."

"Yes indeed," said Dolly fervently, "Wattie is so solid and sensible that one feels Jem is perfectly safe with him."

The two young women would not have been so easy in their minds if they could have seen Jem and Wattie at that moment. The boys had played on the hill all week but today they had decided that they required a change of scene, and they had crossed the ridge and descended into the valley on the other side of it. The river lay at the bottom of this valley, winding along between high red cliffs and black boulders like a glittering silver snake. The boys ran down to the edge and stood there, looking at it.

Jem was enchanted with the river for he had never been on such close terms with a real river before. There was not a creature in sight, and a few white farmhouses miles way on the hills were the only signs of man.

"It's ours!" cried Jem, waving his hands. "The river belongs to us. Nobody else is looking at it. Nobody else wants it."

"They're not wanting it just now," agreed Wattie cautiously.

Jem began to hop about, for there was something tremendously exciting about the river; there was something positively thrilling about the force with which it dashed itself against the boulders and poured in solid masses from pool to pool.

"It's alive!" cried Jem. "It's alive, Wattie!"

"It's just water," Wattie said, but even as he said it he had a strange feeling that Jem was right and that in some way or other the river was alive.

Jem lay down on the stones at the edge of the river and plunged his thin bare arms into a pool; he scooped up handfuls of water and the drops trickled between his fingers, pleasantly chilly. "Lovely!" sighed Jem, "lovely, lovely river!"

Wattie stood and watched him with a smile, and the smile had appeared upon his face because he felt happy to think that the river—which he had provided, of course—was giving so much satisfaction to Jem. Wattie sought for some means of providing Jem with even more pleasure and satisfaction.

"There's trout in it," said Wattie.

"Big trout?"

"Aye, they'll be—they'll be bigger than the fish in the burn. I doot there's a big one doon by yon black rock . . . aye, there it's!"

"Where?" cried Jem. "Oh Wattie, where is it? Did you see it, Wattie?"

"I saw it take a fly."

"But how? But why? Do they eat flies?"

Wattie sighed for he knew that he would have to explain all about trout and flies to his companion, and he was not good at explaining things. Before Jem had appeared on the scene Wattie had imagined that he knew quite a lot about the fauna and flora of his native land but Jem's searching questions had exposed his ignorance. Wattie knew things vaguely and when he tried to put his knowledge into words he floundered about and contradicted himself, and Jem pursued him and had no mercy upon him.

"I'll show ye the falls," suggested Wattie.

"The falls, what's that?"

"The water falls over the rocks."

"High rocks?"

"Aye. They're a wee bit up the river . . . can ye not hear them, Jem?"

Jem listened, and became aware of a dull roar, and to Wattie's delight he forgot about trout and flies and rose to his feet.

"Go on Wattie. Show me," he said eagerly.

They walked up the bank of the river together and at every step the noise became louder, and presently they rounded a bend and saw the river pouring over the ridge of rocks and falling into a deep foamy pool. The noise was now so loud that conversation was impossible, but Wattie pointed and nodded and began to climb up the rocks. Jem followed him and soon they were standing on the bank at the top of the falls, watching the water swirl round and dash down over the barrier of rocks into the pool. The falls were only about twenty feet high, but they seemed grand to Jem. The spray flew into the air and fell in a little shower full of rainbow light.

"It is alive!" Jem shouted. "It's alive just like a tiger . . . and it roars like a tiger, too," and he drew back from the edge of the river with a little shudder.

"Ye're not scared of it, surely?" Wattie enquired.

"Well, yes," said Jem frankly, "it's so fierce, you see. It makes me feel all wobbly inside . . . fancy if you were in it, Wattie."

"But ye're not in it!"

"I know . . . but if you were. It would bash you on the rocks . . . ugh!"

They watched it for a few minutes and then made their way further up the river and climbed out onto a flat rock. The sun was warm and the rock was warm too; they sat down on it and watched the water flow past. Above them was a pool and Wattie saw several trout boil, but he did not mention the fact to Jem. The river curved round the pool and narrowed again, it swirled in a big brown wave round the base of the rock where the boys were sitting.

"How deep is it?" Jem asked.

Wattie considered the question. He had no idea how deep

it was but he knew that it was much less deep than usual, for there had been very little rain during the last few weeks.

"There's not much water in it," Wattie said.

"Not much water!" cried Jem. "But there's gallons and gallons of water . . . whatever do you mean?"

"Ye should see it in spate when the snaw's melting on the hills. It's fine, then."

"It's fine now," declared Jem, who sometimes borrowed Wattie's expressions and made them his own.

There was a short silence.

"Let's wade," said Wattie suddenly.

"Wade!" exclaimed his companion in horror-stricken tones.

"It would be fine," Wattie declared, "there's a wee shallow bit further up. I'll show ye where—"

"No," said Jem firmly.

"It would be fine," repeated Wattie. "It's shallow and there's sand to walk on, and it's not far. Ye can see the place from here . . . Robbie and me waded there one day. I'll show ye, Jem."

Jem shook his head.

"Ye're not frightened?" enquired Wattie in amazement.

"Yes, I am. I told you I was frightened of it."

"But Jem—"

"It's alive like a tiger, you see. I don't *much* like wading in the burn, because I don't like the way it tries to pull your legs away. . . ."

Wattie gazed at him in consternation, for it is always unpleasant to discover that one's idol has feet of clay. "Ye're frightened!" he exclaimed incredulously. "Ye're frightened of wading in a wee shallow bit of the river!"

"Yes," said Jem. "It's so fierce, you see."

"I'll wade masel', then," Wattie declared. He rose and waited to see if this threat would have any effect, but Jem did not move.

"I'll wade masel'," repeated Wattie.

"All right, I'll wait for you," said Jem.

Wattie turned away. He climbed over the rocks and ran along the bank until he came to the shallows where he had waded before, and, divesting himself of his shoes, he stepped in. It was delightful to feel the cool water on his feet and legs, and the soft sand oozing between his toes, but Wattie did not enjoy it so much as he might have done because he was too upset. He had become very fond of Jem and admired him tremendously so it was a frightful blow to discover that he was a coward. The discovery changed Wattie's feelings completely . . . he felt as if he had lost something. . . .

He's just a silly wee coward, thought Wattie miserably.

Presently Wattie began to get tired of wading in the shallows and ventured deeper into the river. He could see where the current ran and he was careful to keep in the slack water for the river was narrow here and, although it was low, there was enough water in it to make it dangerous for a small boy. He skirted the edge of the current, keeping to a ridge of gravel where the gleaming water was less than knee-deep, and made his way along feeling for his foothold at every step. He was sorry now that he had not brought a stick to feel his way, for a little breeze was ruffling the surface of the slack water and the sunshine on the ripples was blinding.

Wattie could see Jem sitting on the rock and he waved to him and shouted that it was "fine" and Jem waved back but did not move.

Then, quite suddenly, something happened . . . Wattie could never remember exactly what it was; whether he put his foot on a slippery stone, or into an unexpected hole . . . he only knew that one moment he was perfectly confident and secure, wading less than knee-deep in the slack water, and the next moment he was struggling for his life in the full force of the current sweeping down towards the falls. He could swim a little, but swimming was useless in this tremendous swirl of

water . . . it closed over his head, and parted again and he
saw the dazzle of spray in the sunlight. The force of the current was amazing and terrifying; it swept him against a rock
and then plucked him away and bore him onward into the
pool. He struggled wildly and opened his mouth to shout,
and immediately his mouth was filled with water . . . and he
was rolled over and over, and his knees and elbows scraped
along the bottom. The force of the current was not so strong
in the pool where the river made a bend but it was much too
strong for Wattie to gain a foothold or to fight against its
onward rush. . . . It *is* like a tiger, he thought, as he felt it
pressing against him and hurling him along . . . and he remembered the jagged rocks at the falls and the great brown
wave that curled over. . . .

Wattie had almost given up hope now, and had ceased to
struggle, for it took him all his time to keep his head above the
water so that he could breathe. He was swept round the pool
like a straw and swept against a low rock . . . and there he
stuck. The current tugged him away but his jersey had caught
on something—Wattie thought it must have caught on a snag
—and the check gave him renewed hope. He stretched out his
arms and seized hold of the edge of the rock which was half
under water and for a few moments he hung there, suspended
in the water, and the current rushed past, bubbling round his
face and tugging at his legs, trying to pull him away.

"Hang on," said a voice in his ear, "hang on, Wattie. It's all
right . . . I've got hold of your jersey. Dig in your toes and
pull yourself up. Wattie, do you hear? *Pull yourself
up.*"

He obeyed, almost unconsciously, and gave himself a tremendous heave . . . and he felt himself hauled over the sub-
merged rock into slack water.

Wattie rose, and looked around in a dazed manner. He said

nothing, and Jem said nothing either. They were both stupefied by the experience through which they had passed.

Jem waded across to the bank and began to peel off his wet clothes. He was almost as wet as Wattie for he had dashed through the water up to his waist and had wedged himself between two boulders to obtain the necessary purchase to stop Wattie's wild career.

Wattie pulled himself together and followed Jem's example, and in a few moments there were two pairs of grey shorts and two jerseys hanging on a tree to dry and two small naked boys sitting in the sun. By this time Wattie had discovered that except for scraped knees and elbows and a large bump which was rising rapidly on his forehead he was perfectly whole. He was surprised at this, for he had felt sure that every bone in his body must be broken.

So far nothing at all had been said, but now Jem broke the silence. He pointed to their clothes and remarked:

"It's lucky there's a nice wind."

"Aye, they'll not take long tae dry," agreed Wattie.

There was another long silence after that. Wattie had a feeling that there was a good deal to say but he did not know how to begin.

"Ye said ye were frightened of it," he said at last in a bewildered voice.

"I *was* frightened."

"Ye went in all the same."

Jem looked at his companion in surprise. "But there wasn't anything else to *do*. I had to go in because you'd have been over the falls in another minute, wouldn't you?"

"It's a wonder we didn't both go over the falls," declared Wattie, and he shivered a little in spite of the hot sun on his back.

"I know," said Jem shortly.

Wattie said no more for a little while. He was thoroughly

bewildered by the psychology of Jem . . . Jem had been frightened to wade in the shallows but he had not hesitated to rush straight into the river up to his waist to effect his rescue . . . there had been no time for hesitation . . . there had been no time for thought. Wattie looked at the river and saw that the place Jem had chosen was the only possible place. He saw the two boulders between which Jem had wedged himself and he saw the current swirling in and then swirling out again to the other bank of the river.

"It was a guid place," said Wattie suddenly, "it was the only place. How did ye think of it?"

"I didn't think," replied Jem. "There wasn't time to think. I'd been watching the river and I saw that all the little twigs and things came bumping up against that rock. . . ."

Wattie saw the idea. He thought about the whole thing very seriously. He was very grateful to Jem but he had no words to thank him—of course he would have done the same for Jem (thought Wattie) if he could have seen exactly what to do. He would have dashed in to save Jem . . . but then he had not been frightened of the river. He was frightened of it now, for he could not look at the swirling water without feeling slightly sick and he wondered whether that was how Jem had felt, "all wobbly inside," and, if so, how he could possibly have gone in.

"I wouldn't go in again tae save the King, himsel'," said Wattie at last.

"You'd *have* to if it was the only way," declared Jem, rising to his feet. "Come on, Wattie," he added, "our clothes will be dry now—or very nearly—and we'll go back to the moor and play at brigands. Don't let's talk about it any more because I don't like talking about it."

"Aye," said Wattie smiling, "aye, we'll play at brigands—" He was feeling quite happy and was once more Jem's faithful slave.

The subject was not mentioned again by either of the boys and they took care not to mention it to their elders. They were aware that if their elders had any idea of the dangers through which they had passed their liberty would be threatened and possibly curtailed. There was only one further mention of the incident, and it took place that night when Jem was preparing for bed. Dolly had gone up to say good night to him and to hear him say his prayers. He said them as usual and then remained on his knees for a few moments longer with his eyes tightly shut . . . then he rose and bounded into bed.

"I was just saying 'thank you' to God," he told his aunt in a casual sort of voice. "It was a little thing He did for me—it didn't take Him a minute, of course."

Dolly was somewhat taken aback. She considered the advisability of improving the occasion . . . and then she realised that the occasion could not be improved, it was perfect as it was. She would have liked to know what particular gift or benefit Jem had received from his Maker, but there was an atmosphere of dignity and reserve about Jem which precluded any questioning upon the subject. Dolly waited for a few moments to see if he would tell her any more, and then she kissed him fondly and went downstairs.

CHAPTER XXXII

WATTIE'S STORY

THERE was one day which stood out alone in Dolly's memory when she looked back at this peaceful interlude in her life. She labelled it in her mind "the last day" for it was the last day that she and Mardie spent together in quiet seclusion. The day started in the usual fashion and there was nothing to herald any change and none of them was aware that Kilnocky days were coming to an end. It was the first of September; Dolly pointed this out at breakfast and added that they had been at Kilnocky for a whole month.

"Nonsense, I can't believe it," Mardie declared. "This month hasn't had the right number of days in it."

"No, it hasn't," agreed Jem. "It can't possibly be a month . . . oh dear, shall we have to go home soon?"

"You can stay as long as Grandfather can do without you," replied Mardie, smiling at him.

Jem thought about this and his face grew grave. "Well, of course," he said slowly, "well, of course I'd like to stay here for ever and ever, but I've got such a lot to learn. I'm not learning anything about how to be a doctor, am I? Wattie's going to be a gamekeeper, you see, so this is a good place for him to be, and he can go on learning all the time. It's different for me."

"Quite different," Mardie agreed.

"Are doctors ever rich?" enquired Jem anxiously.

"Not often."

"It was just—well, I'd like to be rich enough to have a moor, and—and all that. Then Wattie could be my gamekeeper. He *wants* to be my gamekeeper," explained Jem, "he says he'd like that better than anything."

"You might have a river, too," said Dolly, hiding a smile, "and then you could fish all day long."

"No, I shan't have a river," declared Jem. "Just moors and hills with grouse and deer. Can I go now?"

Mardie nodded and he slipped from his chair. "I'm away to find Wattie," he cried, and disappeared like a flash of lightning.

There was a little silence after he had gone and then Mardie smiled, "Jem has caught the infection," she said. "I wonder what Ethel will say when he goes home and produces a Scots accent—'I'm away to find Wattie'—"

Dolly laughed, "He'll soon lose it again. He was bound to pick it up from Wattie, and personally I find it very attractive."

"Ethel won't."

"No, I don't suppose she will," said Dolly with complete indifference.

There was another short silence and then Dolly asked a question which had been troubling her mind a good deal. "What are you going to do?" she enquired, "you aren't going to stay here all winter, are you?"

"Yes, why not?"

"You'll be lonely," Dolly said, "it will be terribly dull for you. Why don't you take rooms in Edinburgh?"

"I'd rather be here among my own belongings," replied Mardie, looking round the room affectionately. "I think when you're all by yourself it helps to have your own things about you; there's a friendliness about chairs and cupboards that have known you all your life."

"But when it snows, Mardie . . . you'll be snowed up!" cried Dolly in dismay.

"I shall just sit down and wait until somebody comes and digs me out, I suppose."

Hoony had come into the room during the last part of the conversation; she had come with her tray to clear away the remains of the breakfast.

"The snaw will not hairm ye," she declared. "It's a nice cosy wee hoose and we've plenty o' logs tae burn. I'd as lief bide here as gang tae Edinburgh—or any ither place. D'ye not have snaw in England?"

"Not very much," admitted Dolly. "We do have snow, of course, but the roads are practically never blocked—at least not in my part of England."

"I was snawed up here for a fortnight," declared Hoony, "yon was the worst snaw I can mind. The road was blocked wi' a sax foot drift and they had tae fetch the ploo from the city. . . . Aye, it snawed and snawed, and the wind screeched in the lum. That was the nicht I got Wattie," she added. "Aye, that was the nicht that Wattie came tae me. It's twa years syne, but I mind it like as if it was yesterday."

Mardie and Dolly looked at each other, and remained silent, for they both knew that here at last was the real tale of Wattie, and from the legitimate source.

"I mind it weel," continued the old woman, shaking her head sadly, "the snaw lay heaped aboot the door, and it was sae deep that it fell in on ma floor when I opened the door tae let the puir bodies come in . . . and dinna ask me how the twa o' them got through the drifts, for I've no conception how they managed it . . . it was sheer desperation I'm thinking."

"Did his mother bring him to you?" Mardie asked.

"Who else?" replied Hoony. "Aye, it was his mither brought him. Eh, it was a wild nicht . . . no fit nicht for a wee boy to be oot, but ye see she didna' ken whaur else tae tak the laddie, sae she was forced tae bring him tae me."

"I see," said Mardie quietly.

"Aye, she was at the end o' her tether, ye see. Puir body, she was at the end of her tether!"

"Did she stay with you?"

"She bided twa days."

"And then?"

"Then dee-ed," said Hoony simply, and she brushed her hand across her forehead and lifted her fine head which had sunk for a moment as if under a heavy load.

There was silence for a few moments and then Hoony said, "I'll maybe better make a clean breast of it while I'm aboot it, for ye've the richt tae ken the truth . . . wee Wattie's ma grandson, Miss Mardie. Aye, he's Alec's son. I've nae proof of it, but it's true none the less. There was proof enough for me in what the lassie told me . . . and in Wattie himsel', for he's the living image of ma ain guid man. I never thought the day would come when I would thank God that ma man had been taken . . . no, I never thought that."

It was difficult to know what to say, for the old woman's attitude did not invite sympathy, it was at once humbled and proud, apologetic and defiant.

Mardie chose her words with care: "Wattie will do well if he takes after his grandfather," she said in a matter-of-fact voice.

Hoony turned away and busied herself at the sideboard. "Oh, Miss Mardie," she said a trifle shakily, "oh Miss Mardie . . . it's guid of ye. I wish I'd had the courage tae speak of it sooner . . . but it's a thing I dinna like tae speak of . . . and that's the truth."

When Hoony had gone, and the two friends were once more alone, they spoke of the little tragedy in low voices.

"It must be dreadful for her," Dolly said. "She's so good and so proud."

"It *is* dreadful for her," agreed Mardie. "She's different, you know. There's something different about her. I felt it before and now I understand it."

"I can't imagine anything worse than to feel that one's own child has behaved badly."

"Perhaps there isn't anything worse," said Mardie slowly and then she added in a lighter tone, "but you must not be unhappy about poor old Hoony, it isn't good for you, my dear. You have your own child to think of, you know."

Dolly smiled at her. "I know," she said, "I don't talk about it much, do I, but I think about it quite a lot. It's very real to me now, and very precious . . . it's a girl, you know."

"Is it?"

"Yes, and I should like to call her Mardie. Would you mind?"

For a moment Mardie felt that she *would* mind, for her name was a family heirloom and she had dreamed so often of a little Mardie of her own. . . . She had wanted children, had wanted them desperately at one time, but Jack had not wanted them. Jack had produced all sorts of reasons why they should wait . . . and Mardie had waited. She saw now that it was fortunate that she had not got her wish for if there had been children and they had shown any signs of being excitable and unstable . . . no, thought Mardie, no, it would have been too much to bear . . . better to be alone, and to look forward to a lonely old age than to bear such a frightful burden as that.

"Would you mind if I called my baby Mardie?" asked Dolly again, and this time Mardie was able to reply to the question:

"I should love it," she declared, taking Dolly's hand and patting it. "I think it would be very pleasant indeed to have a little namesake; it was sweet of you to think of it."

They shopped together as usual that morning and went for a picnic on the moors in the afternoon; Jem and Wattie came with them and carried the baskets and chose a sheltered nook for tea. So far the day had been like other days except for Hoony's confession, but tonight was to be quite different from other nights for it was the night appointed for the Village Dance. Mardie and Dolly had both received invitations to be present at this function but Dolly had decided not to go. Mardie had worn nothing but tweeds for a whole month, and she felt rather strange in the soft golden-brown Liberty frock which she had chosen to wear, but Dolly, who was supervising her toilet declared that she looked delightful.

"You're golden-brown all over," she pointed out, "and all you want now is a golden rose in your hair."

"Kilnocky would have a fit," replied Mardie firmly, as she seized her powder puff and prepared to powder her nose.

"Stop!" cried Dolly. "Good Heavens you can't put white powder on your nose. Haven't you got any rachel powder in your possession?"

"No I haven't. The fact is I haven't powdered my nose once since I settled down here . . . the white stuff matched me beautifully when I came."

Dolly fetched her own powder, and insisted on doing Mardie's hair, and fussed about like a small but exceedingly determined hen with one chicken.

"You'd think I was going to be presented at least," declared Mardie at last, ". . . and you can remove that lipstick from my dressing-table for Kilnocky doesn't approve of made-up women."

"Just the teeniest touch," pleaded Dolly. "Nobody would ever know, and it would finish you off so beautifully."

"No," said Mardie firmly. "Not even the teeniest touch. . . ."

They had their supper early, for the dance was due to begin at eight o'clock, and after they had finished Dolly sat down by the fire and took up her sewing.

"I hate leaving you alone," Mardie declared.

"Nonsense," replied Dolly. "I shall be fine—as Wattie would say. You know, Mardie I think one of the nicest things about Scotland is the custom of having a fire in the evening. Whether it's hot or cold a fire in the evening is a very pleasant thing and I don't believe that even if the temperature rose to ninety in the shade Hoony would forbear to light the sitting-room fire."

"She wouldn't, unless I told her," agreed Mardie smiling,

"but, as a matter of fact, the temperature never rises to that uncomfortable point in Kilnocky."

"I'm glad. I think a fire is lovely. You can't be lonely if you have a fire to look at—that's what I was trying to say. Now off you go, my child, and have a good time, but don't dance too often with the same partner . . . it isn't done in the best Kilnocky circles, I'm sure."

Mardie laughed. "My dear lamb, I shan't dance at all," she declared. "I'm only going because they might be hurt if I didn't go . . . I'll be back early. . . ."

"Away, away!" cried Dolly, waving her hand. "I shall expect you to come in with the milk."

CHAPTER XXXIII

THE VILLAGE DANCE

DOLLY had been sitting by the fire for some time, sewing a small garment which was intended for little Mardie and thinking about Ralph, when suddenly she heard the front-door bell ring. It was an unusual hour for a caller, so she raised her head and listened. She heard Hoony's firm step going to the door, and she heard a murmur of conversation and, after a moment or two, the sitting-room door opened and Kit walked in.

"Kit!" cried Dolly in amazement. "Kit, what are you doing here? Where on earth have you dropped from?"

He came in smiling, and took her hand, and sat down in the other chair and looked at her.

"How are you, Dolly?" he asked.

"Fit as a fiddle," she replied, "but you haven't answered my questions: how and why am I granted this unexpected pleasure?"

"I've come to scold you," he told her. "I'm really very angry with you Dolly, and I've also come to take Jem back to Minfield."

"And to see Mardie?" she asked, a trifle mischievously.

He shook his head.

"No news at all?"

"None."

There was a little pause, and then Kit continued. "I had the greatest difficulty in getting into this house. What a fearsome old woman that is! She terrified me, and I couldn't understand what she said!"

"She's a dear, really," replied Dolly, "but I was a little bit frightened of her at first. They're all dears, and they adore

Mardie. She's a sort of queen here, you know," Dolly told him,
and then she contradicted herself. "No, not a queen . . . she's
too near to them to be a queen. She's more like a mother to
them," said Dolly, raising her peace-filled blue eyes and smiling
gravely at him. "You see, they belong to her . . . and she to
them."

"I see," said Kit.

"She's gone to a dance at the Village Hall. I was to have
gone too . . . but I didn't."

"I'm glad you had that much sense," said Kit dryly.

"I'm very sensible indeed," she declared, "I'm very very good
. . . and very well."

"You look well," he agreed, "but I'm angry with you all the
same. Why didn't you answer my letter?"

"Too lazy."

"But I asked you a question—several questions."

"I know," said Dolly, "but I really have been lazy. I write
to Ralph, of course."

"Oh, of course," agreed Kit smiling at her, "you can find
time and energy to write to Ralph, but you're much too lazy
to write to me, so I have to come four hundred miles to see
you."

"But why?"

"Because we can't go on hiding your condition from your
father . . . the responsibility is too great. I promised that I
wouldn't tell anyone, and I've kept my promise, but I can't go
on keeping it, Dolly. You ought to be under medical super-
vision, you ought to have all your plans cut and dried."

"I haven't made any plans," said Dolly serenely.

"You're hopeless," declared Kit. "Quite hopeless. Give me
your hand."

Dolly held it out to him and he examined it carefully taking
a little magnifying glass from his pocket and looking at the
skin, and the knuckles, and the nails.

"What's the matter with my hand?" she enquired.

"Nothing. . . . It's a very pretty hand, Dolly."

"I know," said Dolly, nodding.

He spread it out and flexed the knuckles thoughtfully and then he bent and kissed it. "I'm very fond of you, Dolly," he said, "you're very precious indeed . . . and we mustn't risk anything. You wouldn't like to risk anything, would you?"

"To risk anything?" repeated Dolly anxiously, "you don't mean my baby—"

"Of course not," declared Kit, "but it's much better to make sure that everything is perfectly normal . . . and then we know for certain that it will be 'all right on the night'."

They talked for a little longer and then Dolly suggested that Kit should go down to the Village Hall and find Mardie, for she was fully aware that although Kit had given two other excellent reasons for his journey to Kilnocky, it was Mardie whom he wanted to see.

"But look at me!" cried Kit. "How can I go to a dance like this? I didn't bring my evening clothes at all because I thought I was coming to the wilds. If I had known that Kilnocky was addicted to night-life I'd have packed my tails of course."

Dolly laughed. "It's the one night in the year when Kilnocky doesn't go to bed at nine," she told him, "and you'll be perfectly all right like that."

Kit shut the gate behind him and turned eastwards towards the village. Now that he was so near to Mardie he was filled with impatience to see her . . . he couldn't do without seeing her. There was no hope in him for the future, but he felt that if he could just see her he could go on . . . if he could just see her face and touch her hand in friendship, that was all he wanted.

It was a warm night, and very still and dark. Kit walked quickly, his impatience growing with every step, and presently he found himself in the main street of the little village. It was easy to find his way to the hall where the dance was in progress, for he could hear the sound of the music in the quietness of the night, and he followed the sound to a long low building—a sort of glorified barn—which stood by itself in a plot of ground with a few fine trees about it. Yes, this was obviously the place for there were bright lights streaming from the uncurtained windows and the sound of revelry grew louder as he approached.

The doors were open, and Kit stood on the threshold watching the fun. His first thought was that they were fine people in a purely physical sense; they were big-boned and well set-up. The girls were handsome rather than pretty, and they looked very clean and wholesome and attractive in their simple, brightly-coloured frocks. The men were ruddy, and their faces shone with honest sweat. They were dressed in lounge suits, tweeds or flannels, so Kit felt quite comfortable about his own attire. He thought they looked rather serious; more as if they were taking part in some important rite than as if they were bent on enjoyment. They were doing a country dance at the moment, and each man had two partners . . . Kit watched them for a little, and saw that the dance had several movements and these were repeated faultlessly by everyone in the room. There was no pushing or scrambling for everyone knew the dance. The men danced to their partners in turn, and then wove a figure with them, and taking their hands led them forward with a proud air. Kit had seen English Country Dances, but this was different; there was more go about it, and the tune was catchy and cheerful and full of verve. The band consisted of a piano and two violins and they played as if they enjoyed playing, stamping their feet and tossing their heads in time to the music.

Presently they stopped, and the floor cleared, and Kit looked about and saw Mardie sitting on a bench at the far end of the room. She was talking to some of the older people—an old man with a rosy face and a white beard, and a pin-cushiony old woman dressed in purple—she looked up suddenly and saw Kit and their eyes met and remained fixed upon each other for a moment, and then Kit walked straight across the empty floor to her.

Mardie came to meet him and held out her hand, and Kit took it and held it. He had no words to say to her—there was nothing to say. He felt that she knew why he had come. She understood. What was the use of words? They stood there together for perhaps ten seconds, and then suddenly the band began to play "Tales of the Vienna Woods" and Kit put his arm round her and they glided off together.

He had never danced with Mardie before, but somehow he had known that she would dance beautifully and he was not disappointed. They danced the old swinging waltz, the steps which suited the gorgeous tune. They dipped and swayed and swung, and Mardie's feet followed Kit's, and her body melted into his, so that they seemed one person, floating on the music, part of the spirit of Strauss. For a few moments they had the room to themselves, but this they hardly knew; nor did they wonder why the other dancers hung back and gave them the floor. The other dancers scarcely knew themselves why they were hesitating and hanging back; perhaps it was because they were a little tired after the rollicking measure of the Country Dance, or perhaps it was because they felt, subconsciously, that something out of the ordinary was taking place before their eyes, something that shouldn't be disturbed or interfered with, something that they were forced to respect, but which they did not understand . . . and then as the swinging tune swelled and blossomed, their feet began to tingle, and gradually, first one couple and then another took the floor . . . and soon the room was full of swirling figures, of swishing skirts, and sliding twinkling feet.

Mardie's mind was a blur. The lights seemed to melt into each other as she swung round, the well-known faces melted and re-formed before her eyes. Her cheeks burned, and her breath came quickly between her parted lips. There was no past, and no future; only the present moment seemed real, Kit's firm arm round her waist and the music which bore them up and sent them whirling round the room.

The last lingering notes died away, and there was a sudden silence, and then a burst of applause; but Mardie and Kit did not wait for more, they had stopped in front of the big doors which stood wide open. He took her hand and they went out together as if they were in a dream—from the lighted room into the dark cool night. The street was very quiet. The trees, which stood about the long low building were quiet too. There was not a whisper of wind in their limply hanging leaves. Beneath the lamp-posts there were pools of yellow light and, far above, the stars were bright and very clear.

So far they had not spoken a single word, not one—there was so little need of words between them—but now as they walked along the street together Mardie began to talk.

"It was queer," she said in a low voice, "it was so queer that at first I couldn't believe it. I had been thinking about you . . . and then you were there. . . ."

Her hand was still in his, and he pressed it gently. "I couldn't stay away," he said.

"Oh, Kit, what are we to do!"

Kit did not reply.

"When we have nothing left to live for we don't die," said Mardie hopelessly. "I think we should die. There's an old Scottish song that rings in my mind—just a few words of it— 'Werena' my heart licht I would dee'—We aren't meant to live without hope, Kit."

"Oh, Mardie!" he said.

"My heart is so heavy," she said, "heavy as lead—but I go on living."

"I make you unhappy?" he asked.

"Oh Kit," she cried, "it's I who make you unhappy—that's the hardest part."

"I'm happy now," he told her. "Just at this moment I'm the happiest man in the world. When I see you . . . well, I don't need anything else . . . not even a future."

"But I want you to have a future," she told him, "why do you bother with me?"

"You know my heart," he said, "you know everything about me, Mardie."

There was a little silence between them, and the tapping of Mardie's heels on the pavement, and the dull thud of Kit's heavier step were the only sounds.

"My brain is tired with thinking," said Mardie at last, "and my thoughts go round in circles and come back to the same place. I could bear it so much more easily if I were not spoiling your life. . . . No, Kit, let me say it. I *am* spoiling your life, my dear. I'm being a dog in the manger. I'm holding onto you and I can never give you anything at all."

He burst out at that, crying incoherently that he wanted nothing except to be with her . . . that it was enough . . . that he could wait. . . .

"But it isn't enough," she said quietly. "It isn't enough for me . . . so it can't be enough for you . . . and waiting is no use at all. I've thought about it, and thought, and thought. I've even wondered whether I should say to you, 'Take me, I'm yours. . . .' "

"Mardie!"

". . . Take me, I'm yours," said Mardie, in a low even voice. "Yes, I've thought of that, for all of me belongs to you, Kit—all of me that matters—but I can't say it."

"Mardie, I wouldn't want that. I'd wait."

"There's no hope," she said, "no hope at all."

"If he's dead—" said Kit in a low voice.

"But he isn't dead. I should know if he were dead."

"You think he's alive? You think he'll come back?"

She hesitated. "It's a feeling, not a think at all," she said slowly, and then she added, "I can't explain it but you know what I mean."

He did know, but his feeling was that Rochester was dead.

"Some day Jack will come back," continued Mardie in a low voice. "Some day . . . and I shall be waiting for him. I couldn't let him down because he's weak, and he wouldn't be able to bear it. He's weak and he needs me . . . I know he went away and left me without a word, but it wasn't really Jack who did that. The real Jack wouldn't have done it. . . . Some day he'll come back and he'll expect to find me waiting for him. I can't let him down."

"He let you down."

"Not the real Jack. It was another Jack who let me down . . . and anyhow . . . even if he did behave badly it doesn't give me the right to behave badly to him. I'm different," she said, "don't you understand, Kit? I can't make you understand. It's a thing you must understand by yourself or not at all."

"It's your pride, Mardie," he said in a low voice.

"Partly, perhaps," she agreed. "It's the way I'm made . . . and the way Jack's made . . . and the way you're made. If we had been made differently. . . ."

"What a tangle!" he said.

"What a tangle!" she repeated with a sigh, and then after a pause she continued, "I'm pledged but you're free. Go away, Kit. Go round the world; go back to America; make a life for yourself, my dear."

They were standing still now, and she looked at him gravely. Her steady eyes were almost on a level with his and they were full of tenderness. "Make a life for yourself," she repeated urgently.

"But Mardie—"

"Yes," she said, "yes. I've wanted to say this to you and now

I've said it. I mean it, Kit. I believe I could bear it if I knew
that you were happy. It would . . . lessen my burden."

"I can't! I can't, Mardie."

"I shouldn't have let you love me," she said.

"You couldn't help it," he told her, "nobody could help it. I
loved you from the first moment I saw you."

"In the garden—"

"Yes, in the garden. You rose up from the path—you sort
of uncurled yourself—and there you were. There was never
any doubt. There was never anybody else that mattered . . .
or anything else at all. . . ."

"Poor Kit!" she said.

"Why d'you say that?"

"You should have loved somebody else—somebody who was
free, or somebody who was brave enough to cut herself free."

"It isn't courage you lack," he said thoughtfully, "you've
got plenty of courage, Mardie. Courage to endure—it's the
hardest kind really—mental courage. You haven't got enough
ruthlessness."

"But we shouldn't be ruthless!" she exclaimed in surprise.

"We should be a little," he said. "At least I think we should.
I think people are soft and sloppy unless they have a tiny pinch
of ruthlessness in their make-up—but I wouldn't have you
different."

"You like me soft and sloppy?" she asked smiling.

"I like you just as you are," he replied.

"Dear Kit!" she said.

"That's better," he told her with an attempt at lightness
which he was far from feeling. "That's much better 'Dear Kit'
is a hundred per cent better than 'Poor Kit'."

She slipped her hand through his arm and they walked on.
They were quite near the little house now, it loomed out of the
darkness in front of them. Kit saw that there was a dim light
shining through the fanlight over the front door. He took the

key from Mardie's hand and opened the door very quietly, and let her in.

"Good-night," he whispered. "I'll go to the hotel—I left my bag here in the hall—where is it?"

Mardie had taken a piece of paper from the hall table and was reading it. She laughed under her breath and passed it to him. He had to hold it near the lamp to read it.

> "My dear Mardie,
>
> I hope the dance was a success and that Kit did not tread on your toes. Hoony and I have prepared the spare room. She was a tiny bit doubtful if it was correct for us to harbour a man for the night, but when I said he was a doctor all was well. She looked at me thoughtfully and asked whether he was 'biding' because if so he might 'come in handy.'
>
> Sleep well, my lamb,
>
> Yours, Dolly."

"Biding means staying for some time," Mardie explained. She paused and then added, "Hoony and I are a little worried about Dolly. Neither of us knows—much about babies."

"She looked well," Kit said quickly.

"I think she ought to go back to Minfield," Mardie said, "I don't want her to go, of course—we're happy together—but —but I feel responsible, you see."

Kit was not surprised. It was exactly what he felt himself. The responsibility was far too great.

"I'll take her back to Minfield," he said. "She ought to go, she ought to be under her father's care."

"If you would," agreed Mardie, "but don't let her think I don't want her, will you?"

CHAPTER XXXIV

A PERFECT DAY

IT WAS decided that Kit should spend a few days at Kilnocky, and that Dolly as well as Jem should accompany him south. Dolly wrote to her father telling him her news and asking if it would be too much trouble to have her. This was merely politeness upon her part (for she knew that Dr. Peabody would insist that his grandchild should be born beneath his roof) but Kit had re-awakened her sense of obligation to her father and she saw that she had treated him somewhat shabbily in delaying her news for so long.

It was still weather for Kit's short holiday, the days had shortened, and there was a misty freshness in the early mornings and gossamer webs floating from the trees. The heather was in full bloom, lying upon the rounded hills like a counterpane of living purple and there was a constant noise of falling water, of running water, for the burns were full.

They spent a few quiet days in the little house together and on the surface they were very merry, but Jem was the only one who was completely happy in his mind and even for him the days of pleasure were faintly tarnished by the shadow of the parting from "Aunt Mardie" and Wattie and the hills.

"Why can't you come too?" he kept saying, swinging Mardie's hand and gazing up into her face. "You'll be lonely without us—I know you will."

Mardie knew it too, but she evaded the thought. She was aware that these days would remain in her memory for ever, and she determined that nothing, no vain regrets or imaginings should spoil them for her. Kit, also, had made up his mind to enjoy them, and he found much to enjoy—Dolly looking after him and Mardie in a grandmotherly sort of way, Dolly encouraging them to go off together for long tramps over the hills, Dolly effacing herself. He wondered what Dolly thought would be the outcome of it all. Perhaps she thought that Rochester was dead, and that he and Mardie would wait for the required number of years, until the law presumed him dead, and then marry. That would be the most sensible thing to do, but he had little hope of convincing Mardie of the fact. The queerest thing of all about Rochester's disappearance was that everyone had his (or her) own theory as to what had happened to the man . . . everyone was interested. Mrs. Colquhoun knew about it too, and sometimes Kit felt her eyes upon him, scrutinising him, and weighing him up, but it was not until the last day of all that she broke through her reserve and spoke to him about it. She was clearing away the breakfast, and Kit was sitting in a chair near the window with the morning paper on his knee. The two girls were upstairs making the beds; he could hear their voices and the sound of their feet as they moved to and fro.

"What's to come of it?" demanded Hoony suddenly, pausing with the marmalade dish in her hand.

Kit looked up and saw her eyes fixed on him—they were suspicious, accusing, anxious.

"I don't know, I'm sure," he said helplessly. "If you could tell me what's to come of it I'd be glad."

"I'm asking," she pointed out.

"I know, but I can't answer you. We must just wait, I suppose."

"Wait for what?"

"Wait for Mr. Rochester to be found."

"The man's deid," declared Hoony firmly. "He'll no' be found noo. It's too late tae talk of finding him, ye should have found oot sooner where he'd gone."

"My goodness!" cried Kit in annoyance. "D'you think I

haven't tried to find the man? I spent weeks hunting for him. I'd go on hunting for him till I dropped if I thought there was the faintest chance of finding him."

"But why?" Hoony asked. "The thing's a sheer waste of time. The man's gone . . . he's deid . . . is she tae spend her life waiting on him tae come back, or what?"

"I suppose so."

"It's madness," Hoony said. "It's sheer madness. Where's the sense in waiting for a deid man tae come back from the grave."

"We've got to find his body before she's free," said Kit bluntly. "D'you understand now?"

Hoony stood for a moment as if turned to stone. "Is that the law?" she asked incredulously.

Kit laughed grimly. "That's the law," he said. "And now perhaps you'll go on clearing the table and leave me to read the paper in peace."

"Ye werena' reading," Hoony pointed out. "Ye were sitting there looking from ye and seeing naught . . . imphm . . . ye needna' trouble to throw dust in ma eyes for I can see as far through a brick wall as maist folks."

After delivering herself of this speech Hoony seized up her tray and departed, shutting the door after her with her foot.

"Well, I'm damned!" exclaimed Kit, and he took up his neglected paper and began to read.

It was very warm and fine in the afternoon and Kit and Mardie decided to take their tea and walk across the moors to Restford Bridge. Jem was anxious to accompany them, but Dolly declared that it would be much too far for him, and that as this was his last day at Kilnocky he had better spend it with Wattie on the hill.

"My last day!" said Jem with a sigh. "Oh dear, I wish it was my first day. Are you going to Restford Bridge, Aunt Dolly?"

"It's too far for me, too," said Dolly smiling.

"Yes," said Jem. "You know, Aunt Dolly, you're getting very old. You can't do all the things you used to."

The words were uttered so sadly and Jem's blue eyes were so full of sympathy for his aged relative that his three hearers collapsed and laughed until they cried.

"I don't see anything funny about it," said Jem. "I think it's very sad."

Fortunately Hoony appeared just at this moment with a couple of thermos flasks and a haversack full of sandwiches and the conversation was changed.

"We shan't be back until late," Mardie told Hoony as they settled the haversacks on their backs. "We'll dine at the Inn at Restford and walk back across the hills in the evening."

"Ye'll no be overdoing it, Miss Mardie," Hoony adjured her, but Mardie laughed and declared that she could walk twice as far without feeling tired.

They set forth together with sticks in their hands. Mardie was wearing thick-nailed shoes and woollen stockings and a short tweed skirt and a jersey. Her head was bare, and the hill breeze blew soft ringlets of dark hair across her face. She looked well, Kit thought, and the shadowed anxious look had disappeared. Her eyes were bright and her skin was tanned to a warm golden brown.

"You're happy here," he said suddenly as they breasted the hill together. "I'm glad I've seen you here amongst your own people. I shall be able to think of you when I go back to Minfield and you won't seem quite so far away."

Mardie answered the first part of his speech. "I'm happy here," she said, "but I was happy at Minfield too, and I had some very good friends there. It's rather sad to think I shall never go back to Minfield again . . . don't let's think of sad things today, Kit."

The path they had taken was narrow and stony and very

steep, it wound up and up to the top of the hill. Presently they stopped and looked back and saw the village of Kilnocky lying far below them, and the reservoir, small and silvery, like a hand-mirror fitted into the surrounding hills. A grouse rose, almost at their feet with a startled cry of "Go-back, go-back, grrrr," and Kit instinctively brought his stick to his shoulder . . . and then turned and smiled at his companion.

"Yes," said Mardie, "if only you could have stayed a little longer I could have got you some shooting . . . but there was no time. Perhaps you'll come back and see me some day."

"I shall come," said Kit. "That's a promise, Mardie."

Mardie sighed . . . her words had been involuntary, for she had not intended to invite Kit again. It was unfair to him, and she had made up her mind to free him from the tangle of her life. She must cut him out of the tangle with a firm hand, and even if it hurt him it would be better for him in the end. I shall write to him, thought Mardie. I shall enjoy myself today . . . we'll both enjoy ourselves . . . and then I shall write and tell him that he is not to think about me any more.

High up on the hillside there was a cluster of pine trees which had been planted as a protection to a sheep-fold, and it was in the shade of these pines that Mardie and Kit sat down to have their tea. They took off their haversacks and opened the packets of sandwiches, and poured the brown liquid out of the thermos flasks.

"It isn't tea," Mardie declared. "Tea in a thermos flask is simply hot brown liquid—it tastes of mouldy hay."

"It's liquid and that's the main thing," replied Kit smiling.

"This moor used to belong to us," said Mardie, after a few moments' silence. "This moor and the next . . . right over to the shoulder of the furthest hill. I know every hill and every stone . . . every little sheep path through the heather. I never shot, of course, but I liked coming out with Father and his friends . . . especially if it was early in the morning. D'you know, Kit, the last time I was here I was with Father. He had come out after black-cock. It was winter then, and it all looked different; there was just a sprinkle of snow on the ground. We sat down here—just here on this very rock—to eat our sandwiches. . . . It's funny, isn't it, Kit, that the rock is still here, so unchanging, and I have changed so much . . . and Father is dead."

"Yes," said Kit in a low voice, "but I don't think you've changed much."

"You didn't know me then," said Mardie smiling. "I was a very raw sort of person . . . I wish you could have met my father. You would have liked each other. Is this boring you, Kit?"

"Boring me? Of course not."

"Well, it might be rather boring to have to sit and listen to me, but I'm glad you're not bored. . . . You see that little white croft over there on the hill? That was where Hoony was born. It belonged to her father and mother. The mother was a terrible old woman and I was frightened of her when I was little. She was so old and wrinkled and so dreadfully ugly that I used to think she was a witch."

When they were just finishing their tea a shepherd passed with a collie slinking at his heels. He called a blithe "Good-day tae ye" as he went by and they could hear him whistling tunefully as he swung off down the hill.

"Come along, Kit, or we shall be too late for dinner at Restford Bridge," said Mardie, as she rose and shook the crumbs from her lap.

From now on their way lay downhill following the course of a burn which tumbled and splashed from rock to rock and from pool to pool in a haphazard manner. The path was wide enough for them to walk abreast and there was no lack of interesting conversation.

"This is flying fish weather!" said Kit suddenly, and when Mardie asked him what he meant he explained that a bright sun and a pleasant breeze was the kind of weather that flying fish liked, and he told her about the Pacific, how blue and shiny it was, and how the flying fish leaped from the waves with rainbows dripping from their outstretched fins. He had always found it easy to talk to Mardie, and today they were so much in sympathy that it was easier than ever before and he went on to tell her about coral islands ringed with surf, and of trade winds rustling through groves of coconut palms.

Mardie liked to hear him talk and she spurred him on by questions about all that he had seen. "We talked about travelling that first day," she said, "d'you remember, Kit? You said that there was nothing so wonderful as the first smell of land after weeks at sea."

Kit remembered every word of that conversation.

The Inn at Restford Bridge was situated on the main Edinburgh road and was surrounded by a group of fine trees. Mardie and Kit dined on the verandah at the back where a fine lawn stretched down to the river, and from here they had a good view of the old bridge which gave the place its name. This bridge was of the hog-backed pattern, made of grey stone and hoary with age, and beneath its high arches the river wound lazily. They dined well, and were waited upon by a rosy-cheeked waitress who seemed very interested in them and was most attentive, and when they were half way through their repast a party of shooters arrived and made their way to another table which was evidently ready for them. One of the party was a tall girl in heather mixture tweeds and as she followed her companions to the table she looked round and her eyes fell on Mardie.

"Hallo, Thea!" said Mardie, smiling at her.

"Mardie!" cried the girl in amazement, "what are you doing

here? Are you at Kilnocky . . . but no, of course you aren't. . . ."

The whole party turned with one accord, and Mardie was surrounded by them, and had her work cut out trying to answer their questions. Kit was introduced and accepted by them with frank friendliness which he found very pleasant. He was glad, however, when the time came to go, for he liked best to have Mardie to himself and there was so little time left that he grudged every moment of it.

"I'm glad you've got friends here," he said as they started off for home, "you won't be so lonely, will you? I liked Miss Simpson very much, in fact they were all nice."

"Yes," agreed Mardie. "But of course I haven't a car, and the distances from one place to another make it a little difficult. I don't suppose I shall see very much of them."

The walk home was almost the best part of that perfect day —or so Kit thought. They took it slowly and in silence with occasional little bursts of talk which served to show the companionship of their minds. It was cool and fresh after the heat of the day and a grey daylight encompassed them (the sun had set behind the hills and this light was the reflection upon the clouds). In this queer half and half light the little cottages that they passed shone with a ghostly sort of radiance and a yellow moon, full and slightly luminous in the white-grey sky, re-minded Mardie of a Chinese paper lantern. It reminded her of a lantern all the more because it hung so low in the sky that sometimes it seemed to hang upon the gnarled branches of a group of fir trees and sometimes, having disappeared altogether for a while, it would swing into view from behind the jutting shoulder of a hill. They passed a little pond, in a rushy meadow full of sleeping cows, and remarked that a white mist hung over it, like a handful of cotton-wool poised in the still grey air.

The church clock was striking ten as Kit and Mardie left the moor and turned southward into Kilnocky village.

"How quiet it is!" Mardie said, "and how loud our footsteps sound."

"It's more lonely than the moor," said Kit. "Everyone has gone to bed."

There were a few lights in the upstairs window of the little houses, but only a few, for Kilnocky folk believed in the ancient proverb "Early to bed and early to rise."

Their day together was almost over and they dawdled a little by common consent. Kit opened the little gate which led into Mardie's garden and paused with his hand on it—"Do you remember when you shut me out?" he asked. "That day when we played tennis at the Furnivals' and I walked home with you across the fields. You said 'Even friends can only come as far as the gate'."

"I remember," Mardie said.

"I've come further now," he declared, coming in as he spoke and shutting the gate behind him, "and I'm going to stay inside, Mardie, it doesn't matter what you say."

She knew then that he had guessed her resolve to shut him out of her life, but her resolve was still firm. She could not speak and tell him her final decision, for her heart melted whenever she looked at him, and the sound of his voice turned her bones to water, but she could write to him and tell him, and she *would* write to him. It was no good waiting and waiting. Her own life was spoiled but he had his life before him and must be free.

They went up together to the little house.

CHAPTER XXXV

JEM'S COUSIN

KIT brought his two charges safely home to Minfield, and they both received a warm welcome from Dr. Peabody. He was delighted to have Jem back, for he had missed him even more than he had expected, and he was delighted to see the child looking so well.

"It's done him a power of good," he declared, gazing at the rosy face of his grandson with a benevolent air.

"A power of good!" echoed Jem, dancing about from one leg to the other in his usual manner when excited. "It's done me a power of good. Why, I can beat Wattie on the hill . . . at least I did beat him one day when he had a stone in his shoe."

Miss Peabody received them more coldly, but even she was glad to have Jem home; it was true that he occasioned a good deal of extra work but she had found the house somewhat dull without him. Kit noticed that she was more lenient with Jem, but her leniency did not extend to himself or Dolly, and in fact the two sisters had scarcely met when they started their usual bickering.

Dr. Peabody had ordained that Dolly was to have the big spare room which had a dressing-room adjoining, instead of her own small bedroom on the top floor, and Ethel considered that the trouble involved in changing the rooms, and in preparing the larger room for Dolly, was unwarranted. She made a tremendous fuss about the extra work and cancelled various engagements in order to see that everything was properly managed.

"I can't play golf with Olive this afternoon," she announced at lunchtime. "I've had to ring her up and tell her I can't come."

"Really?" enquired Dolly with an innocent air, "aren't you feeling well, Ethel? You should be more careful of your diet, my dear. . . . I was afraid that two helpings of ice pudding last night might prove disastrous."

"I'm perfectly well," snapped Ethel, "and it's fortunate that I am, when I have so much to do. Tupman is moving the bed down this afternoon and I must be here to help him."

"I can do it myself, easy," declared Tupman, who had just come in with the pudding. "There's no call for you to give up your playing for that, Miss Ethel. I'm strong, I am."

Ethel glared at the man in an infuriated manner for nothing annoyed her so much as when Tupman saw fit to engage in the conversation at mealtimes. She had done her level best to break him of the habit without avail.

"There, you see, Ethel," said Dr. Peabody, "there's no earthly reason why you should put off your game. You had better ring up at once and tell Miss Sinclair that you can go after all. It's going to be a very pleasant afternoon."

Ethel waited in frigid silence until Tupman had left the room, and then she turned on her father. "Why do you encourage him!" she cried. "How do you expect me to keep Tupman in his proper place when you encourage him like that?"

"What is Tupman's proper place?" Dolly enquired with interest.

The old doctor laughed delightedly. "What, indeed!" he said. "Tupman is Lord High Everything Else in this house and always has been. We couldn't get on without Tupman, that's certain."

"We could get on very well," said Ethel, in a voice which she imagined was too low to reach her father's ears.

"Oh *no!*" cried Jem. "Oh *no,* Aunt Ethel. Who would clean the cars and lay the table and polish the silver and the stair-rods

and sweep the hall? Who would brush Grandfather's clothes
and make the salad-dressing and cut the grass and—"

"Who indeed!" said Dolly, putting a stop to the list of Tupman's activities by the simple expedient of placing her hand
over her nephew's mouth (he was sitting beside her at the
table so the feat was not so difficult as it might sound).

"But Aunt Dolly!" cried Jem, when the hand had been removed, "don't you like to hear about all the things that Tupman
does?"

"No," said Dolly firmly. "It makes me feel such a worm."

Ethel said nothing, and continued to say it in a most dis-
approving manner.

"I wonder when my cousin will arrive," said Jem with an
air of changing the conversation into more pleasant channels.

"Your cousin?" enquired his grandfather is some surprise.

"Yes," said Jem nodding. "My little cousin Mardie is com-
ing to stay. I saw her bed upstairs—a teeny weeny bed—and
Aunt Dolly said that's who it was for. Didn't you, Aunt
Dolly?"

Thus adjured, Dolly admitted with some embarrassment
that she had made some such explanation of the teeny weeny
bed. She looked at her father apologetically.

"Of course," agreed the old man with a twinkle in his eye,
"of course . . . your cousin Mardie. A very nice name too . . .
or perhaps your cousin Martin."

"But she's a little girl," Jem pointed out.

Dr. Peabody said he was glad of that, for a grand-daughter
was exactly what he needed, and he added that he would be
delighted to receive her beneath his roof.

"Yes, it will be nice," agreed Jem. "She's coming from heaven,
you know . . . an angel's bringing her."

Kit looked at Dolly in some surprise (for he had heard her
make the assertion that children should be "told things frankly")
and Dolly had the grace to blush. The fact was that, when her

nephew had demanded how and whence he might expect his young cousin to arrive, she had looked into his large and innocent blue eyes and her heart failed her and she had been thankful to fall back upon the time-honoured explanation, so much deplored by modern students of child psychology.

Ethel registered disgust but made no remark, and the subject was changed by the appearance of Tupman with an urgent message for Dr. Peabody.

Jem's cousin took it into her head to arrive upon the scene some three weeks before her appointed time, but luckily for all concerned the necessary arrangements had been made for her reception and Nurse Winterton was available. Dolly was no stoic—far otherwise in fact—and having decided that her father was her only hope she refused to let him out of her sight for a moment, and Dr. Peabody—usually so impatient with people who were unnecessarily alarmed about their condition—gave in to her whim. Perhaps he remembered another night just twenty-four years ago, when his wife had died in giving birth to Dolly.

Kit looked in, about two o'clock, and saw the old man sitting there with his book beneath the shaded lamp and his steel-rimmed spectacles perched rather crookedly on his big nose. The light shone on his head and Kit noticed that his hair had become much whiter in the last few months, but it was still thick and wavy.

"There you are!" he said, looking up and smiling at Kit. "Stay with her for a few moments, will you, while I go down and get my case book. She doesn't like being left, and Nurse is busy."

Kit went over and looked down at Dolly, and she looked back at him wearily. "It's such a long time," she complained. "Don't leave me, Father."

"Nonsense," declared Dr. Peabody as he rose. "We're getting

on nicely . . . you'll be all right with Kit . . . and I shan't be a minute."

Dolly signalled to Kit to come nearer.

"What is it?" he asked, leaning over her.

"I'm dying," she said in a faint voice.

"Dying!" exclaimed Kit. "Good heavens, no."

"Something has gone wrong," Dolly said, hardly moving her lips, "you and Father are just pretending . . . pretending that everything's all right. It can't be all right, Kit."

"Everything is perfectly normal," declared Kit emphatically, "you're doing splendidly, Dolly."

Dolly shook her head weakly. "It's no good saying that . . . I know I'm dying. I don't mind really . . . I'm so tired . . . it's just poor Ralph . . . you'll write to him, won't you, Kit? Tell him . . . tell him I sent him my love . . . my dear love."

"Dolly, don't be a little goat, everything's all right."

"It can't be," she said. "It can't be all right . . . you don't know what it's like. . . ."

Kit had intended to suggest that he should take Dr. Peabody's place for the remainder of the night, but he saw that she was much better with her father so he left it alone.

"Off to bed with you," Dr. Peabody said, as he settled himself down once more with his casebook and a couple of large ledgers. "Off to bed with you, Kit. I'll send for you when I want you, there's no sense in everybody hanging about all night. . . ."

Kit left them and went to his room. He did not undress but lay down on the bed as he was and tucked the eiderdown round his shoulders. I'll have a half-hour's nap, he decided, and then I'll go back and see how they're getting on.

When Kit opened his eyes after his "half-hour's nap" it was broad daylight, and this although the skies were overcast and the rain coming down in sheets. The "getting-up bell" was ringing through the house and there was a smell of breakfast in the air. He rose hurriedly and ran along the passage to Dolly's room and as he ran he heard the unmistakable "wah—wah—wah" of a newly born infant; Dolly's baby had arrived and they hadn't wakened him! Kit hesitated at the door, and then he realised that the baby's absurd wailing was coming from the dressing-room which adjoined Dolly's bedroom, and he opened the door of the dressing-room and went in.

Nurse Winterton was busy at the chest of drawers; she looked up. "Good morning, Dr. Stone," she said brightly.

"Good morning—look here, why didn't you wake me?"

"There was no need," she replied, smiling. "Dr. Peabody said it would be silly to disturb you. Everything went off very nice."

"It did, did it?"

"Very nice indeed. Dr. Peabody has gone to bed and Mrs. Dorman is sleeping like a top. I've just been in to have a peep at her."

Kit wondered—not for the first time—how on earth nurses managed to do without rest. He had slept for most of the night, and Dr. Peabody had gone to lie down, but Nurse Winterton had been up all night and looked as bright as a bee. Her apron was smooth and starched, her cap hung in crisp folds and she moved briskly about the small room putting everything to rights.

The "wah—wah—wah—" of the new member of the household continued with monotonous regularity, but Nurse Winterton took no notice at all. Kit went over and looked at the baby. "Is it a girl?" he enquired.

"Yes. Seven pounds two ounces. Nice, isn't she?"

She was nice. Kit was fond of small babies and very much interested in them, but as a rule they were extremely ugly. The new Miss Dorman was not ugly at all. She had a small round face like the petal of a pink rose, and dark smooth hair.

Her features were neat and well defined. Kit picked her up in his arms and cuddled her tenderly . . . she stopped crying at once.

"Oh, naughty, naughty!" cried Nurse Winterton. "Who said you could pick her up?"

"She asked me to," declared Kit gravely. "Look at her, Nurse, she's perfectly happy now."

"Bad training," declared Nurse Winterton, but she said it in an amiable voice, for she was very fond of Dr. Stone and could not be angry with him. "Very bad training. How do you think I'm going to train her to be good if people come in and pick her up whenever she cries?"

"She isn't twelve hours old!" he exclaimed. "Surely you might give her a chance to get used to this uncomfortable world before you start training her."

"I start training my babies at once. It's kinder really. Kinder to them and to the people that have to look after them. She *is* a little dear, isn't she?" added the nurse coming over and looking at the baby with loving pride.

The baby was asleep now and Kit laid her down in the basket-cradle very carefully and wrapped the shawl tightly round her. "There," he said, "she's quite happy now . . . and I won't interfere with her training again. She'll have to hurry up and get used to this uncomfortable world because she's a sailor's daughter."

"I don't see why that—"

"Oh don't you," enquired Kit smiling, "I'll tell you, then. This baby will be dragged round the world from port to port in the wake of His Majesty's Ship *Terrible*. She'll spend her time in frousty lodgings, in trains and boats . . . and it won't do her a bit of harm, either. Babies are tremendously strong . . . don't you think so, nurse?"

"Yes," agreed Nurse Winterton doubtfully, "yes, they *are* strong really . . . they come through a lot."

"Of course they do. Think of that baby of Mrs. Faulkner's."

Nurse Winterton thought of it. "What a night that was!" she said, with a little shudder. "I'll never forget that. It's funny how *different* cases are. Last night everything went like clockwork. It's just nature, isn't it, Dr. Stone?"

"It's a miracle," he said thoughtfully. "Or at least it always seems like a miracle to me. Last night there was one person, and this morning there are two. . . ."

"Yes, but I mean—"

"I know what you mean," he declared smiling, "you mean it should always go like clockwork because it's 'just nature', but the greatest miracle is that it should ever go like clockwork at all. We're intended to go on all fours, Nurse Winterton," said Dr. Stone, getting down onto his hands and knees to illustrate his point. "Our organs are constructed on the assumption that we shall spend our lives—or at any rate most of our lives—in this position."

"Lor'!" said Nurse Winterton, giggling involuntarily at the sight of Dr. Stone crawling about the dressing-room floor on his hands and knees.

"You see," said Dr. Stone seriously, "you see when I am in this position my organs are properly supported," and he proceeded to point out to Nurse Winterton where each of his organs was situated and why the position which he had assumed was the correct one for it to function in perfection. It was an interesting lesson, and Nurse Winterton followed it with attention. She knew "her anatomy" of course, but Dr. Stone's theory was new to her, and although she had rejected it at first as "a bit of his nonsense" she now saw that he was serious and that there might be a good deal in it. Ever since that frightful evening when they had battled together for the lives of Mrs. Faulkner and her baby she had cherished an ardent admiration for Dr. Stone. She was fully aware that Mrs. Faulkner owed her life to his skill and courage, and that

she, herself, had played her by no means unimportant part
with her coolness and judgment. The fact that they had battled
together and won through had given them rather a "special
feeling" for each other, and she had been very glad that she
was free to come and undertake this case because she had
realised that she would see a good deal of the young doctor.

"Yes," said Kit, rising and dusting the knees of his trousers,
"yes, if we hadn't been so *proud* of the fact when we discovered that we were able to balance ourselves on our hind legs
and remain balanced upon them indefinitely, we shouldn't
have fallen heirs to so many displacements . . . so if you're
feeling tired, nurse," added Kit with a grave air, "if your legs
or heart or stomach (or any other part of you) is feeling the
effects of remaining too long in the unnatural position which
your ancestors taught themselves to assume, I advise you most
strongly not to sit down in a chair (which I have observed to
be your usual mode of resting) but to resume your natural
position, the position for which your organs were constructed,
and to get down on all fours and remain there as long as
possible."

"Lor', what would my patients say!" cried Nurse Winterton,
laughing delightedly. "Lor', Dr. Stone, you are a card!"

"And now," said Dr. Stone, "now, what about my seeing
Mrs. Dorman—eh? Just a tiny peep at her, nurse?"

"Well, just a tiny peep," agreed Nurse Winterton, who could
have refused him nothing, and would have given him her own
head upon a charger if it would have been the least use to him.

Kit tip-toed into Dolly's room. She was awake now, and
looked cool and comfortable.

"Well!" she said, looking at him with her sky-blue eyes.

"Well . . . everything all right?"

"Everything's marvellous," said Dolly dreamily.

CHAPTER XXXVI

THE REAL ROCHESTER

"THAT'S set all," declared Victor Breeze, mopping his brow with a large white linen handkerchief. "D'you want another straight off, Kit."

"Just as you like," said Kit.

It was Saturday afternoon, and the two men had been playing since three o'clock with an interval for tea. It was very pleasant for tennis, for it was not too hot, at least Kit did not think it was hot—Victor was inclined to be plump and perspired easily. They were evenly matched, for Victor Breeze was the more experienced player and Kit was the more active, and the two sets had gone to fourteen all. Victor had won the first and Kit the second.

"We'd better have an easy one, I think," declared Victor. "We've done pretty well—"

"The light's going a bit," said Kit looking up at the sky, "I don't believe we'd have time for another."

"Unless it was a short one."

"But it never is a short one."

Victor smiled and agreed. "We've had some good games this summer," he said, "but it's getting latish in the year for tennis. There was frost last night."

"Was there?"

"Mhm . . . frost. I hate autumn . . . the end of summer and everything . . . wish I could build a squash court so that I could get *some* exercise, but I can't afford it this year . . . the boys' education and everything. . . ."

"Couldn't you," enquired Kit who thought it would be extremely pleasant if Victor had a squash court. "Would it cost a lot? You could build it over by the garage and use the existing wall for one side."

"Can't afford it this year," declared Victor with a sigh.

They were still standing by the net and were both looking in the same direction—towards the garage where the future squash court might possibly arise—and they both saw a man come out from behind the garage wall and walk slowly up the path.

"Hallo, who's that?" Victor exclaimed in surprise.

Kit did not reply. There was something familiar about the man . . . he felt he had seen him before. They waited for the man to approach, watching him, and they saw that he was dressed in a blue lounge suit and a soft hat, and was carrying a Burberry over his arm.

"What the devil is he doing here?" exclaimed Victor, starting forward to meet him.

Kit put his hand on his friend's arm. "Wait," he said in a low voice.

"But what does he want?"

"Wait a moment . . . I believe I know . . . I believe I know who it is. Let me deal with him, Victor."

"Right-o!" agreed Victor. "Have it your own way. Deal with him faithfully . . . I'll go and have my bath."

He swung off to the house and Kit went forward to meet the stranger alone. He was almost sure that he had seen the man before . . . he was almost sure that it was Rochester. . . .

Kit had only seen Rochester once—in evening clothes—but he had studied the man carefully. If this were Rochester he had changed a good deal in the five months since Kit had seen him . . . he looked younger, and he had filled out a little. His shoulders were squarer. . . . Kit was quite near the man now, near enough to see his face . . . near enough to see his expression . . . and he had a sudden doubt. *It isn't Rochester,* he decided. He hesitated and stood still.

"Good evening," said the man in a pleasant voice, "are you —can you tell me. . . ."

They were face to face now, standing on the path, and Kit's thoughts were in a whirl: It *is* Rochester, he thought, it must be . . . but he's cured. He's perfectly normal. That shifty furtive look has gone. His eyes are perfectly steady. This is the real Rochester . . . the Rochester that Mardie loved. . . .

The man had stopped speaking now and was looking at Kit, and obviously waiting for an answer.

"I'm sorry," said Kit uncomfortably, "I didn't hear what you said."

"Is Mrs. Rochester anywhere about?"

"Well—no. As a matter of fact she's—the house is sublet, you see."

"Oh, I see," said the man. He was silent for a moment and then enquired. "Do you happen to know whether she's gone to Scotland? You see I—I rather wanted to see her."

"Yes, she's in Scotland."

Kit was sure now. Though why he was so sure it would have been difficult to say. He had often imagined a meeting with Rochester, but it had never been like this. Sometimes he had imagined that a message would come for him and he would rush off in the middle of the night and find the man lying ill in a hospital—or dead in a morgue. Sometimes he had imagined that he would meet Rochester in the street, and he would seize hold of the man and call for help and they would have to take him to a mental home. . . . But this man was neither ill nor insane and strangely enough Kit had no angry feelings, no grudge at all against him. Kit did not want to reproach him for all the suffering he had caused, he wanted to help him; for somehow Kit felt that the nerve-ridden creature who had caused so much trouble had nothing at all to do with this quiet-eyed man.

"Would you like Mrs. Rochester's address?" asked Kit at last.

"She's at Kilnocky, I suppose. . . . Yes, of course she would have to give up this place . . . I hadn't thought. . . ."

"You've been ill," Kit said.

"Very ill," Rochester agreed, "I got a knock on the head and I couldn't remember anything for a long time. My brain was an absolute blank—but I don't suppose it would interest you to hear my symptoms," he added with a slight smile.

It interested Kit profoundly. "Please tell me," he said. "I know who you are, you see. I know Mardie."

"You know Mardie?"

"She is . . . waiting for you," said Kit. It was the hardest thing he had ever had to say, and the effort of saying it left him quite limp.

"Poor Mardie!" Rochester said. "I'm beginning to see . . . I thought I had remembered everything, but there are still some things . . . some things. . . ." He paused and put his hand to his head.

"Take it easy," Kit advised him.

"That's what they tell me," Rochester declared, "but it's damned difficult to take it easy. Things come back with a rush and you've got to battle with them . . . then you try to remember more . . . and everything goes." He paused again and then added in a different tone, "There used to be a seat over there—"

The seat had not been moved, and the two of them went over to it and sat down.

Rochester tapped the wood with his knuckles. "It ought to be painted," he said, "but of course . . . of course it has nothing to do with me now. There are new people here."

"Mardie had to give it up because there wasn't enough money," said Kit.

"Money!" he said thoughtfully. "That's another thing I hadn't thought of! She couldn't touch my income, of course . . . poor Mardie!"

Kit remained silent.

"And my partners," continued Rochester, "my partners—Henry Stone and—and John Godfrey—I wonder what they did."

"Where have you been all this time?" Kit enquired; he asked the question partly to change the drift of Rochester's thoughts and partly because he was extremely curious to know the answer. He had searched for Rochester so assiduously that it was difficult to see where he could have remained hidden.

"At Lanstone," replied the other. "It's a sheepfarm on the Sussex Downs. The people there are very kind, and they took me in and nursed me."

"How did you get to Lanstone?"

"I don't know. I can't remember . . . anything," said Rochester vaguely. "Why did I leave here? How did I leave here? How did I happen to be wandering about on the Downs at night? The whole thing is a mystery . . . it's an absolute blank in my memory."

"Very odd!"

"Yes. The farmer was coming home from market and he knocked me down in the road not far from his own gate. He says I was walking in the middle of the road. It was very dark and his lights were bad so he didn't see me. He picked me up and took me home with him . . . but how did I get there at all? Where was I going?"

Kit did not answer for he was busy with his own thoughts and conjectures. He wondered how Rochester had managed to get from Deal to Lanstone—a distance of at least a hundred miles—perhaps some motorist had given him a lift or perhaps he had accomplished the journey by train. Kit thought of the

weary days he had spent searching the country round
Deal. . . .

"We looked everywhere for you," said Kit at last. "We informed the police. There were notices in the papers and messages on the wireless."

"What a lot of trouble I've caused!" he exclaimed.

"But I don't understand it," Kit cried, "why didn't the
farmer let us know? Why didn't he communicate with your
friends?"

"He had no idea who I was."

"He could have informed the police."

"I suppose he should have done so," Rochester agreed
thoughtfully, "but it would never have occurred to him. The
Morleys are very simple country folk; and there's another thing
. . . I mean the farmer had knocked me down with his car
and he may have been afraid he would get into trouble over
it. I don't believe it was his fault because he's a very careful
driver, but still . . ." Rochester paused for a moment and then
continued earnestly. "They're good people, kind and good.
They took me in and nursed me as if I had been their own son.
They would have done the same for the meanest tramp . . .
that's the sort of people they are."

"But the doctor . . . why didn't he. . . ."

"They didn't get a doctor for me. They thought I was just
bruised—not badly hurt at all. I think perhaps I was more seriously injured than they realised. It was my head," he said,
putting up his hand again, "my head was . . . my head
troubled me for a long time, and although my body recovered
quite quickly my head went on buzzing and buzzing. . . .
People like that are different from us. They don't call in a
doctor unless there's something seriously wrong . . . something obvious."

Kit was aware of this. He knew, only too well, that simple

country folk would go on bearing their ailments for months rather than seek medical advice.

"Is this boring you dreadfully?" Rochester enquired.

"No, do go on," replied Kit. "Tell me the whole thing."

"There isn't much more to tell. I was unconscious for a few hours—so they say—and I remember waking up in a strange room. It was a queer shaped room with a low ceiling and a tiny window . . . I didn't remember anything . . . not anything at all. I didn't even know who I was."

"How ghastly!"

"No, it wasn't really," said Rochester slowly. "I didn't seem to mind, you see, and they were all very kind to me. I felt quite calm and contented. The ghastly part came much later when I began to remember. . . ." He bent forward and put his head in his hands. "What a mess!" he said, in a low vibrant voice, "what a hellish mess!"

"But your troubles are over now," Kit pointed out. "The thing is over and done with so you needn't think about it any more. You were ill, and now you're better—that's all. It's wiser not to look back."

"It isn't over . . . you don't understand."

Kit understood very well—or so he thought—he saw that Rochester was still battling with himself and trying to remember all the intricacies of his old life. He saw, but only dimly, what a frightful strain it must be.

"Don't think about it," he said urgently.

"No, I mustn't," Rochester agreed. "When I try to think too hard it all goes blank again. Sometimes when I wake in the morning everything has gone and I have to lie and wait for it to come back."

"Mardie will help you," said Kit.

"Oh, I'm much better," Rochester declared, "I'm practically all right now. I'm feeling better every day."

They were silent for a few moments and then Kit rose from the seat. "Well, what are we going to do?" he enquired. "Where are you staying tonight?"

Rochester looked round somewhat vaguely; it was obvious, of course, that he had intended to stay at the Lynchet.

"You had better come with me," Kit told him.

"Come with you!"

"Yes, Dr. Peabody will give you a bed."

"Dr. Peabody!" said Rochester slowly. "Yes, of course—Dr. Peabody—a nice old man."

"He'll put you up," said Kit.

"But why should he?" Rochester enquired. "I mean I could go to the local pub. The only thing is that I haven't got any money . . . or clothes. I daresay it seems odd, but I thought— I thought Mardie would be here."

"Of course," agreed Kit, "but I can lend you money, and clothes too, for that matter. We're just about the same size."

"Why should you bother?"

"Why shouldn't I?" asked Kit. "Come on, I'll take you to the doctor's house in my car. I'm the doctor's assistant, you know."

"I didn't know he had an assistant," Rochester said in surprise.

Kit thought that Rochester's case was a very interesting one. He had forgotten everything that had happened previous to his departure from the Lynchet—there was a gap in his mind of several months at least—but this was no time to go into any details, or to press for further information as to what he remembered about his previous life. The important thing at the moment was to get the man safely to Dr. Peabody's house. Kit had found Rochester and he intended to stick to him and keep a good hold of him until they could inform Mardie of his return. Dr. Peabody would know what to do . . . Dr. Peabody would help.

"Come on," he said again, "it's getting cold now, and you oughtn't to hang about." (He conquered an almost irresistible impulse to put his hand on Rochester's arm and drag him to the car.) "Come on," he said for the third time.

Rochester followed with some reluctance. "I don't see why you should bother," he declared, "or Dr. Peabody, either. Are you sure he won't mind?"

"Perfectly certain," said Kit.

They got into the car and drove off.

On the way to the doctor's house Kit learned a good deal more about his companion and about all that had happened to him. Some part of Rochester's experiences could never be known—and would always remain a mystery—unless at some future date Rochester remembered them himself. Kit saw that blind chance had played a great part in the affair; it was chance that had sent Rochester to that old farmhouse on the Downs, and just chance that the farmer had knocked him down outside the gate. If Rochester had been knocked down in a town and carried unconscious to a hospital he would have been found by his friends without any difficulty and a great deal of pain and misery would have been saved. It just happened like that, thought Kit; life is made up of strange chances, of queer freaks of fate.

Rochester was talking now, telling Kit about the farmer and his wife. "They're very simple old-fashioned people," he explained. "They're good and gentle. Their minds move slowly, but they have wisdom and a kind of natural dignity. Their faces are peaceful and perhaps this is because they live so close to nature. I spent long days on the Downs with Morley, and helped him with the sheep. It was so quiet and peaceful up there."

Kit began to see the other side of the picture now and he saw that the blind chance which had sent Rochester to that particular farm had been kind to him, at least, for the quiet simplicity of the life had healed him, and the long sunny days on the windswept Downs had completed his cure. Nature's treatment was vastly better than any treatment which man could have devised for Rochester's tortured brain.

Already Kit was wondering what the future held for Rochester. He must never go back to the old life, the hurrying stressful life of the city. Perhaps he would settle down at Kilnocky and he and Mardie would be happy again—as they were when they were first married. He believed that Mardie could be happy again with this man. He believed that she would be able to remake her life. For himself Kit had no hope at all . . . hope was dead. He wondered whether he should stay at Minfield with Dr. Peabody or whether it would be better to do as Mardie had advised and start off on another spell of wandering . . . to Kamchatka or Timbuctoo. . . .

CHAPTER XXXVII

ONE THING AT A TIME

MARDIE was not surprised when she received Dr. Peabody's telegram telling her that Jack had come back, for she had always been certain in her own mind that some day he would return. She had a feeling when she saw the orange envelope that it contained news of Jack and her hands trembled as she took it from the telegraph boy and opened it.

"Is there an answer?" asked the boy, looking at her curiously.

"No answer, thank you," Mardie replied.

She gave him sixpence and watched him go whistling down the path to the gate, and then she turned and went into the house. It happened that Hoony had taken Wattie to Edinburgh for the day—they were going to the dentist in the morning and to the Zoo in the afternoon—so Mardie had the house to herself. She was glad to be alone for a little while for there was a good deal of thinking to be done. The telegram told her that Jack had returned safe and well, and that he was anxious to see her at the earliest opportunity, but it told her no more for Dr. Peabody had been aware that in a small place like Kilnocky telegrams occasion a good deal of interest and the news they contain is often circulated far and wide. Mardie decided to go down to the telephone box in the village and ring up Dr. Peabody to find out all the details and to make plans, but before she could do this she must settle her mind. She found, somewhat to her surprise, that there was a great deal of difference between being certain in her own mind that some day Jack would come back, and hearing that he had come back and was anxious to see her. She found that she was not ready to meet Jack and accept him on the old terms, and she wished that she could put off the meeting and prepare herself for it . . . but that was foolish of course, for she had been waiting for him to come back ever since he went away, hadn't she?

"Yes," said Mardie to herself, "yes, of course I have."

She put the telegram on the table and sat down and thought about Jack. She tried to imagine that he was there. She tried to think what she would say to him. It was impossible, of course, because she had not the slightest idea what Jack would say to her. She did not know what he had been doing all this time, nor what his frame of mind would be. The telegram told her that he was well and this might mean that the old Jack had come back—in fact it must mean exactly that. Mardie tried to think of him as he had been when they were first married, but somehow or other she could not manage it. She could only see him as he was before he had disappeared, irritable, unreasonable, full of fear and misery. She tried to face her future, and to envisage their life together, but she could not do that either, and she had a dreadful suspicion that if she could have envisaged it she would not be able to bear it. All these months she had lived her own life and there had been nobody with any rights over her. She had belonged to herself and had been able to do and say what she liked without having to think first . . . she and Dolly had understood each other admirably, and she had said whatever came into her mind . . . but Jack was different. Mardie was attacked by sheer panic when she thought of her life with Jack. She remembered the frightful strain she had undergone, the necessity of considering carefully before she spoke, the patience which she had needed to deal with his moods.

Mardie had not realised all this at the time, but now, after six months of freedom, she realised it clearly . . . but I must face it and bear it, she told herself, pressing her hands against her burning eyes, Jack is coming back to me . . . and I have been waiting for him. She reminded herself that she was his wife and that she had promised to love and cherish him, and she reminded herself of his weakness and of his dependence upon her. Presently she rose and began to walk up and down for she was so restless and distraught that she could not sit still. Her thoughts were whirling round and round inside her head like bees in a hive. What should she say? What should she do? What would Jack be like? What would he want to do? She tried to compose her thoughts and to think sensibly and quietly, but she could not do it, and after a little while she realised that it would be impossible to think sensibly until she had more information about Jack, and she seized her coat and bag and ran down the path and along the road to the telephone box.

It took Mardie some time to get through to Dr. Peabody's house but she accomplished it at last and was rewarded by hearing the old doctor's voice answering the telephone.

"Yes, he's here," Dr. Peabody said. "He's staying here with me and he's perfectly well . . ." and he proceeded to give her a few brief details of Jack Rochester's illness and recovery and his return to Minfield.

Mardie listened breathlessly. "But how . . . but why?" she asked. "Why did he go away, Dr. Peabody? What does he want to do?"

"He'll tell you what he can," Dr. Peabody replied. "There are a great many things that he can't remember . . . and perhaps it's just as well."

"Yes," said Mardie.

"My suggestion is that he should travel north tomorrow and perhaps you could meet him in Edinburgh."

"Oh, yes . . . yes, of course."

Perhaps Dr. Peabody realised something of what she was feeling for he began to give her some advice. "Now, Mrs. Rochester, don't worry too much," he said in a comforting sort of voice, "you mustn't worry, you know. Just take it easy."

"It's all very well—"

"Oh I know, I know," he declared, "but *take one thing at a time* . . . do you understand what I mean?"

"I think so."

"Don't think of the past. Meet him as if nothing had happened—that will be the best way for both of you—and don't think of the future, either. The future will take care of itself."

Suddenly Mardie felt as if a cool hand had been laid upon her forehead, and the bees stopped buzzing in her brain. "Oh yes, I can do that," she declared, "I *can* do that. How wise you are!"

Dr. Peabody chuckled. "I'm old, you see," he replied. "I'm very old . . . there are some advantages in growing old. You will find that out for yourself one of these days."

The remainder of their talk was concerned with arrangements for the following day. Dr. Peabody promised to send Kit to London with Jack Rochester to see him safely into the train, and Mardie said she would meet him in Edinburgh. Mardie rang off after that; she had spent a small fortune in shillings but she felt that she had got her money's worth.

One thing at a time, thought Mardie as she walked slowly home, and the first thing that she had to do was to meet Jack in an easy manner. Dr. Peabody had given her something definite to do and she felt herself capable of doing it—how wise he is, she thought, how wise and kind! She saw, also, that it would be much easier to meet Jack for the first time in the crowded station and to have their first talk together in the impersonal atmosphere of a big hotel; they would be surrounded by strangers, busy with their own affairs, and this would give Jack and herself the feeling that their own troubles were less important and would help to tide them over the first awkward moments.

Mardie felt calmer now and ready for the ordeal in front
of her, and when Hoony and Wattie returned from Edinburgh she had had her supper and was sitting peacefully by
the fire. The old woman accepted the news of Mr. Rochester's
return in a philosophical manner; she had lived so long and
had seen so much joy and sorrow that she had grown a pro-
tective shell and lived inside it, but she did not approve of
Mardie's plans and, as usual, she announced her feelings in
plain words.

"Ye're off to Edinburgh to meet him!" she cried. "But what's
the use of that? I'm surprised at ye, Miss Mardie. Can ye not
bide quietly at hame and let the man come here? He owes ye
that much after the way he's treated ye."

"He doesn't owe me anything," said Mardie firmly.

"He does so . . . there's not many people would thole the
way he's treated ye . . . leaving ye without sae much as a
word, and never a letter from him tae say if he's alive or deid."

"But Hoony, he was ill. He couldn't help it. You must be
nice to him, Hoony."

"I'll be nice enough," said Hoony with a grim tightening
of her mouth which belied her words. "It's not for the likes of
me tae speak ill words tae a gentleman, whatever I may be
thinking in ma ain mind—imphm!"

"Hoony, you must be *nice*," said Mardie urgently. "I'm meeting him in Edinburgh tomorrow and I shall bring him down
here the next day. I shall be very angry indeed if you're horrid
to him."

"I've told ye I'll be nice enough and I can say nae mair," declared Hoony, with a toss of her proud head, "and ye'd be far
better tae let him come here. What d'ye want tae meet him in
Edinburgh for?"

"I've told you—"

"Ye'll have mair chance of a peaceful talk if the man comes
here. Yon Edinburgh hotels is awful rowdy kind of places."

"I can't do that because it's all settled," said Mardie firmly. "I've settled the whole thing with Dr. Peabody . . . and Hoony, you must promise me that you'll be friendly and kind. He's been very ill, you know."

"Ye needn't worry," replied the old woman dryly. "Ye needn't fash aboot that. Mister Rochester wouldna' care what I said tae him, he's far too high and mighty tae heed *me*."

Mardie was uncomfortably aware that there was a good deal of truth in this. Jack had never liked Hoony or understood her, and the old woman knew this and was always at her worst with him. There would be no peace at Hillside House with Jack and Hoony beneath the same roof and Mardie would be a buffer between their warring personalities. What would Jack want to do? Would he want to go back to the city, or would he be content to vegetate at Kilnocky . . . and if so . . . but it would be absolutely impossible to turn Hoony out of the house which had been her home for so long. . . .

I must not think about it, Mardie decided, Dr. Peabody said I must take one thing at a time. The future must be left to take care of itself.

Mardie had packed her suitcase and caught the train and now she was sitting in the lounge of the big hotel waiting until it was time to meet Jack, and just at the moment she was thinking of her conversation with Hoony, and of how the old woman had tried to persuade her to stay at home. In spite of her troubled mind Mardie could not help smiling at Hoony's description of Edinburgh hotels—"rowdy" was certainly an inept adjective to apply to this big quiet room. It was busy of course, but the people who passed and repassed, bent upon their lawful business, were soft-footed and soft-voiced and the hum of the street was muted by the double windows and the revolving doors.

She was watching the clock so closely now that she began to

think it must have stopped, but her watch told the same time and when she put it to her ear it was still ticking. . . . Jack had been travelling since ten o'clock this morning. It seemed a long time since then. She wondered if he would be very tired. Dr. Peabody had said that Kit would see him safely into the train. She saw that it must have been very hard for Kit . . . the whole thing was dreadful for Kit because he had always hoped that somehow or other things would come right. She had told him not to hope but she knew that he had gone on hoping. Poor Kit . . . but she must not think of Kit. He was strong and brave and he would forget her in a little while and make a life for himself . . . she was sure of that.

The hands of the clock had moved on and it was time to go. Mardie rose and went down in the lift to the platform. People were walking up and down, waiting for the train to come in, and porters were hurrying along with their barrows. Mardie took up her position and waited . . . she was impatient for Jack to come and yet she dreaded the meeting so much that she could scarcely breathe.

The great engine steamed in and the train came to rest at the platform. Jack was the first passenger to alight, he dropped from the step with a small suitcase in his hand and came to meet her.

"Hallo, Mardie!"

"Hallo, Jack!"

He did not attempt to kiss her and she was glad of that, for she would not have been able to bear it. Her heart was thumping uncomfortably and her knees felt weak. It was a moment or two before she could pull herself together, and look at him, but when she did so she was pleasantly surprised, for Jack was smiling at her in a friendly way, and she could see that this was indeed the old Jack. His eyes were clear and candid and the lines of worry and fear and misery had disappeared. It was the old Jack but there was a difference in him, a sort of embarrassment, a reserve which had been foreign to his nature. Mardie could feel this and she put it down to the fact that he had known suffering.

Mardie remembered that she must play her part in this meeting so she smiled back at Jack. "What about your luggage?" she asked, looking round for the luggage van.

"No luggage except this," he replied holding up the small suitcase.

CHAPTER XXXVIII

THE LAST STRAW

JACK and Mardie walked along the platform together and turned into the hotel, talking of commonplace matters. Jack assured her that he had had a good journey and was not over-tired. It was a very good train, and the journey had seemed quite short.

"I had an interesting book," he said, and held up a copy of THE STRANGER PRINCE which he was carrying in his hand. Mardie had read it and enjoyed it immensely. They discussed the book as they went up in the lift.

It was not until they were sitting in a corner of the lounge and had ordered two glasses of sherry, and had lighted their cigarettes that anything important was said.

"I thought we'd stay here tonight," Mardie told him.

He agreed at once. "That will be best," he said.

"And then we can go down to Kilnocky tomorrow morning," Mardie added.

Jack did not reply to that . . . he was watching a fat woman crossing the lounge.

"Would you like to stay at Kilnocky for a little?" Mardie asked him. "It's quite a nice little house. You aren't going back to the city, are you?"

"No," he said. "No, I couldn't go back to the city."

"I'm glad, Jack," she said quickly.

"I shall have very little money," he said.

"It doesn't matter," she told him. "We could be happy on very little—at least I could. I've got enough to go on with. You could have a long rest and then find some sort of job."

He looked down. "I—I've found one, Mardie," he said.

"You've found a job?"

"I want to go back to Lanstone—to the Morleys."

"Of course," said Mardie quickly, "of course . . . whatever you want, Jack. Whatever is best for you."

He was silent for a few moments and then he said in a low voice. "I've treated you very badly."

"It wasn't your fault," she told him. "You were ill, I think you were ill for a long time before . . . before . . . I ought to have seen it, Jack. I ought to have taken a firm stand and made you take a proper long holiday. I blame myself."

"No, Mardie, it was just that I wasn't strong enough to tackle it. The life got hold of me. It would get hold of me again —that's why I can't go back."

"I know," she declared earnestly, "I don't want you to go back. We'll take a tiny house in the country near the Morleys' farm. I don't mind how small it is."

"But I do," Jack said, raising his head. "I mind it for you, I couldn't bear it."

Mardie considered his words. She felt he was trying to tell her something but she had not the faintest idea what it was.

"You aren't used to—to that sort of life," Jack said.

She looked at him earnestly. "What do you want to do?" she asked. "Do you want to go abroad? But no—you said you had found a job at the Morleys' farm."

"Yes," he said. "It's—well, it's just a job as assistant to Mr. Morley; he's getting old and he needs someone to help him, you see. He asked me if I would come . . . he's very anxious for me to come. In fact he said he would take me into partnership—even if I couldn't put any money into the business. It was good of him, wasn't it?"

"Yes," said Mardie.

"He likes me, you see," continued Jack somewhat naïvely, "and I like him. It's just a sheep farm, Mardie. I should have

to help him with the sheep and he would teach me all about
the buying and selling of them, and I could manage the accounts for him."

"Yes," she said. "Well, why not take it, Jack? I've told you
that I don't mind living in a tiny house and being poor. I think
we could be happy."

"No," cried Jack. "No, we couldn't! Mardie, I couldn't bear
it. I should feel all the time that I'd failed you, that I'd dragged
you down. It would mean living in a cottage on the Morleys'
farm. It's right out in the wilds . . . it's high up on the Downs,
miles from anywhere. You would have nothing to do . . . you
wouldn't have a single person of your own sort to speak to."

"But the Morleys—"

"They aren't your sort," said Jack quickly. "They're kind
and good but they're quite simple people, not the sort of people
you could be friends with."

"What do you want to do?" she asked, looking at him in
bewilderment.

"It's so difficult," he said uncomfortably. "You and I . . .
we were happy for a bit . . . and then we . . . weren't
happy."

"You were ill," she pointed out.

"Yes," he replied. "I was ill and you were patient with me."

"I tried to be patient."

"You *were* patient," he declared, "and I knew you were being
patient. That's what made it so hard to bear."

Mardie laughed. "Oh Jack!" she exclaimed. "Oh Jack, I don't
blame you! It would be dreadfully hard to bear . . . somebody being patient with you. Shall I promise not to be patient
any more?"

Jack did not smile at this little joke. "Listen, Mardie," he
said, "I know it was all my fault; but everything went wrong
. . . everything. I want to forget all that part of my life. I
did forget it, you know. I forgot who I was. I was like an

infant with no past at all . . . but I was quite happy and contented. I was quite happy until I began to remember."

"Then you want—what *do* you want, Jack?"

"I want to begin again and make a fresh start."

She did not yet understand what he meant. "We will do
that," she told him, smiling at him encouragingly. "We'll make
a fresh start. I believe we can do it quite successfully. The old
Jack has come back. We'll start again and forget all that has
happened."

"The old Jack hasn't come back, Mardie."

"I think he has."

"No, he's dead."

She looked at him in some alarm for he had spoken the
words seriously, and the thought sprang to her mind that
perhaps he was not cured of the frightful malady, after all. He
was sitting forward in his chair with his knees apart and his
hands folded between them and she saw that his knuckles were
white with the strain of his clenched hands.

"Jack . . ." she began uncertainly.

"I don't know how to make you understand, Mardie," he
said in a low voice. "You are so kind . . . and that makes it
harder still. I couldn't say it to you at all if I thought you really
loved me."

"What do you mean?"

"I want you to divorce me."

Mardie stared at him in amazement. "Do you . . . mean it?"
she asked.

He nodded, keeping his eyes fixed on the floor.

Mardie could not believe that he meant it. She had made up
her mind to take Jack back and to do her best to love him, to
make the very best she could of their new life together . . .
and now . . . she was not needed . . . Jack did not need her
any more.

"But—but why?" she asked, still incredulous.

He did not answer, and for a moment she wondered whether he could possibly have heard anything . . . could Kit have said anything . . . and then she looked at Jack again and saw the flush of embarrassment on his face, his downcast eyes.

"Is there—have you—have you met somebody else?" she stammered.

He nodded again. "I'm sorry," he said, "I know I'm behaving like a cad."

"No," said Mardie quickly, "but please explain—explain everything. I want to understand."

"I feel such a rotter," he said miserably.

"Tell me about it," Mardie urged.

"It's so difficult to tell you," Jack said. "I don't know how to begin . . . it's the Morleys' daughter, Polly. She looked after me when I was ill, and she was so kind and sympathetic. She was the only person who really understood that I couldn't remember anything at all . . . the others were kind too but they didn't understand. Polly and I had jokes together and—and somehow or other we fell in love. Oh, it sounds dreadful, I know," declared Jack, "but it seemed to happen quite naturally, and you see I didn't remember anything . . . not anything at all."

"You didn't remember about me," said Mardie incredulously. "You didn't remember that you were married to me?"

"I didn't even know who I was," he replied.

Mardie was silent. She found it very hard to believe.

"Oh Mardie!" he continued. "Oh Mardie, I know it's a dreadful thing to have done, but I simply couldn't help it. You must believe that."

She saw that he was truly in earnest about it. "Poor Jack!" she exclaimed, "it hasn't been easy for you."

"I've been through hell!" he declared. "When I began to remember who I was and what I was; and about you, and our life together it was almost more than I could bear. You and I were so happy together just at first and I never wanted anyone else. It wouldn't have happened if I had remembered about you."

"We were happy," Mardie agreed.

"Just at first," Jack reminded her. "We were happy at first and then we weren't happy at all. You didn't love me any more . . . you pitied me . . . you despised me."

"No, no," she said hastily. "No, Jack; what a dreadful thing to say!"

"It's true," he told her, "I could feel it. I could feel that you despised me—that was why I tried to make more money."

"But Jack, I didn't want money. I didn't want you to wear yourself out making money. I told you so, I told you over and over again. I never wanted to be rich."

"I know," said Jack. "I knew that all the time, but I wanted to show you what a clever husband you had. I wanted to show you what a fine fellow I was. I wanted your admiration, Mardie."

She was silent, for she had begun to understand and there was nothing she could say. Mardie had never been able to admire Jack's business acumen because she had never been able to understand what he was doing. He hadn't wanted her to understand, but only to admire. She had always felt in a vague way that there was something a trifle dishonest about his activities, for he had boasted so often of "getting the better of the other fellow" that this seemed to be his whole aim. Mardie could not admire that, for she had been brought up to a different way of life and her whole outlook was utterly and completely at variance with such a creed.

"I've been thinking a lot lately," Jack told her, "in fact ever since I began to remember things . . . you have plenty of time for thinking on a sheep farm. I couldn't think at all when I was in the city. I daren't think. It was like a treadmill and you had to keep going or else you were done."

Mardie agreed with that.

"I couldn't go back to it," Jack continued in a thoughtful voice, "because if I went back I should just get caught up in it again—I know I should—so the only hope for me is to make a fresh start." He paused for a moment and smiled. "Polly thinks I'm no end of a fellow," he said.

"Why shouldn't she?" asked Mardie lightly.

"Because I'm not, really; but, you see, it helps me tremendously to know that she thinks I'm wonderful—funny, isn't it?"

"Yes," said Mardie. She had been willing to try to love him, but she was aware that she could never admire him and think him "wonderful" for she saw him too clearly, his limitations and his weaknesses.

"Polly suits me," declared Jack. "I know she isn't half so clever or so high-minded and unselfish as you, but somehow she seems to suit me better. You and I have different points of view—we always had—but Polly is quite content with my point of view. I've thought about it a lot," declared Jack, "and I'm sure it wouldn't be any good going back and trying to patch up our lives together. We wouldn't be happy. You can't go back in life, you must go forward."

Mardie was beginning to look forward and see her own future now, she was beginning to realise that she was free. She had wanted freedom of course (though she had never dared to hope for it) and, by all accounts, she ought to have been delighted to receive it at Jack's hands, but oddly enough her feeling was not one of pure delight—perhaps she would not have been human if she had not felt a trifle hurt to find that after all Jack did not want her.

Jack was looking at her anxiously, "Don't you agree?" he said.

"I expect you're right," she said, "I would have done my best, but I expect you're right."

"You don't really mind very much, do you?"

She shook her head and smiled.

"I believe you're quite glad!" he cried.

"I'm glad you've told me," she answered. She was not going to tell him any more about her own affairs, for they were no concern of his, and it would be unfair to Kit to mention his name. Besides there was so little to tell.

Jack began to talk of ways and means, he asked her what her plans were and whether she could "manage" as regards money. She told him that she would go back to Kilnocky, and that she had sufficient money for her needs.

"I shall have to see Henry Stone," said Jack, "and if there's any money left you must have it."

"I don't want it," Mardie declared emphatically.

They argued a little about that, but Mardie was adamant—not a penny of Jack's money would she touch.

"Have it your own way," said Jack at last. "You always were obstinate when you really minded about anything; the money will be quite useful to me, if there is any. I shall put it into Mr. Morley's farm."

It was all unreal to Mardie and she felt as if she must pinch herself to make sure she was not dreaming. She had made up her mind (though not without inner qualms and struggles) to one sort of future and now her future had suddenly assumed a different aspect. She was almost frightened—but that was foolish and absurd, for there was nothing whatever to be frightened of in a future of complete freedom.

It was a very strange experience to sit here in the hotel lounge with Jack and discuss things in this calm and sensible manner. There was no bitterness in their discussion and no embarrassment. Mardie could not feel embarrassed because Jack was so perfectly natural over the whole affair . . . it struck her suddenly that he was a little *too* natural.

"It's a good thing this has happened," said Jack. "It's a good thing I met Polly—dear little soul—we shall both be much happier now."

"Yes," said Mardie. It *was* a "good thing" of course, but she was angry with Jack for saying it so blithely. Blithe was the exact word for him, thought Mardie, he was perfectly happy and cheerful now that he had got what he wanted . . . and strangely enough she, who had been sorry for him and willing to forget his misdeeds, began to remember them again, and began to remember all the pain and misery he had caused her. She found herself bearing with him patiently—as she had done so often before—and quite suddenly it burst upon her, like a sudden vision of Paradise, that this was the last time she would have to bear with Jack. . . .

"Yes," said Jack cheerfully, "yes, it's all for the best, and how lucky that we haven't any children! Polly wants children —dozens of them—she's a maternal type, you see."

Suddenly Mardie was furiously angry, she felt that this was the last straw, the last and absolutely insupportable insult. She was so angry that she could not trust herself to speak . . . if she began to say anything she would say too much. She rose from her chair with her heart pounding uncomfortably and the blood drumming in her ears.

"Where are you going?" enquired Jack. "What time shall we dine?"

"I'm going to bed."

"To bed!" he exclaimed in amazement.

"Yes, I'm tired. Good-bye, Jack, it will be better if we don't meet again. You'll be going south tomorrow morning, I suppose." She did not wait to see how he took this Parthian shot but walked steadily across the lounge and took the lift to the third floor where her room was.

The bedroom which had been allotted to Mardie in the big hotel was small but very clean and comfortable. There was a telephone standing on a table by the bed, and this was fortunate for she must send a wire to Kit—he deserved it, she thought. Mardie spent some time concocting her message but finally sent an extremely simple one:

"JACK HAS ASKED FOR A DIVORCE."

When that was done she made her few simple preparations and got into bed. She had a book to read, but she did not open it, for her mind was in a whirl and she knew that until she had tidied up the confusion of her thoughts she would not be able to rest.

"I'm free," she said aloud.

That, of course, was the most important thing—in fact it was the only thing that mattered—and she was a fool (so she decided) to cavil at the manner in which this precious gift of freedom had been offered to her. It doesn't matter what Jack says or does now, she told herself, nothing that Jack says or does can hurt me any more. I'm free.

She lay and thought about it for a long time, and the more she thought about it the more clearly she saw that this way was the only way in which freedom could have come to her. Mardie had thought that there was no possible way for freedom to come (for whatever happened she could not have failed Jack) but God had heard her prayers and had seen this way of answering them. Was it wrong to think that this was an answer to her personal supplications? Was it presumptuous to believe that God had worked out her problem for her? Mardie could not answer her own questions, for, on one hand, she believed in the tremendous efficacy of prayer, but on the other hand it seemed presumptuous to believe that the lives of Jack and his Polly had been directed to suit her convenience.

In spite of her unanswered questions and the turbulence of her thoughts, Mardie slept well and awoke refreshed. She rang for breakfast and ordered a satisfying meal for she had had no dinner and was therefore very hungry. The telephone bell rang as she was finishing her meal and she lifted the receiver, wondering if it was a wire from Kit, but it was Jack telephoning from his bedroom to hers.

"I want to see you before I go," he said. "I'm going south by the Pullman at 11:20. Shall we meet in the lounge or where?"

"There's no object in our meeting at all," Mardie replied.

"But I want to see you."

Mardie laughed.

"Are you angry with me?" he enquired.

"No, of course not," said Mardie, and this was true, for Jack did not matter to her any more; she had decided that, and with the decision her angry feelings had vanished. "No, I'm not angry with you," Mardie declared, "and I hope you'll be very happy indeed. I don't want to see you, that's all."

"But Mardie, we must arrange things!"

"I'll tell my solicitor to write to you."

"I *want* to see you," he said again, "there's something special I want to say, and it's difficult to say it on the 'phone."

"Write to me, then," she advised smiling a little at the absurdity of the situation.

"No," said Jack. "No, I'll just have to say it. You see the Morleys are very old-fashioned . . . Mr. and Mrs. Morley don't know that I'm married, you see . . . Polly and I thought . . . we wondered . . ."

"Don't worry," Mardie said, "I shan't do anything, Jack. The Morleys are your affair entirely."

And so they are, thought Mardie as she put down the receiver; they're Jack's affair, not mine.

It was obvious from what Jack had said that he was sinking himself in the social scale, but Mardie thought that he might find true happiness among these simple farmer folk. She thought this first because he had spoken of them with such tenderness, and second because it was evident that they had a sincere affection for him. Jack had always wanted to be admired and respected, it had been his ambition to shine, and he had chosen a milieu where he could shine without any effort. Yes, thought Mardie, yes, he and Polly have every chance of happiness. She is content to accept his point of view, and admire him wholeheartedly, and that is what he needs. I was the wrong person for Jack.

CHAPTER XXXIX

"I CAN TRUST YOU"

MARDIE took the first train home to Kilnocky and arrived there in time for lunch. Somehow or other she had expected a message from Kit—she had expected to find a telegram waiting for her at Hillside House—but no telegram had come. It was rather odd, and she was a trifle—just a trifle—disappointed. She was obliged to tell Hoony her news for it was necessary to account for Jack's non-appearance and Hoony was amazed and indignant.

"Well noo, did ye ever hear the like!" she exclaimed, not once but many times. "Did ye ever hear the like! The man must be mad—that's all I can say."

But unfortunately it was not all that Hoony could say and her well-meant but somewhat tactless denunciations of "yon man" were no less difficult to bear than her embarrassing questions regarding her mistress's future plans and her eulogies of "yon Dr. Stone."

"The man must be demented!" she cried, "and tae think he's been carrying on wi' anither wumman and us all thinking him deid . . . it's fair awful! But I never could abide yon man—and that's the truth, Miss Mardie, if I should dee this meenit—Na, na, he was not worthy of ye, and there's nae need for ye tae fash yersel'. There's as guid fish in the sea as ever came oot of it and just you mind that. Aye, there's plenty that would be prood tae have ye."

"But Hoony, I don't want—"

"Och aye, but never you heed," cried the old woman. "Ye're quit of yon man and that's the main thing, and ye can just

forget him, noo. Have ye thought what ye'll be daeing at all
. . . mebbe ye'll not have had the time, but I was thinking ye
might write a wee line tae yon Dr. Stone. Mebbe he'd like a
wee holiday, Miss Mardie. He liked it fine when he was here,
and he said he'd like fine tae come back. Could ye not send
him a letter?" enquired Hoony, persuasively. "There would
be nae hairm in that, Miss Mardie."

"But Hoony, I don't want—"

"Och aye, but he's a fine open-hairted gentleman is Dr.
Stone, and he's got nae airs and graces . . . he's no like *Mister
Rochester*," declared Hoony, infusing the words with inde-
scribable scorn. "Yon Mister Rochester . . . it fair makes ma
blood boil when I think of the man. Did ye ever hear the
like . . ."

Mardie stood it until she could bear it no longer and then
she seized her coat and fled. "I must have a walk," she declared. "I'll walk down to the village and get some—some
stamps."

Hoony smiled. "Aye," she agreed, "aye, that's the thing.
Away ye go, Miss Mardie. Ye'll be needing stamps for letters,
mebbe, and ye might get a few sausages when ye're aboot it.
I'll fry them for yer supper."

Mardie did not require stamps, but had chosen to walk in
the direction of the village so that if by any chance Kit had
wired to her she would meet the telegraph boy on his way to
Hillside House and receive her message all the sooner. She
walked to the village and bought some stamps and had a little
chat with the post-mistress . . . there was always a chance
that the telegram might arrive while she was there. But it did
not arrive and the post-mistress was so interested in her affairs
and enquired so persistently as to whether she had received
the telegram that had arrived for her the day before yesterday
and whether Mr. Rochester was coming north, and whether he
would be making a long stay at Kilnocky that Mardie was

forced to invent an excuse and fly from the post office as though it were infested with the plague. She bought the sausages—as Hoony had suggested—and walked home very slowly . . . but no telegraph boy overtook her.

Mardie had taken so long over her walk that it was dark by the time she reached Hillside House and Hoony had lighted the lamp and put it upon the table in the sitting-room. Mardie took off her coat and sat down with a book, but she could not concentrate. She was restless and miserable. She got up and moved about the room, and sat down again . . . Hoony had started to fry the sausages in the little kitchen now, and the house was so constructed that Mardie could smell them—she could hear them frizzling if she left the sitting-room door ajar. It was a friendly sound.

I could be happy here like this (she told herself), I could be quite happy alone with Hoony. I could live here quietly and save up my money and go abroad for a month or six weeks every year—I should be quite free. She considered this life which she had envisaged and wondered whether it would be the best solution of her problems. There would be more problems to face if she married Kit—if Kit really wanted her to marry him. Perhaps Kit had realised that it would not be very good for him, professionally, to saddle himself with a woman who had figured in a divorce suit. Kit and I, thought Mardie, Kit and I understand each other *now,* but would our marriage be a success? She remembered that she and Jack had been happy together at first and she remembered that she had failed Jack. She hád tried so hard to be a good wife to Jack but she had not been able to go on loving him . . . perhaps I'm not the sort of person to make a success of marriage, thought Mardie rather miserably.

This thought had just passed through her mind when she heard a step on the path . . . the front door opened . . . and closed again very softly. Mardie rose to her feet, but, before she had taken a step forward, the sitting-room door was pushed open and Kit walked in.

"What a gorgeous smell!" he said. "I hope you've got enough sausages for me."

Suddenly Mardie was laughing and laughing, with tears running down her cheeks. "Oh, Kit, you can have them all," she cried.

"We'll share them," he said. "I want to share everything with you, Mardie. You will let me, won't you?"

They stood there for a few moments looking at each other. Mardie saw his thin eager face smiling at her in the lamp-light—she saw the deep shadows of his eye-sockets, the firm kindly mouth, the jutting chin—there was so *much* in that smile, so much love and friendship and tenderness.

"Oh, I can trust you!" she cried involuntarily.

His smile faded and he replied in a voice strangely deep, "God helping me, I shall never fail you."

EPILOGUE

MRS RALPH DORMAN, having spent the winter—or part of it—at Malta, the spring at Southsea, and the summer at Invergordon, was not in the least perturbed when H.M.S. *Terrible* departed to spend the following winter at Bermuda. She took a small bungalow upon that delectable island and settled down there as contentedly as a bird upon its nest. Dolly was, by this time, so inured to the vagrant life of a Naval Officer's appendage that if Ralph had strolled in to lunch and remarked that the *Terrible* was leaving that night on a voyage to the moon, Dolly would probably have replied, "Yes, darling"; would have packed her trunks and her baby's bed and would have rung up the nearest Steam-Ship Office to enquire when the next boat was due to sail for the lunar regions.

Fortunately, however, this contingency did not arise. The *Terrible* remained, based at Bermuda, with Ralph on board and Dolly saw him frequently; and, if she did not see him frequently enough to satisfy her fond heart, that was not Ralph's fault but was due to the exigencies of the Service.

The bungalow was so near the sea that Dolly could stroll in from her bath in a swimming suit which displayed her charms to the full and left very little to the imagination of the beholder, and one day when she did stroll in (feeling very happy and languorous and pleasantly in need of her lunch) she saw, lying upon the hall table, a letter with an English postmark which had obviously arrived while she was disporting herself in the sea.

"Mardie, at last!" cried Dolly, pouncing upon the letter and tearing off the envelope with impatience to see its contents.

The Fourways,
Minfield.

MY DARLING LITTLE DOLLY,

I expect you are wondering why I have not
written to you before, but I hope you are not very
angry with me. The fact is I have been very busy
indeed and as I knew that this would be a long
letter I put off writing until I had more time.

Our affairs are now settled and we are to be
married in a fortnight—on the 22nd—so you must
think of us on that day if you can spare a thought
from Ralph and my dear wee god-daughter. I feel
as if I needed your thoughts rather badly. I wish
you were here. Somehow or other I find it difficult to believe that I am really free at last and that
I am going to be married to Kit, but he is very
sweet to me and very patient and I know I am a
very lucky woman.

You will see from the address at the head of this
letter that I am staying with the Furnivals. Enid
Furnival has been awfully good to me and has
done everything in her power to make things easy
for both of us. I was dreading the experience of
coming back to Minfield after all that has happened—it might have been rather difficult and uncomfortable—but Enid has been a perfect brick
and it has made a great difference having her as
our very good friend. As you know, everybody
here likes Enid and listens to what she says and
follows her lead, so I have found everybody extremely kind and tactful. Enid is devoted to Kit,
of course, and I believe it is for his sake, rather
than mine, that she is taking such an interest in
our affairs.

You will be glad to hear that Gilbert is very

fit now, he is stationed at Aldershot and comes over in his car when he can manage to get away. You know, Dolly, I always thought you had rather a soft spot in your heart for that young man before you transferred your affections to the Senior Service!

Now I must tell you of our arrangements for the wedding so that you will be able to picture it. Enid insists on having it here which is just another piece of her extraordinary kindness to us. We are only asking a very few people—Kit's brother and his wife, your father and Ethel and Jem and one or two others—it will be very quiet, of course, and Jem is quite disgusted at the prospect; he keeps on saying "Aunt Dolly's wedding was a lovely party," and obviously thinks that Kit and I are very foolish not to take advantage of this opportunity for conviviality. The little wretch is just as sweet and funny as ever, and just as tactless; the other day when I was having lunch at your father's house he enquired suddenly in a piercing voice, "How long will it be before you and Kit get a baby?" I was so completely taken aback that I was dumb, but fortunately your father was equal to the occasion and declared with perfect gravity, "*That* is a purely private matter and should not be discussed." Jem nodded thoughtfully and repeated "A Purely Private Matter" several times, rolling the words on his tongue as if they had a very nice taste. So you see Jem is in good form.

And now I come to the most important part of my letter—our arrangements for the future. I think I told you in my last letter that Kit and I were looking for a little house in Minfield. We wanted a house quite near your father's so that Kit would be available when your father wanted him. We hunted high and low but could find nothing suitable—they were all either much too big, or badly situated or too expensive, or in hopelessly bad repair—and at last we began to think that we should have to build. One day I went to see Ethel about some quite unimportant matter and suddenly she said, "Why don't you come and live here?"

You can imagine my feelings, Dolly! I simply *could not* live in a house run by Ethel, it would be impossible to get on with her.

I was about to refuse to consider her suggestion when she added "then I could get away." She said this with such force that I realised she was simply longing to "get away", and I asked what she wanted to do. It appears that her great friend Olive Sinclair went out to India last winter to stay with some friends in Calcutta, and she has married a banker there, and wants Ethel to go out to her for a long visit. Ethel was very keen to go but she felt she could not leave your father and Jem—it would have been impossible of course.

We all discussed the matter and now it has been decided that Kit and I are to live with your father and allow Ethel to go. I am to keep house for them all and look after Jem. The plan suits everybody. Your father seems very pleased about it and told me privately that he is glad to have Kit in the house because it makes things easier to have him near at hand. Jem is delighted too, so delighted that I have had to sit on him once or twice for showing his pleasure too openly.

Kit is quite pleased and says that we may as well make up our minds to settle down for good and all; he is sure that Ethel will never come back from Calcutta. Kit says that if Miss Sinclair could find somebody willing to marry her he has every hope that Ethel will be able to do the same—he is very naughty about poor Ethel. As a matter of fact Ethel is quite a different person since this has been settled, quite pleasant and kind and happy, so I hope that she will enjoy her trip and find a husband—if that is what she wants.

Of course I am delighted with the plan, for I shall have plenty to do and I would much rather run your father's house and look after Jem and help in various ways than sit in a bungalow on the Hill, waiting for Minfield to call!

I hope you think the plan a good one, Dolly dear, and that you will not think that Kit and I are taking too much advantage of your father's kindness, or too much responsibility in arranging it without consulting you and Mrs. Manson. It will make no difference, of course—I mean this house will always be your home—and it is so large that there will be plenty of room for us all.

Kit and I will be able to look after your father and save him as much as possible. He is getting a little frail I think and is not fit for night work, but he is very well and cheerful, so you need not worry about him.

Do write me a long letter soon and tell me how you are, and all about Ralph and little Mardie

With fondest love,

MARDIE